Between 1984 and 1998 Adrian Churchward lived and
worked in Moscow, Budape
trade lawyer, representing E
corporations. During this p
translating Russian commerc

He was one of the few W
day-to-day arena of President Gorbachev's liberalisation
process of perestroika and glasnost, and which ultimately
resulted in the collapse of communism and disintegration
of the Soviet Union. In 1991, he witnessed the abortive
coup against Gorbachev and in 1993, he was again present
in Moscow when Yeltsin ordered the shelling of the Russian
parliament building, aka the "The Russian White House".

He lives in London, has two daughters, three grandsons
and a cat that eats furniture.

Read more about Adrian at www.adrianchurchward.com

MOSCOW BOUND.★

ADRIAN CHURCHWARD

Best Wishes

Adrian

08.04.14

SilverWood

Published in 2014 by SilverWood Books

SilverWood Books
30 Queen Charlotte Street, Bristol, BS1 4HJ
www.silverwoodbooks.co.uk

ISBN 978-1-78132-200-0 (paperback)
ISBN 978-1-78132-202-4 (hardback)
ISBN 978-1-78132-201-7 (ebook)

British Library Cataloguing in Publication Data
A CIP catalogue record for this book is available from the British Library

Set in Sabon by SilverWood Books
Printed on responsibly sourced paper

In loving memory of my mother and father

Prologue

Moscow: 2013

Yuri Vladimirovich Sokolov was in his living room polishing the frames of his photograph collection when strains of the battle hymn *Johnny I Hardly Knew Ye* invaded the evening's silence on Mosfilmovskaya Street.

They're rolling out the guns again, hurroo, hurroo.

They're rolling out the guns again, hurroo, hurroo.

It was a male voice, singing in English. Sokolov's heart missed a beat. A frame slipped through his arthritic fingers and smashed into pieces on the oak floor.

They're rolling out the guns again.

But they never will take our sons again.

He shuffled over to the window and peeked between the curtains. A sodium street light in the car park cast an eerie haze over the snowflakes as they floated to the ground. Nobody.

No they never will take our sons again.

Johnny I'm swearing to ye—

He edged the curtains wider apart and craned his neck, looking left and right, and left again. A man wearing a fur *ushanka* with the earflaps pulled down over his cheeks appeared from around the corner.

No they never will take our sons again.

Johnny I'm swearing to ye—

Despite the slippery pathway, the singer was marching towards Sokolov's building. Sokolov released the curtains, switched off the light and took to his armchair, where he waited in the darkness.

The singing stopped. He heard the wooden double

doors in the building's lobby being yanked apart, scraping the floor and forced shut again. The residents had been complaining to the maintenance engineer for months to secure the locks.

He tensed. The buzzer to his apartment sounded. Sokolov fought back a reflux of stomach acid in his throat. The buzzer sounded again, this time longer. He shivered. The noise continued. Sokolov cupped his head in his hands and closed his eyes. The buzzing stopped. His palms began to sweat; he'd forgotten to put the security chain on the door for the night.

He heard jingling followed by prodding and clicking sounds; he imagined keys and metal prongs struggling to open the lock. His breathing was shallow and fast. The door creaked open.

They're rolling out the guns again, hurroo, hurroo.

The singing was louder. The door creaked shut.

They're rolling out the guns again, hurroo, hurroo.

The volume increased. The intruder was walking down the hallway towards the open study area. Sokolov's breathing quickened. He was conscious of rasping sounds as the air rushed in and out of his mouth.

They're rolling out the guns again.

But they never will take our sons again.

The voice was louder. The man had reached the study area. Sokolov's legs began to quiver.

No they never will take our sons again.

Johnny I'm swearing to ye—

The man was leaving the study and heading down the corridor, towards the living room.

No they never will take our sons again.

Sokolov began reciting the second verse of the 23rd Psalm.

Yea, though I walk through the valley of the
shadow of death,

I will fear no evil: For thou art with me;
Thy rod and thy staff, they comfort me.
Thou preparest a table before me in the presence
of mine enemies;
Thou annointest my head with oil; My cup runneth
over.

Silence.

Sokolov opened his eyes.

'So many years, so many winters, Yuri Vladimirovich.' The intruder was standing in the half-lit open doorway, smiling. He spoke fluent Russian.

'Who are you?' Sokolov gripped the arms of the chair to stop his hands from trembling. He didn't recognize the face. But he knew what the man wanted.

'I'm the ghost of Christmas past.' The man grinned. 'I've come to give you your present.'

He unzipped his jacket and pulled out a gun.

No they never will take our sons again
Johnny I'm swearing to ye—

Chapter 1

'Nobody fucks the Russian government without paying the price, Scott. The rule of law may operate with you guys in Strasburg but it doesn't work so well on Tverskaya Street.'

Scott Mitchell buckled his seatbelt as British Airways Flight 0233 from London descended through the snowstorm on its final approach into Moscow's Domodyedovo airport. He turned to his middle-aged friend, whose Saville Row suit and twenty-four karat gold cufflinks belied the stereotype of his profession.

'Charlie, forgive me, but I'm the lawyer, you're the IT geek. Okay?' Scott patted his jacket pocket to check the location of his passport. 'Thanks for the advice, but I can look after myself. I'm not a stranger to the Russian psyche.'

'You just kicked the shit out of their military in the European Court of Human Rights – and credit to you. What those bastards did to the Chechens, they should be topped, the lot of them.' Charlie sounded sincere. 'But, your honor, do you think Russian generals spend their leisure time reading law books? You're going to need all the friends you got – and some.' Charlie straightened his Jermyn Street tie. 'Am I right, or am I right?'

Scott didn't mind Charlie's plain speaking. They were from the same mold; the streets of London's East End, where they'd learnt how to take as well as give. He looked around the cabin. The military was trained to settle its disputes on the battlefield, not in the law courts, but so what? A fellow expat across the aisle raised his champagne glass in Scott's direction, mouthed "Well done mate" and downed the contents in one gulp. Lotte, the Dutch investment banker sitting behind the expat and an acquaintance of Scott's, put the final touches to her face, closed her vanity mirror and beamed at him.

Scott winked at them.

'They'll get over it,' he said to Charlie.

'You sure?'

'If they don't, it's their funeral. Not mine.'

'Scott, mate.' Charlie tapped his fingers on Scott's arm. 'How long have we known each other, four, five years?'

'Give or take.' Scott was only half-listening. He was posing for a passenger who was taking his photo on a cellphone. He was used to the media hordes on the court's steps flashing their cameras in his face, but a one-on-one was a special boost for his ego.

'We've had a lot of fun together in this crazy place, yeh?' Charlie said.

'You could say that.' Scott had helped his friend wade through the bureaucratic quagmire that foreign investors were subjected to when trying to start up a business in Russia. After that they'd kept in touch on a social basis. Charlie was the ultimate party organizer. Silvio Berlusconi could learn a lot from him.

'So, don't go getting yourself killed. That's all I'm saying.' Charlie stretched both his arms and exposed the fullness of his double cuffs. 'I've got a lot more years of fun left in me.'

'Don't worry,' Scott said. 'They're not going to kill me. Why should they? With me gone, others will soon take my place.' He squeezed his friend's arm. 'It's cool, Charlie. Really, it's cool. But thanks for your concern.'

The plane's thrusters roared into reverse; its wheels skidding along the icy runway. Scott checked his watch.

It was 2.17pm; still on Greenwich Mean Time; he moved the hands forward to 6.17pm. He lifted the window blind and gazed into the bleak landscape as the aircraft lumbered towards its destination. He squinted and caught the blinking red and green wing lights of another plane taking off in the distance; otherwise darkness. The terminal building was out of sight. If it wasn't for the illuminated runway and the reflected light from the snow they might as well have landed in a black hole. It wasn't a routine touch down. Apart from their late arrival, due to problems on departure, they had left the main runway. The plane taxied for an unusual length of time. The seat belt sign was on, though most of the passengers in the Business Class section were standing and retrieving their luggage from the overhead bins. The cabin staff had disappeared.

He pressed his face against the window, and used his hands as blinkers to shut out the cabin lights. The plane had come to a halt in a remote corner of the airfield. He focused on a series of yellowish dots on the horizon, no more than pinpricks, gradually morphing into flickering lights as they sped across the snow-covered grass. They were heading for BA 0233. Were they fire trucks? A suicide-bomber on board? Within seconds, six canvas-covered trucks slid and skewed to a halt on Scott's side of the Boeing 747's nose cone. Troops dressed in combat gear and wearing balaclavas leapt from the vehicles to form a semi-circle at the foot of the cabin door – Kalashnikovs at the ready. A mobile stairway appeared from under the hull of the aircraft and more troops maneuvered it into place. An FSB colonel, leading four soldiers, stormed up the steps.

The intercom crackled into action. 'Please remain seated ladies and gentlemen. We have come to a stop off the main runway for operational reasons. We shall be continuing on to the terminal building very shortly.' The cabin staff materialized and made their way along the aisles, coaxing the disoriented passengers to replace their luggage in the bins and return to their seats.

Scott watched the FSB colonel as he and his battalion barged into the cabin, accompanied by a rush of cold air. The officer pushed aside a male flight attendant and banged on the cockpit door. The co-pilot opened it immediately; he must have been forewarned. The colonel disappeared inside without giving the passengers a glance. One soldier remained in the open doorway, refusing to respond to the cabin staff's pleas to shut out the Arctic winter. A giant of a trooper swaggered along Scott's aisle to the rear of the aircraft, turned round and stood firm; his automatic clasped in both hands, finger on the trigger. His two comrades-in-arms made their way down the two aisles, scanning from left to right, left to right.

A child cried. A man shouted, 'Will somebody tell me what's going on?' The intercom crackled again. 'Listen all passengers!' a voice thundered in heavily accented English. 'I am Colonel Yakovlev of Russian Federation Security Service! Mr Scott Mitchell, you will surrender to my soldiers!' Scott winced at the sound of his name. He hadn't expected such a welcome. Maybe he'd been too quick to dismiss Charlie's generals. Colonel Yakovlev had the same tone as the Russian commanders in Grozny, the Chechen capital. He'd gone there to obtain testimonies from his clients and he'd personally witnessed a Russian soldier barking orders at a teenager cowering in a shop doorway and then blowing a hole in the wretched lad's head. The murderer wore a balaclava and no evidence of rank.

He sat bolt upright and folded his arms. He wasn't going to let the FSB scare him. This wasn't the front line in a war zone. He scanned the cabin again. The mood had darkened. The other passengers had averted their admiring gazes from him. Sealed lips and bemused faces had replaced their congratulatory smiles. Scott Mitchell's erstwhile devotees no longer wanted to have his babies. They had turned their attention to the armed invaders.

'Looks like freedom of the city of Moscow is out of the question,' Charlie whispered. 'Do you know any decent lawyers?'

'Ha bloody ha.' Scott closed his eyes and recalled the day's extracts from the lead article in *The Independent*:

> Young English lawyer defeats mighty Russian Army at the Battle of Strasburg. Where Napoleon and Hitler failed, Scott Mitchell succeeded. The thirty-three-year-old English human rights lawyer based in Moscow yesterday vanquished the Russian military machine, not with nuclear, smart or conventional weapons, but with words, simple words...

He opened his eyes as the colonel reappeared in the cabin.

> ...In a landmark case a full bench of the European Court of Human Rights unanimously declared that the Russian occupying forces in Chechnya had embarked upon a programme of routine and systematic torture, rape and murder of Scott Mitchell's clients: innocent men, women and children who were unwittingly caught up in President Putin's war on terrorism...

'Seating plan!' The colonel barked to the perky flight attendant who'd earlier written her name and the phone number of her hotel on a menu which she'd slipped into Scott's hand with a Bloody Mary. She glanced at Scott and contorted her face as if to apologize, before stepping into the galley, to return after a few seconds with a piece of paper in her hand. The colonel snatched it from her. Scott had anticipated a difficult time with the authorities when he returned to his Moscow office. He would have to face more than the usual obstacles put in the way of foreigners by the bureaucrats; perhaps they would revoke his work permit. He could handle that. It was all part of the game. But he hadn't gambled on being marched off the plane at gunpoint; especially not in front of a Western audience.

'Seat 5A!' the colonel shouted to his troops.

Before Scott had a chance to think, the titan appeared from the rear of the plane and wrenched Charlie from his aisle seat, heaving him back onto the recoiling passengers in the row behind. Scott took a deep breath, unbuckled and stepped out into the aisle. 'Okay, Colonel,' he said in Russian. 'I'm coming. I'm coming. You can cut out the violence.' He glanced at Charlie. 'You alright?'

Charlie rubbed his neck. 'What's the address of the FSB's Customer Service Department?'

The soldier jabbed the barrel of his Kalashnikov into Scott's back, urging him towards the front of the plane. The constant prodding aggravated a nerve in Scott's spine, sending a searing pain down the lower half of his body and prompting the first mental draft of his pleadings before the Russian Constitutional Court: *there being no possible means of escape the Defendant employed unnecessary and disproportionate force...*

'Hey! Take it easy!' Scott said, again in Russian. 'Get that gun out of my back!' He turned and squared up to the soldier. The FSB wouldn't dare break his bones in front of an audience of foreign business people eager to invest in the precarious Russian economy.

'I said get that—'

The assailant thrust the weapon under Scott's chin, forcing his head up and back. Scott stood on tiptoe. The pain was excruciating. Another millimeter and his jaw would have been separated from his neck. 'Move!'

Scott turned and stumbled up to the colonel, reverting to English for the benefit of the audience. 'Do you mind telling me what you think you're doing? You're breaking every rule in the book. The people on this plane are my witnesses. I'll—'

'Shut your mouth, English human rights lawyer,' Yakovlev said in Russian. He spat out the last four words. 'Shut your mouth and follow me.'

The colonel stepped out onto the mobile stairway, into the darkness.

Chapter 2

Day One: 7.30pm

Scott had been a prisoner of the FSB for over an hour. His locked room, located far from the Domodyedovo terminal building, but still on airport property and within the border guards' jurisdiction, was small and spartan; no windows, pictures or ornaments. Apart from a table and two chairs in the center it was devoid of furniture of any description, not an ashtray or trash can to distract the eye from the monotony of the peeling green paint on the walls, the stained carpet tiles and two clunky concertina radiators. The room was a stubborn relic of the Soviet era under Brezhnev when utility and stagnation were the order of the day. It was worse than a prison cell; there was no toilet. Yakovlev had confiscated Scott's cellphone and left him without food or drink, the radiators were ice cold and he was still wearing the lightweight suit he'd worn during the flight. He hadn't seen his suitcase since it had been loaded onto the luggage carousel at the check-in desk in London. Despite such privations, he remained calm. Nobody was going to kill him or lock him up and throw away the key. The authorities wouldn't dare. He was too high profile. And his discomfort was nothing compared to the sufferings of his wretched Chechen clients. The Russian occupation forces would herd them into overcrowded rat-infested cells, with excreta for mattresses and urine as the only source of running water, or hurl them naked into a slurry pit in the middle of an open field, at the mercy of the elements.

He returned to his pocket notebook on the table and

continued recording the events since the plane touched down on Russian soil; the more contemporaneous the note, the more accurate the recollection. He was building his case against the FSB. The Russian authorities only respected people who stood up to them and fought back. Nonetheless, his hand shook as he wrote and he felt queasy.

The door flew open with a resounding bang, the handle deepening the craters in the wall. Colonel Yakovlev marched in with a black and white spaniel on a lead, followed by a heavily pock-marked teenage soldier, carrying Scott's suitcase. The colonel was no longer wearing his overcoat. His uniform was covered in medals, four rows with six or seven in each. Scott had no doubt that the medals were for show. He returned to his notes, pretending lack of interest while twiddling the pen between his fingers.

The lad plonked the suitcase onto the table, took the leash from his colonel and retreated with the animal to guard the door. He wore the genetic scowl that was so prevalent among the nation's frontiersmen. The FSB colonel was grinning as he fiddled with the broken lock on the suitcase. Scott knew the Russian saying: to smile without reason means you must be crazy.

'Have you informed my embassy of my illegal detention?' Scott addressed the colonel in Russian.

The colonel chortled, unzipped the suitcase and rifled through the contents.

'Do you realize how many of my rights you've infringed by dragging me off the plane in that manner and detaining me without an arrest warrant?' Scott stopped twiddling and tapped the pen on the notebook, one tap per accusation. 'Leaving me in this freezing room for over an hour. Assault and kidnap.' He glanced at the broken lock on his suitcase. 'Malicious damage. Colonel Yakovlev, do you have any idea of the trouble you're in, you're going—'

'Shut your mouth!' The colonel banged a clenched fist on the table.

'Let me save you time,' Scott said. 'The Semtex is concealed in the tube of toothpaste.'

Yakovlev pulled a tin of talcum powder from the suitcase and held it up. 'What's this?'

Scott stared at the tin, glanced at the spaniel, and sat back in his chair. Couldn't the FSB come up with something more original? 'Well, let me put it this way. When I purchased it at Heathrow this morning, it was a tin containing nothing but talcum powder.' He looked at the dog again. 'However, who knows what the effect of atmospheric pressure at 30,000 feet may have had on it.' He turned back to the colonel. 'After all, I'm no pharmacist, just a humble human rights lawyer. So please, educate me in the wonders of science. Has a mysterious in-flight chemical reaction taken place?'

The colonel unscrewed the cap and sprinkled a few grams of white powder onto the floor. The young guard let go of the leash and the spaniel went for the powder, barking frantically.

'Colonel Yakovlev.' Scott poked his pen at the man. 'This won't do. It really won't do. We're not reprising *Midnight Express*. I'm not a drug-trafficker, and you people know it. And I certainly don't take drugs myself.' He dropped the pen onto the table. 'You'll never get away with it'. They could of course. Truth had never stood in the way of the Russian justice system. But Scott wasn't going to betray his doubt. He thrust out his chest. 'You'll never get a conviction.'

'You may understand our language, Mitchell, but you don't understand our psychology. You Westerners never will.' The colonel sat down and smirked. 'I have you.'

'Give me my cellphone please.' Scott held out his hand. 'I'm going to call my embassy. This farce is over.'

'Listen to me, Mr Mitchell.' The colonel's tone was

softer. 'You're a guest in our country. We allow you to live and work here. How do you repay us?'

Scott opened his mouth to speak, but Yakovlev smashed his fist down on the open suitcase and exploded again. 'By representing Chechen terrorists! That's how! Motherfucking Chechens blowing up our men, women and children, on our streets! Who do you think you are, coming to our country and defending this scum?' With a lash of his hand he swept the suitcase from the table and sent it crashing to the floor, followed by the tin of cocaine, which emptied itself over Scott's clothes. The dog jumped on the suitcase and began sniffing vigorously.

Enough was enough. Scott stood up and buttoned his jacket. 'I don't have to put up with this. I'm leaving. You'll be hearing from my embassy.'

Before Scott could take a step Yakovlev sprung up, whipped out his pistol and pressed the barrel hard against Scott's forehead. He dropped his voice to a whisper. 'I don't need any excuse to pull the trigger. You Chechen-loving scumbag.'

He cocked the gun.

'Now…sit…down.'

Scott flinched, the threat seemed real; but he remained standing. He gripped the edge of the table for support and pressed his head into the barrel. He could smell the colonel's hot breath, expelling an odor of oily fish and garlic. A sharp pain radiated to the back of Scott's head. He blocked it out and strained all the muscles in his neck to push his head forward. Yakovlev had to understand that Scott Mitchell wasn't afraid of bully-boy tactics.

The colonel's bottom lip quivered as he increased the pressure of cold steel against Scott's forehead.

The colonel's face reddened. 'I said…sit…down.' He caressed the trigger. His eyes took on a psychotic stare.

Was the man losing control? Scott was no longer on the plane; the only witness to the unfolding events was the sourpuss teenage guard. What if the colonel's finger slipped?

Yakovlev eased the trigger back and began to twist the gun, as if screwing the barrel into Scott's head.

'Now!'

Scott saw out of the corner of his eye that the young guard had approached the table and drawn his pistol. He wanted to call the man's bluff. But was it a bluff? If they shot him, the young lad would support any story the colonel concocted, if only for self-preservation. Scott sat down. He might not have won the battle, but he was determined to win the war.

The colonel replaced the weapon in his holster and sat down.

'Colonel, my clients aren't terrorists. Okay?' Scott's tone was moderate. 'They're innocent men, women and children. And your soldiers tortured, sexually abused and, in many cases, killed them. If you don't believe me, read the judgment of the European Court.'

'Fuck the European Court!' Yakovlev said. 'You're a capitalist pig!' He leant into Scott's face; more offensive breath. Scott recoiled. 'Who's paying you to betray our country?'

'Nobody is paying me. My clients have no money. I'm representing them for nothing. It's what we lawyers call *pro bono*.'

'Oh shit.' The colonel banged the table with his fist and laughed. 'An idealist.'

'Call it what you like,' Scott said. 'I happen to think that people should be treated fairly. We're all equal under the law, Colonel Yakovlev. If you didn't want to comply with the *Helsinki Accords*, you should never have joined the club.' The words came out by rote, rather than because of any conviction that he could persuade the colonel to agree to the reasoning; the colonel didn't seem the type who would listen to arguments with an open mind.

'Don't talk to me about equality!' The colonel clenched

his fists until the blood left his hands. 'Bombing our fucking metro system! Where's your fucking equality in that, Mr Human Rights lawyer?!' His body shook and expanded with rage.

Scott suspected that with each outburst the colonel was becoming more and more frustrated that his orders were limited to frightening the human rights lawyer, and not killing him. Scott's confidence increased. 'I don't agree with the killing and maiming of innocent civilians,' he continued, in a measured manner. 'By any party, for whatever reason. But, and it's a big but, the right and proper course of action is for the aggrieved to pursue their remedies through a court of law. Not by invading the alleged perpetrators' country of origin and reciprocating the alleged crimes.' He held out his hand. 'Colonel Yakovlev, I'm asking you again. Please give me my cellphone. I have the right to call my embassy.'

Yakovlev looked at his watch, squinted at Scott and pursed his lips.

'Colonel. My cellphone please.'

The colonel seemed pre-occupied. Was he relenting?

Yakovlev sneered at him. 'You will stay out of Russian politics,' he said. 'Or a drugs charge and fifty years in the Gulag will be the least of your worries. Do you understand me?'

Scott's hunch had been right. Yakovlev had been instructed only to scare him.

The colonel produced the cellphone from his jacket pocket and handed it to Scott.

The guard moved aside from the door.

Scott rose from the chair and smoothed down his suit. 'Thanks for the advice.' He headed for the door, turned and faced the colonel. 'The rule of law, Colonel Yakovlev, the rule of law. That's what I'm talking about. It applies to the government and the military as much as it does to the man on the street.'

'Next time we meet, Mr Mitchell. I won't be so understanding.' The colonel pointed at the suitcase. 'Don't forget your clothes.'

The spaniel was sniffing the drug remnants on the clothing splayed around the floor. No way was Scott going to risk traveling to his apartment in the center of the city with a suitcase full of clothes smothered in cocaine. The capital's police force might not be as "understanding" as Colonel Yakovlev of the FSB. Lightweight suit or not, Scott preferred to take his chances with the biting cold of the Moscow streets on a single November's evening, than the biting cold of a Siberian prison most of the year round.

'You've got my address,' Scott said. 'Please clean them up and send them on.' He opened the door and left the room.

His clothes were replaceable, his freedom wasn't.

Chapter 3

General Pravda's left ankle tingled the moment he removed the CD from the machine. He'd broken the joint in a botched parachute jump at cadet training and it had never set properly, becoming his harbinger of doom and gloom.

'Got what you came for?' Colonel Yakovlev growled. He was half-sitting, half-standing at the window ledge with his arms folded, and a sneer.

Pravda felt like hurling the buffoon through the closed window. This was the first time he had visited the FSB's third floor offices in the Lubyanka. Being a GRU, military intelligence, general he'd never had the cause or desire to enter the most spine-chilling building in Soviet history. The FSB's method of resolving conflicts was to strike first and ask questions after, if the target was still alive. Pictures of previous FSB/KGB directors from Beriya to Andropov decorated the walls in the colonel's office, which was knee-deep in brown folders of varying thicknesses covered in cigarette ash and plastic coffee cups. 'Are you proud of your interrogation techniques, Colonel?'

'Lieutenant-General Pravda,' he emphasized the lower rank. 'I was only ordered to record the interview for you, not suck your dick. Mitchell belongs to the FSB, not the GRU.'

The mutual loathing and suspiciousness between the two agencies had increased, rather than abated, since the collapse of the Soviet Union and the introduction of *glasnost*, openness. Pravda slipped the disk into his pocket.

'Your kind never learns. You could have cleaned up your act during the Yeltsin years…'

The colonel looked at the ceiling and yawned audibly.

Pravda wouldn't have tolerated such a defiant gesture from a junior GRU officer, but he had no authority within the FSB. Still, one shove. That was all it required. '…Instead you do the mafia's bidding. If you're not laundering their money, you're silencing their competitors. Don't you want your children to grow up in a civilized society?'

'Like I said, I'm not here to su—'

'There are subtler ways to handle the lawyer. Do you really think you've scared him off? If I'd have been there—'

'But you weren't.' Yakovlev smirked and folded his arms. 'He won't be causing us any more trouble. So take your candy and get out of my office.'

'You have no idea how committed to his principles Mitchell is,' Pravda said, shaking his head. Yakovlev's superiors must have known that, even if the idiot himself didn't. Military intelligence had been maintaining an unofficial watching brief on Scott Mitchell for years. The advocate was making more enemies than he realized. However, Pravda understood that Mitchell was only doing his job, and although the legal concept of human rights was new to Russian culture, there was no evidence that the lawyer was politically motivated.

'Have you ever thought, Colonel, that Mitchell and his kind, advocates of human rights and against abuses of power by the state, might one day be beneficial for the Russian people?'

Yakovlev sprung from the window sill and gripped the other side of the table, from where he leant into Pravda. 'If you were under my command, I'd have you shot for treason!'

Pravda stood up. 'If I were under your command, I'd willingly supply the bullets.'

'Wait here,' Yakovlev snarled. 'Somebody will see you get off the premises.' He left the room without offering Pravda his hand.

Pravda's seventeen-year-old Moskvitch was parked in a side street off Lubyankaya Square. Alexei, his No 2, was standing by the driver's door, staring down at the sidewalk and kicking at the ice with his foot.

'Alexei. What are you doing here? What's up?'

'Karat's been murdered.' Alexei's gaze remained fixed on the ground.

An acute pain radiated from the base of Pravda's spine down to his left ankle.

'Karat's been murdered,' Alexei repeated. He looked up at his boss. 'Come on, let's go, Lev. To the Tarasa Shevchenko Embankment.'

'He's been murdered here, in Moscow?' He was supposed to be in Akademgorodok, over 2,500 kilometers east. Pravda gave the keys to Alexei. 'You drive.' Pravda's leg was numb and Alexei was twenty years his junior. His reflexes were quicker.

Karat shouldn't be dead. Karat *couldn't* be dead. He was under Pravda's special protection. It had to be a case of mistaken identity.

'How did he die?' Pravda asked, as they passed the parliament building on their way to the crime scene.

'One shot to the head, that's all we know so far.'

'How did you find out?'

'Sasha's on duty tonight.' Sasha worked for the police department as a crime scene photographer. He was also a member of Pravda's covert team.

'No chance it's a case of mistaken identity?'

'Sasha knows Karat's face.'

'What did you tell the police?'

'That our agency is under new orders to be the first to check the identities of all bodies found in the river, back alleys, parks, brothels, wherever – terrorism awareness and all that bullshit.'

'Bullshit?' Pravda not only disagreed with Alexei's views on their remit, he also feared for the man's outspokenness. Things should have changed by the beginning of the twenty-first century, but they hadn't. It was still prudent for Russians to keep their political thoughts to themselves, especially those in the service of the Motherland.

'You know what I mean. The Chechens are Putin's "reds under the—"'

'Alexei, enough. Protecting our country is a matter of prime importance.'

'Sorry.' Alexei raised his hand. 'Of course, you're absolutely right.'

'Has Sasha been compromised?' Pravda asked, eager to change the subject.

'No, I said we'd picked up their traffic on the police frequency.'

Pravda choked on a lozenge. 'And they believed you?'

'On their measly income? Do they give a toss?'

Indeed, why should they care? While the rich got richer, the poor got poorer. The hardworking key-cutter on Novoslobodskaya Street made an average of 24,000 rubles a month, insufficient to feed his wife, two children and *babushka*, while less than a block away the nation's dollar billionaires were pampering their dogs at the latest pooch parlor with series of ozone bubble treatments costing 400,000 rubles or more. Did the authors of *perestroika* not see it coming?

They parked on the embankment in front of the Mocow City Business Zone. Three uniformed policemen and a man in plain clothes, the supervising detective, were huddled in the biting weather around a body bag down on the riverbank. 'Sasha's moved on?' Pravda asked.

They got out of the vehicle.

'Taken the passport snaps and gone to another job.

Best not to hang around. We'll debrief him later.'

The pair edged their way down the icy steps leading to the riverside. They were wearing their army greatcoats. A light snow began to fall.

'Hurry up, you imbeciles!' Pravda heard the detective say to the hapless policemen, who were lifting the body onto a cradle. 'My lungs have got frostbite!'

Pravda and Alexei approached.

The detective spat into the river.

'Hold it a minute!' Alexei said. 'We want to take a look at the body.'

Two of the uniformed policemen flexed their arms and grabbed the cradle.

'Good evening,' Pravda said to the detective. 'My name is Lieutenant-General Leonid Pravda.' He nodded at the policeman, in purported deference.

'Captain Rostov.' The detective lit a cigarette. 'At the morgue.' He beckoned to his men to carry on.

'I would like to see him now, please Captain,' Pravda said. 'I have to check this one off the list. The morgue would be official.' Which was the last thing Pravda wanted. 'You know, paperwork.' He had yet to meet a man in the field who didn't detest filling out forms, forms that more often than not ended up unread in a filing cabinet until they yellowed and self-destructed through age.

Alexei stepped in front of the men. The police bearers rested the cradle on the side of the bank.

Rostov drew on his cigarette, inhaled deeply and blew out four smoke rings, watching them disappear towards the bright moon, which was peering between two snow clouds. 'Lieutenant-General, with respect,' the detective said in a drawl and without any hint of sincerity. 'You've no authority. This is a police investigation. This is my jurisdiction and I say you can see the body at the morgue.'

Alexei slipped a hand inside his coat pocket. Pravda touched him gently on the arm. He didn't want any more corpses on the riverbank. If Alexei were to pull his gun, Pravda couldn't be sure how the police would react. He and Alexei weren't under threat. There was no need to overdramatize. Alexei withdrew his hand, but remained steadfastly blocking the path. 'Captain, I'm not here to threaten your jurisdiction.' Pravda rubbed his gloved hands together and stamped his feet. 'I'm sure, like me, you don't want to stand on this embankment all night debating such tiresome matters.'

Rostov glanced at the moon.

'You're no doubt aware of my orders,' Pravda continued. 'And like you, I have to obey them.'

Rostov looked away and blew another smoke ring.

'Five seconds. That's all I need,' Pravda said. 'I promise, five seconds. After that I'll be out of your life forever.'

Captain Rostov glared at Alexei; spat into the river again, flicked the cigarette after the sputum. 'Suit yourselves.'

The three policemen moved away from the cradle to allow the intelligence officers to make their inspection. It slipped back towards the river.

'You morons!' Rostov screamed.

One of the policemen preserved the evidence with an outstretched foot. The other two bent down and tugged the cradle back up the slope.

Alexei knelt down and pulled back the zipper of the body bag as far as the waist.

Pravda approached the corpse. It was fully clothed. The head was hairless and the left ear lobe was uniquely malformed, as Pravda had remembered him. One shot in the center of his forehead. Did he see his killer? Did he know his killer? It was all the hardened campaigner could do to stop himself from vomiting. He'd seen hundreds of dead bodies on his tours of duty; he was used to their smell. Death per se wasn't a problem for him. It was the unequivocal confirmation of the death of Fyodor

Sergeyevich Karat that caused his bilious attack.

'Well Lieutenant-General,' the captain of police said. 'Do you know this man? Is he on your list?' He sniffed. 'Of wanted terrorists?'

Pravda looked at Alexei.

The pair turned, walked away from the body and headed up the steps to the Moskvitch.

'No, Captain Rostov,' Pravda said without looking back. 'He is definitely not on our list. I have no idea who the man is. No idea at all.'

Chapter 4

Day Two: 7am

As soon as Scott's Cherokee emerged into the daylight from the car park under his apartment block he was attacked by a crowd of twenty to thirty youths. They bombarded his vehicle with stones hidden in snowballs. They were predominantly boys, but some girls, in their late teens and early twenties. The majority were wearing black leather motor cycle jackets or red and white parkas. Three middle-aged men in heavy winter overcoats stood to one side of the group, laughing and taking photographs of the assault. Some of the youths held placards, which read "Putin is Russia" or "Russian lives, not human rights"; others wielded knuckle-dusters and chains, while a lone figure waved a flag, bearing a white transverse cross on a red background.

They were the thug element of the Putin-backed nationalist youth movement, *Nashi*. They screamed at Scott.

'Mitchell kills Russian babies!'

'Capitalist lackey!'

Scott slowed to negotiate his way through the hostilities. A boy, who looked no older than fifteen or sixteen, scraped a piece of metal along the side of the Cherokee's front passenger door. He banged on the window and ranted, 'Your mother's a whore! Your mother's a whore!'

Two police cars were parked across the street. One was empty, the other contained four officers munching *blinnies* and drinking coffee. They glanced at the furore, but made no effort to interrupt their meals.

The door lock buttons popped up and a swarthy

teenager wearing a hoodie jumped in behind Scott. 'What the...' Scott turned round. 'How did you open the doors? Who are you?'

The lad dangled a key fob on a chain. 'Easy shit. Fuck these Russian bastards, put your foot down.' He looked out of the window and used both hands to give the one-fingered salute to the crowd. 'Drive over them.' The accent was Chechen.

'Who the hell are you?' Scott locked the doors.

'Your *krysha*.' The lad closed the door. 'No charge.'

The *krysha* was the "roof" provided by criminal gangs to protect businesses from unwarranted interference by anybody other than them.

The scraping continued, around to the rear of the Cherokee.

'What you waiting for?' the lad asked. 'The Russian cunt to pimp your ride?'

Scott hesitated. 'Look, I don't think this is a good idea.' He could imagine the media backlash, goaded by the authorities, "Mitchell – an ally of organized crime."

A crowd of the youths gathered at the front of the vehicle.

'Come on! Come on! Let's go!' the Chechen lad said.

Scott was a sitting target. He revved the engine and edged forward. He was reluctant to hit one of the thugs, let alone drive over them.

'For fuck's sake!' the Chechen screamed.

Three of the policemen from across the street got out of their vehicle and ambled towards the youths at the front of the Cherokee. They didn't appear to say anything, but the group parted. Scott stepped on the accelerator. A gap was made for him and he sped away from the scene. He glanced in his rear-view mirror as he approached an intersection. The lights turned red and a hooting vehicle shot across his path. Scott stamped on the brakes and skidded to a halt.

A leather clad youth standing on the street corner with three others stepped off the sidewalk and threw a lead pipe at the vehicle. It bounced off the hood.

'Jesus Christ,' Scott mumbled.

'Chill out lawyer man,' the Chechen said. 'We'll be watching your back.' He opened the door and darted into a housing project.

The lights changed to green and Scott roared off.

'Shit, shit, shit.' No, he didn't want that type of protection. He switched on the radio. It was a phone-in show:

'Next on the line is Maria Pomorova from Khimki. Maria, welcome to Dmitry's Debates. So, what do you have to say about Scott Mitchell?'

'My son was murdered in Grozny by those bastard Chechens. He should be strung up from a street light.'

The line went dead.

'Er, thank you and goodbye Maria Pomorova from the Khimki District of our great city. You're listening to Dmitry's Debates. We're talking about the return to Moscow of the UK human rights lawyer Scott Mitchell after winning his case in the European Courts against our military. The question is: should he be allowed to continue to work in the Motherland? General Schepnikov is calling in. Good morning, General. Are you still a serving officer?'

'No, Dmitry, I'm retired. But I just want to say that I don't understand how the authorities can allow this Mitchell to spit in our faces like this. What is President Putin playing at? This lawyer has shown his true colors. He supports the Chechen terrorists. He's an enemy of the Russian people. He's an enemy of our Motherland. He should be deported immediately.'

'Well General—'

Scott switched off the radio and banged the steering wheel.

The state-controlled media had begun their campaign.

An hour and a half later, after a rigorous bout of tae kwon do in the gym, Scott sat in the locker room trying to stave off creeping self-doubts. Sure, the Russian government was ruthless, maybe nihilistic at times, but it wasn't stupid. The "accidental" death of a high profile foreign advocate on Russian soil would inevitably cause embarrassing questions to be asked, both at home and abroad. In the world of realpolitik the Russians needed the West and vice versa. And whatever its failings, Russia was no North Korea or Iran. He was certain that would be Putin's thinking.

Or would it?

He also wondered whether his supreme self-assurance had driven him right back to where the Russian military wanted him – into the heart of Moscow. The secure confines of the Strasburg Court and the adoring cameras of the world's media were over 2,000 kilometers away. Were Charlie's concerns justified? He closed his eyes. Had the human rights champion been trapped by hubris?

'Are you Scott Mitchell?' a soft, female voice whispered in Russian.

He opened his eyes with a start and blinked, not once, twice. Before him stood a long-haired brunette wearing a black French-style beret, tilted coquettishly. She wore a double-breasted military-style overcoat, tailored to emphasize her figure. It was dark blue, with a black fur collar and cuffs and hung just below the knee. She wasn't of the usual paint-encrusted *nouveaux riches* mold, but an understated *über*-cool siren from the hottest catwalk in Rome.

Instinctively he tightened the large towel around his waist.

'Are you Scott Mitchell?' the woman repeated.

Scott pulled himself up to his full 1.88 meters. 'Who are you?' He tried not to sound too much like the suspicious lawyer.

She offered her business card.

He lingered on her face as he took the card. It was a honey trap. The generals were going to blackmail him. He checked the card and wiped his brow. The words were a blur. How could they blackmail him? He wasn't married, had no current girlfriend and had nothing in the closet to be exposed. His private life had been raked over by the most pugnacious trial lawyers the Russian authorities could hire, all to no avail. 'How did you know I was here?'

'The owners are friends of mine.' She cocked her head to one side and smiled. 'And your return to Moscow is hardly a state secret.'

Scott coughed. The health club was known to be one of six in the city that was managed by a company registered in Cyprus with nominee shareholders: lawyers and accountants. Although Scott didn't know who the beneficial shareholders were, it didn't surprise him that the woman standing before him mixed with people of such apparent wealth. He looked again at the card: *Ekaterina Romanova – Economist* The rest was blank.

A cellphone rang. The ring-tone came from Scott's locker. 'That's mine I believe. Would you please excuse me?' Scott eased by her, taking in the fragrance of her expensive perfume in the process, and hurried over to his locker. He took the phone from the locker and answered the call, while keeping his eyes on his visitor.

'Chief.'

'Rashid.' It was the office gofer.

Scott lowered his voice so that Ms Romanova couldn't hear the conversation. 'What's up?'

'Shit traffic on Smolenskaya. I'll be there in twenty minutes.'

'Okay. No sweat.' Scott disconnected and sat on the

bench. 'My office. I'm without wheels at the moment. Somebody's coming to pick me up.' He had an overwhelming urge to answer questions she hadn't asked. He cleared his throat. 'Okay, Ms Romanova. So, you're an economist.' He flipped the card over. A cellphone number was on the back, nothing else. 'Where do you operate from?'

'It is not relevant to the reason why I am here,' she replied.

Scott scratched his forehead. Is she a lawyer as well as an economist? He grabbed a hand towel, mopped his face and massaged his shoulder blades. 'Look—'

'I want you to help me find my father,' she said.

He jerked his head back. It sounded like a command, but she was smiling plaintively. 'Excuse me, what did you say?'

'I want you to help me find my father.'

He took a few seconds to reflect. 'I'm a lawyer, Ms Romanova, not a detective. I'm not equipped to look for missing persons.'

'I know who you are Mr Mitchell.'

'Then you'll know that I don't—'

'You fight for people who have been abused by our government.' She stepped forward. 'That is why I want you to help me.' Her tone softened and the pleading smile broadened.

'In what way?'

'My father is in prison. He has been in prison for over thirty years. Without a trial.'

Hmmm. She didn't look any older than late twenties. 'Why? On what charge?'

'I don't know.' She raised her shoulders and shook her head.

Scott did a mental calculation. Her father would have been put away during the 70s/early 80s. Brezhnev was General-Secretary of the Communist Party throughout that period. It was a time when it was considered a threat to national security to wear Levi jeans and play Beatles records. Was her father a *politico*?

'Where's he being held?'

'Somewhere in Russia.'

'Huh, that narrows it down a bit. Only eleven time zones to plow through.'

'This is serious, Mr Mitchell.' She fixed Scott with a cold stare.

'Sorry. I didn't mean to make light of the situation.' He would choose his words and tone more carefully. 'But Russia is a very large country. An experienced missing persons' investigator would have problems deciding where to begin the search. So—'

She pushed back her shoulders. 'So you don't want to help me.' It was a statement, not a question.

He stood up. 'Look, Ms Romanova, Ekaterina, it's not a question of "don't want to". I'd like to help you. But I *can't*.' He massaged his neck with his bare hand. 'You need some credible evidence of where your father might be held. And, as I said, I'm not a detective. I've no experience in looking for missing persons, it's not my field. Sorry.'

'My father is not *missing*,' she said. 'The authorities are holding him prisoner. They know where he is.' Her speech stiffened and she raised her voice. 'Human rights. It is a question of human rights. He has not had a trial.'

'I understand that, Ekaterina, honestly, I do.' Scott raised his hands. 'But as I've said, you need a missing per—'

'I am sorry to have wasted your time, Mr Mitchell.' She marched out of the room and let the door slam behind her.

Scott grit his teeth. What was that? Who was this woman's father? Why had he been in prison so long, especially after Yeltsin's mass releases of the 1990s?

And something else gnawed at him: he was sure he'd seen Ekaterina Romanova before, though he couldn't place her. He went to the frosted windows and pulled back a piece of tarpaulin that was temporarily covering a missing pane. Ekaterina Romanova strutted across the car park towards a green BMW 740 Li bearing Italian registration plates. A meter-long red paint mark scarred the offside rear wing; it rested incongruously with the owner's unblemished personal appearance.

She was beautiful, intelligent and assertive – a troublesome combination at the best of times.

Chapter 5

'Are you sure the police have no idea who he was? What was in his pockets?'

'Yeh,' Sasha grunted. 'Nothing. Even the labels ripped from his clothes.'

Pravda had invited the young photographer to his *dacha* for a debriefing of the Karat murder. The property nestled deep in a silver birch forest, north-west of the city twenty-five kilometers from the Kremlin. The retreat was more secure than GRU headquarters on the other side of town. The building at Khodinka airfield, also known as "the Aquarium", was reputed to be held together by hidden cameras and listening devices.

'I don't know about fingerprints though.' Sasha slurped his coffee. 'The killer didn't try to remove them. All fingers intact.'

Pravda said nothing. He was the only person who could gain access to the man's records. There should be no prints in the police databases, nor DNA, for that matter. He got up from the sofa and walked over to the study window. His half-built garden shed was acting as a collecting point for the week's snowfall; he'd been meaning to construct the roof for three years, but something had always distracted him. A recent offer of two years away from the snow, as a visiting Professor of Conflict Resolution at a prestigious university on the US west coast, lay unanswered in his desk. That, too, would now have to wait until he'd found out who'd killed Karat, and why.

'What was the man doing in Moscow?' Sasha wiped his mouth with a greasy handkerchief. 'I mean, wasn't he supposed to be in Akademgorodok in Novosibirsk, or some such?'

It was a key question, and Pravda didn't know the answer, but he wasn't going to discuss it with Sasha. The boy hadn't been wholly taken into Pravda's confidence.

'Why did the killer erase all traces of identification?' Sasha asked.

'He clearly didn't – the finger prints.' Pravda didn't yet have any idea, but this wasn't to be a matter for Sasha's concern.

'Whatever,' Sasha said. 'The labels and stuff, perhaps it's his trade mark. You know...' He made quotation marks signs with his fingers. '...His signature.' Sasha's finger nails were bitten back to the quick. 'Do we have a serial killer in our midst?'

Pravda ignored this conclusion. There was only one body.

Sasha poured another coffee. It spilled over the mug.

'Have they found the bullet?' Pravda asked.

'No. A through and through.'

'A through and through?' Pravda smiled for the first time that morning. 'Have you been watching CSI?'

'I've learnt more forensics from that TV series than I ever did at university,' Sasha said.

'And the criminals too, no doubt,' Pravda replied.

'Sure. Nowadays no self-respecting criminal is seen without his bottle of bleach. Wipe it on, wipe it off – boom boom, the DNA disappears.' Sasha yawned without covering his mouth. 'Leon, I've had so many other shootings this last month. It's been non-stop. You'd think the city'd run out of bullets.' He whistled. 'Or people to shoot.'

Pravda spread the photos on his desk. 'The entry point is clean. I don't see any blast marks or residue by the hole.'

'There's more to come. I forgot to bring the shots of the back of his head. Sorry.'

It wasn't the first time that Sasha had been careless in his duties, and he'd been warned before, but Pravda had more pressing issues to contend with. 'Go on.'

'If you'd turned him over, you'd have seen the shit the bullet collected on the way out. Half the brain was missing and the back of his head had been ripped apart from the skull.'

This was the type of damage done by an armor-piercing bullet.

'I don't think it was done by a mafia weapon,' Sasha said. 'It's not their style.'

He was probably right. Karat had never mixed with gangsters. He was a scientist. Pravda gazed into space. The *siloviki*, the strong men behind the Kremlin. He leant down and scratched his left ankle; it was beginning to twinge.

He had to speak to Yuri Vladimirovich Sokolov.

Chapter 6

Day Two: 12 noon

Scott pushed a button on his office intercom.

'Chief?'

'Rashid, would you come here a moment, please?'

No foreign business could survive in Russia without a gofer who knew where things were and how to get things done, and Scott had one of the most resourceful in the city. Rashid Oziev was a wiry twenty-four-year-old Chechen. He'd appeared on Scott's doorstep three years previously, when Scott was beginning to make a name for himself as the only lawyer in town who would represent people who'd come to the capital from the Caucasus to look for jobs and better housing conditions. They were regarded as parasites. The authorities frequently refused to accept them as Russian citizens and tried to classify them as illegal immigrants, with no rights. Rashid had offered his services to Scott, for expenses only, by way of his people's gratitude. The little man had become indispensable to Scott's law firm. In particular, his working knowledge of five languages predominant in the Caucasus meant that Scott no longer had to rely on outside, and sometimes untrustworthy, interpreters. Rashid was a fully paid-up paralegal.

He appeared in the open doorway.

'So, what news on Chichikov?' Scott asked. He was the local tax inspector. Two days before the Strasburg trial began the Russian tax authorities served a demand on Scott's law firm for unpaid taxes: it was for twenty million rubles, allegedly due in 2010. Scott's average yearly turnover in fees was less than half that amount. The demand was still pending. But instead of disarming him at a crucial time for his clients, it made him more determined.

'He's only the messenger boy,' Rashid said.

'I'd worked that out. What did your cousin's girlfriend say? Who's pulling Chichikov's strings?' She worked in one of the tax collection offices.

'I'm on her case.'

'And?'

'She may be my cousin's girlfriend but she's not yet family. She's an independent negotiator, if you get my meaning.'

'She wants paying.'

'You got it chief.'

'Do what you have to.'

'Music to my ears.' Rashid returned to the outer office.

Scott jotted down notes for a conference call to Irkutsk he'd scheduled for the coming week. His new, Russian, clients were the mothers of reluctant teenage soldiers who'd been maltreated by their superior officers during training; the Russian mother was not to be messed with when her son's welfare was concerned. Throughout both Chechen wars in the 1990s, they were known to travel to the battle-torn front line in Grozny, to negotiate with the Chechens for the release of their captured sons. To their credit, on many occasions they succeeded where the politicians had failed. The Chechens had mothers too.

When he finished he turned on the TV, to catch the midday news. After checking Sky News and CNN he switched to the local broadcasts. A shot of the studio anchor cut to a street scene on Leningradsky Prospect. A breathless female reporter faced the camera. Behind her were two fire engines, at least five police cars, three ambulances and a crowd of onlookers. Scott pointed the remote at the set and turned up the sound.

'It happened at 10.40 this morning. Witnesses say the BMW swerved violently across to the outside lane, exploded and caught fire. The driver's body has not yet been recovered but he or she must have died instantly. The police claim to have found evidence of a bomb, although they are non-committal as to whether it is linked to recent terrorist activities in the capital. The occupants of several neighboring vehicles were seriously injured and at least two are on life support.'

The camera panned around the charred remains of the vehicle. There were traces of green bodywork. The rear registration plate had become detached from the car in one piece; it lay a few feet from a separated broken wheel rim. The camera lingered on both items, the falling snow gradually consuming them. Scott moved closer to the screen. 'Italian plates,' he said aloud.

The shot focused on the rear wing. A ragged red line came into view. 'What the fuck...' he said in English. 'It can't be.' He looked at his watch. It was 12.15. 'Shit, 10.40? But I was with her at nine, half past.' He fumbled in his wallet for Ekaterina's business card and keyed her number into his cellphone. 'No. It can't be. There must be hundreds of green BMWs in the city.'

The phone rang – and rang. A voicemail announcement didn't kick in. He tried again. 'Come on, come on. Answer. Ekaterina, answer the phone.' The ringing continued remorselessly. He saved Ekaterina's number, got up and wandered around the room. Okay, so not all the green BMW L740 Lis had Italian plates, but there must be some: ten? twenty? thirty? Moscow was teeming with imported BMWs. They were as common an accessory for the new Russian *biznizmenni* as were Louis Vuitton handbags for their wives and girlfriends. But how many bore a one-meter-long red paint mark across the rear wing? Fewer. So what? The evidence was circumstantial, insufficient to convict.

His phone rang.

Ekaterina's number flashed on the screen.

'Ekat...?'

'Is that Scott Mitchell, the English lawyer?' It was the voice of an adult Russian male.

'Who are you?'

'It doesn't matter who I am. A friend of mine needs your help.'

'What friend? And what are you doing with E—'

'This morning, the gym.'

'Huh...' Okay, so this guy knew that he and Ekaterina were at the gym earlier. So what? 'Who are you? Where's Ekat—'

'Be at the Luzhniki Stadium at 2pm; the small sports arena. Watch the high school skating competition. Sit in the fifth row down from the main entrance, in the center block. A ticket has been left for you at the gate.'

'What? Okay, but—'

Scott was talking to himself. He stared at his phone. What had happened to Ekaterina Romanova? He refused to allow his mind to fantasize whether the Russian authorities might be setting a trap for him. Instead he took a deep breath, counted to ten and exhaled. He needed back up. 'Rashid!'

The little man appeared in the doorway again.

'Are the Kropotkin twins in the neighborhood?' The brothers were Ukrainian tag wrestlers who'd lost their fighting licenses for committing negligent homicide in the ring – twice.

'They were at two this morning, chief. We were playing roulette. I—'

Scott didn't have time for a running commentary on Rashid's nocturnal activities. 'Right, get them and go to the small sports arena at the Luzhniki Stadium. Get there by 1.30. The high school kid's skating competition. Sit in the first row down from the main entrance, in the center block. I'll be there shortly after. Look out for me, but don't make eye contact. I should be a few rows in front. Watch what happens. If somebody is with me or near to me and I scratch either cheek it means I'm in trouble and you pile in, but only then. If I leave without scratching my cheek, it means I'm okay no matter what happens, no matter who's with me. Understand?'

'Message understood.' Rashid turned to leave.

'And try not to look too conspicuous.' Scott pictured the sight of a slightly-built, diminutive Rashid squeezed in between two gargantuans. What would they be doing at a children's skating competition?

'No problem, chief. Igor's got a ten-year-old daughter, Alisa. We can take her.'

'Shouldn't she be at school?' She was too young for high school.

'She's been sent home for a week – for wrestling her classmates. She's a big gir—'

'Yeh, yeh, okay. I get it.' He waved Rashid away.

Scott arrived at the stadium at 1.45. He noted the location of his allotted seat and climbed the steps to an empty seat high up at the back of the stand, from where he scanned the arena. It was more than three-quarters full. Ten thousand or so spectators were watching the junior teenagers competing in front of their proud parents to the strains of an incongruous mix of Western heavy metal and Russian classical music.

He spotted Rashid sitting next to a young girl, the street-fighting Alisa, though she looked twice the size of Rashid. They were squashed between the twins. He couldn't see Ekaterina, or anybody else sitting near his seat. The row was half empty and there was nobody sitting either directly in front or behind. She must surely be alive; otherwise there would be little point in asking him to come to the stadium. The only other explanation was some crazy entrapment plan by the authorities. He stood up and walked back down the steps, without acknowledging Rashid. He stopped at the entrance to his row, checked his ticket, and edged by the spectators to take his place among a clutch of seven vacant seats. His watch showed 1.55pm. He turned round and checked the seats behind him, again ignoring Rashid who was four rows back, to the left. The five seats immediately behind Scott remained vacant. He turned back to the skating and wondered how many of the kids would grow into lawyers. Would Russia have an indigenous body of dedicated human rights attorneys in ten years' time?

'Hullo, Scott.'

He snapped out of his daydream and swiveled to his right. It was Ekaterina. The beret had been replaced by a silver fur *ushanka*, with its ear flaps tied together across her head. It completely covered her hair. Instead of her military coat she wore a designer red and gray ski jacket.

'Thank you for coming.' She looked around the stadium. She seemed anxious.

Scott wanted to touch her, to make sure she was real. How could she have survived the explosion? 'I saw the car on TV. It was a burnt out wreck. Was it yours? They said the driver was killed instantly. What happened? How did you escape? Why didn't you answer my phone call? Why the Luzhniki?' He couldn't stop the questions. 'Why—?'

'I wasn't in the car.'

'How come? You'd only left me a few min—'

'It was stolen while I was shopping on Tverskaya. It was the thief who was killed.'

'I'm sorry.'

'Why? Was the thief a friend of yours?'

Scott chuckled. The English had a propensity to overuse the word "sorry" and it often amused or puzzled non-native speakers. He raised his hand to scratch his head, and realized that Rashid might mistake it for the alarm signal. He dropped his hand to his lap. 'They said there was an explosion before the car caught fire, a bomb.'

'Yes, it was a bomb,' she said, with a straight face.

Scott didn't want to appear to doubt her, though he had serious misgivings. He nibbled at his lip. 'You're an economist, not a banker refusing credit.' It wasn't unheard of in Russia for uncooperative financiers to be murdered by the mafia. 'Why would anybody want to blow you up?'

She looked away from Scott, at the empty rows immediately behind and in front. 'Please, just accept that they don't want me to find my father.'

'They?'

She lowered her voice. 'The authorities.'

Oh shit. The woman was paranoid. Scott accepted that the Soviets used to lock people up, on the flimsiest of charges, and throw away the key. The world's literature was full of first hand stories of the horrors of the Gulag system. However, cases of the prisoner's children being murdered were few and far between, especially since the death of Stalin.

'You don't believe me,' she said, and laid her gloved hand on his elbow.

Scott looked at her hand. Her fingers tightened on him. He looked into her eyes; the pleading look she had given him in the gym. He removed his elbow and sat up. He would lose nothing if he were to stay and hear her story. 'Okay, how did you find out about your father?'

'From my mother.'

'Can I meet her?'

'No.'

'Why not?'

'She is dead.'

'Oh Ekaterina, I'm sorry, so sor...' He coughed. 'I didn't...When did she die?'

'Two weeks ago.'

Scott coughed again. Ekaterina's tone was matter-of-fact; she had shown no emotion during the exchange. Didn't she get on with her mother?

'She left me a note,' Ekaterina continued. 'Somebody gave it to her.'

'Do you have this note with you?'

She opened her handbag, took out a piece of paper and gave it to him.

Scott read the typed text:

Ekaterina's father lives. He's been held since the 1970s as a prisoner without trial. If you want to learn more, go to Apartment 3 in Building 4 of the old military apartments on Mosfilmovskaya Street.

It was dated four weeks previously. He looked at the other side. Blank. He fiddled with document. 'Have you been to the apartment?'

'I haven't had the time. I only found it in my mother's papers last night.'

'And the first person you thought of was me?'

'I have nobody else to turn to,' she said. It was those eyes again.

Her story didn't stack up. She wasn't the average Russian working woman. She wore expensive clothes and she knew wealthy people – the health club owners. They must have had contacts in the right places, or contacts who knew contacts in the right places, even if she didn't. 'Is that supposed to be a compliment?'

'I mean I can't trust anybody else.' Her hand hovered over Scott's elbow again, but she retracted and rested both her hands on her lap. 'Scott, the government has imprisoned my father for three decades without trial. That is an infringement of his human right to have what you lawyers call "due process". Somebody tried to blow me up. That is an infringement of my human right to live. We do not have coincidences in Russia. The events are connected. The government is responsible for the illegal detention of my father. I do not trust the government. You are not part of the government. You fight the government.' Her tone softened. 'Scott, you beat the government. You're the only person who can help me find my father.' Her shoulders slumped.

It was a well-rehearsed speech and she certainly knew how to whet his appetite. But was it too well-rehearsed? And there she was; the bomb again. Not believing in coincidences was not a rational argument for concluding that the events were connected. He reread the note. 'Was there nothing else among your mother's papers? Something that could shed further light on this?' He folded the document in half and offered it back to her. 'Like, where did it come from?' He'd decided to reserve judgment on her state of mind until he'd heard more.

'Keep it, it's a copy.' She passed over another sheet of paper to him.

Scott looked at it. 'What's this?' It was a photocopy of a handwritten text.

'An extract from the last letter my mother wrote to me.' Scott read it:...

Your papa burst into my life when I was twenty-six. He was tall, dark and handsome (yes really!) and it was love at first sight. He spoke little of himself despite my questions. He said he was a teacher of mathematics in a junior school in Alma Ata where I was at university, but he always managed to turn the conversation around to me. That was why I loved him so much; he was so attentive and unselfish.

We talked of getting married. Then one night, when he had come secretly to my dormitory, four men arrived and took him away. I followed them into the street, crying and screaming. I woke the whole university, but nobody helped me as the men took your papa away in their cars. When I went to the junior school where he worked (it was the first time I had been there) the principal said she'd never heard of him. It wasn't true. I'm sure they were told to erase him from their records for some reason. Yes, it happened in those days, in the 1970s. It wasn't only Stalin who made people disappear...

'Do you have the rest of it? I'd like to read it in context. When was it written? Is it a death bed revelation, or confession?' Scott's misgivings were being tested. The story of the "midnight knock on the door" was well known in Soviet history. Maybe she was right to be wary of the authorities; although that was far from saying that it was the authorities who blew up her car. And neither was he yet convinced that Ekaterina Romanova was an innocent party. She could be an instrument of the Russian military who were trying to entrap him. Was *he* being paranoid?

'It's in my apartment. It was written three weeks ago,' she said.

'Does it refer to this note?' He waved it at her.

'Yes. I'll show it to you later.'

'What's your patronymic?' Russian second names are usually taken from the father's first name.

'My father's first name was Mikhail, if that's what you are after.'

Scott turned and looked at the rows behind. They had filled up except for the three seats immediately behind them. He caught Rashid's eye and glanced away. Why hadn't she brought the complete letter?

'How many cases have you handled that concern our Gulag system?' Ekaterina asked.

It was a reasonable question for a prospective client to ask. How much research had she done into his law practice, apart from the Strasburg case? 'If you mean pre-1991, none. I've concentrated wholly on post-1991 human rights issues, predominantly involving abuses of Russian military power at home and abroad. To be honest, I've never been retained to handle Soviet Gulag cases.'

'I see...' She seemed lost in thought. 'Thank you for your honesty.'

'But...' The case was beginning to intrigue him. He'd read Solzhenitsyn's *One Day in the Life of Ivan Denisovich*, and he'd seen the movie starring Tom Courtney. Such inhumanity. 'I studied Soviet history at university, before I switched to law. I reckon I've a fair insight into Stalin's repression of his people.'

'I doubt it.'

'Ekaterina—'

'But what is more important is that I need someone, a tenacious lawyer preferably, who is not afraid of my government.' She moved closer to him. 'And someone I can trust.'

Scott reread the extract. He tried to imagine how he would feel, if he were in her position. It wasn't a clever approach for a lawyer. Misplaced empathy could stifle the objectivity needed to concentrate on the facts and ignore well-meaning, albeit misguided, speculation. But she seemed to be the proverbial damsel in distress – with a fascinating case. 'I must confess,' he said. 'I would enjoy the challenge.'

'Challenge?' She arched her back. 'This is not a game.' Her voice hardened and she scanned the stadium. 'My life is at stake.'

He bit his tongue. He'd seen her volatility, when she'd dismissed him in the gym. It wouldn't be easy with her; it would be like walking on egg shells. 'I'm sorry, Ekaterina. I didn't mean it to come out like that.' Whatever doubts he'd had, they were disappearing. He was on an adrenalin rush. He wanted the case.

'Okay.' She relaxed her body.

'But,' he said. 'No promises. As I said before, I'm not a private detective. And I've got ground rules. I don't want you to—'

'Leave and go to the back of the stadium, directly opposite from where we're sitting.' She stood up. 'You'll see a maroon Lexus. The driver will be reading an edition of *Argumenty I Fakty*. He won't acknowledge you, but he'll know who you are. Get in the back of the vehicle and wait for me.' She turned and walked out.

Scott closed his eyes.

Was he going to live to regret taking on Ekaterina Romanova as his client?

Chapter 7

Day Two: 3pm

It was one of those extra short winter days when the pregnant snow clouds were dark in the middle of the afternoon and gathering to smother the early evening.

Ekaterina took off her *ushanka*, removed two pins from her hair and shook her long black locks free. Where did she get those cobalt-blue eyes? Her skin was olive, and unblemished; olive skin usually meant brown or green eyes. Scott ran his index finger around the inside of his ear. Hairs were beginning to sprout. It wasn't fair, he was only thirty-three.

'Tolik, take a roundabout route to the apartment,' Ekaterina said to the driver.

'Sure.'

Scott glanced in Tolik's direction.

'You can say whatever you like in front of him,' Ekaterina said. 'He's my brother.'

Scott sat up. 'Your brother?' If that was the case, what did he know of their father?

'Not in the sense you mean,' Ekaterina said. 'He's my cousin. His father, Uncle Vadim, was my mother's brother.'

It was a cultural quirk Scott had noticed when he'd first arrived in the country. Russians often called their cousins, brothers. Still, Tolik might be of help to their quest. 'Does Tolik know anything about your father?'

'Only what I know. We grew up together in Krasnodar. But Tolik's four years younger than me and by the time I was old enough to ask questions Uncle Vadim had divorced my aunt and taken Tolik to live with him in Perm.'

'Any other members of your mother's family who could help?'

'No.' Ekaterina shook her head. 'There was only my mother and Uncle Vadim. He's also dead.'

Scott stared at the floor of the car. Tolik was the obvious person to go to the apartment with Ekaterina on the first visit, not a lawyer.

'What?' she said.

'What am I doing here? I mean, why do you need me, specifically, to come to the apartment with you? You have Tolik.'

'You're a lawyer.' She laid her hand on his arm, again. He kept his arm in place and looked into her eyes. They sparkled. 'Lawyers like to see the whole picture before they give advice. Part of the picture will be the testimony from whomever it is who lives here. You'll have the opportunity to hear that testimony first hand.' She tilted her head and withdrew her hand. 'Does that satisfy you, Scott?'

Another well-rehearsed speech. She had an answer for everything. 'What you say makes sense.' His gut feeling was that she was keeping something back from him; though he was puzzled, rather than deterred.

'It's here, on the left,' Tolik said. He pulled into the car parking area of the residential complex and stopped in the one remaining free space, which was covered in snow.

Scott recognized the development. Eighteen months previously he'd waited in the same parking area while a colleague, a Canadian lawyer, collected his Russian fiancée, a naval officer's daughter, from one of the apartments. Scott had driven them to the airport, at the beginning of their journey to a new life in Montreal. The four ten-story blocks were examples of superior Soviet housing; constructed of brownish-yellow brickwork, instead of the duller gray-green blocks of chipped stone which tended to dominate the city's skyline. The apartments were typical of those allocated to medium grade members of the government and the military. But now, the smarter occupants had advanced their careers and moved on to bigger and better things, some to the wealthier districts of north-west Moscow where many oligarchs lived in sybaritic exclusion. Those who'd remained were predominantly low-grade civil servants – the former *apparatchiks.*

'Building 4 is over there,' Tolik said, pointing a finger. 'In the corner.'

'You've been here before, Tolik?' Scott craned his neck to get a better look at the man in the rear-view mirror; his eyes were brown, almost black, and he spoke with a smoker's rasp.

'Not to that building, but I've been called out to this development.'

'Called out?'

'I'm a paramedic by profession.'

'It's his day off,' Ekaterina said. She leant forward. 'Wait here, please Tolik.' Anything suspicious, ring twice and cut off.'

'Will do.'

She pinned her hair up and put her *ushanka* on. 'Ready?' she asked, grabbing the door handle.

'What do you mean "anything suspicious"?' Scott asked.

'This is Russia. Who knows what might happen?' She opened the door, got out and strode off in the direction of the building.

Scott jumped out and hurried after her. 'Ekaterina, wait.' She seemed to be expecting some danger, yet was prepared literally to march headlong into it.

She stopped and turned to him. 'What?'

'I don't want to dampen your enthusiasm, but have you considered that the note might be a cruel hoax? Some perverted mind, government or otherwise?' He wasn't having second thoughts. He wanted her to be more circumspect. Leaving Tolik to watch the outside was all very well, but he might be better employed as an additional witness to testify what went on in the apartment.

'So what do you want me to do?' Her eyes widened. 'Ignore it?'

'No, but—'

'Tell me.' She folded her arms. 'How is your relationship with your father?'

What was she getting at? 'Fine.'

'Well, I have never met my father. I have never seen my father. I have never seen a photograph of my father. I have never spoken to my father. My father has never written to me. I have never written to my father. I do not know what my father looks like. I do not know where my father is.' She turned and marched towards the entry doors to the building. 'I am very pleased that your relationship with your father is fine.'

'Shit,' he said in English, she's so touchy. He dashed after her.

Ekaterina arrived at the lobby doors first. She pushed at them; they weren't locked. Once inside, Scott stepped ahead of his client and took in the smell of stale urine, the broken light bulbs and the graffiti-clad walls. No more five-year plans, no more maintenance.

Apartment 3 was on the ground floor, tucked away behind the central lift shaft. The faded yellow plastic-covered nameplate was in disrepair and no name was decipherable. He tried the bell push; it was stuck. He raised his hand to knock on the door, but Ekaterina pushed it open. It wasn't properly closed. The hallway was narrow and lit by a low wattage bulb, dangling from the ceiling without a shade. An ancient wooden coat-stand with pegs missing stood against the wall, halfway down the passage. Scott felt uneasy. The lobby doors were unlocked and the apartment door was open. Entry was too convenient.

Ekaterina stepped across the threshold.

'Oh no,' Scott said. He gently took her arm and pulled her back.

'Do you mind?' She yanked her arm free.

He blocked her access. 'Stay behind me.'

'Hullo! Hullo! Anybody here?' Scott called in Russian. 'Hullo!'

Silence.

They continued along the passageway and stopped abruptly in an open doorway at the end. It led into a large study area. The room was a bombsite.

A writing desk had been upturned and one of its spindly legs had snapped off, the drawers and their contents were strewn around the floor. Every book, journal, newspaper, folder and loose paper had been removed from the large breakfront bookcase and lay open or torn in a heap in the middle of the room, as if the perpetrator was going to build a bonfire. The telephone cable had been pulled from the wall and some floorboards had been prized apart, exposing botched Soviet screeding and several years of rat droppings. Half a dozen pictures had been snatched or fallen from the walls and smashed onto the floor; the frames lay in one pile and the torn landscapes in another.

'Hullo! Hullo!' Scott called. 'Anybody here?' Again silence. 'This isn't right. I think we should—'

Ekaterina squeezed by Scott and headed for the pile of documents on the floor, where she bent down and picked through them.

'Ekaterina! Don't touch anything. You haven't got your gloves on.'

She put them on, but otherwise ignored him.

'Ekaterina, this is not for us.' He didn't need the added aggravation to his life of having to explain to the owner, and possibly the police, what they were doing in the apartment. 'Let's get out of here.'

She looked up at him. 'You must be joking.' She returned to sorting through the papers. 'This apartment is the only lead I have.'

'Ekaterina. Please. Be sensible. If the owner comes back, how are we going to explain our presence here?'

'You're a smart lawyer. You'll think of something.'

She'd changed. She was as hard as a rock. It was as though all warmth had been drained from her body. 'Ekaterina, look at me please.'

She did so.

'This is a serious matter. We've come in uninvited. The place has been trashed, and we're right in the middle of it. We're going to be prime suspects. And if you're right about the authorities' involvement, all this could be a set up. We mus—'

'I'm not keeping you.' She took her gloves off again and began to flick through the pages of the books.

'For goodness sake, Ekaterina, your prints are all over the place. Do you want to be caught?' She wouldn't listen to reason. But if he picked her up and forcibly carried her out, she'd probably scream the place down and bring the neighbors running. At least, so far as he was aware, nobody knew they were there. He hoped her fingerprints weren't on any database. She wasn't going to leave until she'd sifted through everything. 'Well put your gloves back on. We don't want to leave trace evidence everywhere.' He stepped around the mess on the floor, careful not to touch anything and headed for the passageway leading from the opposite corner of the room. 'I'll see what else is here.' The passage was dark. The light bulb was missing from the central socket in the ceiling, but the kitchen door was open at the far end and the window provided enough natural light, albeit fading to dusk, to enable him to find his way without mishap. A door to the side was ajar and he edged it further open with his knee. It was the living room. He entered and was immediately repelled by a foul smell. He recoiled.

A fully clothed man was sitting, slumped forward in a chair. His head leant to one side, contorted inwards, and his chin was tucked into the top of his breastbone. The back of his head was exposed and hanging by the barest of threads from his skull. The wall behind him was awash with brain matter, blood and other stains that Scott had seen before in Chechnya. He approached the corpse. A smashed picture frame lay at the man's feet. It was a photograph of an airplane, bearing a decal on the hull comprising a white star on a dark blue circle in the center of a horizontal red line. Scott thought it was a US fighter plane, though he didn't know what type.

He covered his mouth with his handkerchief and took a closer look at the corpse, and retched.

'Have you found anything?' Ekaterina called from the passage.

Scott spun round and reached the doorway in time to push Ekaterina out and slam the door behind him. He headed back to the lobby area. 'Come on.'

Ekaterina stood fast. 'Why?' She opened the door.

'Ekaterina! No! No! Don't go in! Come out!' He charged back, but it was too late to stop her from entering the room. He followed her in.

She stopped a meter from the chair and stared at the corpse.

He looked at her hands. 'You haven't put your gloves on.'

She stood in front of the corpse, shaking her head.

She clasped both cheeks and opened her mouth.

Was she going to scream? Scott grabbed her arm and tugged her towards the door.

'What are you doing?' She tried to wriggle free. 'Take your hands off me!'

'I'm doing what smart lawyers do. Protecting my client.' He pulled her out into the passage. 'Do you want to hang around waiting for those authorities you don't trust so much?' Scott certainly didn't. He dragged her along the corridor. 'Come on. We're out of here.' He heard sirens in the distance, getting louder as they approached. He couldn't tell whether they were the police or some other emergency or state service. It seemed that every government official and oligarch in Moscow had sirens fitted to their vehicles.

Ekaterina's cellphone rang, twice – silence.

Scott released her and she voluntarily hurried after him. They rushed into the building's entrance lobby and Scott slammed the apartment door shut behind them. Two teenage boys came in from the street, wheeling their bikes. Damn. Witnesses. Scott pushed Ekaterina back against the wall and pulled her head towards his.

'What do you think you are you doing?' She struggled.

He smothered her from view and pretended to kiss her.

The boys giggled as they parked the bikes against the opposite wall and entered an apartment.

Scott released his embrace and they headed for the street doors. They could see blue and red flashing lights through the frosted fan light. 'Fuck it,' Scott said, and stopped.

'No wait,' Ekaterina said. She opened one of the doors a few centimeters and peered outside. 'It's okay. Come on.' She disappeared through the doorway.

Scott grit his teeth and followed. Their Lexus was parked at the lobby entrance. Tolik was at the wheel, with the engine running. Blue and red lights spun in their portable roof mountings. Clever; the most natural equipment for a paramedic to have at hand? The nearside passenger doors were open.

Ekaterina jumped in the front and Scott in the rear.

Tolik switched on the sirens and sped out of the complex, passing armed police who were surrounding Building 1. If only they knew what had been going on in Building 4.

Scott collapsed back into his seat.

What the fuck had he got himself into?

Chapter 8

Day Two: 6pm

Pravda had finished debriefing Sasha by midday and spent the afternoon studying Sokolov's case file, in readiness for a meeting he'd hoped to set up with him that evening. If Pravda's fears were justified Sokolov was in mortal danger.

Then the call from Alexei.

Pravda stopped at the makeshift police barrier at the Mosfilmovskaya complex. They were scaling down the domestic incident that had erupted earlier that day in Building 1. A tenant, who could only speak Khanty – a minority language spoken in regions of western Siberia – appeared on the balcony of his apartment with his two-year-old son. He was screaming and, apparently, waving a gun. Nobody understood what he was saying; his wife was out visiting friends. The "gun" was a home-made vacuum attachment.

'Good evening citizen,' a uniformed guard said. 'Your papers please.' Pravda was in civilian clothes in his unmarked Moskvitch. He flashed his GRU identity card. The guard straightened and saluted. 'Sorry sir, I didn't know.' He moved the barrier.

'The domestic over in Building 1?'

'Yes, sir,' the guard said.

'Peacefully?'

'They had to shoot him.'

'How is he?'

'Dead, sir.'

Why was everybody so damned trigger-happy? Pravda

drove on and stopped in the far corner of the parking area, out of site of the activity at Building 1. He stared at the entrance lobby to Building 4. First Karat, now Sokolov. He got out of the car, locked the doors and headed for the building.

Alexei emerged from the apartment as Pravda entered the lobby. He was beaming and carrying a video camera. His hands were shaking, obviously from excitement; he hadn't yet learnt how to conceal his feelings. Perhaps Pravda had promoted him too early. 'Lev, before you go in, look at this download from the surveillance team.'

Pravda moved aside from the open doorway so as not to obstruct the comings and goings of the white-suited SOCOs. An officer handed him a pair of transparent gloves and protective shoes. He put them on and studied Alexei's video. They watched a man and a woman dashing from the building and hurling themselves into a Lexus. The car sped past the police contingent at the other building and out of the complex, with its sirens wailing and emergency lights flashing. Pravda furrowed his brows. 'Scott Mitchell?'

'No question,' Alexei said.

There was no doubt. The surveillance team, specially formed for the particular task, were based in an apartment block directly opposite Building 4. Housed on the third floor, they could pick out the faces of people emerging from the lobby with ease. Though Pravda had never met Mitchell personally, he'd seen him through a telephoto lens on two occasions and on television in media interviews. He also had a gallery of snapshots of the man in the GRU file. Mitchell hadn't hidden his face and there was no mistaking the dimple in the middle of his chin. The identity of the woman, however, was a mystery. She had kept her head down.

'Our sanctimonious human rights lawyer,' Alexei said. 'Caught red-handed.' He replayed the video shot.

'What do these lawyers say? *Inflagrante del*…something.'

'*Delicto, inflagrante delicto*,' Pravda said. 'Except that he wasn't.'

'Lev?'

Pravda looked at Alexei, with a half-smile, as a teacher might look at a student when trying to explain the obvious. 'We have a shot of him coming out of this building, not this apartment. I'm no lawyer, but to my mind this is not evidence of his being *inflagrante*, or *delicto*.'

'But if he wasn't in the apartment,' Alexei said. 'Why did he rush out of the building, jump into the car and do a "Formula 1" exit?'

Scott Mitchell may have had his faults, but Pravda didn't believe for a minute that murder was one of them. Besides, according to Alexei's call, Sokolov had been slaughtered in the same manner as Karat and with a similar weapon. There was nothing in either of their files to connect Mitchell to them. 'A good question and we shall ask him in due course,' Pravda said. 'Meanwhile, I want to examine the body.' They entered the apartment and headed for the study area. Pravda led the way. He hadn't been to the apartment for a year or so, but nothing had changed, in the narrow hallway at least. The door was wide open. Bright arc lights lit the room. Two members of the forensic team who, like the surveillance team, had been specifically chosen for the task, were sitting on the floor sifting through the documents.

'Crate the lot and take it all to the warehouse,' Pravda said. 'I want everything removed for further examination.' One of the team looked up at Pravda and opened his mouth. 'Including the furniture,' Pravda said.

'Leon.' A third member of the team, Galina, appeared from behind a chair in the corner of the room, dangling a transparent evidence bag in front of him. It contained a piece of material. 'It's a woman's glove,' she said. 'A very expensive glove. I found it by the chair.'

Sokolov was unlikely to have entertained any women who wore expensive gloves, be they friends or strangers. 'See if you can get prints,' Pravda said. 'It takes priority.'

'I'm on my way.' She headed for the door.

'And call me as soon as you have any news...whatever it is, whatever time it is.'

'Understood.' Galina left the room.

Things could be looking up. Perhaps he would know who Mitchell's mystery woman was before the night was out. Despite what he'd told Alexei, Pravda too was of the opinion that the human rights lawyer and his female companion had been in the apartment. They weren't the murderers, but they had been there. They must have discovered the body and ran for it. It was the most plausible explanation for their melodramatic exit from the building. 'Where's the body?' Pravda said to Alexei.

'Follow me. In here.'

They walked down the short passageway and into the living room, where three more SOCOs were photographing and examining the body, while two others were taking prints from the furniture and window sills. Pravda bent over Sokolov's body and inspected the gunshot wound.

'We've recovered a 7.62 caliber bullet,' Alexei said. 'It went through his head, the back of the chair, the plasterwork behind, the brick wall and it ended up halfway inside a tree. Armor-piercing payload.'

'And probably from a PSS.' Pravda sighed. 'Definitely the same as Karat.' A PSS was a *pistolet samozaryadne spetsialny*. The specially silenced handgun was reputed to be the quietest weapon in the world. The key factor was that unlike a conventional silencer, which attached to the end of the barrel, the silencer in the PSS was contained in the bullet, the SP-4. The main body of the gun contained a cartridge case that housed the entire explosive material, so no gases escaped to produce a noise or a flash.

Pravda surveyed the crime scene. Apart from the splatter

of the body material, and the smashed photograph on the floor, nothing seemed out of place. The study had been ransacked, to the verge of deconstruction, but the living room was untouched; the table and chairs, the cabinet full of china crockery, the television set, two small side tables and the grandfather clock all appeared to have been unscathed. 'What about the police?' Pravda asked Alexei. He went to the window and peeked through the curtains. A group of uniformed men stood around smoking outside the lobby entrance to Building 1. 'Have they been sniffing around?'

'They asked just before you arrived, but I didn't let them in,' Alexei said. 'I told them we're doing a hush-hush training exercise. If they leave us alone, we'll leave them alone. They killed an unarmed man.' He chuckled. 'Our surveillance team's got it all on film.'

Pravda glared at his number two. 'Come with me.' Pravda walked out of the room. 'To the kitchen.'

Alexei followed.

Pravda slapped his gloves on the kitchen worktop. 'Alexei, the killing of an unarmed man is no laughing matter. I don't want to hear you talking like that again. You must learn to—'

'But, Lev, I wasn't laughing at the killing. It's the fact that we've got the police in the palm of our hands. We can—'

'Enough.' Pravda held up his hand.

'Okay. I'm sorry.'

He looked as though he meant it. 'Now, did our all-seeing surveillance team get Sokolov's murderer on film, by any chance? Coming or going? Because I'm damned sure it wasn't Mitchell or his female companion who killed him,' Pravda said. 'Or wasn't doing the job the team are paid to do exciting enough for them?'

'No. They were...' Alexei stopped. 'I haven't given them a full debriefing yet. Maybe some—'

'Jesus wept!' Pravda slammed his hand down on the worktop. 'We were supposed to be protecting this man!' Alexei was either covering up for the team, misplaced loyalty, or hadn't yet got to the bottom of it. Pravda checked his watch, pulled out his cellphone and punched in a number. 'Volodya? It's Lieutenant-General Pravda.' Volodya was the leader of the surveillance team.

'Yes, sir.'

'I am going to debrief you tomorrow.'

'Yes sir, at what time?'

'2am.'

'That's 2pm tomorrow afternoon, sir?'

'No, Volodya, it's 2am, tomorrow morning.'

'But I'm going to be—'

'My *dacha* at 2am. Don't be late.'

Pravda disconnected.

'That's a bit harsh, Lev.' Alexei had a pleading look in his eyes. That was a plus side to Alexei as far as Pravda was concerned. He had tried to instill in Alexei the need, on occasions, to defend his juniors. But only on the right occasions. And this wasn't a right occasion.

'I'm not going to shoot him,' Pravda said. 'But he needs to learn that actions have consequences.' He slapped his thigh. 'Right. Let's move on. Who is this woman?'

'We're working on it,' Alexei said. 'But it's not easy. As you saw, she kept her head down.'

'Well,' Pravda said. 'Assuming they were in Sokolov's apartment, we can probably also safely assume that she was Mitchell's client and they were there because of her, and not him.'

'Why so?'

'Because,' Pravda said. 'Why else would Mitchell, a lawyer, be there? If it was for a personal reason, he wouldn't have taken the woman along with him. We know he hasn't got any relatives in Russia and he's not currently dating anybody. So—'

'She could be a new member of his firm,' Alexei said.

Pravda stopped in mid-sentence. Alexei was right. 'Okay, let's wait for the prints results on the glove. Where did the Lexus go?'

Alexei shrugged. 'We don't know. We couldn't get backup in time.'

'Understood,' Pravda said. 'Still, we know where Mitchell lives and works. We can bring him in at any time.' He opened a wall cupboard and used a pen to prize apart and search between rows of rice packets. 'Not that he's going to betray his precious attorney-client privilege, if she is a client. He'll clam up.' He closed the cupboard. 'And the car?'

'False plates. Could be any one of a thousand cruising the city. Take your pick.'

'The sirens,' Pravda said. 'Interesting.' He opened and closed a succession of drawers, still using his pen to examine their contents. 'A clever means of escape, bearing in mind what was going on at Building 1.' He looked at Alexei. 'But they couldn't have anticipated the domestic and that the area would be drowned out with police sirens and illuminated with flashing lights.'

'So, they probably regularly carry sirens and flashing lights in the vehicle,' Alexei said.

'It's plausible.'

'The driver, or the woman,' Alexei continued. 'Is connected to one of the emergency services? Government employee?'

'Well, I don't think Scott Mitchell has any reason to possess such equipment.' He took two photos from his pocket. 'Anyway, we'll deal with him later.' He laid the photos on the worktop. They were headshots of Sokolov and Karat; respectively taken three and five years previously. 'We have a more immediate problem.'

Alexei studied them. 'Yes, two down, how many more to go?'

Chapter 9

Day Three: 9am

Scott had spent a fitful night thinking about the body on Mosfilmovskaya. He couldn't get the picture of the bullet hole out of his mind; he had flashbacks to his time in Grozny. In the morning a frightening thought occurred to him: what if it was Ekaterina's father? He looked at the note again. It said that "he's been held since the 1970s…" A simple reading would mean that he's still in prison. But the note was dated four weeks earlier. It was conceivable that her father had been released, or escaped, within that period and had been living at the apartment. What did she say in the car park? "I have never seen my father. I have never seen a photograph of my father." There was no way she could have recognized him.

Inessa, Scott's personal assistant, buzzed him on the intercom. 'Scott, it's the police.'

'What do they want?'

'A Captain Vassiliyev of the Moscow City Police Department wants to talk to you.'

'I don't remember making the appointment.' Scott checked the diary on his computer. 'No, today's clear.'

'Then you're free to see me,' came a voice from the open doorway.

Scott looked up at the figure and pinched himself.

Captain Vassiliyev held up his hand. 'Don't say anything, it's all been said a million times before. But I haven't got a glass eye and I don't smoke cigars, only cigarettes.' He waved a packet at him. 'Do you mind if I sit down?' He sat on the client chair facing Scott.

'Scott?' Inessa's voice came through the intercom.

'It's okay,' Scott said. 'It's okay.' He disconnected and gawped at Lieutenant Columbo's twin; a shade taller, but in all other respects an uncanny resemblance to the American actor Peter Falk. 'It's remarkable. Absolutely remarkable.'

'That's not all,' Vassiliyev said. 'We share the same birthday, September 16, a few years apart, but still the same date. When you think about it, there's, what, six or seven billion people in the world?' He tapped out a cigarette from the pack. 'What are the odds of two people, not twins, looking alike? Pretty good I'd say. And if they both happen to be criminal investigators, homicide detectives to be precise...' He lingered on the word "homicide". 'Well, more credit to our Grand Designer, I say. And it gives the anthropologists something to get their teeth into on a rainy day. Don't you agree?' He held the cigarette up 'May I?'

Scott nibbled at the inside of his cheek. None of his current cases involved homicide. Well, not of the type that would concern the police; they were military matters. He fiddled with his watch strap.

Vassiliyev waved his cigarette at Scott.

'Er, yes, Captain. You may smoke.' Scott took an ashtray from the drawer and slid it across the desk towards the policeman.

Captain Vassiliyev lit his cigarette with his zip lighter, inhaled and blew the smoke out of the side of his mouth, directing it away from Scott's face.

Scott forced a smile. 'So, what can I do for you?'

'What were you doing yesterday afternoon?' Vassiliyev curled his bottom lip. 'Say, between 2 and 5pm?'

Scott wasn't going to jump to any conclusions. If he had to lie, he should stick to as much of the truth as possible. To lie successfully, a person should have a good memory. Scott's wasn't perfect. 'Working on client business.' He tugged at his watch strap.

'Where? Here?'

'No.'

'Where then?'

'Sorry, but I'm not at liberty to tell you.' Scott kept his eyes on Vassiliyev's, trying not to act evasively.

'Client confidentiality?'

'You got it.'

Captain Vassiliyev took a long drag on his cigarette, exhaled and watched the smoke rise to the ceiling. 'Interesting concept, that. Client confidentiality.' He looked at Scott. 'You can use it to hide behind all sorts of...let's say...awkward situations.'

'I'm not hiding behind anything. I'm just doing my job. It's my duty, my obligation, as a lawyer, to keep my client's affairs confidential.'

'Male or female?' Vassiliyev asked.

Scott waved his finger at the detective. 'Nice try, but—'

'Client confidentiality.'

'Afraid so.'

Vassiliyev took another drag and leant forward. 'Do me a favor would you, please, Mr Mitchell?' Smoke appeared, entangled with his words.

'I'm always ready to help the police if I can, Captain Vassiliyev.'

Vassiliyev coughed, squashed the butt of his cigarette in the ashtray and took a brown envelope from inside his coat pocket. He pushed it across the desk to Scott. 'Ask your client, Mr or Mrs Whoever-he-she-may-be, to give you permission to explain this to me.' He stood up and headed for the door.

Scott picked up the envelope and began to open it. 'Captain?'

The detective turned round. 'Yes?'

'No "just one last question Mr Mitchell",' Scott said.

The homicide specialist half closed his eyes. 'Like

I said, "a million times before, a million times before".'
He raised his hand. 'Until we meet again.' He left the
room.

Scott opened the envelope and pulled out a single
photograph. He focused, and his heart fluttered.

It was a timed and dated picture of Ekaterina and
himself entering the apartment block on Mosfilmovskaya.

Chapter 10

Day Three: 10am

Pravda's 2am debriefing of Volodya – at which the young team leader, to his credit, had made no excuses and accepted that he'd messed up – meant that the general's early morning swim had begun late. He was completing his twenty-fifth length of the GRU's Olympic-sized pool when he spotted Yelena waving at him from under one of the water slides. He swam over to her and they rested at the water's edge. Yelena was the only woman in his team, and the best shot by far with a sniper's weapon. And for some obscure reason she had made more free-fall motorcycle parachute jumps from 3,000 meters than anybody else on the planet. The rest of the men joked that she would prefer to have a throbbing Harley Davidson between her legs than a throbbing Mr Davidson. She never sought to disabuse her colleagues of that notion and none of them had ever managed to date her. The apparent ambiguity of her position rattled some of Pravda's predominantly chauvinistic team. Pravda, on the other hand, was of the opinion that conflict bred character, and he did nothing to discourage Yelena's conduct. 'Good news first or bad news?' she asked.

'Always the good news,' Pravda said. 'That way, I'm in a happy frame of mind when I get the bad news.'

'It's Ekaterina Gravchenko or, as she's gone back to using her mother's family name, Ekaterina Romanova.'

'What about her?' Pravda wiped the water from his eyes.

'She's the woman, with Mitchell, in Sokolov's building.'

Pravda wiped his eyes again. Ekaterina Romanova's husband, recently estranged, was Konstantin Gravchenko. He was the country's richest businessman. They had a young daughter. Although Pravda's unit had no official involvement in monitoring domestic commercial operations – that was the responsibility of other agencies – they sometimes checked what Gravchenko was up to, especially if the man had encounters with foreign political and military dignitaries, people whose personal greed had got the better of their public obligations.

The synapses in Pravda's brain began firing. He looked at the other swimmers in the pool. They were a blur. Gravchenko's connections to the Kremlin, Putin in particular, were second to none.

'Mrs Oligarch herself,' Yelena continued.

One step at a time. 'Are you absolutely certain about this?' Pravda asked. 'How did you find out?'

'Extreme hard work on my part, and luck.' She hesitated and grinned. 'One per cent the former and ninety-nine per cent the latter. I'm in the Arbat this morning and I spot her coming out of Gravchenko's office. She's wearing the same very expensive red and gray ski jacket as on our surveillance film.'

'There must be hundreds, if not thousands, of those very expensive, as you call it, ski jackets in Moscow.' He wriggled a finger in his ear to rid it of water. 'If that's your proof, I—'

'Ah, but Lev, she was with daughter Tanya and her cousin Tolik and they got into a Lexus, different registration plates, but the same color as in the film. And Igor in the lab recognized Tolik as the driver in the film. Igor knows him, by sight. Igor's sister works in the same hospital as Tolik, and Igor's seen his sister chatting to Tolik when Igor's been to pick her up.'

'And Igor is sure that Tolik was driving the getaway Lexus?'

'One hundred and fifty per cent. The shot is dead clear.'

It sounded interesting, and it would explain the flashing lights and sirens. Writers of fiction should never employ coincidences to get their protagonists out of trouble, only to get them into it. But that principle didn't always apply to real life situations. Pravda could testify to the fact that many a puzzle was solved because he "got lucky". 'Okay, let's say I'm half convinced,' Pravda said. 'But we need to place her in the apartment, not just the building.'

'Shall I keep up surveillance on her?'

'No, leave her to me.' He was going to test Ekaterina Romanova's mettle.

'Any prints on the glove?' Yelena asked.

'None that are on our databases.'

'What shall I do about Gravchenko?' Yelena said.

Pravda couldn't think what Gravchenko or Romanova would want with Sokolov. The dead man's knowledge was more than twenty years out of date and Gravchenko was a captain of industry. Sokolov's status would have been of no tangible interest to a scheming capitalist. 'Keep up the routine surveillance, but no more. Sokolov's dead. Neither Mr nor Mrs Gravchenko are going to be interested in the apartment now it's been stripped and sanitized.'

Yelena hauled herself out of the pool and sat on the side, dangling her legs in the water. 'Ready for the bad news?'

'Go on.' Pravda remained in the water, with his arms and elbows resting on the side.

'Well, Sasha says that the police precinct is flooded with rumors about the bombing of Romanova's BMW.'

'Which rumors in particular?' Pravda had heard several.

'The preliminary report points a finger at the FSB.'

'Where did this come from?' He knew of that rumor.

'A disgruntled civvy administrator, working in the mayor's office. The mayor wants to blame Chechen terrorists, a random one-off.'

'And where's this disgruntled civvy now?' Pravda asked.

'In hospital.' Yelena stirred up the water with her feet. 'Having his legs removed.'

'What?' Had he misheard? 'I don't understand.'

'It goes like this.' Yelena fidgeted on the edge of the pool, as if to make her seating position more comfortable. 'The civvy is tailgating a large truck on the Garden Ring. It's overloaded, carrying a zillion tree stumps.'

'Tree stumps?'

'Yes, Lev, I know, not an everyday sight on the city's inner ring road.'

'Go on.'

'The truck stops without warning. The civvy slams into the back of the truck. The fastenings holding the stumps loosen. The stumps cascade off the truck, like an avalanche, and wreck the civvy's family Fiat. His legs are crushed under the dashboard.'

'What does the truck driver say about the abrupt braking?'

'Nothing.'

'Why not?'

'Because he's dead.'

Pravda rolled his eyes. 'How?' Maybe she had something.

'He jumps from the driving cab and runs away from the scene, down the center of the road. A car appears out of nowhere and catapults him into the next century. The driver speeds away in a cloud of dust – to his next hit, I reckon.'

So the mayor of Moscow conspired with the FSB to fake a Chechen outrage and target Gravchenko's wife as the innocent victim? No way. The mayor wasn't that stupid. Estranged or not, Konstantin Gravchenko had the wherewithal and connections to pull the city apart to track down the killers of his wife and beloved daughter. But it did sound like a ham-fisted FSB operation; from the BMW bombing to the tree stumps fiasco to the hit and run. That didn't mean the mayor was involved. There was no evidence to indicate his culpability.

Pravda drew a picture in his mind, in the shape of a two-dimensional pyramid. At the apex stood Ekaterina Romanova, looming large over Scott Mitchell who was trapped in a bubble at her side. An arrow descended from her down to the left hand base, where Sokolov's apartment rested. The right hand base housed an exploding BMW, from which an arrow headed upwards towards Romanova. He placed the letters "FSB", followed by a question mark, in the middle of the triangle.

He heaved himself out of the pool. 'It's time for a chat with Aunt Olga.'

By 1pm the cold weather was colonizing the capital with a vengeance; it was minus twenty and falling fast. Pravda wedged his Moskvitch between two intercontinental transporters and kept the engine running while he waited – Russian-made car heaters had a habit of only working in the summer. The quiet cul-de-sac behind the Hotel Ukraina on the Dorogomilovskaya bend of the Moscow River was across the river from the Tarasa Shevchenko Embankment, where the local police had found Karat's body. The Ukraina was one of Stalin's "wedding cake" edifices that had dominated Moscow's skyline until the collapse of the Union in 1991.

A plump woman with large stubby fingers protruding from moth-bitten mittens approached the vehicle. Pravda opened the front passenger door and she maneuvered her bulk into the seat. Pravda kissed her cheek. It was smooth despite her encounters with sixty-seven Russian winters.

'How's Anna…and my little Stepan?'

'Fine, Aunt.' Pravda held out his hand. 'Did you bring them?'

'What's the hurry? Do you youngsters have no time for small talk with your elders anymore?'

'Forgive me, Olga Andreyevna.' Pravda tapped his fingers on the dashboard. 'But this really is a matter of preventing deaths.' And Aunt Olga's information might point him in the right direction.

'Here.' She pulled a red folder from a pocket inside her coat.

He snatched the package.

She lit a Cuban cigar and inhaled to the depths of her lungs.

Pravda opened the folder and pulled out a sheet of paper with five typed paragraphs and two photographs attached. He skimmed through the text and studied the photos. 'Huh. She's a beautiful woman. I can see why Gravchenko married her.'

Aunt Olga whacked him in the chest with the back of her hand; ash fell everywhere. 'And you're married, to my niece, remember?'

He brushed the ash from his lap and rubbed his chest; he would have been bruised were it not for his winter coat. 'Still doing the weights, I see.' He studied Ekaterina Romanova's headshot and pictured a craggy-faced Gravchenko. 'He's got to be twenty, twenty-five years her senior.'

'The media say she's thirty-six or seven,' Aunt Olga said.

He chuckled. 'The things five hundred billion rubles can buy.'

'Not forgetting the father complex.'

'What do you mean?' Pravda turned to her.

'She never knew her father.' Aunt Olga inhaled deeply and blew out the smoke at the windscreen in front of her. 'He died before she was born.'

Pravda pursed his lips. That was news to him. He reread the five paragraphs of text. 'We agree. Mitchell is clean.'

'He is, in the sense that he's no criminal.' She wiped the mist on the windscreen with her fingers. 'No tax dodges. But...' Aunt Olga hesitated.

'But?' Pravda asked.

She turned to him, shaking her head. 'It's not only us, at the FSB, who aren't happy with this Chechen case.'

Pravda sat back and looked ahead. He understood her. 'He's only one man, Aunt. Are you telling me that President Putin is frightened of *one man*?' Putin's KGB career was a matter of public record, as was the composition of his closest advisers, the *siloviki*; they were principally past and present members of the FSB and former KGB. He looked at her. 'Aunt, I—'

'I'm not telling you anything. This meeting isn't taking place.'

He frowned. 'Okay.' She wouldn't say any more about the President. He ran his fingers over the photo of Romanova. 'Why does she need Mitchell's services?'

'You asked for the information. You've put the two together, not us.'

This gnawed at the general. Why didn't the FSB have their agents crawling all over Mitchell after Colonel Yakovlev's fiasco of interrogating him at the airport? He tapped on Romanova's photo. 'And why is there nothing written here about her?' he said. 'Your file is all about Mitchell.'

'Lev, her file has disappeared, except for the picture.' Her body tensed. She clenched her fist and let the ash drop onto her lap from the cigar in her other hand. 'I don't understand it.' She shook her head violently. 'I don't understand it, Lev.'

He could see fear in her eyes. Aunt Olga had been the FSB's chief archivist for years. Her files never went missing. Her refusal to surrender them without a fight was legendary, even within the GRU. He put his hand on her leg. 'Aunt, is this true? Do you really have no idea what's happened to Romanova's file?' He wanted to believe she was being honest with him; that blood was thicker than water.

'You don't believe me?' She seemed genuinely hurt. She opened her door and the rush of cold air caused Pravda to lose his breath. She flicked the lighted cigar across the road and shut the door. 'Lev, you're family. I'm not lying to you.' She began to shake.

Was it the cold, or fear?

Pravda's left leg began to jack-hammer. 'Okay.' He sighed. 'But one last question.'

She grabbed the door handle.

'Please, Aunt.' He leant across her and put his hand on hers. 'Please.'

She looked at him. 'Go on then.'

'There are rumors'. He removed his hand. 'The bombing of Romanova's BMW.'

She smirked. 'Tell me something I didn't know."

'Did the FSB have anything to do with it?' He had to ask the question. The only person within the FSB who might give him a straight answer was his aunt.

She grunted and opened the door. 'If we did, do you think anybody would tell me?'

It was worth the try.

'Goodbye, Lev.' She pecked him on the cheek, got out of the car and disappeared around the corner.

It was time for action.

Chapter 11

It had taken Scott several calls to make contact with Ekaterina after Captain Vassiliyev's visit. She wouldn't come to his office but agreed to meet him on the Sparrow Hills at the foot of the approach road leading to the Moscow University campus, because she would be "in the area" and it was away from the city's crowded center, yet not isolated from civilization.

He arrived first and was alone, apart from a woman motorcyclist videoing the metropolis. Instead of remaining in the warmth and security of his vehicle, he got out and strolled over to the observation point; a favorite spot for newlyweds to have their photos taken, with the sprawling city in the background. If Captain Vassiliyev seriously suspected them of committing the murder, they would be languishing in the cells. Russian state organs paid no respect to the Western liberal notion of client confidentiality. He heard the sound of wheels crunching the snow behind him and turned round.

Ekaterina emerged from a cab. She spoke to the driver and he switched off the ignition.

Scott gave a perfunctory smile as she approached, though he was far from happy. Ekaterina was frowning. He'd only said on the phone that he had "some urgent news". 'Captain Vassiliyev of the Moscow City Police Department gave me this.' He pulled the photograph from his pocket and handed it to her. 'He wants to know what we were doing there.'

She took the photo without looking at it and glanced

over his shoulder. 'Who is that woman?'

'What? I don't know,' Scott said, his eyes fixed on Ekaterina. 'A tourist, maybe?'

'Up here? On a motorbike? In the middle of winter?' Her look hardened.

'Well,' he said. 'Perhaps she's a professional, a film-maker, a geography teacher. How do I know?' He didn't understand her concern. The surveillance photo was far more important to their well-being than somebody videoing the landscape. 'What does it matter? Please, Ekaterina, concentrate on the photograph.'

She glanced at the photo and thrust it back into his hand. 'What did you tell him?' Her voice was distant. She was looking again at the motorcyclist.

'Nothing.'

She glared at Scott.

'Nothing. I said it was a matter of client confidentiality.'

She raised her eyebrows. 'So you told him I was your client.'

'Ekaterina.' Where was she going with this? Vassiliyev didn't know who she was. Scott was more vulnerable.

'What else did you reveal?' She stared at the motor-cyclist again.

'Nothing, I didn't reveal anything.' He felt like a sixth -grader up before the principal. 'What's got into you, Ekaterina?'

She had no time to respond before they heard a revving sound from Scott's Cherokee parked thirty meters away. They both turned and looked at the vehicle. A man in a balaclava was sitting in the driving seat. Two others, also masked, walked towards the pair.

'What the...!' Scott clenched his fists and ran to meet them. 'What the fuck do you think you're doing?'

One of the men whipped out a pistol and pointed it at Scott's face. 'Stop right there, Mr Mitchell.'

Scott halted. Mr Mitchell? An unusually polite form

of address for car thieves.

The other man grabbed him by the arm and marched him back to the Cherokee, followed by the man with the gun. Scott tried to wriggle free, but the grip was too firm. 'Who are you people? Where are you taking me?'

The man holding his arm opened the rear passenger door, pushed Scott inside and got in after him. Before Scott could orient himself, the gunman jumped in next to him from the other side and the vehicle roared away.

Scott looked out of the rear window. Ekaterina was being frog-marched back to the cab by the woman motorcyclist and the cab driver.

When Ekaterina Romanova strutted into the room of the GRU's "safe" apartment, located behind the world famous GUM department store off Red Square, Pravda felt Aunt Olga's heavyweight left hand – and rubbed an imaginary blow to his abdomen. Neither Romanova's rare media photos nor the FSB headshot did her justice.

He waved away her escort and beckoned her to sit down in an armchair by the window. He glanced at his watch and pulled up a chair opposite. The lack of sleep was catching up on him and he had to make a long drive across country later that evening. His helicopter was out of action because of adverse weather conditions.

Romanova was Russian; she wouldn't believe him if he told her that he wasn't out to harm her. Furthermore, she was intelligent; she held two degrees in economics. Small talk wouldn't get him anywhere. 'Why do you need the services of a British human rights lawyer, Ms Romanova, or should I address you as Mrs Gravchenko?'

'Who are you?'

He was in civilian clothes. 'I am Lieutenant-General Pravda of the GRU.'

'I have nothing to discuss with you.'

Her response reminded Pravda of an American film

he'd seen. Two lawyers were trying to negotiate an amicable settlement of a $200,000 contract dispute on behalf of their respective clients. When asked what the debtor party's opening offer was to be, his lawyer replied, "Nothing. Your client can rot in hell for his money." The other lawyer rubbed his hands together and said, "Good, at least we've established the parameters."

'What were you and Scott Mitchell doing yesterday afternoon in Building 4 of the old military apartments on Mosfilmovskaya Street?'

'I have no idea what you are talking about.' She threw her head back.

His bones were aching. He took a small video camera from his pocket, set up the film of the pair dashing from the building and handed it to her.

She took the camera and watched the film, without emotion. 'What about it?' She put the camera on the table.

Pravda kept a straight face, trying not to betray his frustration. 'It's the evidence.'

'That's not me.' She sniffed.

She was cool. The shot of her head was not distinct enough for the facial recognition technology. Still, he persisted. 'Ms Romanova. We have sufficient evidence to place you not only coming out of the building, but also in Apartment 3.' He pointedly stared at the gloves she was holding in her hands. They were of a different color and material to the glove he'd found in the apartment. She didn't move a muscle; there wasn't the slightest sign of discomfort.

'I have things to do.' She stood up. 'I'm leaving.'

'Does the name Yuri Vladimirovich Sokolov mean anything to you?' Pravda asked.

'Not a thing.'

Again, her demeanor betrayed no emotion. Pravda wasn't yet ready to disclose that it was Sokolov who'd been murdered. Or, if she didn't know, that it was his apartment. 'I could lock you up and throw away the key. Nobody would ever know where you were. And you would never see Tanya again.'

For a split second, she furrowed her brows and blinked, twice. 'Goodbye.' She turned and left the room.

Pravda made no attempt to prevent her. It would have taken a month of Sundays to break her. The more aggressive FSB methods of interrogation weren't an option for the civilized military intelligence officer. He made a phone call. 'Bring Mitchell in.' Pravda's men had put the English lawyer in an adjacent apartment while he interrogated Romanova.

Mitchell needed no encouragement to enter the room. He broke free from his two chaperons as he came through the door. He stopped, tilted his head to one side and widened his eyes. Mitchell had recognized him. That didn't surprise Pravda. The lawyer was often making legal requests for disclosures in the Russian Military Archives.

'You're...Where's Ekaterina Romanova? What's going on?'

'Mr Mitchell, take a seat.' Pravda gestured towards Romanova's chair and sat down himself. Mitchell was taller than he looked on film. He stood proud and held his shoulders back. He could have had military training, though Pravda could find no trace of it in his investigations of the man. With his full head of swept back black hair, a pronounced, straight nose and firm, but dimpled, jaw the man was made for the movies. If only Mitchell had chosen such a career, Pravda's life could have been so much easier.

'I'll remain standing,' Mitchell said. 'Now, do you mind telling me what you've done with Ekaterina?'

'We can hold this conversation in English if it's easier for you Mr Mitchell.'

'Answer my questions, will you please?' Mitchell persisted in Russian.

'Where's Ekaterina?'

'I am Lieutenant-General Pravda of the GRU.'

'I know very well who you are,' Mitchell said.

'Mrs Gravchenko is safe,' Pravda said. 'She is probably on her way home.'

Mitchell frowned and he appeared to rock on his feet. 'Mrs Who?'

Pravda didn't betray his mild amusement that Romanova obviously hadn't told Mitchell who her husband was. 'Ekaterina Romanova, as you know her, is Ekaterina Gravchenko, the wife of Konstantin Gravchenko, the oligarch.'

'Yes…I know that. I…I just didn't hear you properly.'

A quick recovery, but not quick enough.

'So tell me, why have you kidnapped us?' Mitchell's eyes darted around the room.

Pravda wasn't ready to interpret Mitchell's apparent agitation as a concern that he and Romanova might have been seen at the apartment. He had no way of knowing about Pravda's film at that moment. Mitchell's edginess could well have been because he was annoyed at the harassment he'd been receiving since returning to Moscow. 'Are you sure you wouldn't like to sit down Mr Mitchell?'

'I've had enough of this nonsense,' Mitchell said. 'I had all this at the airport. When are you people going to learn that you can't scare me out of the country? I'm leaving.' He backed away towards the door.

'Before you go.' Pravda picked up the camera from the table and reset the film again. 'Would you mind telling me what you and Mrs Grav…Ms Romanova, were doing in Apartment 3, Building 4 on Mosfilmovskaya Street yesterday afternoon at around 3pm?' He stretched out and handed the camera to Mitchell.

Mitchell bit his lip as he watched the video.

'Perhaps you will now sit down?' Pravda offered his hand to the vacant armchair.

Mitchell leant forward, put the camera on the table and sat down.

'Now, I repeat the question,' Pravda said. 'What were you and Ms Romanova doing in Apartment 3, Building 4 on Mosfilmovskaya Street?'

'I deny being there.' Mitchell sat up and folded his arms.

Of course the lawyer denied it. The film only showed him emerging from the building. 'I want to help you.' Pravda massaged both his eyes and stifled a yawn. 'Maybe to save your lives.'

'You call kidnapping us on the streets in broad daylight "helping us"?'

'If I had sent you an invitation you wouldn't have accepted or you would have procrastinated like lawyers do, taken weeks to respond and imposed unreasonable preconditions. I don't have the time to play such games.' He leant forward. 'And neither have you. I need answers. Peoples' lives are at risk.'

'So you said. Ours.' Mitchell crossed his legs, cupped his hands in his lap and relaxed back in his chair.

Pravda was losing the lawyer. Mitchell had adjusted to his situation and was gaining in confidence. Why not? That was what he was trained to do. 'Possibly,' he said. 'And others, certainly.'

'How are we in danger?'

'What were you and Ms Romanova doing at the building?' He wasn't going to be sidetracked.

'Sorry. No can tell.' He curled his bottom lip and shook his head.

'What has your client retained you for?'

Mitchell wagged his index finger at Pravda. 'No, no, Lieutenant-General. If I'm her lawyer, and I'm not admitting that I am, any instructions she might have given me would be confidential.' He pulled his legs under the chair and folded his arms again.

Pravda cursed silently.

'Does the name Yuri Vladimirovich Sokolov mean anything to you?'

'No, why? Who is he?'

Mitchell's reply was believable, as was Romanova's, especially as both his FSB and GRU files showed no con-nection to the man. Nonetheless... 'You've been in Moscow for a number of years. You must have met many people in your line of work. How can you be so sure that you don't know the name?'

'You asked if the name *meant* anything to me. It doesn't. If you're asking if I have *heard* of the name, I don't know. As you say, I've met many people in my time in Moscow, but I don't make a habit of trying to remember every single name mentioned in every single document that comes across my desk or is on a conference delegate's identity tag.'

Pravda blinked. A lead weight was attached to his eyelids. He blinked again.

Mitchell stood up. 'Well, if you've no more—'

Pravda also stood up and pulled a plane ticket from his jacket pocket. He handed it to Mitchell.

'What's this?' Mitchell asked.

'Your life line. You will be taking the morning Aeroflot flight from Sheremetyevo to London tomorrow. You will not come back to Russia for the foreseeable future.' Romanova was the key. With Mitchell out of the way, that would be one less person she could turn to for advice and guidance.

'I live in this city.' Mitchell pulled himself up to his full height. He was two or three centimeters taller than Pravda. 'I have a law firm to run. Oppressed clients in your country depend on me to secure their basic human rights. I also have employees that depend on me for their livelihood; mostly Russian employees. I'm not going anywhere.' He offered the ticket back to Pravda and grabbed the door handle. 'If this is part of your government's Chechen—'

'It's got nothing to do with your representation of the Chechens.' Pravda ignored the ticket. 'Nothing whatsoever. I am deporting you for your own good. Keep the ticket. You'll need it for when you change your mind.'

'Deporting me? You can't. You've got no legal right to deport me.' He waved the ticket in the air. 'This isn't a court order. And I won't be changing my mind.' He pocketed the ticket. 'But I'll keep it as evidence for when I sue you lot for harassment.' He opened the door and stepped outside.

'Forget about your legal rights, Mr Mitchell,' Pravda said. 'You are no longer in a court of law.'

Chapter 12

Day Three: 7pm

"Mitchell Caught Fleeing Murder Arrest Warrant."

This potential media headline tormented Scott as he sorted through his case notes from the Strasburg trial. Lieutenant-General Leonid Igorovich Pravda was no fool. Fifteen months previously, Scott put together the CVs and photographs of the military witnesses the Russian government had nominated to give testimony in the European Court. Pravda hadn't been involved in the atrocities; he was to be an expert witness on military operations in the Caucasus. As it happened, the Russians didn't call him to testify and Scott didn't need him. Nonetheless, Scott had done his homework on the man in preparedness for any cross-examination. Pravda had a reputation for being firm but fair.

> A combined surveillance operation involving the FSB, the GRU and the Moscow City Police yesterday morning resulted in the apprehension of the British human rights lawyer at Sheremetyevo Airport who was trying to flee the country after having brutally murdered pensioner Yuri Vladimirovich Sokolov in a Moscow apartment...

This was how the narrative would run if Scott were to fall into Pravda's trap and catch the flight. Human rights organizations could do nothing to save him if Putin put him on trial for murder in front of the world's media. The President would be showing to everybody that Russia was fully committed to the rule of law and due process, and in a highly transparent manner. Meanwhile, the Russian press would have convicted him and the "Chechen-loving" English lawyer would be languishing on remand in a Moscow prison. His life would be over before he ever got to the courtroom. He called Rashid.

'Chief?'

'Rashid, meet me at 8.30 tomorrow morning at the Metropol.'

'Where are we going?'

'Sheremetyevo 2. UK departures.'

'My car's off the road, chief. The surround sound system's being upgraded to super-dooper woofer stat—'

'Yeh, yeh. I get it.' Scott had visions of two gigantic loudspeakers being attached to the wing mirrors. 'And I've put the Cherokee in for service,' Scott said. He'd noticed leaking brake fluid after the kidnapping. 'Use your initiative.' He also wanted the key control unit system reprogrammed. Like his *krysha*, the GRU had used a cloned fob to gain access.

'No problem.'

Scott disconnected. If military intelligence was interested in the slaying on Mosfilmovskaya, its interest would take precedence over Captain Vassiliyev's investigation. However, as Ekaterina had reminded him, this was Russia. Vassiliyev could be investigating the crime in conjunction with the FSB. Ekaterina and Scott could be caught in the middle. Vassiliyev's photograph showed them entering the building. Pravda's film showed them leaving. So why didn't the GRU want to keep him in the country, to face further questions? After all, Pravda was in the intelligence-gathering business and Scott was a source of intelligence.

He packed a suitcase, and called Ekaterina. 'Hello, it's Scott.' He was using a pay-as-you-go phone. 'Everything okay?' He wanted to ask her about Pravda's revelation that she was the wife of Konstantin Gravchenko, but not over the phone.

'Yes, I'm fine.'

'Do you trust me?' He had to clear the air. He didn't want to be treated like a child again, as per her contempt for his lack of concern for the motorcyclist; although she'd been right to be suspicious.

Silence.

'Ekaterin—'

'Yes. I trust you.'

'Thank you. Now listen to me and don't ask any questions,' he said. 'This is very important. Do you understand?' Pravda wasn't the only one who could play games.

'Yes.'

'Pack an overnight bag. Enough for two or three days and meet me in the lobby of the Metropol Hotel tomorrow at 8.30 tomorrow morning. Is that clear?'

'Yes.'

'And bring your external passport with you. Will you do that?' If the GRU had the ability to track his pay-as-you-go phone calls, Pravda might not be too happy if Ekaterina also left the country. That should give the general something to think about.

Silence.

'Ekaterina? Did you hear me?'

'Yes.'

'Will you do as I ask?'

Silence.

'Ekaterina, will you?'

'Yes.'

'Right. I'll see you tomorrow. Bye.'

'Bye.'

Scott walked into the lobby of the Metropol Hotel at 8.20am, his eyes were everywhere. Tour groups were waiting for coaches to take them to the city's airports for their homeward journeys, others comprised bleary-eyed arrivals sleepwalking to the registration desk. He spotted his client sitting in the corner opposite the reception desk, reading a Russian *Vogue* magazine and looking every square millimeter the focused unflappable beauty. She knew nothing of his plan and where they were going. 'Thanks for coming, Ekaterina.'

She stood up and air-kissed him lightly on both cheeks. 'I'm intrigued,' she whispered.

'There are a couple of things I need to discuss with you.'

She put a finger to his lips and shook her head. 'Not here.'

Rashid arrived, breathless and late. 'Sorry chief, puncture.'

'Where is it and what is it?' Scott asked.

'Shalyapin Bar exit. Behind the tour bus. It's the crimson Audi Quattro.'

'Where did you get it?' None of the firm's employees had an Audi.

'Borrowed it from my brother.'

'Hmm. As you haven't got a brother, a real brother that is,' Scott said. 'I assume you borrowed it from one of your cousins.'

'Brother, sister, uncle, aunt, *babushka*; who cares?'

Ekaterina broke into a broad smile.

'Are you insured to drive the vehicle?' Scott had to ask the question, although in Russia most driving-without-insurance problems, criminal or civil, were settled at the roadside with an open wallet rather than in open courts.

'For any driver, chief.'

Scott wasn't going to get anywhere pursuing the matter. 'Let's go.' The trio headed for the exit and got into the car; Rashid in the driving seat with Scott next to him and Ekaterina in the back. 'Take the most direct route to

Sheremetyevo 2, but don't rush.' He wanted to see if they were being followed. They headed north-west out along Tverskaya across the Garden Ring, on to Leningradsky Prospect and Leningradsky Highway en route for the M10/E105, the main city artery to the Sheremetyevo Airport complex and ultimately St Petersburg. The sky was cloudless and the brilliant sun was trying unsuccessfully to create the illusion that the temperature had risen above freezing.

Rashid swerved to avoid a pothole and the Audi flattened a wooden "danger" sign. 'Did you see that?' he said. 'It came straight for us.'

The glove compartment popped open. A torrent of CDs cascaded out and crashed onto the floor. 'What's all this?' Scott sifted through them. They comprised an eclectic mix of UK and US 60s rock and pop, Spanish flamenco, Chilean pipes and Zumba fitness music. The titles were handwritten in English, with many spelling mistakes.

'My samples,' Rashid said.

'Samples? It's not your car.'

'Yeh chief. But us capitalists can't let logistical hurdles get in the way of economic growth. Got to keep commodities in circulation. Supply and demand. Essential for market liquidity.'

Scott heard Ekaterina clear her throat.

He examined an Eagles CD. The titles were Eagles' records, but he didn't recognize the photo of the group. They looked like the English 60s group, the Kinks. 'Are these pirated?'

Rashid bared his tombstone teeth. 'I'm not saying anything without my lawyer.'

Scott glanced in the rear-view mirror. Ekaterina was smiling. He returned to the collection and found Tom Petty's *I Won't Back Down*. 'This one's for you Lieutenant-General Leonid Igorovich Pravda. Take a note of the title my GRU buddy.' He loaded it. 'When I've played this, I'm going to throw all this contraband out the window.'

'You can't chief.'

'Why not?'

'Pollution laws.'

Scott pressed the button and the song began.

'Bandits at six-thirty,' Rashid said.

Scott checked his wing mirror. A black Jaguar was on their tail. The woman at the wheel wore sunglasses; her front seat passenger was a man. Both looked to be in their mid-thirties. 'Are you sure?'

'Positive, Chief. They stopped and watched me while I was repairing the puncture. Moscow Mafiosi types; soldier level. All bling-bling and no brains.'

'The mafia's not interested in us Rashid. It's the GRU. They're making sure that I leave the country.' Or, perhaps they would be the arresting officers when Scott attempted to pass through immigration control.

'Chief. What's all this about?' Rashid, like Ekaterina, didn't yet know Scott's plans.

'Later.'

The traffic to the airport was much heavier than usual. They arrived at the terminal with only a few minutes to the end of check-in time for the Aeroflot flight. As they approached the up-ramp to the departures hall, a tourist bus broke down and narrowed the main access way, forcing the impatient travelers and their global-warming combustion engines to funnel their way through the tightest of gaps. Rashid's deft maneuvering enabled the Audi to steal a few places on its competitors and he managed to tuck the vehicle neatly into a confined space between two tourist buses. They were within touching distance of the automatic glass entrance doors to the building. Scott turned to Ekaterina. He could see over her shoulder through the rear windscreen. 'Take my cue.' The bling-blings' Jaguar was parked half on the road and half on the forecourt, with a vacant space in front of it and a coach behind. A third bus pulled up and began disgorging its full load in the middle of the narrow roadway, adding to the chaos. The two goons left their vehicle and hovered near the other set of entrance doors, failing to be inconspicuous.

'Rashid, when Ekaterina and I leave, drive out and come back up the ramp again. If there's still a space in front of the Jag, slide in and reverse until you touch bumpers. Get out and go for a walk. If the space is occupied, double park by the Jag and break down.'

Rashid banged the steering wheel with his fist and beamed. 'Oh boy. Is this going to be my day!'

Ekaterina and Scott grabbed their luggage, got out and jostled their way through the early morning beggars and illegal taxi drivers milling around the doors, into the departure area. They stopped at the indicator board and checked the flight departures.

'What do you have in mind?' Ekaterina asked.

'Keep looking at the destination board,' Scott said. 'We're going on a trip.'

'Where to?'

'Trust me. And follow my lead to the check-in desk; it's closing shortly.'

'So we *are* leaving Russia?' She raised her eyebrows. 'A ticket might be useful.'

'Walk with me to the desk and nod as I talk to you.' Scott kept his eyes on their stalkers. 'The male goon is to our right by the doors. The woman is at the check-in. When we reach the desk, we say goodbye and you go down to the arrivals hall. Grab a cab and wait with the engine running. Call me with the details.'

'So, Mr Bond. You're not the stuffy English lawyer after all.'

They stopped at the check-in desk. The queue of departing passengers was down to the last few stragglers.

Scott put his suitcase on the floor and turned to Ekaterina. He pecked her on both cheeks. She reciprocated. Her right hand gently touched Scott's elbow. 'Go,' Scott whispered.

Ekaterina picked up her overnight bag and merged into the crowd.

'Are you for the Aeroflot flight, sir?'

Scott's eyes momentarily, and unsuccessfully, tried to follow Ekaterina all the way to the exit.

'Sir, are you for the Aeroflot flight to London?'

It was the check-in clerk. 'They're closing the gate, sir.'

'I'm with you,' he said. 'I'm with you.' Scott was the last person to check in. The female goon was standing at the adjacent desk talking with two uniformed airline staff. He looked around. The male goon was no longer standing at the entrance doors. Scott assumed that Rashid had completed his task and was involved in a robust exchange of driving philosophies with an irate spook. Scott's phone rang.

'Three vehicles to the left of the first exit.' It was Ekaterina. 'We'll flash once when we see you.'

He was impressed. She was as aware of the possibility of their phones being bugged as he was. She'd made no mention of the make and color of the cab.

'Shit,' he said to the check-in clerk. 'I've left my passport in the car. My driver's double-parked, he can't leave the vehicle.' He put his suitcase on the X-ray belt. 'Take a look at this while I nip out and get it.' He turned and ran full pace down the escalators, across the arrivals hall, out to the street and into Ekaterina's beckoning cab. 'Go to Sheremetyevo 1,' he instructed the driver. 'Make two slow circuits around the car park, exit and make your way across town to the M7.' He wanted to be certain they weren't being followed this time.

Forty-five minutes later they were heading east on

the Moskovskaya Koltsevaya auto route, the capital's large outer ring road, towards the Volga Highway, which would take them to the towns of the "Golden Ring".

Chapter 13

Day Four: 1pm

Scott woke up in the cab two and a half hours later, in blizzard conditions. He'd fallen asleep as they left Moscow's city limits and joined the M7, after he was sure they weren't being followed. They were approaching the woodlands surrounding the numerous convents and monasteries of the town of Suzdal, some 215 kilometers north-east of Moscow. It was part of the "Golden Ring" of religious towns on the outskirts of the capital; the others included Rostov and Vladimir.

Ekaterina was still sleeping.

Scott's *dacha* nestled in a row of eight town houses. It was located outside the town with a distant view of the wooden cottages of the Pokrovsky Convent. He had taken the terraced cottage on a ten-year lease from a Swedish owner who'd bought the house in 1990 for a fortune and was immediately banned from the country on trumped up charges of "hooliganism": the Soviet crime of engaging in any act or omission to which the powers-that-be happened at any particular moment to take objection.

The cottage owners paid extortionate monthly fees to a security company for the dubious peace of mind of knowing that the only people who would steal their possessions would be the employees of the security company. New England clapboard in style, their first owners had been the local corrupt Communist Party *apparatchiks*. They sold the properties on to naïve foreigners at inflated prices. It was no different to capitalist property speculation in some ways, except that in the West legal title to the property could be guaranteed; whereas in the Soviet Union, and to a lesser extent in the new democratic Russia, the question of whether anybody other than the state could own freehold land tested Mensa's finest minds.

The cab driver remained seated while the pair got out. He slid down the window. 'That'll be $600.'

'What!' Scott said. 'You said $300.'

'That's right, $300 for bringing you, and $300 for denying it.' The driver was no more than early twenties, yet his heavily lined face showed a worldliness that matched his extortion techniques.

'Thieving bastard.'

'Perhaps. But what are you?'

'It's not legal tender.' Scott counted out six $100 bills and dropped them onto the driver's lap. 'Rubles are your currency, you bandit.' Despite the legalities, no self-respecting foreigner in Russia would travel the country without easy access to the world's reserve currency.

The driver scooped up the money. 'I don't suppose you want a receipt.' He laughed and roared away.

Ekaterina coughed.

Scott turned and looked at her.

'You realize,' she said. 'If your Captain Vassiliyev leaks it to the media that we're wanted for questioning in connection with the Mosfilmovskaya murder, the cabbie will cash in on it.'

'What was I supposed to do?' Why did she say that? 'Give him a tip?' Scott picked up her holdall from the curbside and hurried towards the house.

'It probably wouldn't have made any difference,' Ekaterina said and followed him into the house and through to a large living room.

A framed picture of Stockholm harbor dominated the wall over a real wood-burning hearth. Two three-seater green leather sofas faced each other at ninety degrees to the fireplace, separated by a deep-piled white rug on polished mahogany flooring. A Scandinavian pine coffee table stood in the center of the rug. Scott's eye caught several classic car magazines that were scattered on one of the sofas, where he'd left them a few months before. A half empty jug of water stood on his writing desk. The cleaners hadn't been, again. Perhaps they thought he'd never be allowed back in the country.

'It looks like an IKEA showroom,' Ekaterina said.

'I believe the correct term is minimalist,' Scott said. 'But I think we've more important things that concern us at the moment.' In particular, he wanted to know if Pravda had been telling the truth about her being Konstantin Gravchenko's wife. 'Ekaterina, I want to ask you about your—'

'Why did you leave your suitcase at the airport?' she asked.

He blinked. 'There was no other way I could think of to convince the goons that I'd be back.'

'But you'll need your things.'

'Only old clothes. I've got plenty in the *dacha*. Besides, it's getting to be a habit of mine, leaving suitcases full of clothes at airports.'

'What do you mean?'

'Later. Ekaterina—'

She turned away from him and studied the picture of Stockholm harbor. 'Do you own this property?'

'Long lease, well longish.'

'Who knows you come here?'

'You want to know how vulnerable we are to discovery?' It was a fair question.

'Yes.'

'Apart from the landlord, who lives in Sweden, and the estate managers, only me – and any nosy neighbors, I suppose.'

She looked at him. 'Come on, you're a lawyer.'

Scott bit his top lip. It was a gentle cross-examination.

'Hmm. The cab driver, and, of course, you. Why?'

'Rashid?'

'Rashid. Now—'

'You forgot to tell him we were coming here,' she said. What was she playing at? 'I'll call him later. Now—'

Ekaterina sat on the edge of the sofa and crossed her arms. 'Why have you brought me here, Scott?' Her eyes narrowed. 'What are we going to do here that we can't do in Moscow?'

She was a tricky woman; distraction tactics.

'I need to get away from Moscow,' he said. 'From the attentions of the GRU, and from the possibility of being taken in for questioning by Captain Vassiliyev.' He scratched the back of his head. 'I don't need any distractions. I want to concentrate on trying to find your father.'

'But why do you want *me* with you, specifically now? They can't deport me and I've not been interviewed by the police.' She shook her head. 'Captain Vassiliyev probably doesn't know who I am.'

Indeed, and aren't you the lucky lady? 'Unless Pravda has told him.' Scott seized the opening he'd made for himself. 'You know our interrogator was Lieutenant-General Pravda of the GRU, don't you?'

'Yes.'

He moved closer to her. 'Ekaterina, I have to ask you something, before we go any further.'

She took off her overcoat, draped it over the back of the sofa and sank into the cushions. 'Go on.' Her look softened.

'Pravda told me—'

'By the way,' she said. 'I almost forgot to tell you. I have arranged for Tolik to transfer 2.5 million rubles to your account tomorrow.'

'What on earth for?'

'On account of your fees.'

'But that's much too much, at least at this stage.

I don't…' Was she still trying to distract him? He threw his coat over a chair and sat on the sofa opposite Ekaterina. What the hell. It's not as if he didn't need the money. 'Okay, I'll call my office later today and tell them to set it up with Tolik.'

'Now.' Ekaterina smoothed her skirt over her legs. 'What did you want to ask me?'

Scott licked his lips and took in a deep breath. 'You're married to Konstantin Gravchenko. Is that true?'

'Married, but separated.' It was a matter-of-fact response; no indication of surprise. She used both hands to push her fringe back over her forehead and lifted her hair over her ears with her thumbs. She stretched her neck. Scott noticed a small black mole under her right ear. He hadn't seen it before, when her hair was up, either at the stadium or in the Lexus on the drive to the apartment.

'Is it relevant?' she asked.

'I don't know. It might be.' The car bombing was beginning to make sense. Gravchenko would undoubtedly have made enemies on his way to mega wealth. 'Have you parted on good terms?'

'Yes. But in anticipation of your next question, he won't help me look for my father.'

'Politics?'

'Perceptive.'

It was more like common sense. Russia was all politics, in one form or another. 'It's what you're paying me for.'

'He doesn't want to get on the wrong side of Putin,' she said.

'And knocking on Gulag doors is a sure fire way of doing it.'

'That's what he says.'

'There's a daughter, I—'

'Tanya, she's four,' Ekaterina said.

'And the chance of finding Tanya's grandfather won't budge your husband?'

She winced. 'He doesn't think she needs one.'

'Does he know you've hired me?'

'Yes.'

'What did he say when you told him?'

She hesitated. 'Good luck.'

That was double-edged. Gravchenko could have meant that he wished her success or he thought that a foreigner, especially Scott Mitchell – public enemy number one – would never be able to penetrate the Gulag labyrinth.

'Scott,' Ekaterina said. 'Do you honestly think you can find my father?' Was she having second thoughts? 'I mean.' She leant forward and her shoulders drooped. Her self-assurance had gone. 'I'm certain Kostya has all the right connections, and without his help, you're going to have a very difficult time.' She looked at him, pleading.

She was right. The oligarch was reputed to dine with Putin's right-hand men frequently, and on two or three occasions with the President himself. 'I can't give you any assurances.' He stood up. 'Other than to say that I shall do my very best. However, you have to trust me. Do you understand?'

'Thank you again, for being honest with me.' She relaxed back into the sofa. 'And yes, I trust you.' She sounded convincing. 'How long are we going to stay here?' she continued.

'A couple of days,' Scott said. 'If we're left alone. Let's see how it goes.'

She frowned.

'No, don't get me wrong.' He held up his hand. 'This is strictly business.'

She tilted her head.

Was she playing with him or ridiculing him, thinking that he was contemplating hitting on her? Which he wasn't. He saw no point in pursuing the subject. 'Do you want to call anybody, tell them where you are? Although your cellphone might be bugged.'

'I'm okay for a few days,' she said. 'Tolik will call me in an emergency.' She got up and walked towards the door. 'I'd like to freshen up. Where's my bedroom, and the bathroom?'

'Follow me. You can have the main bedroom. It's on the second floor. Bathroom's en suite. I'll take the other room on the third floor.'

The log fire was crackling in the living room when Ekaterina returned, thirty minutes later. Slacks had replaced the skirt. She sat on the sofa opposite Scott, with a photograph clasped in her hand.

'What's that in your hand?' Scott asked.

'A photograph.'

'I can see that. What of?' He leant forward.

She handed it to him.

'Two men standing on a river bank, carrying hunting rifles.' Scott flipped it over and read out the handwritten scrawl, which was in Russian: "A-16 Summer 1979." He flipped it back again and looked at Ekaterina. 'So, what does it mean? Where did you get it? What's it got to do with your father?'

'I found it in the apartment,' she said matter-of-factly. 'On the floor, in the pile of books.'

'Ekaterina!' Scott dropped the picture onto the sofa as if it was contaminated. 'What's wrong with you?' He picked up the snapshot with his handkerchief and wiped both sides. He was brushing off the prints; more a gut reaction, than out of concern that the authorities would find it. He had no intention of returning it to the apartment. 'Haven't we got enough aggravation?' he continued. 'Do you realize that taking stuff from a crime scene is a criminal offense?'

She coughed. 'Your respect for the law is commendable, and much needed in Russia, but you're going to have to compromise some of your principles if we're going to make any progress.'

'Please don't lecture me on my principles.' He didn't like being patronized. 'After all, isn't that another reason why you hired me? Because I'm a man of principle.'

She raised her hand. 'Alright, but please remember that I want to find my father.'

'Okay,' Scott said. 'But what makes you think this photograph will help you?' He got up and went to his desk, where he removed a transparent plastic folder from a drawer. He popped the photograph inside the folder and sat down at the desk chair.

'It was hidden in a book.'

'What book?'

'It was called *Histoire du Roy Henry Le Grand*. It was published in Amsterdam in 1659.'

'Henry Le Grand?'

'Henry the Fourth, King of France.'

'And?' So what?

'I found two photo albums on the floor. They had pictures of aircraft. Some had Soviet markings, but most were foreign. There were shots of groups of pilots standing by a plane, but I didn't know what nationality they were.'

'Ekaterina.' She was straying. 'What's the connection to this French book?'

'Well, this photo. It was the only one I found that wasn't in an album.'

'So?' Scott still didn't understand her thread.

'So, why was this particular photo hidden in a book that had no connection to 1979, or Russia? All the photos were of airplanes and pilots, except this one,' she said. 'And in an album.'

'What attracted you to the French book in the first place?'

'Apart from the fact that I learnt French at school, nothing in particular. It was just one of the many I flicked through.'

He waved the photo at her. 'Why did you say, it was *hidden* in the book?'

'People put photographs in albums or drawers, not books.'

'Or wallets,' Scott added. 'Anyway, perhaps it was being used as a bookmark.'

'Perhaps.'

'Have you any more surprises up your sleeve?' Scott booted up the computer.

'You'll get over it.' Ekaterina got up and approached the desk.

'Come and sit behind me,' Scott said. 'You can see what I'm doing.'

She pulled up a second chair and sat down.

Scott pointed at the photo. 'Could either of these men be the murdered man in the apartment?' He was thinking aloud.

'The photo is thirty-four years old,' Ekaterina said. 'The man in the apartment was disfigured. The bullet—'

'Understood.' He turned to her. 'Ekaterina. There's something I need to say to you.' Was it the right moment? The man's brains had been blown out, literally. Would there ever be a right moment?

'Yes?' She looked at him, innocently.

'The man in the apartment...we can't be sure that—'

'He's not my father?' Faint creases appeared at the corner of her mouth, as if she was going to smile, or cry.

Scott felt the hairs stand up on the back of his neck. 'Yes, but how—'

'It was my first thought when I saw him.'

Scott remembered how she'd clasped both cheeks and opened her mouth as though she was about to scream. 'So you—'

'But I have discounted the possibility. The note said he was still in prison, and it was signed just four weeks previously.' She shook her head. 'You saw the place. It had been lived in for much longer than a month.' She shook her head again. 'It wasn't my father.'

Scott stroked her arm. 'Yes. Think positively.' He turned back to the photo and squinted at the smaller man. 'What's this?' He pointed to a lightly shaded object above the smaller man's shirt pocket. 'That. It looks like it's made of metal.'

'I don't know,' Ekaterina said. 'Does it matter?'

'It doesn't look like part of the shirt,' he said. He turned the picture over again. 'Do you know what A-16 means?'

'No.'

He laid the snapshot on the desk with the picture face down, so the handwritten "A-16 Summer 1979" was exposed. He logged on to the net.

'If you type A-16 into the search engine, you'll get millions of results,' Ekaterina said.

'I know that. But I belong to the school of surfers who lose patience after scrolling through the first twenty or so hits. So don't worry, we won't be here for the rest of our lives.'

'That's nice to know,' she said.

He googled the expression in the format "A-16" and hit the search button. He chuckled. 'It could be worse, only 2,970,000 results.'

'What does it say on the first page?' she asked.

'Don't you know *any* English?' Scott asked, concentrating on the screen.

'The alphabet and some words.'

'Why did you opt for French at school?'

'They have better ski runs in France.' She nudged him in the back.

He looked over his shoulder, smiled at her and returned to the screen. 'It's picked out not only "A-16" but "a 16", "A16", "a 16 year old", "a 16-bit" and a host of other combinations. They refer to such topics as a US government Executive Order, a modern-day anarchist and anti-capitalist group, a piece of computer software, a restaurant, a UK government public health table, an alpha-sulfur structure and many other items. I doubt if any of them have a connection to the legend on the back our photograph.' Scott snatched up the photo and flipped it over and back, over and back. He repeated the phrase "A-16 Summer 1979". 'Aha, what do people usually write on the back of photos?'

'The place and the year,' Ekaterina said.

'Indeed. And we have the year – summer 1979.'

'So, A-16 is a place,' she said.

'Worth a try. Could be an abbreviation for it, you know, like UK for the United Kingdom, LA for Los Angeles. After all, A-16 by itself would be a strange name for a place.'

'Not in my country.' Ekaterina stood up and moved round to the front of the desk.

'Meaning?' Scott asked.

'It's all coming back to me now. We had closed cities in the Soviet Union. They were involved in secret works, usually manufacturing armaments. They were never on any maps and the public wasn't supposed to know of their existence.'

'But they did?'

'Of course,' she said. 'Everybody knew. It was one of the best kept open secrets in the Soviet Union.'

'Such as?'

'I was a child, but I remember people talking about Chelyabinsk.' She frowned. 'Yes, that's it. Chelyabinsk was C something and Krasnoyarsk, it was K-20 or 30. They gave these letters and names to all the secret cities.' She moved back around the desk and stood by Scott's side. 'I'm positive.' She rapped her fingers on his shoulder. 'Come on, come on.'

'Great,' Scott said. 'But why didn't you mention this earlier?'

'Because, as I've just said, it's only just occurred to me.'

'Hmm.' He shrugged and typed in "Russian cities". He scanned the first page. 'Look, a reference to a list of all Russian cities on the web.' He clicked on it. A comprehensive list appeared. Thirteen began with the letter "A". 'This shouldn't take too long.' He clicked on the first one. 'It's Akademgorodok.' He studied the name. 'Hang on. If A-16 is a secret city it's not going to be on the web, for all to see, is it? Open secret or not, the Soviet Union may no longer exist but Russian secrecy is still alive and kicking.'

'So find the city of Sarov,' Ekaterina said.

'Sarov? Why?'

'My mother mentioned it in her letter to me.'

Scott turned to her. 'What letter?'

The letter I showed you at the stadium.'

'Extract, you mean. You only showed me an extract. And it didn't mention Sarov in the text.'

'Didn't it?'

'Fuck!' He punched the top of his knee and sighed. She knew she hadn't shown him the whole letter. 'Ekaterina, why do you keep drip-feeding information to me? I thought you trusted me. How can I—'

'Scott.' She squeezed his shoulder. 'I'm sorry, truly I am, but I have to be certain.' She sounded contrite.

'I don't understand you.' He turned back to the screen. 'But I've got a job to do. Now, what did your mother say? Can you be more specific? Better still, do you have the letter, a copy, with you?'

'No. I'm sorry. I forgot to pack it.'

She's at it again. He closed his eyes and massaged his forehead.

'Honestly, Scott. I really did forget.'

'Okay.' He looked at the screen, only half-believing her. 'Can you remember what your mother said about Sarov?'

'Yes, she overheard the men talking.'

'What men?'

'The KGB who took my father away. They said they were going back to Sarov with him.'

Scott kept his eyes on the screen. 'Alright, but that by itself doesn't necessarily mean—'

Ekaterina grabbed the mouse from him and guided the cursor down to the city of Sarov. She knew the English name. She clicked on it. 'What does it say?'

'Forbidden – you don't have permission to access on this server,' Scott said.

'Why not?'

'God knows. But don't worry; maybe we can get at the information another way.' He typed "Sarov" into the search engine and scrolled through the opening pages, which mostly comprised references to St Seraphim of Sarov. 'Look, a site on Sarov, something to do with nuclear weapons. And look here.' He tapped the screen. 'It's had other names: Kremlyov, Moscow-300, Arzamas-75 and...and...Arzamas-16.'

'I knew it!' she said. She repeatedly tapped Scott on the shoulder. 'I knew the photo had something to do with my father.'

'Not so fast.' Scott held her fingers on his shoulder, to calm her. He was warming towards her again. 'This reference is a long way short of convincing evidence of any connection to your father.'

She withdrew her hand.

'Sorry, Ekaterina,' Scott continued. 'But we need much more than this if we are to join the dots between the apartment, the photo, A-16, Sarov and your father.'

Before she could respond, Scott entered the website and speed-read a lengthy overview of the city. He paraphrased the opening words for her in Russian:

Formerly known as Sarov, it was renamed Arzamas-16
in 1946, until 1991. It was the location of the Soviet
Union's nuclear weapons research and development

facilities. In 1991 it was renamed Kremlyov and then in 1995 Yeltsin signed a law which changed it back to Sarov. He whizzed through the many pages.

'Where is it?' she asked.

'One hundred kilometers south of Nizhny Novgorod, plus or minus. I'll print this stuff out and go through it in detail. It'll be in English. Do you want to have a lie down for a while? We've been up since dawn. This may take some time. I'll also check all the other cities beginning with "A", for the sake of completeness.'

'You're right. I must be patient.' She patted him on the shoulder again. 'And I do feel tired. Wake me in three hours.' She headed for the door.

'Two questions, before you go, Ekaterina.'

She turned. 'Yes?'

'If Sarov was known as Arzamas-16 between 1946 and 1991, how come that in the 1970s your mother heard the KGB guys saying they were taking your father back to Sarov, or so she thought?'

'I don't know.' She shrugged. 'Maybe they were trained not to mention the name Arzamas-16 in public places.'

Possibly. After all, it was a secret city and, according to the information Scott had just read, all mention of Arzamas-16 was wiped from all maps and statistical documents. 'Okay.' He would accept her explanation until he found a more convincing one. 'Second question.'

'Yes?'

'What year were you born in?'

'1976. Why?'

'Which month?'

'March, why?'

'So, if I remember my biology lessons correctly, your father must have been imprisoned no later than, say, June 1975.'

'I agree.' She disappeared from the room. 'See you later.'

Scott began to skim through the reams of information downloaded from the various websites. Sarov, or Arzamas-16, was a secret "installation" where bombs were designed. It was the location of the All-Russian Scientific and Research Institute of Experimental Physics (VNIEF), which was the oldest of Russia's two principal warhead design institutes. Arzamas was nicknamed "Los Arzamas" after its American prototype, Los Alamos. There were reports of important events at Arzamas throughout the 1990s: shady plutonium deals; factory fires in danger of spreading to chambers allegedly containing uranium-235 residue; a Russian tourist attempt to get into the still-closed city. This information was followed by details of an FSB warning of Chechen infiltration in the area; insider thefts of uranium and precious metals; suspicious deaths of security personnel; concerns over safety issues; accidental radiation death of an employee; cadmium leak injuring employees. But he couldn't find anything for the earlier decades, especially the 1970s, other than turgid statistics concerning the Soviet nuclear arms industry.

Persistence paid off in the end, however. His trawling netted a report called *Downsizing Russia's Nuclear Warhead Production Infrastructure*. It was published in *The Nonproliferation Review*. Table 1 in the report dealt with Soviet nuclear weapons production complexes in the 1980s; it referred to Sarov/Arzamas-16, as well as the cities Ekaterina mentioned: Chelyabinsk-65 and Krasnoyarsk-45. Table 2 was the clincher; it specifically referred to "A-16", "C-65" and other similarly described places. All the named complexes in Table 1 had been replaced by the same format – a single letter followed by a number comprising one or two digits. A-16 was Arzamas-16. Scott congratulated himself with a large vodka and picked up the photograph again.

Okay comrades, so who are you and what were you doing in Arzamas-16 in 1979?

Chapter 14

Day Four: 9.45pm

The blizzard had persisted since midday and only the passenger-side windscreen wiper on Pravda's Moskvitch was working. He was traveling east on the southern section of the M7 which forked at Vladimir, going north to Ivanovo via Suzdal and east to Nizhni Novgorod. Visibility was limited to the end of the vehicle's hood, yet trucks still managed to pass him at suicidal speeds. He was coming to the end of a 500-kilometer obstacle course.

The best laid plans. He failed to achieve his objective to begin the journey in the early hours of the morning after the brief and fruitless interrogations of Romanova and Mitchell. First, his car refused to move until an eleventh hour engine overhaul by two squabbling GRU mechanics and second, the Aeroflot flight headed for London without the maverick lawyer. The dramatics at the airport were cleverly conceived, well executed – and stupid. More stupid, though, were the two incompetent FSB agents tailing them. Yelena had been watching the action from a distance. Had an officious traffic cop not shown an interest in her customized motorbike, she would have been able to keep observation on the lawyer and his client. Ekaterina Romanova should have known better; the wife of Konstantin Gravchenko was supposed to be streetwise. As for Mitchell, Pravda could only think that the Strasburg victory had gone to the man's head. They couldn't hope to match the GRU's resources; they must have realized that. The GRU had planted a tracking device in the Cherokee while Pravda had been interviewing Romanova and Mitchell at the safe house. The general felt duty-bound to remain in the capital until mid-morning and monitor the search for the pair, but as soon as it became clear they had disappeared, leaving the Cherokee in the city, he set out on his solitary cross-country journey to Arzamas-16. His team in Moscow would continue the search for the runaways.

In Soviet times, the country's leading scientists regularly churned out weapons of mass destruction from the hidden colony. Working in the strictest secrecy, they were rewarded with the best health care, the highest wages and the widest choice of consumer goods obtainable in the USSR. Perestroika and glasnost, however, had done nothing to improve their living conditions. Their situation had deteriorated in the new Russia of the 1990s and was continuing to do so. The lack of state funding brought on by the collapse of communism meant that the workers went without their wages for months at a time; essential repairs to the city's nuclear reactors were routinely ignored. Yet, one advantage of living in such a closed society was the low crime rate; the inhabitants could sleep with their front doors unlocked, fearing nothing but the cold. Only the bravest and most desperate criminal would operate in the shadow of ill-maintained nuclear installations.

Nonetheless, scientists were still working in the city; there were over 20,000 people working in the All-Russian Scientific and Research Institute and a further 10,000 in the Avangard plant, where the warheads were assembled and disassembled. Nobody could leave Arzamas-16 without special permission and relatives were rarely allowed to visit their resident families; all telephone calls were monitored. The fifty-kilometer perimeter comprised a double, barbed wire fence patrolled by the Russian army, with dogs, and armed watchtowers.

It was approaching midnight when Pravda stopped in an isolated country road on the edge of a copse. Nobody was expecting him, which was how it had to be. It had stopped snowing. Dark clouds shielded the light from the moon and the stars. He used his pencil torch to check the map "Uncle Nikolai", his supervisor, cadet commander and mentor, had scribbled out three decades previously, when the old soldier had been secretly called out to the same city – that time on a false alarm. This was Pravda's first visit to the city and the first time he'd come face-to-face with the men he was going to see.

He clicked off the torch, stuffed the map into a purpose-made tear in the lining of his left boot and drove on. He estimated he was a few kilometers from the turn-off: a makeshift pathway leading through the dense birch forest to the railway tracks that entered the Avangard complex on the south-eastern side of the city. The path was doubtless no longer in use and overgrown, but it would be the easiest way to get into the city unnoticed. The area would be knee-deep in snow and difficult to find. He hunted for the marker – a "kissing" seat carved out of two resolute tree trunks at the side of the pathway by the road. The towpath came into view sooner than expected. He parked the car in a thicket and with a compass, the torch and wire cutters, cautiously made his way on foot through the trees to the barbed wire. The snow was recently trodden, probably by guards, so his own footprints would be undetectable.

He stopped in a cluster of small shrubs which extended the remaining five meters to the outer fence; then ten meters of no-man's-land – pristine with untrampled snow – to the inner fence. The nearest watchtower was seventy-five or so meters to his right, with the buffer zone to his left carving an unobstructed channel deep into the forest. The searchlight at the watchtower was switched on and pointing in his direction, though not roving. Pravda wasn't concerned; he had years of experience in the field sneaking past guards without being seen. He listened for the signs of life, human or dogs. There was silence; not a whimper. He released the retaining clasp on the cutters and edged forward.

'Put your hands above your head!' It was a youthful voice from behind.

Pravda's heart sank. The man with years of experience had been caught out through over confidence; an elementary mistake that could have cost him his life in other circumstances. He dropped the cutters in front of him and raised his hands, turning slowly so as not to frighten the child, whose inexperienced finger would be caressing the trigger. 'Why not put the weapon down, soldier and I'll come quietly.'

A conscript, still in his teens, was standing two meters from Pravda and pointing an unsteady automatic at his face. Pravda could smell drink. Not the odorless real vodka, but the poor man's version, *samogon* – homemade firewater. The boy's *ushanka* clung lopsidedly to the back of his head. 'I have to speak to your commanding officer,' Pravda said. He took half a step towards the boy.

'No! Stay right where you are! The raw recruit stumbled back and tried to hold the weapon in position. 'Don't move!'

Pravda didn't move. An agitated teenager full of drink was pointing a loaded weapon at him.

'That's it. Stay there.' The kid hesitated, as if he was uncertain what to do next. He nodded and muttered, 'Don't move, don't move.' It was a pitiful sight. The boy was no more than a babe-in-arms. His parents probably didn't have the money or the influence to keep him out of the army.

'So, what do you want me to do?' Pravda shuffled forward.

The conscript swayed.

'Your safety catch is on, soldier.' The split second it took the recruit to check his gun was long enough for

Pravda to land a knockout punch to the boy's temple. He fell to the ground in a drunken heap, his fall cushioned by the snow. Pravda snatched up the automatic, unloaded it and laid it back down by the kid's side. He didn't wish any more harm on him than was necessary. The penalty for losing a weapon in the Russian army was so Draconian that summary execution was considered light relief. The soldier could always say he used the ammunition chasing rabbits for food or defending himself against bears. Pravda rummaged through the kid's pockets and found a small, half empty bottle of the *samogon*. He unscrewed the cap and poured the contents into the groggy kid's mouth. Firewater or not, the soldier had to go to sleep for a couple of hours.

The boy woke up and began to splutter. 'What the...'

'Here drink some more.'

The callow youth obliged.

When the bottle was empty, Pravda knocked him out again. 'Sorry son, but you'll be okay in a few hours and your only memory of this incident will be the pulsating headache.' Pravda picked up the cutters, moved on through the shrubs, and closed in on the fence.

He looked up at the watchtower; still no sign of movement. The guards could be asleep or drunk, or it could be unmanned. He crouched and remained still. He could hear faint voices, followed by raucous laughter. At least two men. They began singing. They sounded drunk.

Pravda couldn't wait any longer.

He snipped at the wire, stopping and listening after each cut. Could the guards hear him? Probably not. Within thirty seconds, he'd crawled through the hole and into no-man's-land. He lay face down in the snow, motionless for ten seconds, listening for any noise indicating that the guards had discovered his presence.

Only the raucous singing invaded the silence.

He eased himself up. With slow and silent hand

movements he smoothed the snow over his few discernible tracks through the fence and, after a further glance at the watchtower, he headed for the other fence in a semi-crouching position, using his feet to scuff out the footprints as he made the crossing. He stopped at the inner fence and dropped to the ground, where again he lay silent for a few seconds.

A voice cried from the watchtower and the searchlight began moving. Pravda's heart raced. The guards were trained to fire warning shots in the air before shouting their commands. They were stimulated and impaired by vodka.

Pravda gripped handfuls of snow and tensed.

The light moved away and Pravda was in darkness. He turned his head. The shouting morphed into laughter as the searchlight jerked and zigzagged across the sky. Pravda cut his way through the second fence, hastily smothered his tracks with the snow and dashed towards a cluster of trees inside the secret city.

He walked through the small copse and stopped on the edge of an industrial site comprising modern-looking warehouse units. The grassy terrain of the woods surrendered to a concrete access road leading to the buildings. There was no security fencing. Beyond the industrial site, to his left, the rail tracks led towards the Avangard installation. The street lighting was minimal. There was no sign of life.

He reached the comparative safety of one of the warehouses, edged around the building, and entered a deserted residential street. Despite the 90,000 inhabitants private cars were rare. He had to maintain a low profile if he was to succeed in his mission: in and out within an hour or two, three at the most.

Half a dozen young troops appeared from around the corner 300 meters down the street, pushing and pulling each other, larking around. They weren't looking where they were going but they were fast approaching Pravda. These troops were not naïve army conscripts, but highly-trained members of the Ministry of the Interior (MVD) – primarily from the 94th Sarovsky Division, which went by the cover-name Military Unit (V/Ch) 3274.

Pravda pressed himself flat against the doorway of an apartment block; it afforded him little protection from discovery. He looked up and down the street. All the street doors appeared to be flush with their windows; there were no entrance lobbies in which to hide. He had to chance it. He darted across the road and down a side street, taking care not to look back. He ran the full length of the street, half a kilometer to the end, where he found a passageway leading into a quadrangle bounded by modern residential apartments. But there were too many lights in the rooms with their drapes open, for him to risk spending more than a minute or so in the square to catch his breath. With renewed vigor, he checked he hadn't been followed and crossed the desolate street to the rail yard opposite, where he slid down the embankment and landed on the tracks leading to the rail sheds. A freight train was stationed half out of its shed; it afforded him cover from the street as he trudged along the side of the wagons.

A floodlight was switched on. It temporarily blinded Pravda.

A hail of bullets flew over his head.

'Stop right there and put your hands in the air!'

Pravda froze and closed his eyes. The voice was mature and determined, not that of a drunken young conscript.

'Put your hands in the air!'

He blinked and stared ahead. The outlines of shadowy figures came into focus. The horse-playing soldiers from the deserted street by the warehouse stood fifteen meters in front of him, weapons raised and concentrated on their target's heart, not a trembling hand among them. They were led by a fresh-faced major.

'Put up your hands or we'll fire!' The major repeated.

Pravda raised his hands above his head. The soldiers needed no provocation to fill him full of holes – an order from their commanding officer would be sufficient.

'Now walk towards us! And keep your hands above your head!'

Pravda wasn't in uniform; he had to reveal his identity. 'Major. I am Lieutenant-General Pravda of the GRU. I have come to—'

'Shut up! Keep your mouth shut!'

'Major, you don't understand. I am—'

A burst of gunfire screamed past his right ear.

'I said, shut up!'

'Look,' Pravda persisted. 'I'm a general with the GRU.'

Another round seared his left ear.

'One more word and you'll be a dead general with the GRU!'

The general with the GRU kept his lips sealed and surrendered to the major with the MVD.

Chapter 15

Day Four: 10pm

Ekaterina lay sprawled on the sofa. Scott watched her sipping a glass of Jack Daniels; the flickering flames of the fire reflecting in her gaze. A long day was coming to an end and Scott had difficulty keeping his eyes open. 'Jack Daniels, not vodka? That's not very patriotic,' Scott teased. He flipped through the remaining A-16 printouts.

'What's the national drink in the UK?'

'Curry, probably,' Scott said. He rubbed his eyes with both hands, and returned to the scattered sheets of paper covering the rug.

'What are we going to do?' Ekaterina asked. 'Are we going back to Moscow tomorrow?'

'Well.' He scooped up the documents and arranged them into piles on the desk. 'We think we've established a link between the apartment and Arzamas. I can't see that we can do much else here.'

'Are you having second thoughts about coming? We could have found out this information back in Moscow.'

She was right. Despite his earlier explanation as to why they had come to the dacha, it did now seem a little pointless. He'd allowed his fear of Pravda laying a trap for him at the airport to affect his reasoning.

'I've an idea,' she said.

'What?'

'Well, we're never going to get into Arzamas.'

He nodded.

'So, the only other place left to go, is back to the apartment. What do you think?'

She wasn't smiling. Scott rubbed his eyes again. John McEnroe's classic rants in the Wimbledon Finals came to mind, "you cannot be serious". Had he heard her correctly? 'What do I think?'

'Yes.'

'I don't think it would be a wise move. That's what I think.' He chose his words carefully. It was too late in the evening for a heated argument.

'Why?' She put her glass of whiskey on the table. 'Pravda knows we didn't murder the man,' she said in a dismissive tone. 'And Captain Vassiliyev would have arrested you if he thought you were the murderer. Besides...' She stopped.

'What?'

'I can't find one of the gloves I was wearing at the apartment.'

'Great.' Scott gave out a loud sigh. 'That's great. Not only do you steal evidence from the crime scene, you leave your calling card. Didn't I tell you to keep your gloves on?'

'I'm not saying I definitely left it there,' she said testily. 'Just that I may ha—'

'Okay, okay. I'm sorry. But, Ekaterina, forensics would have cleared the place of its contents and taken the stuff away for examination. If your glove was there, it's not going to be there now.'

'But—'

He held up his hand. 'Please, let's think this through. I'll do some more research when we get back to Moscow; find out more about Arzamas...and how to trace people lost in the former Soviet Gulag system. 'I could—'

She sat up. 'No. You must not mention what we are doing...to anybody.'

He could see the fear in her eyes.

'I know. Your fear of the authorities.' He sat on the opposite sofa, cupping the glass in both hands as if he was warming an after-dinner cognac. 'Give me some credit, please. I'm not daft enough to mention any names.' Nonetheless, he was sure she was overdramatizing her plight. 'However, I really do think—'

'You think I'm paranoid, don't you?' she asked.

'Well,' Scott said. 'I believe you're frightened that if the authorities, whoever they may be, find out you're looking for your father, they will try to stop you. But—'

'The bomb under my car.'

'Possibly. But why would they want to stop you. You don't yet know why he was imprisoned, so why do you think the authorities want to stop you from finding him?'

'Scott, I am Russian, not Western.' She held out her hands, palms upward, fingers splayed, as if to give force to her argument. 'Our cultures and histories are so different. We've had five hundred years of Tsarist repression followed by seventy years of totalitarian communism. The people have absolutely no trust in the authorities, none whatsoever. We never have had and we never will have.' She nodded. 'Do you really think the bomb under my car was an isolated act of a madman, or terrorists? How do you explain the body in an apartment that both Pravda and Captain Vassiliyev happen to be watching?' She looked at him, wide-eyed. 'Scott, you of all people should know about our government cover ups.' She took a sip of whiskey and sat back. 'If you don't think my paranoia is justified, ask my husband.'

'Justified paranoia?'

'You know what I mean.'

'What will your husband tell me? You said he won't help us.'

'I mean, ask him about how our system really works. How everybody, even Russia's richest man, is constantly having to look over his shoulder.'

Scott wasn't convinced. 'Anyway, you could have been

targeted because of your marriage to him, not because of your father.'

'Please Scott, accept what I say. I know what I am talking about.'

'Okay'. He didn't. He was sure there was more to her so-called fear. 'But even corrupt power-hungry officials have, what is to them, rational explanations for their behavior. They must have a reason for wanting to keep your father hidden.' Was he a threat, or an embarrassment to those in power?

Ekaterina gazed into space, and said nothing.

No matter how cold it was outside, Scott always slept with a window open. Ekaterina's history lesson had brought their conversation to a close and they had both retired soon after. Scott fell asleep immediately.

A cat's screeches woke him with a start.

He checked the clock; it was 11.20pm. He slipped out of bed and went to the window. It was no longer snowing. The landscape was a white blanket. The screeching stopped and the immediate silence was both seductive and reassuring. Nature, apart from the cat, was at peace with itself. He focused and something caught his attention. Large pristine footprints had disturbed the snow on the lawn. They were too large for the cat or a dog, and unlike a bear's; they must have been human. They tracked across Scott's land from one side of the front garden, towards the front window, and back out to the other side to the neighboring plot in a large "v" shape. Had the owner meant to walk straight across the garden, changed his mind and deviated to look in the window? The dacha was the last but one in the terrace. The footprints trailed across the final plot and disappeared around the corner, to an unmade pathway leading to the back gardens.

Scott put on a robe, grabbed the torch from his bedside table and went down the stairs to investigate.

He heard the sound of crunching footsteps coming from outside the patio doors in the living room.

His stomach turned.

He switched off the torch and crept into the kitchen, where he took a Glock pistol with a faulty trigger mechanism from the bread-bin, using the green display lights from the digital clocks on the microwave oven and the worktop radio to guide him. A year or so previously his personal trainer had forced the weapon on him, for protection. He'd taken a few lessons on a firing range for self-defense purposes but had never shown any real enthusiasm for owning such weaponry. He'd witnessed the damage guns could do. He brought the pistol to the dacha – where it would be out of sight and out of mind. There were scratching sounds on the patio doors. He could he feel his heart pumping. He edged out of the kitchen and stopped by the open doorway leading into the living room, where he peered through the crack between the door and the frame. There were no curtains; the moon lit the scene. His pulse rate increased. A stocky male figure, hatless, slid back the locked patio doors and slipped in with ease. He was shorter than Scott, probably only 1.74 meters.

The intruder raised a pencil thin torch and panned the room. He settled on the Arzamas papers lying on Scott's desk and flicked through the documents.

Scott licked his lips; dehydration. He didn't know if it was the evening's alcohol or fear. Had Putin's men decided to terminate him? The figure looked up, and in Scott's direction. Scott took a deep breath, smashed the door further open, switched on the light and pointed the gun at the trespasser. 'Put your hands on your head!' he said in Russian.

The uninvited guest, mid-sixties, had a buzz-cut hairstyle, similar to that worn by military personnel the world over. 'C'mon Scott,' he said in American-English.

'Put that thing down. You and I know you're not gonna shoot me.'

Scott had no idea who the guy was. He was certain he'd never seen him before. He raised the gun in a determined fashion and spoke in English. 'I said put your hands on your head!'

The intruder began to raise his arms.

Scott caressed the trigger without thinking, and sent a bullet whizzing past the man's cheek. It sounded like a loud knock on an oak door with a hammer.

The intruder whistled.

Scott's hand trembled.

'Okay, you got me. Look, hands on head. Please counselor, point that thing away from me before you do some real damage.'

Scott kept the gun on his target, steadying it with both hands. 'Who are you? How do you know my name? What are you doing here?'

'Mind if I sit down?' the intruder asked. He moved towards the desk.

'No, you stay where you are and keep your hands on your head.'

'Sure thing. You're the boss.'

'Who are you?'

'My name is Frank Ferlito. I'm a commercial attaché at the US Embassy in Moscow.' The man spoke in a confident, matter-of-fact tone.

'And I'm the Dalai Lama.' That was bullshit. 'Now tell me, before my finger slips again, who are you?'

'I got ID.' Ferlito lowered his hands.

'On your head!'

Ferlito obliged.

'What's the phone number of your department?' Scott asked.

'The Commercial Section is Moscow 725 5580. Call them, if you doubt me.'

'At this time of night?'

'You'll get a recorded message of confirmation.'

'What's the address of your Consular Section, where they process the visa applications?' Scott reasoned that while an impostor would make sure he knew the telephone number of his own alleged department he probably wouldn't be thorough enough to memorize much other information.

'It's on Novinskiy Bulvar, 19/23, zip 123242, tel—'

'Okay, okay.' Could he really be from the US Embassy? 'What's Wrigley Field?'

'Which one?' Ferlito shot back.

Scott's lips moved but no sound came out; was there more than one Wrigley Field? He moved around to get a better look at the man, at the same time hoping to hide his ignorance.

'I'll put you out of your misery. Wrigley Field Chicago, home of the Cubs. Wrigley Field LA home of the Angels. It shut down in '66.'

The man's accent seemed genuine. He doubted if a native Russian, no matter how brilliant a linguist, could speak American-English without a trace of an Eastern European accent and have an in-depth knowledge of such trivia as the two Wrigley Fields. Of course, being American wasn't by itself conclusive evidence that the man was a commercial attaché, or not out to harm him.

'You surprise me.' Ferlito removed his hands from his head. 'I didn't think you Brits knew anything about baseball.'

Scott kept a tight grip on the gun and dropped his arm to his side. If he accidentally let another bullet fly it would only put a hole in the teak flooring, not Ferlito's head. 'How do you know my name? And what's a US commercial attaché, if that's what you are, doing breaking into my house at this hour?'

'You're the number one lawyer this side of the Urals

129

at the moment Scotty boy, the top guy, the main man.' He grinned. 'Well, for some. For others, you're a corpse waiting to happen.'

'Have you seen his ID?' Ekaterina asked.

Scott and Ferlito both turned to the doorway.

Ekaterina was wearing one of Scott's robes. She was disheveled with tousled bed hair and looked as sexy as hell.

'It's okay,' Scott said in Russian. 'He seems genuine.'

'Good evening, Ekaterina,' Ferlito said, also in Russian. 'How's Kostya?'

Ekaterina glared at him.

Scott glanced from Ekaterina to Ferlito, and back to Ekaterina. 'Ekaterina?' There was a hint of recognition in her face.

She hurried back upstairs without further comment.

'Ekaterina?' He looked at Ferlito. 'Do you two know each other?'

Ferlito edged to one of the sofas, where he began smoothing the material, as if it contained creases. 'You and the Lady Gravchenko are in deep shit. You know that? Terminal shit.' He stared at Scott. 'You got real big troubles ahead.'

'Ferlito. It's midnight and I've had a very long and tiring day.' He kept tapping the side of his thigh with his gun hand. He didn't know how much longer his patience would last. He watched Ferlito, who kept his eyes on Scott's waving hand. 'What the hell are you doing breaking into my property like this?'

Ferlito nodded at the documents on the desk. 'What's your interest in Arzamas-16?'

'Oh no. That's not why you're here. You couldn't possibly have known that those papers would be here.'

'Smart lawyer. I can see why you piss off the Russkies.'

'So answer the question.' He raised the gun, stopping short of pointing it at Ferlito. 'What are you doing here?'

'I wanna show you something. It's in my jacket.' Ferlito reached into the left inside pocket of his overcoat with his right hand.

'With your left hand.' Scott pointed the gun at the man. 'Easy does it. Easy.'

'Yeh, yeh. Okay. But point that thing away from me.'

'You have to earn it Ferlito. The quicker you take whatever it is out of your pocket, the quicker I lower the gun.'

Ferlito switched hands and fumbled around; with his left hand trying to reach into the inside left pocket. 'How am I supposed to do this, Scott? I'm not a magician.'

'You can do it, believe me. It's amazing what obstacles people can overcome when they have a gun trained at their head.'

'Okay.' The attaché grinned and nodded at Scott. 'You win.' He pulled out the photo with ease.

'There's a good boy,' Scott said.

'Here, take a look at it.' Ferlito held it out and moved towards Scott.

Scott stepped back. 'Put it on the desk.' He kept the gun on his target.

Ferlito did as he was told and stepped back. 'I'm impressed. Have you been watching *Law and Order*?'

Scott edged to the desk, while covering Ferlito with the gun. He glanced at the picture. 'Where did you get this?' It was identical to the photograph given to him by Captain Vassiliyev: the timed and dated snapshot of Ekaterina and Scott entering the apartment block on Mosfilmovskaya.

'I can see why you guys don't want to show your faces in Moscow. Your DNA must be decorating that apartment.'

Scott winced.

'Did you find what you were looking for?' Ferlito continued.

That was it. The man had to go. 'Right! Out! Get out!' He waved the gun at Ferlito. 'Your time's up Mr self-appointed commercial attaché.'

'Sure,' Ferlito shrugged. 'If that's what you want.'

'That's *exactly* what I want.'

Ferlito left the room and headed for the front door at the point of the gun. 'Why the hell you wanna get mixed up with Gravchenko's woman, sure beats me.' He opened the door. 'Still, it's your funeral.' He turned his back on Scott and trudged across the garden. '*Hasta la vista, amigo.*'

Scott returned to the kitchen, shaking and bemused, where he put the gun back in the bread-bin and poured himself a glass of water. If the guy was genuine, the Americans were interested in Mosfilmovskaya and, maybe, Arzamas-16. He bounded upstairs to Ekaterina's bedroom, knocked once and entered the room without waiting for an invitation.

She lay on her side, apparently asleep.

'Ekaterina. Ekaterina.' He rustled the duvet. 'Wake up. Please. Wake up.'

She opened her eyes. They were wide, not sleepy.

'Ekaterina, how do you know this Ferlito guy?'

'It can wait until the morning.' She turned away.

'But—'

'In the morning.' She buried her head in the pillow. 'Goodnight Scott.'

Chapter 16

'Spetsnaz. A tough guy…from Moscow,' Colonel Kisletski flicked through the pages of Pravda's documents. 'Impressive, very impressive.'

Pravda had read the GRU file on Kisletski before he'd embarked on his journey. In the 1990s, at the beginning of the Second Chechen War, Kisletski had burnt down a Chechen village on a drunken whim, sodomized, and murdered two eleven-year-old twin boys whom he falsely accused of being terrorist snipers. The Russian armed forces had a rule that serving personnel could only be arrested with the permission of their superior officers, irrespective of how heinous the offense was. Not one of Kisletski's superior officers would give the prosecutor's office permission to arrest him. He had protection, but Pravda didn't know why. He could only presume that the man knew too much about some powerful people, and had managed to escape a bullet. However, the Kremlin ultimately deferred to the voices of revulsion from the ranks and arranged for Kisletski to serve his time out of harm's way as the commander of the Arzamas-16 installations. Kisletski was FSB, not MVD, but the MVD's protestations to the Kremlin, about having "such an animal" in charge, were ignored.

'We're honored,' Kisletski said, with a contorted smile. 'Honored to have a Spetsnaz general in our midst. The bulbous-nosed and red-faced colonel passed Pravda's ID papers back over his head to the major standing behind him. 'Aren't we, Major?'

'Yes sir, Colonel,' the major said, glancing at them with no sign of interest. 'Honored.'

Pravda sat opposite the monster, biting his tongue. He'd spent the night in solitary confinement in one of Kisletski's stinking cells. The colonel had ordered his detention less than an hour after he'd been captured and made no sign of wanting to interrogate him. The cell had four walls and a hole in the ground; nothing else; no iron cot to lie on. He hadn't received any food or water. The lieutenant-general accepted his situation without visible complaint. He'd trained for much worse privations. His one concern was that Kisletski had confiscated his cellphone and he was unable to contact Alexei, the only person who knew he was in Arzamas. If Pravda didn't call or text Alexei by 3.30pm that day, Alexei was to inform Uncle Nikolai. Pravda's superior had enough clout to secure Pravda's release by official methods, if he couldn't arrange it by other means.

Kisletski clasped his hands. 'Now, tell me, General Pravda, what brings you down from your ivory tower on such an inclement day? He grimaced and exposed two gold teeth. 'Hardly the weather for gathering mushrooms. What have we done to deserve this honor?'

Pravda's superior rank meant nothing to Kisletski; with his protection, he had nothing to fear. Although Pravda didn't have a weapon, he could easily take the vodka-sodden colonel out, but the young major behind him was a different matter. He was the trigger-happy soldier who'd caressed his earlobes at the railway sidings. He glanced at the clock above the former Soviet flag on the wall behind the colonel.

'Do you have an appointment, General?' Kisletski asked. 'Am I keeping you from something?'

'You don't understand Colonel Kisletski. I—'

'Don't talk down to me!' the colonel screamed. He stamped both his feet hard on the floor. The major flinched.

'Or I will have you taken out and shot!' The veins on the colonel's neck swelled up into pulsating purple balloons. 'Do you understand me, General Pravda? Do not talk down to me!'

'I apologize, Colonel,' Pravda said calmly. He was getting the measure of the man, and his insecurities. 'I didn't mean to sound patronizing.'

The veins on Kisletski's neck retreated into their skin folds.

'Perhaps we could have a word in private,' Pravda continued, and narrowed his eyes as if conspiring with the colonel. Pravda hoped his suggestion would restore the feeling of self-importance to Kisletski and calm him down. People often liked to think that they knew something their colleagues didn't.

'A word in private?'

'Yes, Colonel. In private.'

The FSB chief curled his bottom lip. 'In private,' he said again.

'Yes. Colonel.'

Kisletski waved his hand over his shoulder. 'Wait outside, Major.'

The junior officer sneered at Pravda, but obeyed the order without question.

Kisletski opened a drawer on the left side of his desk and removed a vodka bottle with two tumblers. He pulled out a.9mm Makarov automatic from a drawer on the right side. He placed the items either side of him on the desk top, leant back in his chair and folded his arms. 'Well, General Spetsnaz, I'm listening.'

'I have a letter for you, Colonel.' This was Pravda's escape route.

He moved his right hand towards his inside jacket pocket.

Kisletski leant forward, his hand hovering over the Makarov.

'I'm not armed.' Pravda said. 'Your men have checked.' He'd been stripped searched.

The hovering continued.

Pravda took two pieces of paper from his pocket and handed one across the desk.

The colonel unfolded it and read it aloud.

To whom it may concern. You are instructed to extend to the bearer of this letter, Lieutenant-General Leonid Igorovich Pravda, the fullest possible cooperation without question.

It was dated October 2013 and signed by Army-General Pyotr Mikhailovich Bezrukhov.

General Bezrukhov was neither FSB nor military intelligence. He was a mediator between the two warring factions. Twenty years previously, he had settled a dispute involving a KGB (FSB) assassination attempt on a senior GRU general. As such, both sides grudgingly accepted him, at the Kremlin's direction, as a disinterested figure with some authority. Pravda counted on two things: first, if the colonel wanted to authenticate the document, he wouldn't be able to do so for some time. Pravda had checked with the general's aides while in Moscow and they'd confirmed that he was out of the country on a personal jolly in Shanghai. He was building a property portfolio for himself and his cronies with their shares of the profits from illegal arms sales in the early Yeltsin years. China's adoption of capitalism was attracting a motley crew of investors and Beijing wasn't concerned with the sources of their funding. Second, the forgery was the handiwork of one Yuri Rostov, Moscow's leading "documentologist"; servant to the highest bidder. It was so masterful that Pravda defied anybody to detect the facsimile copy and the alteration to the year, including Bezrukhov himself. The rest of the document was genuine. In 2012 Pravda had undertaken a real mission for the Army-General.

The colonel threw the letter back at him. 'It's a photocopy. I wouldn't wipe my ass with it.' His hand returned to the air space above the Makarov.

Pravda edged the original version across the desk, but kept both hands firmly on the document. 'This is the original.' Kisletski tried to pick it up, but Pravda held it fast. They were behaving like schoolchildren.

The colonel read it. 'Give me back the copy,' he barked.

Pravda suppressed a smile and handed it to him.

'Major!'

The door crashed open and the young terrier burst in, gun drawn. His face confirmed his disappointment at seeing no reason to shoot the prisoner. 'Yes sir?'

'Verify this.' The colonel thrust the copy letter at him.

'Sir.' The major grabbed it and left the room.

Kisletski filled the two glasses with vodka and pushed one in Pravda's direction. Pravda needed to keep a clear head and was not in the mood for drinking, especially with a sodomite, but on this occasion his principles would have to defer to pragmatism. Kisletski picked up the drink and downed it in one go. Pravda did likewise and Kisletski refilled the tumblers. The colonel again gulped his drink down in one go, and promptly topped up his glass for a third time. Not once did Kisletski take his eyes off Pravda and not once did his right hand stray from its hovering position over the Makarov. 'As I said, I'm listening, Lieutenant-General.'

'I need to interview two of your residents.' How many obstacles would the colonel put in his way?

'You're not drinking.' Kisletski pushed the vodka bottle across the desk.

Pravda drank the second glass and pushed it aside.

'Don't be polite, General Pravda.' The colonel leant

across the desk, grabbed the bottle and filled Pravda's glass to the top for the third time. 'I have plenty more where this comes from.'

Pravda ignored the glass.

The two soldiers glared at each other.

'Colonel Kisletski, I have to interview Mikhail Konstantinovich Danilov and Igor Alekseyevich Petrov.' He studied the colonel's face for the slightest hint of any suspicion as to what was behind Pravda's visit to Arzamas. Kisletski's ruddy demeanor betrayed nothing, except an excess of alcohol being pumped around his system.

'Why?' Kisletski downed his third shot and poured himself a fourth. He moved his right hand away from the Makarov and rested it on the desktop; presumably to mask an alcohol-induced tremor. 'You're not drinking General.'

'I am sorry, Colonel, but Army-General Bezrukhov has ordered me not to divulge the reason…to anybody.' Pravda pointedly pushed his glass further away from him. Their roles were reversing.

'You don't like vodka?' Kisletski's eyelids were beginning to droop. 'Maybe you prefer Western cat's piss?' He smirked. 'You know, Lieutenant-General Leonid Igorovich Pravda, we have a file on you and your American friends.'

Surprise, surprise. The FSB had files on everybody – especially each other. Pravda had visited the CIA's headquarters in Langley, Virginia five years previously. He'd had to obtain authorization from the GRU top brass to go there; it was never meant to be a state secret. The FSB would have picked it up in the press, if they hadn't been told directly. 'I have a long drive back to Moscow. So, if we—'

'You've no fucking right to call yourself a Russian!' Kisletski thumped the desk with his fist. 'No fucking right!'

Instead of grinding the colonel's manhood into the electric pencil sharpener on his desk, Pravda retained his cool. 'Colonel Kisletski, if you could please—'

The major entered the room. 'We can't contact General Bezrukhov, sir. He's abroad.'

'Where is the asshole?'

'They thought he was in Shanghai, sir. But they can't find him.'

'Shanghai! Have they no telephones in that yellow-skinned dog-eaters' shit hole?'

'They have no idea where he is, sir.'

'Screwing some village whore's grandmother!' Kisletski stamped both his feet again, and his knees hit the underside of his desk, making the pistol jump.

The major fidgeted in the background.

'State fucking security!' Kisletski poured himself his fifth vodka.

'Colonel.' Pravda looked at the clock on the wall again. 'I must be on my way back to Moscow as soon as possible.' He couldn't risk Kisletski suggesting that he extend his stay in Arzamas until Bezrukhov returned from his trip. That would have been signing his own death warrant.

'Pick up Danilov and Petrov and bring them to me,' the city's commander said to the major.

'Yes, sir.'

Pravda swallowed hard and tried not to display his concern. 'That's very kind of you, Colonel, but if you don't mind I would prefer to interview the men in their apartments.' The last place he wanted to discuss the deaths of Karat and Sokolov was in an FSB commandant's headquarters.

'Why?' Kisletski demanded.

'They mustn't feel oppressed. They need to be in relaxed surroundings.' He hesitated. 'It's a very delicate matter.'

'You think I'm oppressive?' The colonel raised his eyebrows, as if offended.

Pravda didn't believe the colonel cared a fig what a GRU general thought of him. 'No. It's just that—'

Kisletski turned to the major.

'Call Danilov and tell him that he and Petrov will be having a visitor in twenty minutes.'

'Thank you, Colonel,' Pravda said with an inward sigh of relief.

The major left the room, again with a disapproving glare at Pravda.

'I'll get hold of Bezrukhov.' Kisletski bared his teeth. 'And if your letter's a forgery...' He knocked back the vodka in one gulp and picked up the Makarov. 'You won't live long enough to regret the day you were born! Do you understand me, Lieutenant-General Leonid Igorovich Pravda of the GRU?'

'Loud and clear, Colonel Kisletski. Loud and clear.'

Pravda leant across the sink in Danilov's kitchen and peered through the window. The major was across the street, talking on his cellphone. Pravda couldn't help thinking that Kisletski had given in too easily. Bezrukhov's orders or not, the man should have put up more of a fight. After all, he was the apparently untouchable "Butcher of Grozny".

He turned to Danilov. Despite never having met in person, the two had spoken on secure telephone lines on numerous occasions over the years. 'Is your apartment bugged?' The scientist was tall and agile, with a shiny scalp showing through white wispy hair. Pravda was surprised; Danilov's smooth baby-skin face helped present him as a man in his mid-fifties, rather than his sixty-three years.

'Kisletski thinks it is.' Danilov laughed. 'Wine or spirits?'

'I've had my fill of vodka today.'

Danilov brought a bottle of Côtes du Rhône, some

borscht, black bread, half a cucumber and crisps to the table. 'Sorry, but my wife has been looking after an expectant mother for the past week. Shopping isn't my favorite hobby.'

Pravda glanced at the food. 'That looks good. I've not eaten for almost twenty-four hours.' He looked out at the major again. He was still on the phone. 'I'll get straight to the point, Mikhail Konstantinovich. We have a serious problem.'

'Then we'd better not discuss it on an empty stomach, especially yours.' Danilov poured some wine and sat down. 'Come away from that window and let's eat.'

Pravda joined Danilov, who proposed a toast. 'To absent friends.'

'To absent friends.' Pravda winced. 'That's why I'm here, Mikhail.' He braced himself. 'I have no other way to tell you this.'

Danilov bore a warm unsuspecting grin.

'Karat and Sokolov are dead. Murdered in Moscow. In the last ten days.'

Danilov put his glass down. 'Sokolov? Murdered? In Moscow?' He shook his head. 'No Leon, that's not possible. Not possible at all. He was here, in Arzamas.' He paused. 'Yes. Last Tuesday fortnight. How could—'

'What?' Pravda's grip tightened around his glass. Sokolov had never visited Arzamas, or anywhere else. Until his transfer to Moscow in 1999 he'd been living at Vilyuchinsk in the Kamchatka Region, thousands of kilometers east of Arzamas and Moscow. What was he doing in Arzamas? They were to have been kept apart, with Danilov being the only member of the group knowing the whole picture.

'Yes,' Danilov continued. 'He came to see Igor Alekseyevich.'

'Sorry, Mikhail, but I can't begin to imagine what you're saying.' Pravda's head was spinning, and not through the drink. 'How did Sokolov know of Petrov's whereabouts?' He rubbed his leg.

'Leon, it doesn't matter. Igor is ill. Very, very ill. He could die at any moment. Sokolov found out, I don't know how, we were never alone for him to tell me how. He persuaded the FSB that he should be allowed to visit his old friend on compassionate grounds.' He shrugged. 'Don't ask me why, but they agreed.'

Petrov dying? The FSB compassionate? This was the mother of all nightmares. 'Our cousins aren't supposed to know anything about you people.' If the FSB knew the truth they would have used the knowledge, but they hadn't mentioned a word.

'That's what we like to think, my friend.'

Petrov would have the answer. 'What's wrong with Igor Alekseyevich?' Pravda asked.

'He has unstable angina.'

'And?' Pravda knew it had something to do with clogged arteries, but sufferers could lead reasonable lives if they had the right medicine or operation.

'A thrombus...a clot...in a narrow blood vessel.'

'How serious is it?'

'Here, in Arzamas, life-threatening. He could die from a heart attack at any moment, without warning.'

'Surely they can do something for him?' A by-pass operation or those beta-blocker things. Igor Alekseyevich Petrov had been Uncle Nicolai's favorite of the ten. 'He has served this country well.'

'He needs first class cardiac care,' Danilov said, shaking his head. 'We don't have that degree of specialty in Arzamas. He needs Moscow's finest heart doctors, and they won't, or can't, come to Arzamas.' He took out a handkerchief and blew his nose. 'We could lose him, Leon.' His hands shook as he wiped his eyes.

'How long has he got?' This was sad news indeed.

'How long is a piece of string? He could die tonight.

On the other hand he could live for years.' Danilov pushed his plate aside, the food half-eaten. 'It's as if he's living on a knife edge.' He leant forward. 'Can't you do something, Leon? Please.'

Driving or not, Pravda poured himself a large glass of wine, and took some bread and crisps to soak up the alcohol. He resolved to take immediate action with Petrov, but he wanted to solve the riddle. 'The FSB is no way compassionate. Why did they let Sokolov into this city? It doesn't add up.'

Danilov shrugged again.

Pravda wandered around the kitchen.

'I never met Karat,' Danilov said. 'He was a name on a list to me.' He reached out and picked at the food. 'Although, of course, I knew he was one of us.'

'Your lives are in serious danger,' Pravda said. 'Apart from you and Petrov, Grushchenko is the only member of the group still alive.'

'Where is he?'

'Safe.' He was living 1,700 kilometers east of Moscow, in Snezhinsk, Chelyabinsk Oblast.

Danilov looked at Pravda. 'We're also safe, Leon. Nobody can get at us. Kisletski may be a drunkard but his men are no fools.'

'It was easy enough for me to get through the perimeter fence.'

'And straight into Kisletski's arms,' Danilov replied.

'You have to take the threat seriously,' Pravda said. 'The killer is on a mission. I'm certain of it. You all belong to the same group. That's the connection. I refuse to believe that the slaying of Sokolov and Karat within days of each other and by the same MO is a mere coincidence.'

'Of course you do, Leon.'

'What do you mean?' Pravda studied Danilov's face. Was the scientist mocking him?

'You're an intelligence officer. Your default position is that everybody is a security risk and must prove their innocence. Me, I'm only a simple old scientist who searches for proof before reaching any conclusion.'

No. Pravda's extensive experience as an intelligence officer told him that his hunch was right. 'I have enough proof, Mikhail. You have to take extra precautions until the killer is caught.'

Danilov sighed. 'Okay. Let's assume somebody *is* out to kill us all. But why us? And why now?'

'Indeed.' Pravda sat down again and took some bread. He hadn't yet worked out the killer's motive.

'Don't worry. We'll be okay.' Danilov extended his hand to Pravda. 'We will. I know what a low-life Kisletski is—'

'You do?'

'Yes, Leon. I should imagine that most of us in the city know the story of the Butcher of Grozny.'

'Does he know you know?'

'Of course. In his more drunken moments he positively revels in it.'

'Bastard.'

'We're sorry for his victims, it goes without saying,' Danilov said. 'But he doesn't cause us any problems.'

'I still refuse to believe the FSB acted out of compassion when they let Sokolov come here,' Pravda said. 'It's against their ethos. They wouldn't recognize compassion if it smacked them in the face.'

'Maybe some things are best left unexplained, Leon.'

Pravda was beginning to think the unthinkable. Danilov could be playing both sides. He dismissed the notion. 'I'm taking Petrov back to Moscow with me, for medical treatment. Where is he? I want to talk to him.'

Danilov cleared his throat. 'Leon, when I asked you to do something, I didn't mean take him to Moscow, today.'

'So what *did* you mean?' Pravda asked. Didn't Danilov

want the best treatment for his friend, who was "living on a knife edge"?

'Your heart is ruling your head,' Danilov said. 'Our humanitarian commandant won't allow his own shadow out of the city without the right papers. Anyway, the car journey will probably kill him.'

'You say the man needs specialist treatment by Mocow doctors if he is to have any chance of a decent life.'

'Leon, think this through.'

'I have.'

'Have you?

'What do you mean?'

'As I said, your heart is ruling your head.'

What was the man getting at? Petrov could die at any moment without the correct treatment. 'What do you expect me to do?'

Danilov clasped his hands together. 'Taking him to Moscow will expose him to the elements.' His eyes steeled. 'Elements, which neither you nor Uncle Nikolai, could control.'

'The FSB? The Kremlin?'

'Kisletski is one thing,' Danilov said. 'But if Moscow gets hold of him, who knows what might happen? You need to plan the move.'

Was Danilov threatening or warning him? 'You tell me that Petrov will die unless I get him to Moscow.'

'Yes, but—'

'Well, that's good enough for me,' Pravda said. He'd failed to protect Sokolov and Karat. He wasn't prepared to let another member of the group die, without at least doing all that was humanly possible to try to save him. 'Now, where is he?'

'Okay, I've said all I have to say.' Danilov got up. 'His apartment is in the next block, on the third floor. I'll take you there. But he might be drowsy. He's taking sleeping pills for restless nights.' He sighed. 'The trouble is, they only seem to work during the day.'

Pravda walked over to the window. The major was still standing across the street, this time smoking. It must have been minus ten. Had he made contact with General Bezrukhov? Was he waiting for backup? He turned to Danilov. 'Do you still have a secure phone?'

'We're scientists. What do you think?' He got up. 'Follow me. I hope you know what you're doing.'

They went into the bedroom. Danilov opened the wardrobe and removed a false panel from under a pile of clothes at the bottom. He pulled out an old-fashioned red Soviet style telephone on a long lead and laid it on the bed. 'It's safe. Untraceable.'

'Who pays the bill?' Pravda asked as he dialed a number.

'I can see why you're the intelligence officer and I'm the scientist,' Danilov said. 'It's never crossed my mind.'

The phone connected to a distant line.

'Aunt Olga?'

'Lev?'

'Yes.'

'You sound distant. Where are you?'

'Sarov. Arzamas-16.'

He expected an immediate response.

He got it.

Silence.

'Aunt?'

'Yes.'

'I need a favor, a very special favor.'

'Go on. I'm listening.' Her voice was slow and the tone was measured. Every call to FSB headquarters was recorded, as a matter of routine. Whether anybody listened, was debatable; though Pravda didn't discount the possibility that Kisletski had already bragged to his protectors in the Kremlin that he'd caught a GRU general invading his fiefdom.

He straightened up, as if she was in the room with

him. 'I'm on a special mission for General Bezrukhov.'

'So?'

'I need to bring somebody to Moscow. He needs immediate life-saving treatment.'

'So?'

What else should she have said?

'Colonel Kisletski, the commandant of the city, won't let the patient go.'

'Why don't you ask General Bezrukhov to intervene?'

'He's abroad. Out of contact.'

'What do you expect from me?'

'Who is Kisletski's immediate superior in your organization?'

'Major-General Dorogin,' she said.

'Do you know him?' Pravda had met him once, at a reception. Unusually in Pravda's experience, the FSB major seemed to be a reasonable man.

'Not personally. But I have a line through to his aide.'

'Aunt Olga, this man will die if I don't get him to Moscow immediately for expert medical treatment.'

'Do you have a copy of General Bezrukhov's orders?'

'I can fax them to you in thirty minutes, from Colonel Kisletski's office.'

'Do that. What is your patient's name?'

'Igor Alekseyevich Petrov.'

Pravda waited for the next question: *who is he?*

But Aunt Olga disconnected with a curt "okay" and nothing more.

The call had gone smoothly; perhaps too smoothly. Pravda repeated the mantra - blood is thicker than water, blood is thicker than water.

Pravda was relieved the major was out of the room and he was alone with Kisletski when he had sent the fax to Aunt Olga. He could assert himself. 'Colonel, Petrov is seriously ill. I have to take him back to Moscow with me.'

Petrov was asleep when Pravda visited him. The man's pale color and the plethora of pills and medicine bottles surrounding him, coupled with Danilov's report, was more than enough to convince Pravda that Petrov had to be transferred to Moscow without delay.

Kisletski laughed. 'So you're a doctor now, as well as being a Spetsnaz tough guy.' He poured, himself a vodka without inviting Pravda to drink with him.

'No, Colonel, but I think I can recognize a seriously ill person when I see one.'

They eyed each other across the desk. Pravda expected Aunt Olga's return fax bearing Major-General Dorogin's instruction to release the ailing Petrov into Pravda's custody to arrive any minute. The commandant's face was as red as a beetroot; it could have been the vodka, or it could have been consummate anger.

'What's the point?' Kisletski smirked. 'He'll be dead before you get him to Moscow. He won't last the journey, not in that shit heap of yours.'

Pravda smelt victory. 'Please let me have my cell-phone, Colonel.' He held out his hand. 'I want to arrange for a helicopter to collect us.' It was only 2pm; he had time to check in with Alexei. 'The weather's eased.' One of the helicopter team would drive his Moskvitch back to the capital.

The fax machine came to life and delivered its message. Kisletski turned round and hastily pulled the printed matter from the tray. He read the contents to himself. His hands quivered and the veins in his neck came out from hiding.

'Satisfied?' Pravda asked.

Colonel Kisletski grit his teeth and crumpled his instructions into a ball.

'May I remind you, Colonel,' Pravda said. 'This is a secret mission.'

Kisletski poured himself another vodka. 'And may

I remind you, my high and mighty Spetsnaz General, if you show your uninvited Moscow face in my city again I shall shoot you dead – secret mission or no secret mission.' He picked up the Makarov and pointed it at Pravda.

Pravda held his breath. The colonel's hand was shaking.

'Your health, comrade General!' Kisletski downed the vodka and threw the empty glass over his shoulder, grinning dementedly as it shattered against the hammer and sickle on the flag.

He pulled the trigger.

'Bang! Bang!' he shouted.

Pravda flinched.

The gun was empty.

It was a race against time. Which would arrive first – Pravda's helicopter or Army-General Bezrukhov's return phone call?

Chapter 17

Ekaterina's promised discussion of her acquaintance with Frank Ferlito had failed to materialize. They'd risen early, had a quick breakfast and slept for most of the cab journey back to Moscow. Scott wasn't concerned. The issue of Ferlito's relationship with the Gravchenkos could wait a further day or so; he had a more pressing issue on his mind. He hadn't slept well after Ferlito left. He could no longer be wholly objective in the search for Ekaterina's father, because he was no longer a disinterested party. The GRU, the police and, if Ferlito was to be believed, a US commercial attaché, could place him at the scene of a brutal murder, apparently without any lawful reason. Lawyers often spent so much time concentrating on their clients' affairs that they neglected their own well-being. A person who represents himself has a fool for a lawyer.

He needed to take his own counsel.

The sign on the apartment door was in Russian, it read, "Sophie Menke, Legal Counsel. Hired gun at US $500 an hour – bullets extra". A sense of humor was essential for those doing business in Moscow.

Sophie greeted Scott wearing no more than a loosely tied bathrobe that exposed the top half of her fulsome breasts, and a hint of the right nipple. She kissed him full on the lips without warning.

He followed her into the kitchen.

'A spot of bother, you said on the phone?' She chuckled and handed him a mug of coffee.

Scott pushed a single dollar bill across the breakfast bar. 'Your retainer as my counsel.'

She fondled the note. 'Is this all our friendship is worth?'

'Switch the radio on, will you?' Sophie was the only blond woman he ever recalled having slept with; a drunken one-night stand on their second or third meeting, some years previously. He preferred brunettes. However, their post-coital relationship had deepened, platonically, and they looked out for each other like devoted siblings. She selected a sports discussion program.

He told her the story so far, every detail.

'Well, well.' Sophie licked her lips. 'As a former US District Attorney, and now a consultant compliance counsel, I should march you off to the local police department for questioning. After all, you've not yet been formally discounted as a murder suspect.'

This wasn't a joking matter.

'And I bet there's a bounty on your head.' She giggled. 'On the other hand, my biggest clients are capital investment fund managers, I suppose I should be looking out for suitable projects for them.' She leant forward and whispered. 'We'll handle the film rights, Scotty baby.'

'Sophie, I think you're straying from the center of gravity of my narrative.'

She jerked back. 'Where did that shit come from? "Straying from the center of gravity of my narrative". This is me, Sophie Menke, you're addressing, not some fusty old Strasburg judge.' She refilled Scott's mug. 'Seriously Scott, you've got yourself into some shit; exciting, but real deep, black hole deep. You know what I'm saying?'

'That's why I'm here,' Scott said testily. 'So tell me, what's my next step? My objectivity is disintegrating before my eyes.'

'Okay. Here's how it goes.' She held up her right hand and began counting off her fingers with the index finger of her left hand. 'One, you've upset the Russian government and the military, with your Chechen loyalties at Strasburg. Two, you and that Romanova woman have probably left all sorts of trace evidence in the apartment on Mosfilmovskaya despite your amateur forensic efforts. Three, Pravda, Vassiliyev and Ferlito can all place you at the building. Four, the GRU have ordered you to leave the country.' She smiled. 'Is that central enough for your narrative?'

Her summation was accurate, too accurate. It felt like a kick in the stomach.

'But hey,' she continued. 'You're the hot-shot lawyer. You're supposed to know all this.'

'I do. So please, let's try to be constructive.'

Sophie shook her head. 'Unless you're prepared to close down your law firm in Moscow today, this minute, and go back to the UK to advise on safe subjects, like corporate pension schemes and city zoning laws, you're in for a hell of a ride, no matter what I say, *capeesh*?' She reached out and touched Scott's arm. 'This is Russia. Why screw around with court cases when it's cheaper and less time-consuming to put a bullet through your head...? with no need for all those appeal costs.'

Scott winced.

'Look at the investigative journalist, Anna Politkovskaya,' she said. 'The bastards killed her. And that guy in London, Alexei Litvinenko. He was one of their own for Chrissakes, ex FSB; yet they still killed him.' She took his hands in hers. 'Please, Scott baby. Take the GRU's advice and go home.'

Scott slipped his hands from Sophie, closed his eyes and massaged his temples with his thumbs. 'Sophie, our legal journals are full of articles supporting human rights lawyers all over the world; lawyers who are in danger, prison, being tortured, whatever. If they can stick it out, so can I.' He thumped the worktop. 'Damn it. Ekaterina's father has been imprisoned for thirty years without a trial. If this isn't a classic human rights case, I don't know what is.'

'Shit!' Sophie said. 'Who the hell do you think you are?' Sophie reached out for the coffee refill. 'Aung San Suu Kyi? Haven't you done enough for the world's oppressed? Or are you on a suicide mission?'

She was being melodramatic. 'My life hasn't been threatened and—'

'Your client's has...the car bomb.'

'No. This isn't the answer.' If he was prepared to risk going to Grozny in the middle of a war, he should have no qualms with walking Moscow's streets. Sophie wasn't only a bright lawyer; she had a keen understanding of how the Russians operated. He wanted her to come up with suggestions as to what she thought was going on and how he should handle it. He didn't want her to tell him to run away.

'Okay, you won't listen to reason,' she said. 'So let's at least try some damage limitation. If the GRU are involved with the homicide on Mosfilmovskaya, they're not gonna want Moscow's finest trampling all over their turf and poking their snouts in troughs that don't concern them. These spook guys are ultra-possessive...' She hesitated.

Was she expecting him to contradict her? 'Okay,' Scott said. 'I don't disagree. Go on.'

'The GRU'll do whatever it takes to keep the murder under wraps. For sure, they'd like to know what you guys were doing in the apartment; but again, if they tried to deport you, they can't be too concerned with *your* involvement. That Romanova woman though, well she's got them guessing.' Sophie's eyes widened. 'And they're not gonna sleep 'til they found out what her story is.'

'I realize that.' He was waiting for an angle he hadn't considered. 'How many cents left on my dollar?'

'What concerns me,' Sophie said. 'Is that that oil-slick Frank Ferlito has joined the gang.'

'He's a commercial attaché, right?'

'Yeh, right.' She sniggered. 'I've met the guy at our embassy on a few occasions. And that's definitely what it says on his business card. But I got more idea of the rules of your crazy game of croquet than he has of revolving letters of credit and freight-forwarding contracts.'

'I think you're referring to cricket?'

'Baseball on lithium, whatever.'

'Is he CIA?'

'Possibly.' She didn't sound too convinced.

'Something else? National Security Agency?'

She threw up her hands.

'But what can Ferlito and the GRU have in common at Mosfilmovskaya?' Scott asked.

'Forget it.' Sophie shook her head. 'You'll end up in the rat-infested netherworld of international spookery where the shadows haven't a clue who they are or where they're going. Don't try to figure that one out. Leave it to the paranoid fuckwits who provide fodder for le Carré.'

'Easier said than done. Mosfilmovskaya is Ekaterina's starting point. And that's where she found the Arzamas photo.'

Sophie took in a deep breath and revealed more of her cleavage. Scott enjoyed a momentary flashback.

'Scott, your objectivity has...dematerialized. She picked out one photo from the apartment. How many others were there? Ten, twenty, one hundred? You've no idea. Why should that particular photo be relevant? What are the odds of the only one she picks up being the relevant one? Arzamas could be a complete red herring.' She rapped her knuckles on her temple. 'Use this, counselor.'

'That was my thinking, at first,' Scott said. 'But you're forgetting two things. Ekaterina's mother referred in her letter to the men saying they were taking her father back to Sarov. That's Arzamas. And Ferlito was pouring over my Arzamas downloads at the *dacha*.'

'Is she sure it was Sarov? Some place that sounded like it? Saratov, perhaps?'

'We'll never know,' Scott replied.

They sat in silence for a few minutes, gazing into their coffees.

'What do you know about Arzamas?' Scott asked. 'Apart from the internet stuff I've just told you about.'

'Zilch. Never heard of it.'

'That photo bugs me.' Scott tapped his index finger on the worktop.

'What do you mean?'

'I think Ekaterina may well be right. Perhaps it was hidden, and not in that French book by chance.' The finger tapping became more pronounced. 'What do they say, "follow the money"? Well, I say, "follow the photo". It's the key.'

Sophie rolled her eyes. 'Not again. Have you listened to anything I've said?'

'You're a lawyer Sophie. You have to be cautious.'

'So what do you do for a living Mr Mitchell?' She looked at him. There was pity in her eyes. 'Okay, how secure are your files?'

Scott pulled a buff legal folder from his briefcase and handed it to her. 'Duplicate file. For safe keeping. I'll copy everything over to you in future.'

'Where do you keep the originals?' She flicked through the folder.

'Most of the routine stuff has been scanned onto a hard drive and the unwanted originals shredded. Ekaterina keeps the originals of the letter, note and photo in her bank safe deposit box.'

'You trust Russian banks?' Sophie raised her eyebrows.

'Ekaterina does.'

'Her funeral.' Sophie smirked.

'Hang on,' Scott said. 'She's no ordinary citizen.

Who's going to interfere with Mrs Gravchenko's bank accounts?'

'Two words.'

'What?'

'Car...bomb.'

'Touché.' Scott tapped the folder. 'Anyway, you've got a running narrative in this lot.'

'Send any hard copies here to my apartment, not to my office,' Sophie said. 'And use my personal e-mail for attachments.'

Sophie and Scott stood up; she approached him.

'Watch your back Scott and don't let that Romanova woman lead you astray.' She beamed at him. 'Sophie loves you, you crazy Brit.'

'I'll be okay, don't worry.'

'You promise?'

'I promise.' He kissed her gently on the lips. 'I now know what I have to do.'

Follow the photo.

Chapter 18

Day Five: 9pm

The secret encampment consisted of a series of small, wooden cottages dotted among the sky-scraping silver birch trees and connected by snow-covered asphalt pathways. It was located twenty kilometers due-north of the capital.

The Mi-8MTV helicopter hovered over a small ring of red landing lights in the clearing. Pravda checked his watch and thanked the Chinese for encouraging private enterprise; Kisletski had been unable to contact Army-General Bezrukhov. He looked at the young freckle-faced doctor, Andrei. The medic had a scar on his chin; it was a bullet wound that hadn't healed properly. Pravda's mind strayed to Scott Mitchell's dimple. Had lawyer and client found whatever it was they were looking for in the apartment?

The chopper touched down and Pravda jumped out into the sub-zero temperature of the Moscow woodland. The hatch slammed shut behind him. He was taking no chances. His patient would remain on board until he could be sure the area was secure. The last leg of the journey would have to be made by road. Pravda was taking Petrov to a small, insignificant-looking GRU hospital – one that was used to secrecy – that didn't have a helipad.

His men were taking up their positions in the forest. They didn't know who their special charge was. It wasn't that Pravda didn't trust them, but this mission was like no other; they didn't need the information. The less they knew, the less they would have to lie if questioned by the Kremlin. Alexei was the only member of the team who knew that Petrov was coming to Moscow. Aunt Olga, Kisletski and Major-General Dorogin also knew, though they weren't aware of the details of Pravda's itinerary.

Pravda hadn't slept properly for thirty, forty, fifty hours? He'd lost count. His reactions were slowing down. 'Go!' Pravda said to two heavily armed men who had climbed out with him. They trekked away towards the corner of the clearing where an ambulance and three Zil limousines were waiting. He rapped twice, sharply, on the side of the helicopter. The hatch slid back and Andrei shivered in the doorway. 'I'm from Georgia,' he said. 'This is cruel and unusual punishment.'

'How is he?' Pravda was in no mood for their usual light-hearted banter.

'Asleep.'

Four vehicles crawled across the white grassland towards the helicopter, their engine noises muffled by the deep powdery snow. 'Can we keep him that way until we reach hospital?'

'It's in the hands of the gods,' Andrei said. 'He's had enough sedative for this trip.'

'It couldn't be helped,' Pravda snapped.

'Merely an observation.'

'Get him ready.' Each of Pravda's eyelids weighed a kilo. He took in a series of deep gulps of the frosty air and forced it down to the bottom of his lungs, hoping to keep alert until they reached their destination. The final leg of the journey would be the most hazardous; they were on the ground.

Andrei retreated into the hull of the big bird.

A Zil pulled up first and three men carrying Kalashnikovs scrambled out, leaving the driver at the wheel with the engine running. The three made a protective arc around the open hatch. The ambulance followed closely behind and maneuvered itself into position, edging its own sliding doors flush with the helicopter's. Four men squeezed out. Two remained with Pravda while the other two trudged round to the other side of the helicopter. The second and third Zils stopped behind the ambulance. Two men, bearing only holstered pistols, emerged from the second Zil and waited by the helicopter to receive the patient's cradle from the doctor. Three more men with automatic weapons climbed out of the final vehicle and joined the arc, facing away from the helicopter and scouring the area.

Pravda made a 360 degree scan of their location with his binoculars. All four vehicle engines were kept running. He had another fifteen men secreted in the forest.

'Okay,' he said, rapping on the side of the helicopter again. 'Ready.' The hatch slid open for the second time.

Andrei and an assistant stood before the armed group, holding a cradle. It contained a secured mound of clothing plumped up to look like a body. Two of the men on the ground grabbed the end of the cradle and gently guided it into the ambulance. Pravda surveyed the area again. 'Right,' he said.

Andrei and his assistant disappeared inside the hull for twenty seconds and emerged with another cradle, this time bearing the ailing and sleeping Igor Alekseyevich Petrov.

The arc closed in, so as to make it impossible for anybody to see what was going on from a distance. One of the men opened the middle door of the second limousine and climbed inside. With two other men, he eased Petrov and his cradle into a coffin-shaped, bulletproof box that had replaced the rear seats, but lengthwise, front to back. The first man squeezed behind the coffin and took up his position as the rear gunner. The remaining two men climbed into the front; one driving, the other riding shotgun. Pravda and Andrei slipped into makeshift seats behind them, one either side of the front of the coffin. The ambulance doors closed and the rest of the team piled back into their vehicles.

'Wait for the command,' Pravda said to the driver of the lead vehicle via his headphones. It was a Russian custom for those ready to travel to sit silently on their luggage for a few minutes, in contemplation. On this occasion the luggage was definitely not for sitting on. 'Go,' Pravda ordered after twenty-five seconds.

The convoy crawled out of the forest and made for the Dimitrovskoe Highway where they would travel due-south to Moscow's outer ring road and turn east at Savelovksya. The snowfall was mild, but the city's evening traffic would make it slow going. Pravda's eyes closed.

Ekaterina Romanova was the reason for the pair being at Mosfilmovskaya. The thought played on his mind, over and over again. What did she want from Sokolov? He half-opened his eyes and checked his patient; he was still breathing, though not awake. Andrei was also asleep. Pravda's eyes alternated between closing and opening in an attempt to fight off sleep. But she had said, convincingly, that she'd never heard of Sokolov. It didn't make sense. Pravda's thought processes were interrupted when a flash of light from the top of an office building caught his eye.

He blinked.

It wasn't the moon or street lights reflecting on a window. He sat up and squinted at the light source. 'Shit!' A man was on the roof with what could be a weapon.

Andrei woke up. 'What? What's happening?'

'Drive! Drive! Drive!' Pravda shouted at his driver, Sergei. His ankle locked up. The vehicle screeched away from behind the ambulance and roared towards the oncoming traffic, Pravda looked back. An explosion destroyed the rear Zil. Bullets from nearby buildings tore into the ambulance. It swerved onto the sidewalk, crushed the bodies of three hapless pedestrians and pushed them through a shop window. A second explosion reduced the ambulance to a smoldering wreck of twisted metal. The occupants couldn't have survived.

The windows either side of Pravda and Andrei, and the rear window, also took the blast and shattered. Splintering glass showered the occupants and the cold air rushed in.

Pravda called Alexei on his cellphone. His headset's range was limited to the members of the convoy. 'Alexei! Sandstorm! Sandstorm!' It was the code for a pre-arranged rescue. Alexei had two teams located along the route at different points: Sandstorm and Mistral. Sandstorm was a deserted industrial estate three kilometers from their current position.

Pravda looked over his shoulder again. Their blood-spattered rear gunner sat crumbled lifeless in his seat.

The lead Zil had disappeared. Pravda shouted at Sergei, 'Sandstorm! Now!' Sergei accelerated towards the oncoming traffic, forcing a gap between two of the lanes.

Andrei put a protective arm on the sleeping Petrov.

'Is he still alive?' Pravda asked.

'He's breathing.'

A truck headed straight for them. Sergei held his position, compelling the truck driver to swerve into the inside lane and crash into a line of cars. Two motorcyclists with helmets and reflective visors sped out from a side street and raced along with the limousine. Each carried an automatic assault weapon. They sprayed the Zil with bullets, powerful enough to penetrate the toughened windows of each front door and blow Pravda's shotgun rider's face off. Another showering of shattered glass and rush of cold air. Andrei and Pravda dropped to the floor.

Sergei slammed on the brakes.

Pravda felt their vehicle lurch forward, followed by a muffled sound. He peeked up. One of the motorcyclists was sprawled on the hood. Sergei had braked to allow the cyclist to overtake, and then swerved into him. A hail of bullets from the other cyclist tore into the vehicle.

Pravda ducked down again.

The Zil swerved to the right. 'Here's where we drop you off, my friend!' Sergei shouted. Their vehicle roared away. There was a soft bump as they drove over what Pravda presumed to be the motorcyclist's body. The other assailant kept shooting from behind.

The streets were alive with sirens.

Andrei popped his head up without warning and took a bullet in the back of the neck. The doctor's head slumped forward and his body tilted sideways, coming to rest over Petrov's "coffin". Bullets ricocheted around the inside of the vehicle. Pravda felt he was in a pinball machine. But Petrov seemed to be sleeping soundly through the mêlée.

The shooting stopped.

There was an explosion behind. He turned and looked out of the windowless rear compartment. Flames engulfed the second motorcyclist and his machine. Armed police stood watching from a distance; nobody wanted to risk being caught in a second explosion. More by luck than judgment, Sergei and Pravda emerged unscathed, though blood trickled down Petrov's neck. 'Step on it!' Pravda stared at the blood.

When the Zil arrived at Sandstorm, Alexei's team was waiting. It comprised two heavily armed fire trucks, each containing nine GRU men dressed as firefighters. They were supported by six armed GRU motor cycle outriders in police uniforms.

The war had begun.

If only Pravda could be sure who his enemy was.

Chapter 19

Day Five: 11.15pm

The four men in the front Zil had disappeared with their vehicle. Pravda didn't know if they were injured or dead. Two of them, Vladislav and Eduard, were permanent members of his team, but the other two were last minute stand-ins for two regulars who'd cried off due to illness. Pravda suspected the newcomers of being involved with the instigators of the attack. The loyalty of his regular members was beyond question. If he was right, Vladislav and Eduard would also be dead.

The GRU's hospital was located in Moscow's outer southern suburbs, on the way to Domodyedovo airport, and within walking distance of the Tsaritsyno Museum. The building stood at the end of a narrow drive leading from the road. Two three-story apartment blocks, built in the 1930s, flanked the access way. The residential tenants were unable to see over the high walls and into the hospital grounds; in any event, most of them were former Communist Party members in their twilight years and grew up learning not to ask questions. The sign "State Bread Factory No 27" hung on the double wrought-iron gates at the entrance. For over fifty years until the 1980s that was what any enquiring mind was entitled to know. During Soviet times, the building housed "enemies of the people" who were on their way to the Gulag in the sub-zero temperatures of Siberia if they were lucky – and to psychiatric asylums for drug experiments, if they were unlucky. These "dead souls" would arrive straight from the back door of a court house, or the infamous

Lubyanka, in windowless blue vans with the word "Bread" painted on the side. In the final few decades of the twentieth century, the in-patients comprised military personnel injured on deniable missions, mostly abroad. Though the principals in the Cold War no longer sought to subvert each other's political philosophies, they both invested heavily in trying to discover each other's commercial secrets, using the experience and resources of the military where appropriate.

Pravda and Alexei walked behind Petrov's gurney, with three paramedics and a physician guiding their patient through a maze of corridors to the assessment room. Petrov was still breathing, but when they'd moved him onto the stretcher Pravda saw that the blood on his head was seeping from a bullet entry wound. 'Get a team onto the lead car immediately,' Pravda said. 'If Eduard and Vladislav have been killed—'

'Already actioned,' Alexei said.

Pravda slowed down and began to drag his left leg.

'When did you last get some decent sleep, Lev?'

Pravda stopped. 'I can't remember.' He closed his eyes and massaged his eyelids with finger and thumb of one hand.

'Lev.' Alexei touched him on the elbow. 'General Bezrukhov is back from China and he wants to see you. He was on the plane home when Kisletski tried to contact him, but now the bastard butcher has told him what happened at Arzamas.'

Pravda opened his eyes and looked at his watch. 'Now? It's gone 11.'

'Now,' Alexei said. 'I told him about the ambush,' Alexei continued. 'But he still wants to see you.'

Pravda accepted he would be ordered to report to the general at some time, but not at that particular moment. He wanted to prepare his case. It was too soon. He was reeking of cordite.

'I can make excuses,' Alexei said. 'You're still recovering—'

No. Pravda remembered he'd insisted on debriefing Volodya, the leader of his surveillance team, at 2am, after the fiasco at the Mosfilmovskaya apartment, and he'd told Alexei that actions have consequences. He couldn't complain that Bezrukhov wanted to do the same to him. 'No.' He walked on. 'I'll go.'

Alexei kept pace with him. 'But you're down on your feet.'

'It's my responsibility. I have to deal with it. Besides, it's not that important. I've taken a few liberties, but I'm sure Bezrukhov will understand. Hurt pride, nothing more.' He didn't believe what he was saying to Alexei. The old man was no fool.

'Okay, but you're in no fit state to drive. I'll get you a driver.'

'Alright. But call me the second you have a report on the bullet wound. I faxed a summary of Petrov's medical history to Dr Glasunov from Arzamas.'

'What else do the medics know?'

'About his non-medical history?' Pravda asked. 'Nothing, absolutely nothing. And it must stay that way.'

Army-General Bezrukhov was writing on a pad, when Pravda entered the room. He didn't look up, but gestured with a shaking right hand for Pravda to sit down in the chair on the other side of his desk. Large brown age spots dominated the general's balding head. Pravda sat down.

Bezrukhov's office was in a former Soviet Ministry building off Staropanksy Street, behind the Supreme Court. It was a few minutes' walk from the Kremlin. His room retained the Soviet style; with its emphasis on size and not the furnishings – to denote the perceived importance of the successive occupants. A twenty-two-seater redwood table commanded the middle of the room, with ten chairs either side, and one at each end. There was a large map of the world on the wall behind the old man. Two of the other walls were bedecked only with the regulation brown wood paneling. The remaining wall comprised a line of windows with their blinds permanently closed. The threadbare dark green carpet could have been a relic from the days of Catherine the Great.

'General Bezrukhov.'

The old man raised a hand and carried on writing.

Pravda strained to keep his eyes open.

Bezrukhov took off his half-moon glasses and looked up. His face was drawn and jaundiced. He had cadaverous jowls bearded with white tufts. His head twitched periodically. He looked ten to fifteen years older than the seventy-two Pravda knew him to be. 'You're not making it easy for me. Kisletki's supporters in the Kremlin want your soul.' His voice was soft, though croaking. He appeared to be having difficulty breathing. This was a different man to the one Pravda had met on previous occasions.

'General Bezrukhov, I—'

The general held up his hand. 'Let me continue.'

'General.'

'You assaulted a young recruit. That by itself is enough to hang you in most Western societies.'

Pravda restrained a smile. Western societies didn't execute officers if they knocked recruits unconscious. More to the point, neither did Russia.

'You tried to enter Arzamas surreptitiously and without authority. You forged my orders and you removed one of the scientists against Kisletki's wishes.'

Pravda opened his mouth to respond.

The general waved him down again. 'Your actions are indefensible. Kisletki demands that you be court-martialed and shot.'

'He thinks the process of first securing a conviction to be too liberal?'

'This is not a joke, Lieutenant-General. Some in the Kremlin would go further than Kisletski – and dispense with the court martial.'

Those days had long disappeared, but all the same Pravda understood Bezrukhov's point.

'General Pravda, the ice is melting beneath your skates.' He closed his eyes, as if to sleep, then opened them again. His breathing was heavy. 'So give me something to work with, give me some reason to justify your continued existence in military intelligence.'

Did Bezrukhov know anything about their mission?

'Tell me, Leonid Igorovich.' Bezrukhov tugged at an ear lobe. 'Why did you go to Arzamas? Who is this Petrov and why did you bring him to Moscow?'

The wily old codger could have been testing him with the questions. Pravda had to make an instant decision: tell the old man about the secret mission and hope to gain his sympathy or keep quiet and risk the consequences.

'Well?'

If Bezrukhov knew who Petrov was, Pravda had no need to tell him. But, there was a killer on the loose and Petrov may be the next target. The more people who knew who Petrov was, the more chance there was of a leak. 'I'm sorry, General Bezrukhov. I don't want to be disrespectful of your authority but I can't answer the first two questions. The third? Well, Petrov needs to see a heart specialist in Moscow.'

'Are you a doctor, as well as an intelligence officer?' Bezrukhov asked. He sounded exasperated.

'No, sir. But his medical records confirm that he has unstable angina. It is—'

Bezrukhov fiddled with his notepad. 'I know what it is, General.' The man's thin body seemed to collapse before Pravda's eyes as the old man gazed into the distance. 'I know what it is.' Bezrukhov picked up his glasses and rose from the chair. 'Lieutenant-General. I can do nothing more for you.' He was unsteady on his feet. 'You will bring Petrov to me, at this office.' He looked at his watch. 'At 2pm this afternoon.'

Pravda also checked his watch. It was 12.55am.

'I shall personally arrange for him to be returned to Arzamas.'

Pravda also stood up. 'I'm sorry General Bezrukhov, but I can't do that. He is seriously ill. He needs urgent medical treatment, in Moscow. You've heard that he was shot in the ambush a few hours ago. The bullet is still in him. If he is moved again, coupled with the angina…well, he could die.' Pravda stopped breathing, while waiting for the general's flak.

'I shall take responsibility for Petrov's welfare,' Bezrukhov said. He pointed a quivering index finger at Pravda. 'You will do as I command.'

He shuffled across the room and disappeared into the corridor.

Chapter 20

Day Six: 10am

Scott took a copy of the "A-16" photograph from the office safe. He'd made several copies of the picture of the two men on the riverbank, but not the legend on the back. It was easy to remember. He'd been given a state-of-the-art copier/scanner by the Chechen community. He studied the picture for the thousandth time. The metal-like object on the smaller man's shirt fascinated him. He punched in a number on his cellphone.

'Yep?' The response was in English.

'Charlie, it's me, Scott.'

'I know that, mate. You're on my screen. So Colonel Yakovlev hasn't shot you yet.'

'Very funny. I need your help. Can you enlarge a photograph to pick out some indistinct detail?'

'No problemo.'

'You haven't seen it.'

'You're talking to Charlie Birch.'

'I need it done urgently.'

'When?'

'Today, if possible.'

'No time like the present. Come over. I'm in my new office on Kutuzovsky. You know where it is.'

'Thanks, Charlie.' Although Scott knew where it was, he'd never been there. 'You're a star.'

Charlie's office was located on the first floor of a three-story building in a courtyard which was hidden from the world on Kutuzovsky Prospect. Rumor had it that the Brezhnev family had occupied most of the buildings during the country's years of stagnation. Terraced blocks populated each side of the courtyard. They comprised a mixture of offices on the first floor, with apartments on the three or four floors above. The masonry, originally brown and green, was covered with centuries of grime. Only the first floor office windows had any semblance of twenty-first century attention with their double-glazed PVC frames. Decades of Russia's harsh winters had reduced the upper floor frames to strips of rotting gray timber. The asphalt yard was overgrown with weeds and was used as a dumping ground for domestic waste.

Crossing the threshold into Charlie's office, however, was to cross time dimensions. Beyond the heavy nineteenth-century wooden-slatted double doors lay a technological complex that put the flight deck of *Starship Enterprise* to shame. The office was one of six on the floor. The door to Charlie's office was made of silver colored metal and had a spy-hole. The name tag on the wall by the buzzer said, in Russian, "Universal Technology Inc. Registered in Cyprus". Scott raised a finger to press the buzzer, but was beaten by the sound of bolts on the inside being pulled back.

Charlie opened the door and beamed. 'Look above your head.'

There was a small black protuberance between the top of the door frame and the ceiling.

'CCTV,' Charlie said. 'Follow me.'

They went into a large open plan office. Charlie worked alone. A waist-high wooden bench ran along two walls of the room. On top sat numerous computers, with their processing units and spaghetti-like wiring housed on the floor under the worktop. They comprised a mixture of Apples, PCs and laptops. Three screens were working: one with a series of English brand logos floating around, another with lines of numbers and letters scrolling across the screen; they looked like computer codes to Scott. The last screen was taken up with what looked like a surveillance headshot of a man whose face Scott recognized, but he couldn't put a name to it. He walked over for a closer look.

'It's Yevgeny Strelnikov,' Charlie said. 'Chairman of Inter-Commerce Trade Bank.'

'What's your interest in him?' Scott asked. Inter-Commerce was in the news. It had recently pulled out of a financing deal for a joint oil and gas venture between the Russian government and the Ukraine.

Charlie feigned a serious look. 'Come now, counselor, have you never heard of client confidentiality?'

Scott continued his survey of the room. A long metal table was pushed against the third wall. An array of cameras, cellphones, iPads, iPods, tablets, and other equipment that Scott didn't recognize, lay on top. He looked at Charlie and pointed at rows of DVDs on the shelves of the fourth wall. They were contained in plain brown covers.

'Sorry mate,' Charlie said. 'Client confidentiality.'

'Does any of this stuff ever get nicked?'

'Who's got the guts to steal from Charlie Birch? Everybody knows my punters. They wouldn't dare.'

The ex-commodity trader from London's East End reveled in his job, satisfying the insatiable demands of the free-market converts who dominated the world's capital of state-organized crime. Charlie gathered commercial and financial intelligence for his clients. He collected information on anything, anywhere, including: real estate, equities, commodities, currency swaps, media invest-ment, intellectual property, overt and covert political funding, municipal infrastructure building. The Russian entrepreneurs who capitalised on their country's disint-egration were masters at turning thin air into money, preferring dollars to rubles. Much of London's expensive real estate had been bought by the new Russian *biznizmenni*. Scott glanced at the photo of a beautiful Russian girl on his desk.

'Valentina, my latest,' Charlie said.

She was late teens/early twenties, at the most. 'And if you dump her,' Scott said. 'She might want revenge.'

'No worries on that score, my friend. The gorgeous dame loves Charlie Birch. He's a true master of the universe.'

'Russian *biznizmenni* and a beautiful young woman.' Scott nodded slowly. 'A recipe for disaster.'

'Why are you lawyers so cynical?' the security expert said, rubbing his hands together. 'Come on, judge, let's get this show on the road. What have you got for me?'

Scott showed him the copy of the photograph.

'Anything on the back?' Charlie flipped the picture over.

'Nothing.'

'What about the original? Date? Place?'

'Nothing.'

'Okay, you're the boss.' Charlie grinned. 'So what's your target? This metal-looking bit, here, on the little guy's shirt?'

'How did you know that?'

'What else on the photo can't you decipher?'

'Hmm, you're not just an ugly face,' Scott said. 'What do you reckon? Can you do anything with it? Can you enlarge it?'

'Follow me, Your Honor.'

Charlie went into a small dark side room and flicked on the light switch. He sat down in front of an 86cm flat screen monitor. Scott pulled up a chair next to him. Charlie laid the photograph on a scanner.

'Hold on,' Scott said. 'Use this.' He took a flash drive from his pocket and put it on the desk. 'Save it to this, not your hard drive.'

'Tut, tut,' Charlie said. 'You don't trust Charlie Birch? A fellow East Ender.'

'It's *because* you're a fellow East Ender that I don't trust you.' Scott laughed and slapped Charlie on the back. 'No, it's for your own protection. It's better if you have no traceable record of it.'

Charlie picked up the photo and studied it again. 'This must be some shit.'

'That's what I'm hoping to find out.' He took it from Charlie's hand and placed it back on the scanner.

Charlie inserted the flash drive, pushed a few buttons on the various bits of hardware attached to the monitor, sat back and waited. 'Where does it come from?'

'Why do you want to know?' Scott chuckled. 'You never give up.'

'Knowing its provenance might help me tease out whatever it is you expect to find.' Charlie said with a straight face.

'I can't tell you.'

'Client confidentiality?'

'You got it,' Scott said and carried on looking at the screen. The photo got bigger but lost its sharpness. 'Can you make it clearer?'

'Sure, some.' Charlie tapped a few keys and pushed the pointer. 'It's better, but still distorted.'

'Can you zoom?'

'*Mais oui.*'

'Right!' Scott stabbed his index finger at the metal-looking object. It was below the hand of the taller man. His arm was draped over his pal's shoulder. 'Zoom again.'

Charlie brought it in stages up to maximum. It looked like a badge or pendant. It was engraved with numbers and letters; maybe four or five rows. The letters were English but none of the rows was complete. He squinted at the object. There was something sticking out of the top. It wasn't attached to the smaller guy's shirt. It was a chain. The big guy was holding the badge, pendant, in his hand.

'Satisfied?' Charlie asked. 'You know what it is?'

'No, I don't.' Scott reckoned he knew what it was, though he wasn't going to tell Charlie. But it didn't make sense. If he was right, it would be out of context in the photograph.

Follow the photo.

Maybe a second visit to Mosfilmovskaya was a risk worth taking. If not to the apartment itself, to the neighbors, to see what they knew about the occupant.

'How many copies?' Charlie asked.

'Just the one, enlarged.' He would print it off later.

'My, my,' Charlie said. He saved the copy and handed back the flash drive to Scott. 'This is real cloak and dagger stuff.'

'What's the damage?' Scott asked.

'On the house, judge.' Charlie beamed at Scott. 'You never know, I might need the favor returned someday.'

'I'd love to, Charlie.' Scott grit his teeth. He was thankful that commercial law wasn't his field; especially Russian commercial law. 'But what do I know about your line of business?'

'You got contacts, my friend. Contacts.' Charlie tapped the side of his nose in true *Monty Python* fashion. 'Know what I mean? Know what I mean? Nudge, nudge.'

Chapter 21

Pravda parked his car in a side street and walked the final few hundred meters to the hospital entrance, checking for unusual activity. The doctor had called him; there was a problem, but he'd refused to discuss it on the phone. He would only confirm that Petrov was still alive. Dr Fyodor Konstantinovich Glasunov was an old friend of Pravda's and he was used to military intelligence's need for secrecy. Petrov's medical records confirmed that he was fortunate enough to have suffered no more than a double hernia in his earlier life and his angina was a relatively recent diagnosis, but Pravda hadn't revealed any further information about the patient.

Pravda approached the security guard on the front gate. It was Yuli, one of his team. The electronic gate opened and Pravda walked through. He peered into the small guardhouse. Nobody else was there. He turned to Yuli. 'Nobody is to come in,' Pravda said. 'Or leave, except emergency vehicles. Do you understand? Nobody.' It was a dramatic gesture, but until he knew what was troubling Glasunov it was better to be safe than sorry. 'Call me if anybody objects.'

'Yes, Leon.' The guard pressed a button and the gate closed.

The front desk was unstaffed. Pravda kicked the structure. It was supposed to be manned twenty-four hours a day. The civilian receptionist with a high-level security clearance was probably moonlighting. He dashed up the stairs and along the brightly lit, but eerily empty, second floor corridor. The doors to the secluded wards were closed except for the room at the end of the corridor. It was Petrov's. The door was wide open and the light was on.

Dr Glasunov emerged from the room, wearing a physician's white coat. He was a couple of centimeters taller than Pravda, with an athletic build, a sprinter rather than weightlifter. He was stroking his goatee beard and his glasses were perched on his head.

'Fyodor,' Pravda said. 'You've got your puzzled face on. What's happened?'

'Come with me, Leon, I want to show you something.' He led Pravda into a side room, where he pulled a cord that operated two strips of neon lighting on the wall.

'Who's with him?'

'The nurse.'

'Who is she?'

'Don't worry, she's cleared,' he said. 'And, your colleague is with her.'

Fyodor sounded contemptuous. Pravda's white-coated colleague was Gregor; what he lacked in medical knowledge he made up for with street-fighting skills.

Fyodor held an X-ray up to the light and lowered his glasses on to his nose.

'What's this?' Pravda asked.

'It's your patient's brain.'

'And?'

'See that?' Fyodor pointed to a small, thin, cylinder-shaped object.

'The bullet?'

'The bullet.'

'Can you remove it?'

'If I want to kill the man.' Fyodor narrowed his eyes. 'Yes.' He wasn't joking.

'And what if you don't remove it?' Pravda's heart rate increased.

'It's not my field, but I suppose it's possible that any

sudden movement of the head could dislodge it. Then,' he shrugged. 'Who knows?'

Pravda imagined Petrov stretching across to his bedside table to get a glass of water, a simple movement – yet dying as a result.

'How much damage has it done?'

'That depends on your point of view.'

'Please explain.'

'It looks like the bullet is lodged in the rhinal cortex.'

Pravda had heard of that part of the brain, but had no idea what its function was. 'With what effect?'

'Again, it's not my field, but his memory may be impaired.'

'Amnesia?'

'It's possible.'

'Has he come out of the coma?'

'Yes.'

Pravda glared at Fyodor. 'I told you, I was to be at his bedside when it happened.'

Fyodor took off his glasses and poked them into the top pocket of his coat. He blew out a gust of air. 'Leon, I called you as soon as I could.'

'Okay, okay, sorry.' It was an ill-considered statement. 'Has he said anything?'

'Yes and no.'

'Fyodor, I'm in no mood for riddles.'

'Who is this man?'

'Tell me what he said,' Pravda continued.

Fyodor took a small cassette recorder from his pocket and pressed a button.

Shit! Shit! We've been hit. Tracers! Six thou…Five thou…Shit! What's the fucking…!

He was speaking in English. The accent was American.

Pravda's heart stopped. 'Are you sure this is Petrov?'

'Of course, I'm sure. What do you—'

'When did he say this?' Pravda snatched the machine from his friend.

'As he was coming out of the coma. Are you going to tell me who he is?

'Why did you record it?' Pravda was snapping as his friend. 'I didn't say you could.'

Fyodor stepped back. 'It's standard procedure, Leon.' He looked offended. 'As soon as a coma patient shows signs of life, we record them. It could be helpful in their treatment.'

'Was Gregor present when this happened?' If so, why hadn't the boy called him immediately?

'No, he wasn't. He was in the canteen.'

Pravda closed his eyes and screwed his face up.

'I don't think I've ever seen you so physically expressive. Will you please tell me who this man is?'

Pravda opened his eyes. 'Who else knows of the existence of this?' It was time for drastic measures.

Fyodor stood his ground. 'My nurse and your colleague.'

'Right.' Pravda waved the cassette at his friend. 'Is this the only recording?'

'Yes.'

Pravda hurried from the room and into the corridor.

Fyodor overtook Pravda and blocked his entrance into Petrov's room by raising both his hands, palms facing Pravda. 'Why won't you tell me who he is? What have you got me mixed up in?'

Pravda brushed his friend aside without replying and entered the room. The nurse was sitting by Petrov's bed, sponging sweat from the man's face. Petrov's eyes were half closed. He was mumbling incoherently. Gregor was sitting in the corner of the room by the washbasin, reading a book. Pravda waved the nurse away, took the flannel from her and carried on from where she had left off. He leant into Petrov's face and whispered in Russian.

'Igor Alekseyevich, can you hear me? It is—'

'Where...am I?' Petrov mumbled, in Russian.

'In hospital,' Pravda said, relieved.

'Hospital?' Petrov strained his neck and tried to look around the room, but his head fell back on the pillow and he closed his eyes. 'Where?' Both his eyelids were covered in minute skin tags and rivers of veins covered his nose. The whites of his eyes were graying. He looked much older than Danilov, despite being five years his junior.

Gregor looked up from his book.

'Moscow,' Pravda replied. He laid his hand on Petrov's forehead in an attempt to hold his head still.

'Moscow?' He opened his eyes.

'Yes. I brought you here so the specialists could treat your angina.'

'Where's Danilov?'

Fyodor and the nurse were standing at the foot of the bed, listening to the exchange.

'Would you please leave us alone for a few minutes, Fyodor?' Pravda looked at Gregor. The soldier jumped up and ushered the hesitating doctor and nurse from the room, closing the door behind all three of them.

'Igor.' Pravda lowered his voice and sponged Petrov's face and hair, again trying to keep the man's head still. 'Danilov is in Arzamas, waiting for you. As soon as you're better I'll take you back to him.'

'Doctor,' Petrov said.

'Yes?' Pravda saw no reason to disabuse Petrov of the notion.

'My head hurts.' He turned to one side.

Pravda laid the sponge on the bedside cabinet and tiptoed out of the room. Gregor was on sentry duty, sitting in another chair and again buried in his book. Fyodor was chatting to the nurse in hushed tones on the opposite side of the corridor. 'Fyodor, how certain are you that a sudden movement of his head could kill him?'

'I never mentioned any certainty. I'm not a brain specialist. I—'

'Alright.' Pravda had an idea. 'But it's a possibility, no matter how remote?'

'Yes, that is what I said.'

'So, can we minimize the risk by giving him a strong sleeping draft and keeping him immobile?'

Fyodor closed his eyes and shook his head vigorously. 'We can't keep him sedated forever.' He opened his eyes and shook his hands up and down in jerks. 'He'll have to move his head some time, if not in his sleep. Can't you see that?'

'Yes, yes, I'm aware of that. But the sedation should give us time to decide how to deal with him.'

'What do you mean?' Fyodor straightened. 'It's a simple decision. He needs a brain surgeon to remove the bullet, sooner rather than later.'

Pravda felt a lead weight crushing his left ankle. He checked his watch. 'I'll get back to you. Meanwhile I—'

'When?' Fyodor asked. 'I don't want to play Russian roulette with this man's life.'

'And neither do I.' The criticism was unnecessary. 'Neither do I.' He gestured for Fyodor to accompany him to the stairwell. 'Who's this nurse?' he whispered. 'Can she be trusted?'

'Svetlana? She understands the rules.'

'Yes, but does she respect them?'

'She's my niece.' Fyodor stared at Pravda. 'Satisfied?'

'Okay. Okay. No more recordings. Do you understand?'

'And what if I deem them to be a help in his diagnosis or prognosis?'

They stopped at the top of the stairs. 'It's a question of priorities.' Pravda put a hand on his friend's shoulder. 'Fyodor. The removal of the bullet is priority number one, not any suspected amnesia.'

Fyodor nodded.

'I'll arrange for the brain specialist team,' Pravda said. 'I have some people in mind. It shouldn't take long to get them here.'

'As fast as you can, please, Leon.'

Pravda put a foot on the first stair, stopped and turned to Fyodor. 'One further thing.'

'Yes?'

'No other doctors or nurses are to look after him. You must take it in shifts with Svetlana.'

'Leonid Igorovich,' Fyodor said, raising his voice. 'Other patients need our attention. We're short-staffed as it is. You're not being—'

'Please, Fyodor, no arguments.' He carried on walking. 'And I must be called again, immediately he wakes up. No matter where I am.' He checked his watch. It was 12.15pm. Under two hours to Bezrukhov's deadline. 'You know how to reach me, any time, day or night.'

Pravda stood on the hospital forecourt. An accidental jerk of Petrov's head was all that it would take – and his troubles would be over, no more worries for Lieutenant-General Leonid Igorovich Pravda.

He inhaled the freezing air.

Chapter 22

Day Six: 12 noon

It was a blessing that the traffic on Novy Arbat was crawling along at less than fifteen kilometers an hour, because Scott's mind was paying scant attention to the driving conditions. Ekaterina hadn't needed any convincing to return to the apartment, but Scott had another concern. He cleared his throat and glanced at her. 'Are you ready to talk about Frank Ferlito?'

'There's nothing to say. He knows Kostya.' Ekaterina eyes remained fixed on the enlarged version of the photo. 'That's all.'

'So he's done business with your husband?'

'I believe so,' she said.

Scott watched out of the corner of his eye as she rested the photo on her lap, laid her hands on top and turned to him. 'But it's got nothing to do with my father.'

They turned onto the Novoarbastkiy Bridge and the snow began to fall. If this was her idea of trusting him, he wasn't impressed. 'Ekaterina, Ferlito has done business with your husband and Ferlito wants to know about our interest in the apartment and Arzamas. Please, I'm trying to see if I can join the dots.'

She watched the traffic ahead. 'There are no dots to join.'

He made a last second swerve, to avoid killing an errant dog. 'I'm not asking you to disclose confidential information about your husband's business affairs. I just want—'

'I don't know anything about my husband's business affairs.' Her tone was abrupt.

The traffic thinned out once they'd crossed the bridge. They speeded up. Scott wasn't going to get anywhere at that moment. He'd try later. 'Okay. The client knows best.'

'Yes she does.'

'But you don't make my life easy, Ekaterina.'

'You're being paid well for the inconvenience.'

'I'll reserve judgment on that, as we lawyers say.' A client who wasn't completely open with her counsel could lead the pair of them into all sorts of trouble.

'Where are we going?' Ekaterina asked. 'We've passed the complex.'

Scott steered the Cherokee into another apartment complex, several hundred meters further along the road. 'We're returning to a recent murder scene. We've no idea what we're in for,' he said. 'I don't want witnesses taking the vehicle's registration number.' He drove towards a corner of the compound by the side of the last building, near the road. 'I'll park here, for a quick getaway.'

Ekaterina folded the photo, put it into her handbag and grabbed the door handle. 'It won't open. It's stuck.'

The central locking system was still engaged.

'I want to set the ground rules,' Scott said.

'Where have I heard that before?' Ekaterina turned to him. 'I'm not a child.' She turned back to the door handle. 'Come on, open it.'

'No, you're not a child, but you're damned head-strong.'

She glared at him and folded her arms. 'So what's happened to "the client knows best"?'

'I deliberately omitted the word "always".'

She sighed. 'Okay, get on with it.'

'Don't forget why we're here,' Scott said. 'To ask the neighbors if they know, knew, anything about the occupant, especially his name. We're not here to break into the apartment in the vain hope that the authorities may have left something there for us to find. Is that clear?'

'Abundantly.' She looked up at the headlining. 'Can we go?'

'And if I say leave, we leave. No arguments, no foot-dragging. Okay?' He didn't care that she was a native Russian and probably had a greater sense of danger in her little finger than he had in the whole of his body. She had shown herself not to respect the danger. He wasn't prepared to let either of them get arrested, or worse, because of her recklessness. 'Right, let's go.' He unlocked the doors.

She again outpaced him as they trudged through the week's snow fall back along Mosfilmovskaya to the complex on the other side of the road. She was steady on her feet in the biting wind, whereas Scott was gasping for breath when he caught up with her in the car parking area. He would speak to his personal trainer about a different regime. 'Wait,' he said 'Wait.' He tugged on her arm. 'Look, there's no need to rush, let's take it easy.'

She pulled her arm away and stepped back. 'After you.' She smiled at him for the first time that day. 'You're in charge.' She changed moods so quickly.

'I'm being serious,' Scott said.

She bowed her head and waved him on.

The front doors were open. The lobby was silent. Ekaterina marched over to the apartment.

'No,' Scott said. 'Come back.'

She remained at the door. 'The lock is new. There are two of them. And the buzzer has been replaced, without a name.'

Scott followed her. 'What have I just said?'

She shrugged.

He had an uneasy feeling. It was only three days since they found the body yet there was no "crime scene" tape across the door. In the movies the tape would stay there for at least a week, to give all the interested parties time to undertake their different investigations. Yet in this case Pravda, or Vassiliyev, had apparently finished their tasks in record time.

Ekaterina raised her arm, as if to knock on the door.

Scott pulled it down. 'No, that's not why we've come here. Let's see what the neighbors can tell us.'

A door opened and they both turned round. A man in his early twenties appeared in the doorway of the apartment opposite. 'Are you from the agents? Have you come to view the apartment?'

'Yes.' Ekaterina stepped forward. 'We might want to rent it.'

Scott was impressed, she didn't pause for breath.

'Wait here, please. I've something for you.' He disappeared back into his apartment.

The pair exchanged glances, saying nothing.

The neighbor reappeared with a bunch of keys in one hand and a crinkled brown envelope in the other, the flap was only partially sealed. 'Would you please give these to the agents, for the owner? He's moved on without leaving a forwarding address.'

Ekaterina took the keys and Scott took the envelope.

'Sure,' Scott said. 'Can you give me the owner's name, so I can write it on the envelope?'

'Sorry,' the lad said. 'I don't know it. I don't live here. It's my mother's apartment. She's been rushed to hospital. Both kidneys have failed. I've just got here from Kiev to be with her.' He pointed at the keys. 'The decorators gave them to my mother, to give to prospective tenants if the agents weren't available.'

'And what's this envelope?' Ekaterina asked.

'The old man who lived here left it with my mother years ago, in case of emergency I suppose.'

'Okay. And don't you worry,' Ekaterina said. 'We'll make sure the agents get these. And we hope your mother makes a full recovery.'

'Thank you,' the lad said, and returned to his apartment.

Despite his ground rules, Scott couldn't resist the temptation. He took the keys from Ekaterina and the pair returned to the other apartment. He hesitated at the door.

'What are we waiting for?' Ekaterina asked.

'Better safe than sorry,' Scott said. He pressed the buzzer. It sounded inside. He counted ten seconds. Nothing. He pressed it again. Another ten seconds. Nothing. He tried the keys until he unlocked the door. They stepped inside the hallway, Scott first. There was a strong smell of paint and the walls were pristine white. The hat-stand had gone and the single light bulb was shrouded by a Chinese, pagoda style lampshade.

Ekaterina tried to edge past Scott. 'Take it easy,' he said, and stepped in front of her.

They entered the study area. 'Well, well,' Scott said in English. The room was empty; every item of furniture had been removed, plus the books and papers. The broken floorboards had been replaced and the walls and woodwork given a coat of paint. 'Somebody was in a hell of a hurry to sanitize this place,' Scott said, in Russian. 'I mean, I know real estate agents like owners to smarten up the place before it goes on the market, but this is ridiculous. Two, three days? The poor guy's probably still warm in his grave, if he's not still in the morgue.'

Ekaterina strutted past him and headed into the corridor that led to the living room, bedroom, bathroom and kitchen. She wasn't happy. She hadn't said a word since they'd come in. He followed her as they inspected the other rooms, all similarly cleared of furniture and redecorated. They ended up in the kitchen, where the cupboards had been emptied.

'Nothing,' she said, shaking her head. 'There's nothing here.' She gazed out of the kitchen window. 'Nothing.'

Scott walked up behind her and let his hands hover over her shoulders. He wanted to try to comfort her. She turned round before he could touch her. He withdrew his hands. 'Not necessarily.' He waved the envelope at her. 'Let's see what we've got here.' He tore it open and pulled out a single sheet of paper. They stood side-by-side examining it.

It contained a list of Russian names, in Russian script, numbers and letters:

1. Alekseyev, Sergei Yurevich (5) 204800 N
2. Grushchenko, Mikhail Semeonovich (3) 112447 N
3. Kulachenko, Vladimir Grigoryevich (7) 144630 N
4. Karat, Fyodor Sergeyevich (10) 160400 N
5. Redchenko, Anatoli Igorovich (8) 155500 N
6. Petrov, Igor Alekseyevich (1) 165800 N
7. Lapin, Andrei Nikolayevich (9) 110432 N
8. Poltoranin, Gleb Mikhailovich (6) 204500 N
9. Danilov, Mikhail Konstantinovich (4) 163226 N
10. Sokolov, Yuri Vladimirovich (2) 141458 N

'Look at the final name,' Scott said. 'Number 10, at the bottom: Sokolov, Yuri Vladimirovich. That's the name mentioned by General Pravda. He could be the owner.'

'Or the dead body,' Ekaterina said.

'Or both.'

'Or neither.'

'I wonder what the numbers and letters stand for,' Scott said.

'Bank accounts,' Ekaterina replied.

She was a Russian economist married to an oligarch. How could they be anything else to her? 'Possibly,' he said. He ran his finger across the names and down the column of "Ns". 'The names are in Cyrillic, but the letter "N" at the end is English. You have no equivalent shaped letter in the Russian alphabet.'

'Offshore bank accounts,' Ekaterina said.

'Is that what they call lateral thinking?' He shook

his head as he studied the document. 'I've seen similar number and letter sequences before. But I can't remember in what circumstances.' And what do the single numbers in brackets mean?

'Hi folks!'

They both spun round.

Frank Ferlito stood in the open doorway to the kitchen.

'Do you make a habit of breaking into people's property?' Scott asked, stuffing the list of names into his inside jacket pocket and zipping it up.

'You left the door open.' Ferlito patted his chest. 'Cold?'

'What do you want Ferlito?' Ekaterina said.

'I thought we could share some information.'

'Such as?' Scott asked.

'This apartment.' He tilted his head. 'And maybe Arzamas.'

'We've nothing to say to you,' Ekaterina said.

'I'll find out, Mrs Gravchenko. One way or the other. You bet I will.'

'I am leaving.' Ekaterina pushed past Ferlito and headed for the door.

'We don't need you, Ferlito,' Scott added, and followed Ekaterina.

'You're way out of your depth you guys,' Ferlito said. 'Way out! You don't know what you're playing with!'

Scott dropped Ekaterina off at Tolik's apartment, to collect her daughter Tanya, at 3.30pm. He used Tolik's fax/copier to make two copies of the list of names; he would make more later. Ekaterina would put the original in her bank safe deposit.

It was on the drive back to his apartment that he had a hunch as to what the numbers, and letter "N", might represent. There was a large billboard at the intersection of Tverskaya Street and Tsvetnoy Boulevard. It bore a holograph of the world rotating on its axis, with lights flashing along horizontal and vertical lines circumnavigating the globe; red for horizontal, green for vertical and a legend which said "Globalization and the Death of the Nation State".

Check and double check: that was the philosophy employed by Woodward and Bernstein while they were investigating the Watergate affair: *check and double check*.

And he knew just the man to go to.

The Montecristo was one of Moscow's finest private cigar clubs; located behind Komsomolskaya Square where the famous "Three-Stations": the Leningradsky, Kazansky and Yaroslavsky termini, met. It came complete with a walk-in humidor, Kashmir carpets and a high efficiency ventilation system. It was a place only for the well-heeled. Scott waited in one of the high-winged chairs. He could have been in a gentlemen's club in St James's in London, such was the Montecristo's peaceful and luxurious ambience. His silver-haired guest arrived and sat in the equally sumptuous armchair opposite him.

'Thanks for seeing me at such short notice,' Scott said.

A waiter approached.

Scott ordered a large glass of red wine for his guest and a vodka and orange for himself.

'No, thank *you*, Scott. It's not that often I get to spend a depressing Moscow evening dining in the Montecristo with a superstar lawyer – at his expense.'

'For the first time in my life I don't know what to say,' Scott was joking, but he hadn't yet decided how much he was going to tell his friend.

'Lawyer lost for words. Some headline. That should get me the Nobel Prize for Journalism.' Tom was the Washington Post's chief of station in Moscow. He'd been in the capital for three years and, workloads permitting, Scott and Tom lunched or dined together every couple of months.

Scott fidgeted in his seat. He was having second thoughts. Ekaterina was adamant about not letting any information get to the authorities. He trusted Tom, but the more people who knew what Ekaterina's quest was, the more risk there was of a leak.

'You look troubled,' Tom said.

'This has to be off the record.'

'Unless you've got evidence of another 9/11 attack on the States, I can live with that. Go ahead.'

Scott stretched his arms along the wings of the chair, tapping his fingers on the edges. It wasn't too late. Tom was an experienced reporter. He would understand the last minute change of mind.

The waiter brought the drinks and placed them on the table separating the two chairs.

'Before you say anything,' Tom said. 'Take a drink.'

Scott clinked glasses with his friend and downed his drink, not Russian style – all in one go – but enough to cause him to choke. 'Excuse me.'

'Take your time.' Tom's tone was that of a carer trying to put his charge at ease.

'I'm breaching my client's confidence, but I think it's in the client's best interest to do so.'

'His or hers?'

'I'd rather not say. At the moment.'

'Understood.'

'Tom, you've traveled some in your fifty-three years,' Scott said.

Tom smiled. 'Well, since my late teens I've been to every continent except Antarctica.'

Scott nibbled at his bottom lip.

'This is off the record, Scott. Your secrets are safe with me.'

Scott had another drink. 'Yeh, okay.' He took the list of Russian names from his pocket and passed it over to Tom. 'What do you think the numbers followed by the letter "N" represent?' He also had a copy of the "A-16" photograph in his pocket, but he wasn't ready to discuss the metal object with anybody at the moment.

Tom studied the document for an undue length of time, or so it seemed to Scott. 'They look like latitudes,' Tom said finally.

'I agree,' Scott replied. He pictured the globalization billboard.

'I only said look like.' Tom raised his eyebrows. 'They could signify something else entirely.'

Tom was right. 'I appreciate that, but what?'

'I don't know.' Tom made a clicking sound with his tongue. 'A code, maybe. Bank account numbers. Something scientific. An arrangement of characters like this could mean anything.' He studied it again. 'Do you know who these people are?'

A sudden impulse made Scott lean forward and gently extract the list from Tom's clutches. He had a crazy, and baseless, notion that his investigative journalist buddy might have been trying to memorize the names.

Tom looked surprised at the action, but said nothing and released the list without objection.

'I understand what you're saying Tom, but these numbers are followed by the English letter "N". It's not a Cyrillic letter, which you would expect it to be if the numbers were indicative of some Russian code.'

'Indeed.'

'Are latitude designations in a standard international format...English?' Scott asked.

'Interesting question.' Tom pursed his lips. 'I've never given it any thought.'

'They just have to be latitudes,' Scott said.

'Why?'

Scott laughed. 'Because it would be easier for my client and me to trace their geographical locations, than it would be to trace the whereabouts of any secret bank accounts or to decipher them if they had some other obscure meaning à la Da Vinci Code.'

'And that's the hot-shot lawyerly reasoning you use to win your cases?' Tom asked.

'You better believe it.'

'Of course, if they are latitudes,' Tom said. 'They aren't much use to you without the corresponding longitudes.' He sipped some wine.

The waiter reappeared. 'Your table is ready, Mr Mitchell.'

'Ten minutes?' Scott needed their current privacy. The dining tables were too close together.

'No problem, Mr Mitchell.'

'Thanks.'

Scott lowered his voice. 'I can get an idea where the locations are if I plot a band around the world between the northern and southernmost latitudes.'

'If the equator's involved it could be a zone of 25,000 miles in length,' Tom said.

'It's a start.'

'So where are the longitudes?' Tom frowned. 'And why would they be in two separate lists?'

'My next hurdle.' And it was some hurdle. He hadn't a clue where to begin to look for the second list. 'And what if the longitude list has been lost or destroyed?'

'What indeed,' Tom said. He raised his eyebrows. 'If so, my friend, and this case is so important to you, you might as well give up, go home to the UK and spend the rest of your life advising on automobile crash compensation claims.'

'At least that would be more exciting than pensions and zoning law.'

'Excuse me?'

'Nothing. It was something another American philosopher said to me recently.'

'So,' Tom slapped both his knees. 'When do I get exclusivity on whatever it is you and your client are investigating?'

Scott polished off the vodka and stood up.

'I wish I knew, Tom. I wish I knew.'

Chapter 23

The main-frame server in Scott's office crashed, rendering the computer and internet systems out of action. He could access the internet from his cellphone, though net connectivity wasn't that great. Despite manufacturers' and service providers' efficiency boasts, cellphone internet access was still prone to failure, by crashing or buffering, when the user most needed it. He wondered why countries in the twenty-first century resorted to armed conflict to defeat each other, when all they had to do was to concentrate a cyber-attack on the opponent's servers. The IT technician couldn't make it to the office until late afternoon but Scott was eager for information. Rashid had borrowed the Cherokee, so Scott spent the morning crisscrossing the city using the metro, looking in bookshops for the solution to his problem. The exercise had its benefits; nothing compared to the limb-numbing cold air of a Moscow winter morning to clear his head, coupled with the sensual pleasure he received from the feel and smell of paper and ink.

Moscow boasted over 200 bookshops. By midday he felt as if he'd visited most of them: including the famously Soviet-built and disorganized *Dom Knigi*, The House of Books, on Novy Arbat Street; the American Book Store opposite the Italian Embassy and *Biblio-Globus* next to the Mayakovsky Museum across the Lubiyanka Square, where suspicious sales staff were known to mingle with the customers to check their purchase receipts.

But despite his trudging and trekking through the

day's first layer of snow, he failed to find what he was looking for – until he visited the *Russian State Library*, formerly the *Lenin Library*, on Vozdvizhenka Street; a stone's throw from the Kremlin grounds. A staff member made several trips to and from the elevators to deliver fifteen large books and maps to Scott while he waited patiently at the reading desk. He spent an hour plowing through the charts until he found a printed map of the world showing latitudes and longitudes. It was part of a donation to the library by a firm of cartographer-publishers in Hungary.

It had taken Scott some time during his teenage years to appreciate that although latitudes were marked on maps horizontally – east to west, their directional positioning was designated north or south with an "N" or "S" at the end of the series of numbers, to indicate whether it was north or south of the equator. Similarly, the longitudes were marked vertically – north to south, yet their directional positioning was designated east or west with an "E" or "W", to indicate whether they were east or west of London's Greenwich meridian. It seemed counterintuitive to his non-scientific mind.

He checked the northernmost and southernmost latitudes on the map against his list. The sequence of numbers on the list all ended with an "N". The northernmost and farthest from the equator was Alekseyev with 204800, i.e. 20 degrees 48.00 minutes. The nearest to the equator, but still north of it, was Lapin with 110432, i.e. 11 degrees 04.32 minutes. Beginning at the Arabian Gulf, Scott tracked the two latitudes around the world, going west. This took him on a journey through Ethiopia, Senegal, across the Atlantic to Central America, across the Pacific to Asia, Burma, India and back to the Arabian Gulf. He recalled Tom's words, "If the equator's involved it could be a zone of 25,000 miles in length." Being north of the equator, the distance was short of that figure, though not by any significant amount. Without knowing the longitudes, his task was going to be formidable, if not impossible.

But he had to begin somewhere.

The list. The owner of the apartment had left it with the neighbor for safe keeping. People anticipating the midnight knock on the door from the KGB would often leave their important or incriminating papers with their neighbors. Of course, Stalin's enforcers knew of the culture, but they rarely had the time or resources to turn every apartment in the neighborhood upside down. How important, or incriminating, was the list? He closed the book and headed for the elevator down to the first floor, without making a copy of the map. He'd committed the principal territories covered by the latitudes to memory; he didn't want to leave a paper trail of his investigations if he didn't have to.

Back on the street, he called Ekaterina. He wanted to meet her later that day and tell her that the numbers on the list could be latitudes. She didn't answer; he left a voicemail and opted to walk part of the way back to his office and take the metro when his legs gave out. He tracked north along Mokhovaya Street, with his mind firmly fixed on trying to solve the riddle of the latitude locations and the whereabouts of a list of corresponding longitudes.

Then again, they might not be latitudes.

Think positive.

'A few minutes of your time, please Mr Mitchell.' Pravda had stopped on Mokhovaya Street, where he'd been watching Mitchell after the lawyer had emerged from the Lenin Library. He was waiting for confirmation of when the brain specialists he'd selected would be available to treat Petrov, so he decided meanwhile to have another conversation with the English lawyer. Mitchell hadn't made any attempt to lower his profile on his return to the city and it wasn't difficult for Pravda's team to resume surveillance on him. Pravda wasn't annoyed at the man's refusal to leave the country. He'd changed his mind; it should be easier to crack Mitchell than Romanova; she was Russian, she wouldn't trust authority.

Mitchell peered into the vehicle.

Pravda opened the passenger door.

Mitchell wavered on the curbside, looking up and down the street.

'I'm alone,' Pravda said. 'The place is full of pedestrians. I'm not here to kidnap you.' He opened the door wider. 'Please.'

'Well, as you've said the magic word this time.' Mitchell got in the car.

Pravda drove around for ten minutes, looking for somewhere to park.

'I don't need a guided tour of the city,' Mitchell said. 'If we're going to the airport, I haven't got my passport with me.' He sounded edgy.

'It's a no-parking zone back there,' Pravda said.

'No special dispensation for a GRU Lieutenant-General?'

'Unfortunately not.' Pravda edged into a space opposite the Bolshoi Theatre on Teatralnaya Square and switched off the ignition. 'May I call you Scott?'

'Call me what you like. Get to the point.'

Pravda ignored Mitchell's brusqueness and adopted a soft tone. 'I really need to know what you and Ekaterina Romanova were doing at the apartment on Mosfilmovskaya.' He'd asked the question before, but perhaps he could wear Mitchell down.

'I admit that we were in the building,' Mitchell said in an off-hand manner. 'If you want to know why we were there, you'll have to ask my client.'

Mitchell and Romanova had disappeared from Moscow

a few days earlier. Pravda hoped that lawyer and client had spent some time during their absence reflecting on the seriousness of their position and considering his offer to help them. They must have realized that the GRU wouldn't be involved for no good reason. 'I'm trying to protect you and your client.' Pravda sighed, audibly. 'Can't you see that?'

Mitchell raised his eyebrows. 'Who is this man Sokolov?' Mitchell asked. 'Or should it be was? And what's the GRU's connection to the apartment. Who is it who wants to kill us? And why?'

Pravda waited a few seconds. 'Finished?'

'For the moment.'

'I'm sorry, I can't tell you. It's a matter of state security. But you mus—'

'And I can't tell you anything more, General Pravda.' Mitchell's face contorted with a supercilious smile. 'It's a matter of client confidentiality.'

Pravda had lost him, again. 'I'm asking you to please accept what I say at face value.'

'Hmm,' Mitchell said. 'That's your second "please", General.' He widened his eyes. 'A courteous GRU officer. That's a new one.'

Mitchell's flippancy didn't irritate Pravda. The threat of arrest wouldn't deter the lawyer. Arranging for the police to detain him for a few days, or weeks, on suspicion of murder, would make him more intransigent. The only way to get through would be to try to reason with him. 'Scott, you and your client could be unwittingly caught up in something far more life-threatening than your human rights activities. Believe me, you—'

Mitchell held up his hand. 'General, forgive me, but this is effectively a rehash of what you told me before, when you wanted to deport me. It's all generalization.' He turned away and looked out of the window. 'Unless you've got something specific to tell m—'

'It was Sokolov who was murdered,' Pravda said. He wasn't revealing much. A tenacious lawyer like Mitchell could find out by making enquiries of the neighbors.

Mitchell continued gazing out of the window. Was he hiding his reaction?

'Did you hear me, Scott?'

'Yes, General.' Mitchell turned to him. 'Who was Sokolov? Why was he killed?'

No, Mitchell. It's your turn to give me something. 'Perhaps if you were to tell me why you and your client were in the apartment, I might decide that the answers to your questions wouldn't be a breach of national security.' Pravda closed his mouth and grit his teeth. In his frustration, he'd spoken without thinking. He was insulting Mitchell's intelligence. The man wasn't going to be persuaded by such sophistry.

'Nice try, General. But I've admitted to being in the building, not the apartment.'

That was it. No more Mr Nice Guy. 'I'm not going to waste my time splitting hairs.' Pravda's tone harshened. 'Just give me a straight answer.'

'No, I'm sorry, I can't.' Mitchell left his mouth open, as if he was going to add something.

'Yes?' Pravda said.

'Nothing.'

'Goodbye, Mr Mitchell.' Pravda leant across the lawyer's lap and opened the passenger door. 'We have different destinations.'

Scott headed back to his office on foot, picturing the map in his mind and mulling over Pravda's sudden appearance. He was going to tell Pravda that he might ask Ekaterina for permission to reveal why they'd been at the apartment, in the hope that he could get more information from the man about what the GRU's interest in the apartment was. But his instinct told him to hold back for the time being.

He was trying Ekaterina on his cellphone again – he could now add Pravda's comments about Sokolov to his news update for her – when Rashid called.

'Rashid?'

'Chief, we need a meet, urgent.'

'I'm on Kamergeskiy,' Scott said. If Rashid said something was urgent, it was urgent. 'I'll be back in the office in twenty minutes.'

'No, chief. Not the office. I'm in the National,' Rashid said. 'Alexandrovsky Bar.'

'Okay, ten minutes.' Scott ended the call.

When he arrived in the winter garden surroundings of the Alexandrovsky Bar, his gofer was scoffing a plateful of eggs, beans, sausages and too many rashers of processed bacon. Scott sat down and ordered a coffee. 'Okay, so what's the drama?'

'The gunfight on the Outer Ring.'

'What about it?'

'It was a hit. A failed one.'

'The mafia?' Scott's mind began to stray in Gravchenko's direction. Not all oligarchs were Mafiosi, but they were often accused of being so.

'Not this time chief. The government.' He puffed out his cheeks. 'The army, or some such.'

'Rashid,' Scott said. 'I'm prepared to accept most things you say, as outrageous as they sometimes first appear to be, because more often than not they turn out to be true. But the army? Come off it. Why on earth would the Russian army stage an attack like that?' He paused. 'Who are they going to blame it on? Your people?' Rashid had to be mistaken.

'And that's not all.' Rashid continued eating, and appeared not to take offense at Scott's doubts. 'The target was a special patient being taken to a secret hospital in the city.'

'Where's this fairy tale leading to? What's the moral?'

'And this special patient was in a coma, but he's come out of it.'

'I'm happy for him, and his family, but would you please get to the point?'

'And chief, guess what?'

'Please, Rashid.' He'd never lost his patience with his gofer before, but everything had its limits. 'I've got things to do.' Contact Ekaterina.

'The guy in charge of him is your kidnapper, Lieutenant-General Pravda of the Spetsnaz.'

Scott's choked on his coffee. 'Say that again.'

'Your friend, General Pravda, has a patient stashed away in a secret hospital somewhere in this city.'

'What's the patient's name?'

'Petrov.'

'Petrov?' It sounded familiar. Scott took the list from his pocket. His eyes sped down the names. Number 6 – Petrov, Igor Alekseyevich.

'How common is the name Petrov in Russia?'

Rashid smirked. 'Do I look like I give a fuck?' He pushed a fork full of sausage into his mouth.

The last thing his Chechen gofer would be interested in was a demographic survey of the Russian nation. Still, Scott wanted an answer. 'Humor me. You know this country much better than I do.'

'Not uncommon.' Half-masticated sausage skin followed Rashid's words out of his mouth.

A possible connection: Pravda to the list, via Sokolov and Petrov. But, would this lead to Ekaterina's allegedly imprisoned father? 'Rashid.' Scott stood up. 'Where is this secret hospital?'

'I don't know.'

'Okay my friend,' Scott said. 'Time for action.' Sokolov was dead, but Petrov was alive. 'I want you to find the hospital. I don't care how you do it or what it costs.' Ekaterina could afford it. 'But find it.'

'What, now?' Rashid pointed at his unfinished meal. 'Chief?'

'Now, please, Rashid. If you find Petrov, I'll buy you ten meals. Come on, you can keep the Cherokee, but get moving. The quicker we find the hospital, the quicker I can plan the next step.'

Rashid's face dropped. He pushed the half empty platter aside and stood up.

Scott called Ekaterina's cellphone again. A third piece of news: Petrov. Still no response. He called her land line. No response. He left the same message on both phones. 'Ekaterina. When you get this message, please, please, call me, immediately.' He disconnected and his phone rang.

Rashid picked up his fork and began scooping up the remaining eggs.

The screen flashed up. "Inessa".

'Hi Inessa what's up?'

'Scott, you must come to the office.' Her voice was a whisper. 'I can't stop them.' She sounded distressed.

'Stop them? Stop who? Stop what? What's going on?'

'They're going through your files. I can't stop them, Scott. You must come. It's that—'

'Okay, okay. I'm on my way – fifteen minutes max.' He finished the call. Going through his files?

'What's up, chief?' A sliver of egg white fell from Rashid's mouth and landed on his shirt.

'It's got to be that idiot Chichikov,' Scott said. 'He threatened to call in the tax police. Now they're raiding the office.'

'Let's go.' The gofer made stabbing actions with his fork.

'No, Rashid. I'll deal with Inspector Chichikov and his band of forty thieves. You find that hospital.' Scott handed him the list of latitudes. 'And guard this with your life. I might be searched.'

Inessa was standing in reception, in tears, when Scott walked in. 'Scott, I'm sorry. I couldn't do anything.

Nothing. They won't let anybody into your room. They're turning the place upside down. They're pigs. Absolute pigs. You know, that man—'

'It's not your fault,' Scott said. 'Don't worry. I'll deal with them.' He marched through the general office area. His three associate attorneys were at their desks, speaking in hushed tones, with fitful glances at Scott's office and head-shaking. Scott nodded and smiled to reassure them, and pressed on towards his office. He could see a hazy figure through the frosted glass partition; it was standing at a filing cabinet, emptying the drawers, throwing the files onto the floor, one by one. Scott flung the door open.

'What the hell do you people think you're doing? Where's your warrant!'

The figure at the cabinet, a giant of a man, ignored him and carried on scattering the files around the room. Scott's high-backed chair was facing the window. He could see the back of somebody's head; it was mostly bald. A deep, authoritative voice said calmly, 'I don't answer questions, Mr Mitchell.'

The chair spun round.

'I ask them.'

Scott stood still. It wasn't Chichikov, whom he'd met once before. The occupant's smile was ice cold.

'My name is Konstantin Gravchenko.'

Scott had seen the man on the television news and pictures in the press. In the flesh Gravchenko was every inch the stereotype Russian *biznizman*: bald, bull-neck, thick set, probably no taller than 1.77-78 meters. Scott couldn't see if he had any tattoos, the mark of criminality in certain Russian circles.

Gravchenko threw a cream business card across the desk.

Scott picked it up. His name was on one side and a cellphone number on the other. Otherwise, the card was bare, similar to Ekaterina's.

'My daughter Tanya and that lunatic mother of hers are missing, Mr Mitchell. I want your file on the mother.'

What did he say? Missing? 'Ekaterina, missing? She can't be. I only saw her yesterday afternoon. She wasn't missing then.' He shook his head. 'No, Mr Gravchenko. Surely you must be mistaken. Have you—'

'Mitchell, don't try my patience,' Gravchenko replied, his voice hardening. 'If I say they're missing, they're missing.'

'What about Tolik? Have you spoken to him? Perh—'

'It was Tolik who told me they were missing!' Gravchenko banged the desk with a clenched fist. 'I won't ask you again. Give me the file.'

'Yes, but how does he know they're missing?' Scott refused to believe it. 'They might have gone away for a short break.' He began punching in her number on his cellphone. Maybe she would answer now. 'Anyway, I can't let you have the file. Client confidentiality.'

'Gleb,' Gravchenko said in a whisper.

Before Scott could utter another syllable, Gravchenko spun round in the chair to face the window again while Gleb interrupted his filing duties and grabbed Scott's right wrist. There was a burning sensation and it felt as if a vice was crushing bones. He dropped the cellphone to the floor.

'Hey, let go, what do you think you're doing?'

Gleb forced Scott's hand onto the desk, palm down, fingers splayed. Scott tried to pull away, but he was no match for the man who produced a retractable knife and eased the cold steel blade onto the base of Scott's right thumb. Scott was physically restrained and mentally frozen. Gravchenko remained facing the window, ensconced in the "deniable scenario" position. He could genuinely testify that he didn't see what Gleb was doing to the lawyer. 'Okay! Okay! I'll give you the file.' Fear of imminent physical mutilation was an understandable and forgivable reason to breach a client's confidence. 'But it's not here.' Gravchenko said nothing. Gleb extended the caress of the knife to cover all Scott's fingers.

'I'm telling you the truth, Mr Gravchenko. It's not in my office. Well, not at the moment. It's on my computer but our server crashed this morning and the whole system's down. We're waiting for the engineer.'

Gleb squeezed Scott's wrist and he cried out in agony.

'I've got a backup. I can make a phone call.'

Gravchenko turned back in the chair to face Scott while Gleb released his grip on the hand and put the knife away.

'That wasn't necessary.' Scott rubbed his wrist and flexed his fingers and thumb, making sure that they were all in one piece and functioning as nature intended.

'Make the call,' Gravchenko said. 'And make it in Russian.'

Scott keyed in the numbers.

'Sophie. It's Scott.'

'Yo, counselor. Am I billing you or are you billing me for this call?'

'Sophie, listen to me. It's serious. I need the package, immediately, on disk. I want to meet you at your apartment block, in the front lobby, and collect it. Traffic permitting, say, forty, fifty, minutes?'

'Why are you speaking with me in Russian?' Sophie said in English. 'Are you alright Scott? Where are you?'

Scott continued in Russian. 'I'm in my office. Everything's fine. My client needs the package, urgently Sophie.'

Silence.

'Sophie?'

'Yeh. Okay, fifty minutes. That's fine.'

Scott finished the call and turned to Gravchenko. 'Satisfied?'

Gravchenko got up, put his hefty arm around Scott's shoulder and squeezed hard. Despite the difference in height, the smaller oligarch inflicted excruciating neck pain on his wife's lawyer. He whispered in Scott's ear, 'Let us both hope, Mr Mitchell, that your confidential file leads to the safe return of my daughter.'

Scott sat next to Gravchenko in the back of the oligarch's limousine as Gleb drove them to Sophie's apartment in Krylatskoye District, west of the city center. Gravchenko studied a document, while making and taking phone calls. They sounded like business conversations. Scott couldn't detect anything to show that Gravchenko was looking for Ekaterina and Tanya. 'Why won't you help Ekaterina search for Tanya's grandfather?' Scott asked during a break in the calls.

'My daughter's got *me*,' Gravchenko said, without looking up from the document. 'She doesn't need anyone else.'

'And Ekaterina? Doesn't she need to know what happened to her father?'

Gravchenko turned to Scott. 'Mitchell. Don't let your Strasburg victory go to your head. In Russia we do things our way.'

'I understand that, but—'

'Our politics and your rules of law don't mix,' the oligarch said. 'You understand that, and you might just survive here.' He dropped the document onto his lap and punched a number into his phone. 'Then again, you might not.'

Scott gazed out of his window for the rest of the journey. Gravchenko was a cold man. It seemed that business matters were more important to him than the well-being of his loved ones.

They pulled into Sophie's residential complex and parked in front of the main doors to her block. Scott jumped out and Gravchenko followed him, but stopped at the hood, where he lit a cigarette.

'Be quick,' Gravchenko said.

Scott hurried into the building. Sophie approached him from the elevator. She had an envelope in her hand. 'What's going on, Scott?' She looked over his shoulder. 'Jesus! That looks like Gravchenko.'

'The man himself,' Scott said.

'Has that Romanova woman got back with him?'

'No, Ekaterina hasn't got back with him. The opposite in fact. She's missing.' He stepped back and shrugged. 'Well, so Gravchenko says.'

Sophie's shoulders slumped. 'Oh fuck.'

'What?' Scot said. 'What is it?'

'Gravchenko's no fool and he doesn't jump to conclusions. If he says she's missing, you better take that as gospel.' She handed him the envelope. 'And baby Tanya? Where's she?'

Scott opened the envelope and pulled out a CD. 'She's missing too.'

'Double fuck.'

'Is this everything?' Scott asked.

'Sure, I think so.'

'Including the list?'

'What list?'

'A list of ten Russian names and latitudes. I e-mailed it to you last night.'

She shook her head. 'I haven't received it.'

Shit. Where was it? Had he sent it to the wrong address? 'When did you last check your Inbox?'

'Last night, about eight.'

'There's your answer.' Scott sighed with relief. 'I sent it at midnight.' On second thoughts, maybe it wasn't so bad that Sophie hadn't been able to transfer it to the disk for Gravchenko. Scott didn't relish the idea of the oligarch trying to find out who the names were, yet. They could be an embarrassment to Putin for some reason and Gravchenko might use the list to curry favor with the

President. And that in turn might frustrate Ekaterina's ability to find her father. All supposition.

'What's the password?' Scott asked.

'Sugarpussy69.' Sophie said with a straight face.

Typical Sophie. 'That'll give hackers something to smile about,' Scott said.

'Ah,' she said. 'But the first and third "S" are "$" signs.'

'Here, take it back a minute.' He handed the disk to Sophie and took out a pen.

'Why, what are you doing?'

'I'm writing the password on the envelope. I'm not going to spell it out and try to explain its meaning to Gravchenko.'

Sophie laughed, gave the disk back and hugged him tightly. 'Watch yourself, Scott. It's getting hot in the kitchen.'

He put the disk in the envelope and kissed Sophie on the forehead. 'I'll be fine.'

Scott emerged from the building. Gravchenko had disappeared. The limousine's black-tinted rear window slid down. 'Here you are, Mr Gravchenko.' Scott handed the envelope to him. 'The password is written on the envelope.' Scott began to walk round to the other passenger door.

'Wait there,' Gravchenko said.

Scott hovered on the curbside, with a feeling of pubescent anticipation, while Gravchenko read the password. The man remained expressionless. 'If there's anything on the disk you need explaining, Mr Gravchenko, don't hesitate to ask.' Except the meaning of the password of course. 'And if you want me to help you find Ekaterina and Tanya, please—'

'You've done enough damage,' Gravchenko said. 'Stay away from my family.' The window closed and before Scott could move or say anything more, the Lincoln sped away.

'Well thank you, Mr Gravchenko. Thank you very

much.' Scott watched the vehicle disappear at the inter-section as he walked back to the apartment building to get the concierge to call a local cab service. His phone rang. He didn't recognize the number. But it could be Ekaterina. 'Yes?'

'Scott? Scott Mitchell?' It was a Russian man. The voice sounded familiar.

'Who's asking?'

'Tolik. Ekaterina's cousin. She gave me your number.'

Jesus, that was close. Scott watched Gravchenko's car merge with the traffic. 'Do you know where Ekaterina and Tanya are?' Scott asked. 'Mr Gravchenko says they're missing.' Screw the oligarch's warning; he wanted to know where his client and her child were.

'They are. We need to talk. Not on the phone. You know the *Lenin's Tomb* bar?'

'I've heard of it, but I've never been there.'

'It's off Delegatskaya, behind the Museum of Decorative and Folk Art. Where are you?'

'Krylatskoye,' Scott said.

'I'll be at the bar in thirty minutes,' Tolik said. 'I'll wait for you.'

'Okay.' Gravchenko could go to hell.

Scott spotted Tolik sitting in a wood-paneled booth, enclosed on three sides. He was nursing two opened bottles of German lager. True to its name, the bar was underground, dark and decorated with photographs of Lenin and the storming of the Winter Palace. Eisenstein's film, The Battleship Potemkin, was playing on the largest wall monitor Scott had ever seen. They shook hands and Scott sat down.

'This okay?' Tolik pushed a bottle towards Scott.

'Fine.'

Ekaterina's cousin was smoking French cigarettes; a packet of Gauloise lay on the table between them. He had a full head of wavy hair, dark brown, and a small crooked, or maybe broken, nose, that Scott hadn't noticed when Tolik was driving them to the apartment.

Tolik nodded at the packet of cigarettes.

'No thanks,' Scott said. 'Gave it up after I took my first drag when I was seven.'

Tolik's face hardened. He tapped the ridge of a glass ashtray with his cigarette and watched the ash fall off. 'Last night,' he said. 'Just after 9, Katya called me. There was a gas leak in her apartment block. They were evacuated. She didn't know how long they would have to stay out, so we arranged for her and Tanya to spend the night with us.' He looked at Scott. 'That's me, my wife and daughter, Kristiana.' He took a swig of beer and swished it around his mouth.

'Go on,' Scott said. He too took a swig.

'They never turned up. I called and called her cellphone.' He shrugged. 'It kept defaulting to voicemail. I rang the concierge at her apartment block. It was a false alarm; kids or somebody playing with gas canisters. Anyway, they were all back in the building within an hour. The concierge remembered talking to her in the lobby. He told her to go to the assembly point at the opening to the underground car park. He never saw them again.'

'He could have missed them as they all went back in,' Scott said.

Tolik stubbed out the cigarette and the man's hand quivered as he immediately lit another. He wasn't acting. It was genuine fear. 'No, I told the concierge she would have called me to say she wasn't coming if she'd changed her mind.' He took a deep drag. 'The guy called her land line, knocked on her door and used the master key to go inside. There was no sign of them. Last night or today.'

'So you told Mr Gravchenko.'

'Of course, last night, after the concierge had done his bit, and again this morning.'

'What do you think has happened to them?' It was Scott's turn to be concerned. Could her fear of the authorities be justified? 'Tolik, would she go off with Tanya without telling anyone?'

'No way.' Tolik shook his head vigorously. 'No way. We talk every night. Apart from our two children we have no other blood relatives.'

'Ekaterina seems paranoid with her mistrust of the authorities.'

'Show me a Russian who *does* trust them.' Tolik blew a raspberry. 'The corrupt bastards don't even trust each other.' He pulled some folded sheets of paper from his pocket and passed them to Scott. 'She asked me to give you this letter.'

It comprised three sheets and was handwritten. Scott looked for the final signature. It was the full text of her mother's deathbed letter:

My dearest darling Katyushka
If you are reading this, the cancer has won the war.

You must understand how difficult this is for me.

I have lived through difficult times. To survive in the Soviet Union everybody had to lie. People who had the courage to speak out and tell the truth were put into psychiatric hospitals, or worse! And their children were split up and put in orphanages; they were branded "children of enemies of the people" and denied all rights to join the Pioneers, the Komsomol and study at the best institutes. They were damned for life.

In private, it was different. We couldn't keep our true feelings pent up inside of us for generation after generation. Everybody needs somebody they can trust and before I had you I promised myself I would never lie to a child of mine. That's why

I brought you up not to lie to people you trust.

And now I'm asking you to forgive me for having lied to you for over thirty years about your father. Please try to understand, Katyushka darling. This is very, very difficult for me.

Your papa burst into my life when I was twenty-six. He was tall, dark and handsome (yes really!) and it was love at first sight. He spoke little of himself despite my questions. He said he was a teacher of mathematics in a junior school in Alma Ata where I was at university, but he always managed to turn the conversation around to me. That was why I loved him so much; he was so attentive and unselfish.

We talked of getting married. Then one day, when he had come secretly to my dormitory, four men arrived in the middle of the night and took him away. I followed them into the street, crying and screaming. I woke the whole university, but nobody helped me as the men took your papa away in their cars. When I went to the junior school where he worked (it was the first time I had been there) the principal said she'd never heard of him. It wasn't true. I'm sure they were told to erase him from their records for some reason. Yes, it happened even in those days, in the 1970s. It wasn't only Stalin who made people disappear.

I never found out anything more: who he was, why they had taken him, what he was supposed to have done, where they had taken him, nothing. I never saw or heard from him again. It was like he'd never existed. The KGB – I don't know who else it could have been – even refused to admit that anybody had come to my dormitory that night and taken him! The university authorities and the police said they knew nothing about it, *even though I screamed and shouted so much that it must have been reported to them. I thought I was going mad. Maybe they were right, maybe he was a figment of my imagination – until you came along, then I knew he existed.*

When you were thirteen, I had a visit from one of the men who had taken your papa. He said he didn't like what the KGB had done. Gorbachev had come to power. People felt freer to speak their mind. Though he couldn't or wouldn't tell me where your papa was he promised to get a photo of you to him. I gave him one of your school photos. I had several developed of the one taken when you were eleven. I never heard anything more from the KGB man and I have no idea whether your papa ever received the photo.

Last week somebody slipped a note under the apartment door telling me that your papa is still alive and living somewhere in Russia, as a prisoner without trial...Katyushka my darling, I've hidden the note in the usual place, with a copy of the photo I gave to the KGB.

Please forgive me for keeping this secret from you all these years. But I only did what I thought was best for you. Not knowing if he was alive or dead while you were growing up was torment for me, but I didn't dare raise your hopes. And I couldn't guarantee we would find out where he was or get any information to him.

If you go in search of your papa you should know some personal things. He said his name was Misha, Mikhail Alexandrov. I don't know. I never saw his papers. He had a seven-centimeter scar on his lower right arm. He said it was from a motor bike accident. He spoke Russian fluently but he had a slight accent. I've have no idea where it came from, maybe beyond the Urals, but he didn't look Asian. Possibly pre-Baltica, I don't know. As I said, he rarely spoke of himself. When the KGB men were putting him in the car one of them said they were taking him back to Sarov that night.

I am so sorry for hiding this from you. Please forgive me my darling. I only did what I thought was best for you.

Goodbye my dear, dear sweet Katyushka. I am so proud of you. Give Tanyushka a million hugs and kisses from me. Don't let her grow up too quickly.

Your ever-loving Mama xxxxx

'I don't understand Tolik. When did she ask you?'

'It was her idea. If she fails to call me by midnight on any day, or get a message to me that she's okay, I'm to give this letter to you.'

'To me. Not to Mr Gravchenko?'

'To you.'

Scott collapsed back against the wooden panel and sighed. Would she ever forgive him for his remark about "justified paranoia"? He waved the letter at Tolik. 'Won't you be in trouble with Mr Gravchenko, if he finds out you've given me this? He's warned me off.'

'Kostya knows me inside out, and he knows I love Katya like a sister and Tanya like my own.' He took another swig of beer and wiped his mouth with the back of his hand. 'No, he'll be a bit rattled, but in the end he'll understand the way I feel...but I'm not so sure about you.'

Chapter 24

Day Seven: 5.45pm

Rashid popped his head around Scott's office door.

'Irkutsk, chief.'

Scott wasn't listening. He was making notes about the day's events, with Ekaterina's disappearing act prominent in his mind.

'Chief?'

'What?'

'Irkutsk.'

'What about it?'

'They've postponed tomorrow's conference call.'

'Did they say why?' Scott wasn't disappointed. So much had happened during the day that he hadn't had time to prepare his brief for the call.

'They couldn't get hold of somebody they wanted you to talk to. They'll reschedule.'

'Okay. You may as well go home. You can—'

'No can do chief.' Rashid beamed. 'I've got a lead on Petrov's hospital.'

'What?'

'I think I know where Petrov's hospital is.'

Scott perked up. 'Good man.' He rubbed his hands together. 'Call me as soon as you have confirmation. Any time.'

'Will do.' Rashid hurried from the office.

Scott was finishing the notes when his eyes caught a small headline on the front page of the English language newspaper, *Moscow Times*, which was lying on his desk. It said: *Murder on Mosfilmovskaya – P7*. His stomach turned. The apartment had been sanitized; the media couldn't have known about Sokolov. He turned to page seven:

Police yesterday discovered the battered corpse of a young man in a garbage bin at the rear of the old military apartments on Mosfilmovskaya Street. According to identity papers found on the dead man he was twenty-two-year-old Dmitry Yatsenko, a resident of Kiev. Police enquiries reveal that he came to Moscow to visit his mother who is in hospital for a kidney operation. The cause of death has not yet been determined...

Scott massaged his temples. Not Sokolov, but the lad from Kiev who'd given them the list. His cellphone rang. 'Yeh?'

'Scott, hi, this is Frank Ferlito. How—'

'Ferlito?' Not again. What was it with this man? 'I thought I told you—'

'Hear me out, counselor.'

Scott raised his voice. 'Ferlito, I said—'

Silence.

'Ferlito?'

'Scott, don't worry, we're safe. Listen to Ferlito's story. And check it out for me.'

'Ekaterina? Is that you?'

Silence again.

'Ekaterina!'

'Easy boy,' Ferlito said. 'I'm taking good care of them. Besides, she wants to lie low for a couple of days.'

'What do you mean? What's going on?'

'*You* can't look after them,' Ferlito said. 'So *I* have to.'

Scott held his cellphone in front of him and stared at it. Lie low? Look after them?

'I've been trying to warn you, Scott. You two are in deep shit. They're not gonna stop until they get the list.'

'List? What list?' Scott recalled the moment when he and Ekaterina were studying the list in the kitchen at Mosfilmovskaya. Ferlito appeared in the doorway. How long had he been standing there? Scott stuffed the list into his inside pocket and zipped up his jacket. He could see Ferlito looking at him, patting his own chest and saying, "Cold?". 'Who's not going to stop? Who are you talking about?'

'Meet me in the *House of Mirrors* in an hour and I'll explain,' Ferlito said. 'And don't worry. As long as she's with me, your client, and the kid, are safe. They won't come to any harm.'

The conversation was bordering on the bizarre. 'I want to speak to Ekaterina. Put her—'

'But don't tell Gravchenko,' Ferlito said. 'He'll have a different sense of priorities.'

'Stop talking in riddles. Let me talk to Ekaterina.'

'The *House of Mirrors*. One hour.'

'I said—'

The line went dead. Scott tried last number redial. The phone kept ringing.

He got up and paced around the room. Ekaterina's voice had been calm; there was no hint of anxiety. Ferlito could have drugged her. But his choice of venue, though unusual, was a public place. There was no point in telling Gravchenko about the call until Scott had found out what the diplomat was playing at.

The *House of Mirrors* was situated south-east of the Kremlin off the Garden Ring, in a recently constructed amusement park behind a late night shopping center. Scott made his way through hordes of excited kids enjoying themselves on the attractions, under the watchful eyes of their *babushkas*, while their parents trawled the shopping mall. The next day was a school holiday and the winter cold was no bar to the park's extended opening hours.

The sign on the door of the *House of Mirrors* read: "Closed for Repairs". What was Ferlito playing at? 'Shit!' He kicked at the door. It opened.

He hesitated before stepping inside.

An array of multi-colored lamps hung from the ceiling, strategically placed so that each picked out the contorted face or figure of one of the clowns and harlequins whose pictures covered the four high walls. He didn't see any evidence of the place undergoing repairs.

A young receptionist sat at the pay-desk, watching a Spanish soap on the wall-mounted TV screen. She was dressed in the style of a Persian Blue cat with a bowtie, and smoking a cigarette. 'He's waiting for you,' she said, without taking her eyes from the screen. 'In there.' She raised her arm in the direction of the opposite wall, where Scott could see the outline of a door secreted between the lower torsos of two giant psychedelic clowns painted on the wall.

'What about the repairs?' Scott asked.

The Persian Blue shook her head, still staring at the screen.

Scott approached the door. He pushed a small button, the door opened and he stepped across the threshold into the pitch black of another world. The door slammed shut behind him. 'Ferlito?'

Scott's eyes adjusted to the darkness. He was in a corridor. A blinding light shone ahead of him. The walls were no more than two body widths apart. He used them for support as he groped his way towards the light.

'Ferlito? Where are you?'

Strange gloomy shapes and images appeared and disappeared on either side.

'Frank Ferlito! Answer me!'

Periodic blasts of cold air from behind prompted him along the corridor until he reached a brightly lit room at the end. There was no door. He looked back. The walls were made of mirrors. The strange shapes had been his amorphous body.

He stepped into the room, no more than five meters by four, he guessed. All four walls, together with the ceiling and the floor, were covered with mirrors. They were different shapes and sizes: flat, convex, concave – or so it seemed. His own image appeared in some of the mirrors, but not others. He was fat, thin, tall, small, all head, all legs; those shapes he could understand – but the nothingness, the absence of a reflection of any part of his body, no matter that he stood in front of the mirror and pressed his face against it. How could it be?

'Scott, hi. Good of you to come.'

Scott spun round and scanned the room.

'Ferlito?' All he could see were the grotesque distortions of his own body. 'Ferlito. Show yourself. Stop fucking around.'

'Now you see me, now you don't.' The attaché's image came and went as he stepped from one mirror to another along the length of the wall opposite and vanished into the corner, like Hitchcock's cameo roles in his own films. Scott turned round to see if the man was behind him; he wasn't.

'Ferlito!'

'Up here, Scott.'

Scott looked up at the ceiling. Ferlito's reflection was in the largest mirror in the room, which occupied over half the ceiling. Scott looked down at the floor, to see where Ferlito should have been lying to enable his image to be reflected onto the ceiling – nothing. 'What are you doing with Ekaterina and Tanya? You must be out of your tiny mind.' Scott felt like a caged animal. He roamed around the room, from end to end, corner to corner, running his hands along the mirrors in search of a way through, banging on the glass. 'Come on Ferlito. Show yourself.'

'Behind you.'

'What?'

'Look behind you.'

Scott spun round and stared at the mirror at the far end of the room. Ferlito, or his image, was sitting in an armchair. Scott ran to it and banged on the glass. Ferlito smiled. Scott ran his hands around the edge of the mirror, looking for an opening mechanism. He looked back towards the other end of the room where the "real" Ferlito should be sitting – again, nothing.

'Mirrors without smoke.' Ferlito beamed.

'Yeh, sure,' Scott said. 'You've got a hidden camera somewhere in this place, and you're behind the walls, projecting yourself onto a computer screen.'

'What did Churchill say?' Ferlito asked. 'The Soviet Empire is "an enigma in a puzzle wrapped in a riddle." Well, amigo, *plus ça change* in the new Russia.'

'Stop playing these stupid games,' Scott said. 'Where's Ekaterina? I want to talk to her.' He stood erect in front of Ferlito, with clenched fists at his side and his feet apart.

'Calm down.' Ferlito raised his hands, with the palms facing Scott and motioned as if to push him away. 'Calm down.' Ferlito smiled plaintively. 'We're on the same side.'

Scott dropped his shoulders and relaxed the tension in his body. The man's eyes were open wide, he bore a half-smile; he looked sincere. No harm would be done by letting him continue. Besides, there was nothing else Scott could do. He couldn't physically assault an image.

'You and your client have no idea what you've gotten yourselves into with that list of names. You're holding an unexploded bomb, counselor. And the bad guys don't care if it blows up in your faces. Which it will do, if you don't hand it over to the good guys.'

A picture of Ekaterina's burnt out BMW flashed through Scott's mind at the mention of the word "bomb." 'What bad guys?'

'People who'll stop at nothing to get the list.'

Scott thought of the *Moscow Times'* article about

the murder of Dmitry Yatsenko. He swallowed hard. 'You know about the list from the neighbor's son at Mosfilmovskaya, don't you?' Ekaterina could also have told him. But if she had, and Ferlito was one of the good guys, she would have given him a copy of the list. That was why she had asked Scott to check the man's story; she wanted to be sure.

Ferlito nodded, then shook his head. 'Yeh, but I didn't kill him, if that's what you're getting at.'

'Why did he tell you about the list?'

Ferlito smiled. 'He was coming out his apartment when I got there. He told me you were next door, prospective tenants or whatever. He thought I'd also come to view the place. I didn't have to say anything. He was one of those guys who'd tell you his life story without prompting.'

That was true. The lad had been as forthcoming when he and Ekaterina had turned up. 'Why were you following us?'

'Someone's gotta watch your backs.'

It was a smug response, and told Scott nothing. 'Fer...' No, let the man finish.

'Anyway, he came out with a sob story about his mother's illness,' Ferlito continued. 'I gave him $1,000 for her medical fees. You know this country's health system. If you don't have the cash, you get to see a witch doctor. I pumped him about you guys. He told me about the envelope. He said he only glanced inside and thought it contained a list of names. He didn't know anything else.'

'And you believed him?'

'Sure. I can tell when somebody's telling the truth. Scott, my friend, you mustn't go through life mistrusting everybody.' Ferlito's eyes narrowed. 'That's how paranoia sets in. Some of us tell the truth...I never laid a finger on the kid.'

Scott had interviewed hundreds of clients and witnesses. He reckoned, like Ferlito, he could more often than not tell when somebody was telling the truth. More important, Scott didn't have a shred of evidence to implicate Ferlito in a murder. 'So your bad guys killed him for the list?'

'You got it,' Ferlito said.

'And you think those same bad guys are going to kill Ekaterina and me?'

'You better believe it. They'd kill their own mothers to get the list.'

Ten Russian names are promoting a murder spree. 'Why is this list so important to everybody…and you in particular?'

'Not to me personally, but my employer, the United States government,' Ferlito said.

The plot was thickening. 'Why does the US government want this document?'

Ferlito shuffled in his chair, as if to get more comfortable. His tone softened. 'Scott, what's your knowledge of the Vietnam War?'

'Why? What's the Vietnam War got to do with anything?' Was this another one of Ferlito's damn riddles? 'Get to the point.'

'Humor me.' He nodded and smiled.

'Okay.' It had better be good. 'Only what little I've read. It was before my time.'

'There are over 2,000 American GIs unaccounted for. They're designated MIAs,' Ferlito continued.

'MIAs?' Scott had an idea what the initials meant, but he wanted Ferlito to confirm it.

'Missing in action. They either died in the conflict and their bodies never recovered, or got lost in the POW system.'

'And?' Scott's own war crimes investigations had revealed that combatants in action sometimes disappeared without a trace.

'After the war ended the North Vietnamese kept some back, as bargaining tools in the reparation negotiations that followed.'

But Scott's patience was wearing thin. 'What's all this got to do with the list?'

Ferlito leant forward. His voice dropped several decibels. 'It's a list of ten American GIs who were captured by the North Vietnamese and brought to the Soviet Union during or after the war.'

Scott's heart sank. He thought the conversation had been going somewhere. That's what you think Mr Ferlito. My list contains Russian names. Hadn't the kid from Kiev mentioned that simple fact? Scott sighed. Ferlito was either wrong or he had more to tell. Scott decided not to reveal the discrepancy, yet. 'The war was between the Americans and the North Vietnamese. What have the Soviets got to do with it?'

'The captured GIs were part of the price the Vietnamese had to pay for the Soviet advice and weapons supplies. These captives were hi-tech guys, pilots flying state-of-the-art Phantoms and stuff. The Russkies were desperate for the technology.'

Scott took a few seconds to digest what Ferlito was saying. He'd read of Churchill's negotiations with Stalin at the end of the Second World War. The British rounded up thousands of Russians, primarily Cossacks who had sought asylum in Austria. Churchill tricked them into going back to Russia, and certain death, in exchange for some territorial indulgences from Stalin. Though not the same as Ferlito's story, it showed how governments were prepared to sacrifice innocent people when it suited them. 'What's the US government going to do with this list?'

'Scott, I've come to Moscow to find out what happened to these men.' He raised his eyebrows. 'Maybe some of them are still alive.'

Scott shuffled his feet. He was marshaling his thoughts. A list of captured American airmen was a long way from Ekaterina's father.

'Think of those poor GIs,' Ferlito said. 'Think of their families back home. Don't they have the right to know what happened to their husbands and sons?' He eased back. 'Scott. You and me, we're their last hope. We gotta help these guys...to get justice and closure.'

Ferlito was persuasive. He might just be telling the truth. But Scott had two problems: he wasn't currently looking for another human rights case to investigate and they had to be talking about two different lists. 'What would happen if I were to call your embassy and ask somebody for confirmation of your story?'

'If you know anything about what goes on in embassies you'll appreciate that information is disseminated on a need-to-know basis. Nobody at the embassy knows what I'm doing here.'

'That includes the ambassador?'

'Sure.'

Scott didn't understand why the US Ambassador, at least, wouldn't have known what his commercial attaché's true task was. 'Let me get this straight. Your mission is so secret that nobody at your embassy knows what you're doing, the ambassador and your CIA colleagues included...' He paused for Ferlito's response.

'It's highly classified,' Ferlito said.

'That, I think I understand,' Scott said. 'Except you're prepared to confide everything in me, this highly classified information, a complete stranger. And a non-American one at that.' There had to be more to it. 'You want me to believe that I'm in your need-to-know group?'

'A complete stranger maybe, but a stranger who has the list.'

Yes, indeed. A list that had come into Scott and Ekaterina's possession while they were searching for her father. 'And this list, you say, is a ticking bomb while it's in our hands?'

'You got it.'

If Ferlito was right, Scott's priority had to be to try

to prevent Ekaterina from being killed – and himself of course. The search for her father would have to come second. 'Okay, Ferlito. But don't you think that Gravchenko is in a better position to ensure his wife's safety than you are?'

Ferlito smiled. 'BMW.'

Scott wasn't convinced. 'The BMW bombing happened before we got the list.'

'Proves my point,' Ferlito said. 'Doesn't that just show how Gravchenko can't protect his wife and daughter? They both could have been killed.'

It was arguable. 'But—'

Ferlito held his index finger up. 'There's more. If it's of value to the Russian authorities, it's of value to Gravchenko.'

'How so?'

'Scott, I've done deals with Gravchenko. I know how he operates; what makes him tick.'

Aha, the truth was now coming out. Perhaps Scott would find out what Ekaterina had been refusing to tell him about Gravchenko's business relationship with Ferlito. 'So, you—'

'Gravchenko could make a fortune out of the list of names if he thought the Russian government wanted it so desperately,' Ferlito said. 'Which it does.'

The implication from what Ferlito was saying was ludicrous. 'Gravchenko's one of your bad guys and he's going to kill his wife, the mother of his beloved daughter, if I don't give it to him?' Scott laughed. 'Give me some credit, Ferlito.'

'You've misunderstood me.' Ferlito narrowed his eyes. 'I'm not talking about him killing his wife. Although I'm sure you know as well as I do that he can be a violent man.'

Scott flexed his fingers.

'No, Scott. Not even beating up on her. I'm talking about the mental torment and abuse he could put her through, if he thought she had access to the list, not to mention the economic hardship. He could reduce her to begging on the streets at the drop of a hat.'

Scott wasn't convinced that Gravchenko would hold his wife to ransom, estranged or not. He did, though, believe that if the Russian authorities were to get their hands on the list, they might well ensure that any of the GIs who were still alive were never found; not kill them, but destroy the paper trails and send them deeper into exile.

'You haven't yet told me what you and Ekaterina were doing at the apartment and why you're interested in Arzamas,' Ferlito said suddenly.

That was none of Ferlito's business. 'If Ekaterina hasn't told you, I'm certainly not going to.'

'Have it your way.' Ferlito stood up. 'I'll call you in the next forty-eight hours—'

'Why forty-eight hours? Why the delay?' Scott asked.

'As I said, I gotta watch your backs, I need to shake off the Russkie surveillance.'

Scott was under no illusion; the Russian authorities would have been keeping track of his movements since his return to Moscow, if only to check his contacts with the Chechens. But being tracked by Ferlito's bad guys, who were also supposed to be the Russian authorities, raised an interesting conundrum: were Ferlito's bad guy watchers also watching those who were watching Scott?

'So when I'm sure it's safe,' Ferlito continued. 'We'll all meet up. We'll get the list to the States. The Russkies will be presented with *a fait accompli* and the heat will be off you and your client.' He picked up the chair. 'As I said, we gotta make sure our boys and their families in the States get the closure they deserve.' He turned and vanished.

If Ferlito's story of the MIAs was true, what the Soviets had done was horrific: keeping the American GIs in

Russia for thirty or forty years against their will; not a word to their families. They weren't Russia's prisoners of war. And the so-called new Russian democratic regime, with all its exhortations of transparency, was compounding the felony of its predecessors by continuing the cover up. Whether or not the list of Russian names had anything to do with Ferlito's MIAs story, Ekaterina and Tanya didn't seem to be in any danger. Gravchenko had refused to help with the search for her father and she and Tanya had narrowly escaped being blown up by a bomb. Scott could well imagine his highly-focused client taking a few days away, without telling anybody, to gather her thoughts. *Check and double check.*

Scott left the room and returned along the corridor to the entrance lobby. The Persian Blue had gone and the TV was switched off. Back out in the real world, in front of the *House of Mirrors*, he punched some numbers into his cellphone. 'Tom? It's Scott. I know it's getting late.' It was 9.30pm. 'But I really need an hour of your time. Tonight if possible.'

'Sure. Come over now if you like.'

'What do you know about the Vietnam War?'

'I thought you lawyers were trained to be specific,' Tom said.

Tom's living room resembled a small Dickensian library instead of an expat's up-market Moscow apartment. Three of the walls, including either side of the door, were covered with wooden shelves of differing sizes and quality, haphazardly crammed with books and papers. It was a mystery to Scott how Tom was ever able to locate anything. A black oak dining table was stationed against the fourth wall beneath the window. Tom used it as his writing desk and repository for books that couldn't find a home on the shelves. The only surrender to orderliness, and expense, was Tom's pride and joy: a George III,

Sheraton period, mahogany glazed corner cupboard, which displayed framed photographs of his wife, who'd died in a car crash in the States four years previously, his two married daughters, their husbands and the five grandchildren. Scott wondered if he would one day present his parents with grandchildren.

Tom poured two glasses of red wine and gestured to a plate of nibbles on the coffee table between them. 'Help yourself.'

'Thanks.' Scott took a handful of cheese balls and a napkin. 'I've not eaten since breakfast.'

'Do you want something more substantial?' Tom asked. 'I can easily rustle up some—'

'No thanks. It's fine.' Scott didn't want any distractions. 'It won't do me any harm to go without a couple of meals occasionally.'

Tom nodded. 'Okay. So what aspect of the War are you talking about?'

'POWs that never came home. MIAs I think they're called.'

'Missing in action? That's a strange question. Why do you want to know?'

Sophie's counsel on his situation had been limited to his current predicament; Scott now needed historical information. Tom was a student in the 60s; he must have known more about Vietnam than Scott would ever know. 'Can you put some music on?' A Washington journalist of Tom's caliber was ripe for FSB bugging.

Tom picked up the remote control from the coffee table and pointed it at his CD changer. 'Crosby, Stills and Nash okay?'

'Fine.'

Tom nestled back in his chair. 'Okay,' he said. 'What's going on?'

'We're still off the record.'

'Until you say otherwise,' Tom said.

Scott told him everything; from the minute he met Ekaterina, to the "A-16" photo – which he fiddled with in his pocket, to Pravda and his patient Petrov, from Ekaterina's going missing to Gravchenko's demand for the file and Ferlito's revelations in the *House of Mirrors*.

Tom listened patiently and without interruption.

Scott finished and took a drink. 'What do you think?'

Tom breathed in deeply and let out a soft whistle. 'Well, Frank Ferlito is definitely not a bona fide commercial attaché. I know that for sure.'

Scott knew better than to ask how he could be so certain.

'Probably CIA,' Tom said. 'And it's the sort of mission he could be on. But I doubt it's the whole story.' He chuckled.

'Why do you say it's a mission he could be on?' Scott asked. He was looking for any hint of a possible connection to Ekaterina's father.

'Well.' The investigative reporter relaxed back in his chair. 'I seem to recall that shortly after Yeltsin was elected President of the new Russia, he came to the States and gave an interview to NBC's *Dateline*. He said Soviet archives show that US POWs from Vietnam had ended up in the Soviet Union and were kept in labor camps. He said the same in an address to Congress.'

'What happened?'

'At first the US and Russian governments publicly labeled Yeltsin a drunkard who didn't know what he was talking about. However, in the early 90s those governments set up a Joint Commission on POWs and MIAs. It was to investigate whether any American servicemen weren't repatriated from the various wars since the Second World War, including Vietnam.'

'With what results?'

Tom shook his head. 'I haven't heard much about it since the initial excitement.' He took a drink. 'But maybe the US government has got some new information and wants to revive the investigations. Hence, Mr Ferlito's presence in Moscow.'

And Ferlito had taken an interest in the Arzamas printouts at the *dacha*. Now was the time. Scott took the enlarged copy of the "A-16" photo from his pocket and handed it to Tom. The reverse side remained blank.

'Is this picture connected to the list of latitudes?' Tom asked.

'I'm hoping you can tell me.'

'Any idea when and where this was taken?' Tom looked at the back and waved the photo at him.

'No.' Scott took out his pen and pocket notebook and wrote down *A-16 (Arzamas, closed city) Summer 1979.* 'No idea at all.' He ripped the page out and handed it to Tom.

Tom read it, and put it through the shredder on his desk. 'I'm going to the head for a leak. But before I do, I think I can complete a small part of your jigsaw,' Tom said. 'This badge-like object you're interested in.'

'What about it?'

'Well,' Tom said. 'The letters aren't Cyrillic, Russian; they're English. And seeing as we're talking of American GIs, the US dog tag contains five lines, like this one: last name, forenames, social security number, blood type and religious preference.'

'Maybe,' Scott said. He was playing the devil's advocate. 'But there are many languages that use the English alphabet, give or take a few letters and accents. It would take a leap of faith to link this particular photo of a dog tag to a supposed list of American GIs.' The only connection was that the photo and list had both come from the apartment where Sokolov was murdered. 'And don't forget, Australia and New Zealand also took part in the Vietnam War.'

'Yeh,' Tom said. 'But nowhere near on the scale that the US did. And how many of them flew state-of-the-art Phantoms?'

'I'm a lawyer, Tom. I have to examine all the evidence, if only to discount it.'

'Of course. So before we jump to any conclusions we need to get these characters deciphered and checked out.' Tom dropped the photo onto the table. 'May I keep it? You have copies?' He stood up. 'I'll send it to my geek friends in Washington. They claim they can spot neutrons in a peanut on Pluto's landscape.'

'No, Tom.' Scott's heart stopped. 'Thanks but no thanks.' He picked up the photo. After Ferlito's story, he couldn't risk it being intercepted by the Russian authorities on its way out of the country.

'Look, Scott, you and I don't have access in this country to the equipment that's needed to tease out this object.'

Charlie Birch probably had access to the technology to clarify the characters, but if it was an American dog tag Washington might be able to find out the name of its owner.

'So,' Tom said. 'If the photo is as crucial to your client's search as you think it is, shouldn't we try to get to the bottom of it?'

'Yes, but—'

'And, there's something else.'

'What?' Scott asked.

'Don't you think the US government should be given the opportunity to examine it? If only to discount it, as you lawyers say.'

Tom was persuasive.

'And don't worry,' Tom said. 'Security isn't a problem. We may not be diplomats, but the press has its own methods of getting stuff out of the country. It'll be safe from prying eyes.' He left the room. 'I'd stake my life on it!'

Chapter 25

Day Eight: 8.30am

The Moskvitch shuddered to a halt in the inevitable gridlock of the early morning commuter traffic on the Garden Ring. Capitalism might have brought more privately-owned automobiles onto Moscow's streets – but it had also brought more frustrations. Two days had passed since Pravda had been required to deliver up Petrov, though Bezrukhov hadn't been in contact with him. This had given Pravda an opportunity to contact the brain surgery team he preferred, via Skype. He knew them to be discreet. They were 3,000 kilometers away in Novosibirsk carrying out post-operative monitoring on a soldier accidentally shot through the head while on maneuvers. They should be available within three days. Meanwhile, Petrov was under mild sedation and spending most of the time sleeping, with no further outbursts in English.

Pravda rested his head against the door window and closed his eyes, the energy draining from his body. Somebody rapped on his window. Pravda opened his eyes with a start. A body in an army greatcoat was standing beside the Moskvitch in the middle of the road. Pravda lowered the window and popped his head out to get a better look.

'Lieutenant-General Pravda, would you please come with me, sir. General Bezrukhov wants to see you.' A flushed-faced regular army major was hovering in the outside lane.

So, that was the Army-General's tactic; public humiliation, in the center of the city in broad daylight.

'Major, as you can see, I'm unable to move. The traffic is at a standstill.'

'We'll look after your vehicle, sir. Please get out and come with me.' A young captain opened the front passenger door and got in, uninvited. He tilted his head in deference to Pravda.

'Do I have any option?' Pravda said to the major.

'No, sir, you do not,' the major said.

He turned to the captain. 'Where will you take my car?'

'I'll bring it to the hospital, Lieutenant-General sir.'

'Hospital?' Alexei was on duty, yet he hadn't called Pravda to warn him.

'General Bezrukhov has collapsed, sir,' the captain said.

'It's very serious,' the major continued. 'His organs are failing. He's dying. He wants to see you.'

Torrents of relief flooded Pravda's veins and threatened to overwhelm him. It was stemmed only by his contradictory feelings of guilt. It was a cold and dismal winter's day – not a pleasant time for the endearing old rogue to die.

The major led Pravda to a black Mercedes parked on the shoulder of the road. They weaved in and out of the traffic along Kutuzovsky Prospect on the wrong side of the road with the headlights blazing, the siren screaming and the red lamp on the roof spinning. 'How long has he got, Major?'

'The doctors doubt he'll survive the next twenty-four hours, sir.'

'How long has he been ill?'

'Several months.'

Pravda recalled Bezrukhov's frail demeanor at their "Petrov" meeting. 'Have you been with him long?'

'Not long enough, sir.' The major's mouth drooped.

As corrupt as the ageing wheeler-dealer was, Pravda

had never heard anyone criticize the way he'd treated his subordinate officers or, indeed, the conscripts. He had looked after his men, despite having occasionally dragged them along with him on his questionable schemes. 'Which hospital?'

'Central Clinical, General.'

'Good.' The Moscow Central Clinical Hospital was the most advanced medical facility in the country; so many of the political elite were its patients that it was nicknamed *Kremlyovka*, the Kremlin Hospital. At least the old boy wouldn't be dying through the incompetence of medical staff or for lack of the proper medicines and equipment.

The Mercedes screeched to a halt at the hospital entrance. A group of soldiers lounging on the steps dropped their cigarettes and straightened up when they saw the two officers arrive. Two of them peeled off and rushed to open the car doors. Pravda jumped out, gave a perfunctory salute and hurried inside the complex with the major. The lifts were busy. Pravda followed the major as they bounded up four flights of stairs to the private ward where the general lay attached to an array of tubes and monitors. An orderly was washing his hands in the sink. He turned and smiled at Pravda; it was a smile tinged with sadness.

Pravda pulled up a chair and sat down. The old man's eyes were closed. His lips were covered in sores and his cheeks sunken. Pravda spoke softly to the general, while the major waited at a discreet distance and waved the orderly out of the room. 'General Bezrukhov. It's Leon Pravda. Can you hear me?'

'Yes,' the general whispered. His eyes remained closed. 'Come closer.'

Pravda put his ear next to the general's mouth. 'Yes, General. I'm here.' The general's breath smelt like a rotting corpse. It reminded him of the battlefields in the

Soviet-Afghan War. Pravda blew out air to minimize the nauseous effect of the odor.

'Leon...watch...your...back.' Bezrukhov gasped for air. 'I can...no longer...help you.'

Help me? 'What do you mean, General?' Were Kisletski's friends in the Kremlin a real threat to him? 'General, tell me. Who do I have to watch out for?'

'Your enemies...are many.' The general collapsed and began coughing up sputum.

'Try to preserve your strength, General.' Pravda pulled a handful of tissues from a box on the bedside locker, mopped the general's brow and wiped his mouth. "Your enemies are many". So it wasn't only Kisletski's friends who were out to get him.

Bezrukhov raised his arm and snatched at Pravda's wrist, but failed to keep hold of it. 'F—'

Pravda leant forward again. 'Yes, General? What are you trying to say?'

'Fer...' Bezrukhov choked, gasped and collapsed.

The heart monitor flat-lined.

'Doctor!' Pravda jumped up. 'Get the doctor!' He pushed the emergency button above the bed and the major rushed from the room.

'General Bezrukhov! General!' Pravda put his cheek to the man's lips; no apparent breathing. He felt for a pulse in his neck. Nothing. The flat-lining continued.

The major returned with a doctor and two nurses.

Pravda withdrew from the bed, and watched with the major while the medics tried to resuscitate their patient. The doctor shook her head and looked at her pocket watch. 'Time of death, 9.27am.' The two attendant nurses nodded in agreement.

Pravda stared at the dead body. A wave of nausea came over him. He would never know how much the old man knew of Petrov. And what did "Fer..." mean?

'Would you please come outside, sir?' the major

whispered. 'General Bezrukhov asked me to tell you something if he didn't get to talk to you in person.' The major's eyes were watering. Pravda followed him into the corridor. The major blew his nose and walked a few meters from the ward, to the seclusion of an alcove. 'General Bezrukhov was working on a particular investigation, sir.'

Pravda felt a twinge in his leg. 'Go on, Major.'

The major blew his nose again. 'I don't know much about it, sir, none of us did.' He dropped his voice. 'But it had something to do with a commercial attaché at the American Embassy called Frank Ferlito.'

Pravda was puzzled. He knew of the name, vaguely, though he suspected that the information the GRU had on the man would be old and unreliable. The FSB were responsible for monitoring foreign embassy personnel; their files would be comprehensive and up-to-date. 'He definitely said Frank Ferlito?'

'Yes, sir.'

'And that's all he said? Nothing else?'

'Yes, sir, Frank Ferlito, that's all. I hope I've pronounced it correctly.'

So that explains the "Fer...". But there must be more. Bezrukhov knew that Ferlito was within the FSB's remit, not the GRU's. Pravda moved closer to the officer and lowered his voice. 'Did he leave you any papers to give to me?'

'No, sir, nothing.'

'Do you know where his investigation files might be?'

'No, sir. He never kept anything about it in the office.'

'Not on his computer?'

The major wiped his eyes. 'General Bezrukhov and computers weren't compatible, sir.'

Pravda knew the feeling. The only point of passing on Ferlito's name was that Bezrukhov hadn't completed his investigation and he wanted Pravda, not the FSB, to finish it.

He had no time, or desire, to call for Aunt Olga's help again. It wasn't that he distrusted her after the ambush, necessarily, but he couldn't be one hundred per cent certain that somebody powerful within the FSB wasn't playing her.

Pravda wouldn't risk calling Alexei either on a landline or on his cellphone. The captain and the Moskvitch were stuck in traffic, so he borrowed the major's Mercedes, switched on the sirens and sped south around the outer ring road to the hospital where he'd installed Petrov.

Alexei was talking to Fyodor at the entrance to Petrov's ward when Pravda arrived. 'Fyodor, would you please excuse us for a few minutes?' Pravda asked.

Fyodor stood his ground. 'Your patient is sleeping, if you're interested. But he needs to see the specialist without delay. That bullet concerns me.'

'Yes, Fyodor, I *am* interested, and thank you for the update. I've arranged the specialist team and I'll explain after I've spoken to Alexei. Now, would you please excuse us?' He ushered his number two into the ward and closed the door.

The patient's eyes were closed; Pravda lowered his voice nonetheless. 'Alexei. I want you to contact Morpheus immediately and get everything he has on Frank Ferlito, the US commercial attaché here.' Morpheus was the GRU's man in Washington. He was their highest placed mole in the US and was only ever used in extraordinary circumstances. As far as Pravda was aware, the last time was during the abortive coup in August 1991, when Gorbachev was under house arrest at his *dacha* in the Crimea and Yeltsin wanted to know what the American government and the Pentagon's unpublished views and plans were.

'Morpheus?' Alexei frowned. 'You sure, Lev?'

'Yes, I am sure.' But it wasn't such a daft question;

Morpheus could be exposed in his efforts. Anonymity didn't always last forever.

'It's the middle of the night in the USA.'

'Alexei, for goodness sake. I don't care if Washington is in the middle of Hurricane Apocalypse, I want the information yesterday.'

Alexei left the room.

Pravda pulled up a chair beside the bed.

Petrov opened his eyes. 'Who's Frank Ferlito?' he said in Russian.

'What?' Pravda said. How much had he overheard?

'You want me to say it in English, Lieutenant-General Pravda? That is your name, isn't it?'

Pravda's leg seized.

Chapter 26

Day Eight: 9am

'For fuck's sake, Boris.' Scott kicked the wheel of his Cherokee. 'Are you trying to kill me?' He'd returned the vehicle to his local garage; the brake fluid was leaking again.

'I'm sorry, Scott,' the garage owner said. 'We used a temporary mechanic. I got rid of him. I'll fix it myself. Give me forty-five minutes, an hour at most.'

'An hour, no more. And I'll wait here while you do it.'

'No problem.' Boris drove the vehicle into the workshop and Scott went into the adjoining office, where he grabbed a coffee from the machine and flicked through a classic car magazine. There was a tapping on the window. Scott looked up. It was Rashid beckoning him outside. Scott waved him inside; there was nobody else in the room. Rashid shook his head. Scott nodded and went outside. It must be important, for Rashid to turn down the warmth of the office and a free quadruple latte.

The gofer was wearing a black leather jacket and a kipper tie. The predominant pattern on the tie was one of red white and blue diagonal stripes with a picture of David Beckham in the middle, sporting a Manchester United shirt and standing proudly under an archway with his arms folded and one leg on a football. He was wearing a crown. The archway bore the logo: *The Great United British Kingdom*. David Beckham no longer played for Manchester United, but of more interest to Scott was the revolutionary description of his homeland. He pointed at the tie. 'Where did you study geography, Rashid?'

'Zakan-Yurt.'

'Where's that?'

'Where did *you* study geography, chief?'

'Touché,' Scott said.

'I've found Pravda's hospital,' Rashid said. He spread his arms and bowed, as if expecting plaudits.

'Good man.' Scott gave him a high five. 'Where is it?'

'South, by the Tsaritsyno.'

'And you're sure Petrov's there?'

Rashid pointed to his tie. 'Is this David Beckham?'

'Right. Find out how I can get in to interview the man.' It was a long shot, but if anybody could do it, his gofer could.

'Sure.' Rashid's face contorted. 'And do you want me to convert North Korea to capitalism, while I'm about it?'

'Rashid, I've the utmost faith in you.' Scott waved him back to his vehicle. 'On your way.'

Rashid walked off, shoulders slumped and muttering in what Scott assumed was an attempt at a North Korean accent. 'Now students, lesson one. If there's no profit in the deal, you're fucked. That's capitalism.'

Scott's cellphone rang. Tom Huxley's name was on the screen. 'Tom?'

'We must meet. Sooner rather than later.' The tone was clipped and Tom's usual paternal air was missing.

'Sure, where?' Scott asked. 'Are you okay, Tom?

'I'm fine. I'm out at Khimki, the IKEA store, picking up some bookshelves. Can you get here by noon?'

It was a Moscow suburb, about twenty kilometers from the garage. 'Yes, I should be able to make it. Are you sure you're—'

'Good. I'll finish my shopping and wait in the car. I'm parked near the entry barrier.'

'Okay.'

Tom disconnected. Something was up.

'Boris…!'

It was 12.30 when Scott pulled into a parking bay at IKEA and turned off the engine. Tom appeared within seconds and Scott let him in.

'I've got a response from Stateside.'

'I'm listening.'

Tom's eyes narrowed and his faced creased. The man didn't seem to be in physical pain; more like mild agitation, concern. 'We've stumbled on something.'

'Go on.'

'They've warned me off,' Tom said.

'Who have?'

'The suits in Washington.'

'Who precisely?' Scott asked. 'Politicians? Bureaucrats? Military?'

Tom shook his head. 'I don't know.'

'I don't understand. What did your people say?'

'Nothing yet. I didn't get a chance to speak with them.'

'I'm none the wiser.'

'As soon as you left last night I sent the photo by way of an encrypted e-mail to my contacts. It would have been about 2pm Eastern Standard time. At five this morning I got a knock on my apartment door.'

'Hmm,' Scott said. 'Somebody was in a hurry.' It would have been 8 or 9pm the previous day in Washington; the same day the photo would have arrived.

'It was an American. Mid-thirties, retro Tom Selleck moustache, arrogant as hell. I've never seen him before and he wouldn't confirm who he was. He refused to give any ID.'

'But you let him in.'

'No way.'

'So what did he say?' Scott pictured the scene of the "suit" hovering awkwardly on Tom's threshold.

'That some people in Washington wanted to know why I was so interested in the photograph.'

'I can imagine your reply at five in the morning.' Scott laughed.

'And you'd be right, Scott.' Tom smiled for the first time. 'As he left he told me that it wouldn't be in my best interests for me to ask any more questions about the photo.'

'He used those exact words, "some people in Washington" and "best interests"?'

'You bet.'

'He's been watching too many "B" movies.' Scott rapped his fingers on the steering wheel and watched the cars coming and going. Sophie's "rat-infested netherworld of international spookery where the shadows haven't a clue who they are" entered his mind. His heart raced. He didn't know whether it was excitement or anxiety. 'They don't know it's A-16.' Scott turned to Tom. 'Do they?' Scott's instinct, and it was nothing more than that, told him that the "A-16" legend had to remain secret until he could find out before anybody else if it was connected to the list of names.

The journalist sighed. 'What do you take me for, Scott?'

'Sorry.' Scott remembered, Tom had torn up the note and shredded the pieces in front of him. 'So, you've hit a dead end.'

'No way,' Tom said, and perked up. 'I've got another idea.'

'What do you mean?' Scott didn't want Tom to do any more investigating until they'd had a chance to think things through. 'First, we need to—'

'You're frowning,' Tom said. 'Don't worry. I'll be fine.' He slapped his friend on the thigh. 'You owe me a scoop; remember? This could be my *Watergate*.'

'Yes, but—'

'I have to go. I'll catch you later.' Tom got out and disappeared behind a row of cars.

'Shit!' Scott banged the steering wheel. He felt as if a series of alarm bell clangers was about to smash against the inside of his head. 'Shit, shit, shit.' He called Sophie. He wanted to tell her about Ferlito's revelation.

'Hi, counselor,' she said. 'You must be psychic. We need to play catch-up.'

'Can we meet?' Scott asked.

'I'm in the Sheraton Palace, Piano Bar.'

'I thought they frowned on smoking there?' Sophie liked to top up her liquor with nicotine.

'Huh. Why hasn't anybody told me?'

'Scott!' Sophie caught his eye as he entered the bar. 'Over here!' She said something to her two young male admirers. They picked up their drinks and left with a nod and forced smiles in Scott's direction. He responded with a sympathetic grin; he'd spoiled their entertainment. He grabbed the chair opposite the American attorney.

She thrust out her chest and summoned the waiter. Her blouse had one too many buttons undone. 'Another screwdriver for me and...' She glanced at Scott.

'A small lager please,' he said to the waiter.

The waiter nodded and left.

'People don't drink small lagers...' Sophie mimicked an upper class English accent, '...in the Sheraton Palace, my dear.' It wasn't Lady Bracknell, but a passable attempt for an American with an excess of screwdrivers agitating her blood cells.

'Ekaterina and Tanya are staying with Ferlito,' Scott said. 'I've spoken to her. She and Tanya are okay. Ferlito says the pair of us are in danger.'

Sophie choked on her cigarette. 'You'd better explain.'

Scott told her Ferlito's story.

'And you believe this crock of shit?' Sophie asked, stubbing out her cigarette in an ashtray.

The waiter brought the drinks.

'I'm inclined to. It makes a lot of sense.'

'Huh, what part?' Sophie asked. 'The bit about your list of *Russian* names, being *American* GIs, or the bit about Gravchenko being the homicidal maniac?' She lit another cigarette.

'Sophie, cut the melodrama.' Scott was irritated. She knew better than that. 'Ferlito didn't say anything about Gravchenko wanting to kill Ekaterina. But the guy's in a position to exert strong persuasive power over her. Anyway, look at the bombing of her BMW. Somebody out there has already tried to kill her, and Gravchenko wasn't able to prevent it.' He took a drink. 'She's always said that she feared the Russian authorities getting wind of the search for her father. Ferlito's doing her a favor; he's keeping her out of harm's way. Besides, when I spoke with her, she was cool, calm and collected. She's smart enough to have given me a signal if she and Tanya were in any danger. No, her enemies are Russian, not an American diplomat, spook or whatever.'

'Scott, I got news for you. Governments, diplomats, spooks, whatever, don't do favors.'

'Maybe.'

Check and double check.

'Sophie, put your prejudices aside for a moment. Does Ferlito's story stack up?'

Sophie shrugged and smiled. 'I guess you got a few cents left on your dollar.'

'Last night,' Scott said. 'I googled the individual names on the list, in the Russian language and in English transliteration, but there were so many hits and combinations, it would take the proverbial million monkeys a million years to throw up anything relevant.'

'I don't know about your list of names, but our guys, taken by the Russkies? Sure, it's possible.' She lost the smile and her eyes glazed over. 'My dad was a grunt in the war.'

'Grunt?'

'Your basic foot soldier, aka "crunchy" or "ground pounder".' She finished off her drink and signaled the waiter with her hand for a repeat round. 'I don't know what I know.' She screwed up her face. 'Maybe zilch. Dad never talked about the war.' She lowered her voice. 'He committed suicide when I was eighteen.'

'Ah shit,' Scott said. 'Soph,' He reached out a hand to her. 'I'm sorry. I didn't know. You never told me.'

'It's okay.' She stroked Scott's hand. 'It's always been a no-go area...until now.'

'Look, if you don't want to talk—'

'No, no. It's okay.' She blew her nose. 'They treated him like shit.'

'Who?'

'The US government. Him and thousands of others.'

'I don't understand,' Scott said. 'Why?'

'Politics. The country turned against the war and anybody connected with it. The electorate gave it the big thumbs down. So when our boys came home, the government dumped on them.'

'How so?'

'Lack of sufficient funding for their psychological as well as physical wounds. Little or no help to get them back to work, or even to readjust to civilized society. Stuff like that.' She laughed sardonically. 'There sure weren't any votes in supporting these guys...despite the fucking suicides. It was left to the families, Vets' associations, and charities, to look after them, best they could.'

The waiter brought more drinks.

'They were real bad news for the White House,' Sophie continued. 'Too many body-bags. It was in your face. On TV. Night after night. Who needed all that shit? Not Nixon, that's for sure. He had his own demons to contend with.'

Tom had told Scott that the US-Russia Joint Commission on POWs and MIAs hadn't been set up until 1992.

'So,' Scott said. 'The North Vietnamese could indeed have sent some of the soldiers to the Soviet Union and, if the US government knew about it, they may have decided to do nothing for, let's say…geopolitical, international relations, reasons?' And they'd probably been hindered by the ongoing Cold War.

'I don't know, for a fact, what our government knew.' Sophie's head dropped and she played with her glass. 'But my opinion is that the GIs could have been sent anywhere: Russia, China, North Korea, North Pole, Jupiter, and good old Uncle Sam would have done jack shit about it… It costs tax dollars to investigate something like that.' She took a drink. 'And tax dollars means votes.'

Scott took Sophie's hand in his. She was understandably bitter, and no doubt her judgment was clouded. But he hadn't meant to bring back sad memories for her. 'Sophie, I'm really sor—'

'I'm okay.' She sniffed and took a long drink. 'So, counselor, what do you think Ferlito's going to do when he finds out that the names on your list are Russian, and not American?' She narrowed her eyes. 'In fact, what are you and Ekaterina going to do, if your list is not the list Ferlito is talking about? The one that everybody and their mother wants to kill you two for. If he's telling the truth, you'd both continue to be in danger.'

Scott had been turning the questions over and over in his mind.

He hadn't a clue.

Chapter 27

Day Eight: 12 noon

Ferlito was occupying Pravda's mind when he drove off the gas station forecourt, stepped on the accelerator instead of the brake pedal, and shot across the Garden Ring. Luckily for Pravda, the clockwise lane was empty; the traffic was being held at stop lights some 300 kilometers away. The anticlockwise lane was under partial repair, so the oncoming vehicles were approaching at a snail's pace. The dice with life and death persuaded him to park for a few minutes, to regain his composure.

His cellphone rang. He answered without looking at the screen. 'Pravda.'

'Raskolnikov.'

Pravda's heart missed a beat.

The code name. It couldn't be.

'What do you see?' Pravda asked, following the pre-arranged sequence.

'Green shadows.'

Pravda stared at the screen. He thought he knew who it was, but he couldn't be sure; he wasn't in the habit of remembering cellphone numbers. His only communication with the man in seven years had been to pass on code words and phone numbers for emergencies.

This was the first emergency call.

Pravda continued.

'Where are these shadows?'

'In the rivers of Babylon.'

It had to be Grushchenko, the third and only other surviving member of the group. 'Where are you?'

'At Afonsin's.'

Grushchenko was in Moscow, in the Novodevichye Cemetery, where Major-General Semen Afonsin was buried. Sightseers were attracted to the three-meter-long tank mounted on top of his tombstone. Grushchenko was 1,700 kilometers from home. Pravda closed his eyes and rested his head on the steering wheel.

'Did you hear me?' Grushchenko asked.

'Forty minutes,' Pravda said. 'I'll meet at you at the front gate.' Pravda disconnected and called Alexei. 'Raskolnikov's in Moscow,' he said.

'What the fu—'

'I'm picking him up now. I'll take him to the apartment in Lefortovo.' It was one of the GRU safe houses. 'Get somebody to meet me there with the keys.'

'You can't Lev, not for a couple of days. The block has no running water...or heating. Burst pipes. They're supposed to be fixing them this week.'

'Damn. Okay. I'll put him on the barge.' The GRU used a converted Dutch barge as a staging post in emergency cases. Permanently moored on the Moscow River, a few kilometers from the Novodevichye Cemetery, it was occupied by an "eccentric old man", Gennady, who hoisted the skull and crossbones every morning but otherwise kept himself to himself. He was a retired GRU foot soldier who helped his former employers whenever the need arose. Two weeks previously Pravda had allowed Gennady to take a six week vacation in the warmer climes of Sochi – because nothing was happening in Moscow. 'I'll call you when we get there.' Pravda continued. 'Inform Uncle Nikolai and tell him I must see him later today.' The situation was in danger of overwhelming Pravda. He needed Uncle Nikolai's counsel.

'Will do, take care.'

Pravda didn't recognize the man who got into his Moskvitch at the gates of the cemetery, and collapsed. He was bald, had two black eyes and an open bloodied gash running from the base of his right ear to the corner of his mouth. Two upper front teeth were missing and both hands were severely grazed.

'It took five days and three muggings to get here, Leon.'

Pravda handed him a bottle of water. 'Give me your cellphone.'

Grushchenko gave him the SIM card. 'I've just chucked the phone down a hole in the ice in the lake.'

Pravda switched on the ignition and moved off. 'So what's the story?'

Grushchenko gulped down half the bottle and coughed the contents back out of his mouth and through his nose. 'I'm on the run, Leon. I've not slept for three days.' He was shaking.

'From what?' The wretched man was desperate with fear. Had the killer of Sokolov and Karat been stalking him?

'I killed my wife, eight months ago.'

Pravda stamped on the brakes and turned to look at his passenger. Grushchenko's head was bowed, his chin resting on his chest. He was fiddling with his fingers. 'You'd better explain,' Pravda said. 'And look at me.' He wanted to see if Grushchenko was telling the truth.

Grushchenko obliged; his face pleading. 'You've got to believe me, Leon. It was a mercy-killing.'

The vehicles behind began honking. Pravda drove on.

'Luda, my wife, she had advanced multiple sclerosis. She couldn't take it anymore. She asked me to end it for her.' Grushchenko's eyes glazed over. 'So I smothered her with a pillow.'

One of Pravda's cousins had died with multiple sclerosis. The wretched soul and his loved ones had suffered hell for thirty years. 'Go on.'

'My lawyer's got friends in the prosecutor's office. She

says the prosecutor's got it in for me. I won't get a fair trial. They're going to lock me up and throw away the key.' He blew out air. 'They've refused to let the family doctor testify for me.'

Pravda hissed. Many trials in Russia were still "political": the procedures were outside the rule of law and convictions and sentences were subject to non-judicial influences.

Had the FSB found out who Grushchenko was?

Pravda's ankle throbbed the moment they boarded the barge. The cabin door key wasn't in its usual place, taped inside the housing for the mooring ropes, and the door was unlocked.

He looked at Grushchenko.

'Get back on the street and wait until I've searched the cabin.'

Grushchenko turned towards the gangplank.

Pravda felt a crashing blow on the back of his head. His legs gave way and everything went dark.

'Wake up, Lev, wake up!'

Alexei was dragging Pravda across the floor of the cabin when he came round.

'Wh…what…what's going on?'

'Quick! Get out of here! There's a bomb!' Alexei said, helping Pravda to his feet.

Pravda stood up and looked around, while massaging the back of his head. Grushchenko was slumped in a chair in the center of the cabin. There was a single bullet hole in his forehead and segments of brain were splattered over the wall. Two wires led from inside Grushchenko's coat and down to a sports bag under the chair.

'Lev, don't hang around! It's ticking!'

'I'm with you,' Pravda said.

Alexei was away first, with Pravda close behind him.

When they reached the sidewalk the bomb exploded. The noise was deafening.

Pravda dropped to the ground, alongside Alexei, and they covered their heads with their arms. A dense pall of smoke enveloped them and Pravda gasped for air. The ground shook as the heat penetrated his winter coat and seared into his bones. Burning debris rained down.

Silence.

The smoke began to clear. Pravda looked round. In place of the colorfully-decorated barge, lay a smoldering, splintered hull. Grushchenko's body and any other usable forensic evidence would have disappeared into the ether.

He got up and hauled Alexei to his feet. The occupants of passing vehicles were rubbernecking. The pair brushed themselves down and walked briskly away.

'I'll double the security on Petrov,' Alexei said.

'No.' Pravda stopped. 'We're not going to attract any more attention than we already have.' He touched Alexei on the shoulder. 'We can handle the situation, as it is.'

Alexei said nothing.

The bombing brought Pravda back to the TV pictures of Romanova's charred BMW. 'There's a rumor that Ekaterina Romanova has gone missing. If she has, I want to know why. Check it out.'

The eleven car passenger express, headed by a TEP70 diesel locomotive, emerged from the tunnel at over 150 kilometers an hour and crashed head on into a stationary freight train comprising fifty-two wagons. The freight train was on the wrong track. The engine and front three cars of the passenger express up-ended and toppled down the embankment, pulling another six cars with them. There were many dead and injured. The driver of the freight train was also killed in the catastrophe, but its wagons stubbornly remained on the track.

'You see,' Uncle Nikolai said. 'This is what happens

when you take your eye off the ball – and forget to switch the points.' He picked up the damaged engine and cars and laid them one by one on the shelf, as if returning sleeping babies to their cribs. 'Some I can mend, but the others...' He grimaced.

Uncle Nikolai was Russia's premier model railway enthusiast. Pictures of his track layouts and his articles regularly appeared in the world's most prestigious journals devoted to the subject. Much to the annoyance of his wife of sixty years, Uncle Nikolai's obsession occupied the entire upper floor of their penthouse suite in the Kudrinskaya Square Building, one of the famous seven Stalinist "wedding cake" constructions in Moscow.

'How long have you been collecting, Nikolai Sergeyevich?' Pravda asked.

'This is my seventh decade.' The portly eighty-five-year-old beamed at his protégé. 'No one in the country can touch me.' His full head of white hair and bushy black eyebrows took twenty years off his age. 'People come from all corners of the globe.' He beckoned Pravda with a wave to sit down; a stump where his pinkie finger should have been.

Pravda pulled up a faded green leather armchair and watched as Uncle Nikolai inspected the damaged cars, individually.

'Another PSS used and a bomb,' Uncle Nikolai said. 'That's a departure. There's nothing like overkill.' He smiled at Pravda. 'Excuse the pun.'

'FSB?' He was surprised at Uncle Nikolai's flippancy over the slaying. His former superior used to have more respect for his charges.

Uncle Nikolai turned and faced Pravda. He held a damaged passenger car in his hand. 'I don't think so.'

'Oh?'

'All three members of the group have been killed by the same MO,' Uncle Nikolai said.

'Apart from the bomb,' Pravda said.

'The PSS bullet through the center of the forehead which takes half the brain with it on the way out.' The old man waved the damaged car at Pravda. 'This is personal.'

'How so?'

'It's not a simple case of wanting them dead. The killer wanted to remove their brains, to dehumanize them. Erase their identities.' Uncle Nikolai returned the car to the shelf. 'That's personal.'

'But why not the FSB?'

'Think about it,' Uncle Nikolai said. 'You and I know that it can't be personal with the FSB.'

That was true. The men that he and Uncle Nikolai were protecting had never done anything to make the FSB want to take their actions personally; even assuming the FSB knew of their existence. 'Okay, so if it's not the FSB, who wants them dead? And why has the MO changed? Grushchenko was killed by the bullet; there was no need for the bomb.' A sharp pain shot down his leg. He understood. 'It was meant for me, wasn't it?' Somebody had connected Pravda to the dead men. He scratched his left thigh.

'I can't answer that,' Uncle Nikolai said.

Pravda was keen to change the subject. 'The FSB have removed Ekaterina Romanova's file from their database. Why do you think they would do that?'

'Don't waste your energies on trying to figure out why the FSB do things,' Uncle Nikolai said without turning round. 'Better minds than ours have tried before – and failed.'

But Pravda's mind was beginning to wander. His mentor was giving in too easily. Unless Grushchenko was being stalked, only Alexei and Uncle Nikolai knew that he and Grushchenko were at the barge. "Your enemies are many", Bezrukhov had said. Alexei would give his life for Pravda, but where did the old man's loyalties lie? Nikolai

Sergeyevich Dvornikov had been a career GRU operative, and a trusted confidant of successive Communist Party Secretaries from the 1950s to his retirement in 1991. Unlike Pravda, he was a political animal. To have survived for so long in the Machiavellian culture of the Kremlin Uncle Nikolai would have to have worked with everybody, especially the FSB – Putin's shield.

'And don't worry about this Romanova woman,' Uncle Nikolai said. 'Now Sokolov's apartment has been sanitized she needs you more than you need her. She'll soon come running.' He turned round to face Pravda, spinning the wheel of a freight wagon. 'She's nowhere else to go.'

'She could be a front for Gravchenko,' Pravda said. His men were going through the books and papers they found in the apartment, in search of connections between Sokolov and the oligarch.

'It's always a possibility of course, but I don't see how Gravchenko could make money out of your operation.' The train enthusiast spun the wheels of a second car with his three fingers and nodded as they operated without obstruction. 'It would be too speculative for him.' He put the car back on the track and rubbed both his eyes under his glasses.

Uncle Nikolai had a point. Okay, so it must be something personal for Romanova. But what did he say? *Your* operation? Not, *our* operation? This was classic Soviet politics: when things get hot, disengage, find a scapegoat and run for cover.

Uncle Nikolai shuffled to the far end of the layout where he pressed two buttons on a control board and stood back. A third train left a station and headed towards a replica of the Kiev Station terminus in Moscow. 'Let her come to you.'

'What do you know about Frank Ferlito, Nikolai Sergeyevich?'

'Only what you've told me,' Uncle Nikolai said. 'I've

never heard of him.' There was no sign of recognition in his voice, and he kept his eyes on the model train. But the art of deception was second nature to Uncle Nikolai. The limited amount of information on the GRU file about Ferlito confirmed that the American had appeared in Russia in the late 1990s, years after Uncle Nikolai's retirement at the end of 1991. So the old man's statement could be true, but...

'See what Morpheus says first.' Uncle Nikolai turned and looked at Pravda, his eyes narrowing. 'Before you make any moves in this man Ferlito's direction.'

But why should he wait? Uncle Nikolai had just said that he'd never heard of Ferlito. Pravda decided not to pursue the point. 'That leaves Petrov,' he said.

'And he's your immediate problem.' Uncle Nikolai sat on a wooden bench, which he had acquired from a real rural train station.

Your immediate problem? That was the second time.

'Speaking English coming out of a coma?' Uncle Nikolai continued. 'To mix my metaphors, Leon my dear boy...the genie has poked his head above the parapet.'

Pravda searched for transparency in his mentor's face and speech. All he could think of was the Latin phrase: *Quis custodiet ipsos custodies?*

Who watches the watchers?

Chapter 28

Day Eight: 5pm

Despite being alone in the apartment – Anna and Stepan were spending a few days with their *babushka* – General Pravda locked himself inside his study; old habits...Pravda pushed the desk and chair aside, exposing a rubber foot mat partly covering a threadbare carpet; his GRU status counted for nothing in the domestic comfort stakes. He slipped the mat to one side and peeled away a square meter of the carpet. Only the keenest eye would have detected that the strip had been previously cut out and re-laid. He placed the palm of his right hand on the exposed floorboards and slid it under the carpet until he came to a ridge, which would normally have been hidden under the base of the desk drawers. He teased the ridge up with the tips of his fingers and felt his way into a hole in the floorboards, from which he pulled out a small rectangular metal box. He took out a computer hard drive, substituted it for the existing drive in his desktop PC and booted up.

He wasn't becoming paranoid about Uncle Nikolai's choice of words, but he wanted to be certain that the information was still on his computer. The tension was telling on him, he wasn't thinking clearly. He hit the wrong key five or six times on his way through a series of password levels. On each occasion he was booted out of the system and had to begin again. He finally opened a subfolder to reveal a list of names and numbers:

1. Pickering, David James (6) 1065500 E
2. Slowe, Ronald (10) 1073759 E

3. Wilson, Robert John Ear (2) 1061041 E
4. Berkowitz, David Scott (9) 1074138 E
5. Gregg, Michael Sutherland (1) 1052900 E
6. Vincent, Jacob (8) 1045953 E
7. Leadbetter, Lance (3) 1073905 E
8. Huntsman, Robert David (5) 1082000 E
9. Damon, George Petersfield (7) 1064530 E
10. Church, Bernard William (4) 1081300 E

He relaxed and returned the disk drive to its hiding place. The corresponding list, with the Russian aliases and latitudes, went missing years before Pravda's time. Although Pravda occasionally wondered about it, he realized that even if whoever had it worked out what it meant, it would be useless without the American names and longitudes. The original hard copy of Pravda's list was buried in a lead-container in the back yard at his *dacha*; so a computer crash or theft, though inconvenient, wouldn't be fatal. Nobody, including Alexei, knew where it was.

He opened the GRU's only file note on Frank Ferlito:

American citizen, Caucasian. Sixty-nine years old, ex-special forces officer in Asia during the Vietnam War; honorable discharge; ex-CIA, left under a cloud for 'over enthusiastic' interrogation techniques; fluent Russian speaker; began visiting Russia in the late 1990s, setting up technology exhibitions; currently a commercial attaché at the US Embassy.

Pravda had no doubt that he was still CIA, or perhaps NSA. Now that monitoring Ferlito was the FSB's task – a legacy from perestroika – he would have to rely on Morpheus to fill in the gaps. The FSB's attention to detail left a lot to be desired.

He left the study, locked the door and headed for the living room, where he switched on the TV and poured a scotch, a fine malt. The moment he put his feet up the entrance lobby intercom buzzed. He was expecting to be left alone that evening. His team would phone in an emergency; they certainly wouldn't have called round uninvited. He checked the receiver in the hall. 'Yes?'

'It's Tom, Leon, Tom Huxley. I was in the neighborhood, so I thought I'd look up my old friend.'

An experienced American investigative reporter was the last person Pravda wanted to see. On the other hand, Huxley had been the person who'd recommended Pravda for the university posting in the United States. Huxley knew the Dean. 'I've got the scotch on ice, Tom,' he lied. 'Please come up.' Pravda waited at the open door. He had first met Huxley two or three years earlier at a US Embassy function; where "openness" was supposed to be the philosophy, but everybody suspected that everybody else was a spy, the media representatives included.

Why had Bezrukhov been investigating Ferlito?

Tom arrived, panting, with flushed cheeks. 'Why don't elevators ever work in your apartment blocks?'

'It's our state-enforced fitness regime. Besides, it's only five floors.' Pravda led him into the living room. 'English or Russian?'

'If you don't mind, Leon, it's too late in the day for me to think in Russian.'

'Drink?' Pravda asked.

'Scotch is fine.'

Pravda gestured for him to sit down.

'Ready for the States?' Huxley asked.

'It is a big decision. Anna and me, we have much to think of.' And Pravda still had Danilov and Petrov's welfare to protect.

'Sure, I understand.'

Pravda studied Huxley as he handed him the drink. The journalist had regained his composure and his eyes were darting around the room. Huxley had been in the apartment before; he wasn't taking a furniture inventory. Pravda didn't want to initiate the conversation. He wanted his friend to come clean about his real reason for being "in the neighborhood" at that time of the evening.

'By the way,' Huxley said. 'I suppose you're aware of the rumors on the street?' He took a sip of the whiskey. 'Your Gun Fight at the OK Corral – on the Outer Ring. This mysterious hospital patient of yours. A Russian who speaks English in his sleep. They're all over town.'

'Sorry, Tom. What did you say?' Pravda was pretending to watch a series of news clips on the TV. Yes, he'd heard those particular rumors. So much for Fyodor Glasunov's niece "understanding the rules". Headshots of Ekaterina and Tanya Romanova appeared on the screen. Pravda glanced at Huxley. He was staring at the TV. The scrolling word delivery at the foot of the screen read:

Wife and daughter of billionaire business man Konstantin Gravchenko disappear...

Pravda turned up the volume. A woman newscaster was speaking:

'The police have confirmed that Ekaterina Romanova and her daughter Tanya have disappeared. They were last seen the day before yesterday, in the evening, outside their apartment block, with a white male getting into a foreign-make SUV. Friends say she failed to make two appointments yesterday and is not answering any of her phones. The vehicle was dark blue, bore no registration plates and its windows were blackened. It's not known if the incident is related to Mr Gravchenko's business activities...'

Pravda's eyes met his friend's. Huxley's face was blank. The journalist knew enough Russian to have understood what the newscaster was saying, but his thoughts were difficult to assess.

'Do you know the Romanova woman Leon?' Huxley's expression remained neutral.

'Why do you ask?'

'Are the rumors true?' Huxley asked.

Pravda glanced back at the screen. A sports item appeared. He looked again at Huxley. The man was jumping from the rumors to the disappearance and back to the rumors. Seasoned investigative reporters like Huxley were often as skillful as experienced cross-examining attorneys at hiding their thought processes. 'They are rumors. Nothing more.'

'Look, Leon, I know you've been avoiding me for the past week or so.' Huxley sipped again at his scotch. 'You've not been available for our periodic chinwags. What's going on? If you want it off the record it's okay by me.'

On or off the record, friend or no friend, Pravda wasn't about to reveal anything to Huxley that couldn't already be found in the public domain, with a little effort.

'I know his name is Petrov,' Huxley continued. 'Who is he?'

Pravda curled his toes until he got cramp. What else was out there? He sighed. The questions would continue. He had to give his friend something. 'Off the record.' He refilled Huxley's glass. The reporter was being a nuisance, but he was honorable.

'Agreed, shoot.'

'How much else do you know?'

'*Quid pro quo*, comrade,' Huxley said. 'Your turn.'

'His life is in danger.'

'From what?'

'A bullet in his brain.'

'Self-inflicted?'

'No.'

'Who shot him?'

'I think it was the Clantons and the McLaurys.'

Huxley smiled. 'Your knowledge of classic American films is impressive, especially for a Russian. Is it a fatal wound?'

'He can be saved.' Pravda paused and focused on the journalist. 'If he is left in peace.'

'Why should anybody want to disturb him?'

Because that's what inquisitive journalists do – disturb people. 'You must answer *my* questions, please, Tom.'

'I won't reveal my sources.'

'What will you do with your information of Petrov? Not what I am telling you. We have agreed it is off the record. The other information, your rumors?'

Huxley swished the drink around in his glass. 'Is Petrov from Sarov? Arzamas-16 to be precise?'

Pravda's heart stopped. He hesitated for a moment and reverted to his native tongue. 'Tom. I hope you understand what I'm saying.' He eased the half empty glass from Huxley's hand. 'I don't expect you to reveal your sources. I know it's your journalists' code. I understand you believe it goes to the heart of a democratic society and I respect that. But the *quid pro quo*, as you say, is that you must understand, and respect, that codes also bind me. I must protect what I believe to be our national interests.' He indicated with a polite smile that the discussion was over and guided his friend to the door.

'Thanks, my friend.' Huxley shook hands. 'You've told me all I need to know.'

'Goodnight, Tom.' Pravda closed the door.

Friend or not, Huxley was becoming a serious problem.

Chapter 29

Day Nine: 8.30am

Scott sat in an internet café off Red Square, continuing his website searches for any connections between the MIAs and Arzamas-16. He hit on a site called *POW/ MIA Freedom Fighters*, quoting an ABC Radio Australia News report posted on February 18, 2003. The Moscow Interfax news agency had reported that Russian Military Archives revealed that more than fifty US pilots who were captured during the Vietnam War were transferred to the USSR. Only seven of the men had been identified; the fate of the others was unknown. The Soviets wanted the pilots for their technological knowledge and equipment. However, according to another article, published by "The Vietnam News" – quoting its source as The Associated Press, although the archives revealed instances of Soviet Intelligence officers interrogating American POWs in North Vietnam, there was no evidence that the Americans were transferred to the USSR. Though, it was known that the Soviets gave logistical support to the North Vietnamese during the war. Were the pilots the *quid pro quo*?

Frank Ferlito's story might not be that incredible after all. But the warning from Washington was bugging him. The US government, or military, didn't want somebody of Tom's experience and status to investigate the dog tag. Scott wanted to know why. He called Tom's cellphone.

'Allo,' said a Russian voice Scott didn't recognize.

'Sorry, wrong number.'

He tried again.

'Allo.' The same voice.

Scott hesitated. 'Is that Tom Huxley's number?'

'Who?'

'Tom Huxley; the American journalist working for *The Washington Post*.'

'Who is this?'

'Scott Mitchell. Tell him it's Scott Mitchell.'

Another voice came on the phone. 'Mr Mitchell. This is Captain Vassiliyev. Please tell me why you want to speak to Mr Huxley.'

'What? Captain Vassiliyev? What's going on? What are you doing with Tom's phone? Put him on please.' Maybe Tom needed counsel. Had there been a murder? 'I'm his lawyer, Captain Vassiliyev. I want to speak to my client.'

'What is your business with Mr Huxley?'

'Let me speak to my client, *please*.'

'That's not possible.'

'How not possible? He's entitled to legal representation while in custody, Captain, even in Russia.'

'He's not in custody Mr Mitchell...Mr Huxley is dead.'

Scott's stomach lurched.

'Did you hear me Mr Mitchell? Your client is dead. Murdered, to be precise. A bullet through the center of his brain.'

Scott didn't have to go to the police precinct house. Scott didn't want to go to the police precinct house. He didn't want to have to lie to the police. He was bound to be found out at some stage. But when Captain Vassiliyev suggested that a lawyer might like to help the authorities find out who'd murdered his client, and friend, Scott couldn't refuse the invitation. He parked in a car park across the street from the police building and called Rashid.

'Yes, chief?'

'Rashid. Tom Huxley's dead, murdered. I'm going to

see Captain Vassiliyev in a few minutes. I—'

'Wow, is he doing you for that as well?'

'Rashid, listen to me. He's not "doing" me for anything. You understand? He's asking for my help, that's all.'

'Sorry, chief…And about Tom Huxley. Sorry.'

'Okay. You know where the precinct house is. The café nearby. It's called the *Russkiy Izbar*. Meet me there in two hours. If I'm late, wait for me.'

'How long?'

'As long as it takes.'

'Will do.'

'Where were you yesterday afternoon and evening, Mr Mitchell?'

The interview room at the precinct house was not unlike the interrogation room at Domodyedovo Airport. True it had four chairs instead of two, three full ashtrays on the table, a cracked jug of water and a picture of Putin on the wall, but the rest of the place was, again, Soviet utility à la Brezhnev.

Scott was alone with the detective. Their conversation, interrogation, or whatever it was supposed to be, was taking place without any witnesses and no apparent recording device, and the detective wasn't taking notes. 'I came here to help you, Captain, not to be interrogated as a suspect.' He leant forward. 'And before you ask, no I don't go around murdering my friends, or my clients.' He paused. 'Although in the latter case, sometimes I feel like doing so.'

The captain grinned. 'Help me tick the boxes for my superiors, Mr Mitchell, please.'

Captain Vassiliyev lacked the feral aggression of Colonel Yakovlev and displayed instead the calm resignation exhibited by somebody who'd seen and done it all and was looking forward to retirement without any hassle. 'I was with Tom at about 12.30 for ten minutes or so. Then I drove back into town, first to my office, then to the Sheraton Hotel, where I met with an American lawyer friend. We had drinks and a meal. I left about seven and went home for the night.'

'Anybody with you, at home?'

'No.'

Vassiliyev took a long drag on his cigarette. 'What was your business with Mr Huxley, during those ten minutes or so?' He held up his hand. 'And please don't waste my time with all that client confidentiality garbage again. I'm trying to solve a murder, not steal your client's investment portfolio.'

'Point taken.' Scott clasped his hands. He'd worked out his story on the drive to the precinct house. 'It wasn't legal business anyway. He was doing me a friendly favor.'

'What favor?'

'My nephew in England collects information on army dog tags. It's a hobby. He sent me a photograph of a damaged dog tag that he thought might be Russian. He asked me to check it out.'

'And was it?'

'No. I had the photograph enlarged and I could read some letters, English, not Russian. So I showed it to Tom. He said it could be an American dog tag.'

'Why did he think that?'

'Because of the placing of the letters and numbers. He said he'd send a copy to his contacts in Washington for verification. We met yesterday for an update.'

'Where did you meet?'

'IKEA, out at Khimki.'

Vassiliyev raised his eyebrows. 'What did his contacts in Washington say?'

'I don't know. He didn't yet have an answer from the States. That's why I called him this morning, to see if he'd received the response.'

Vassiliyev nodded slowly. 'It was a long way to go, just for no news. He could have called you.'

Scott fidgeted and plucked at his watch strap. 'We were both in the area.' He had to brave it out.

'Shopping?'

'Tom was. I was scouting the district…for real estate investment opportunities.'

Vassiliyev cleared his throat. 'Tired of human rights, Mr Mitchell?'

'We all need a pension fund.'

The detective fiddled around in his jacket pocket and withdrew a transparent folder, which contained the enlarged "A-16" photograph. He slid it across the table. 'This the photo?'

Scott picked up the folder and studied the photograph. He was tempted to flip it over, but decided not to and slid it back to the captain. 'Similar.' The second he'd done it, he realized that it would have been a natural reaction for him, the inquisitive lawyer, to have turned it over to see if there was anything on the other side. Would Vassiliyev comment on that?

'Similar?' Vassiliyev asked.

'That's what I said.'

They studied each other while the policeman rocked backward and forward in between long drags on his cigarette.

'Why did your nephew think it might be Russian?'

Scott leant back in his chair. He felt the worst was over. 'One of his school friends was on an exchange visit with a Russian student. When the young lad came to England he brought some photographs with him. He left this one behind apparently.'

'Deliberately?'

'No idea.'

Vassiliyev scratched the top of his head with his thumb, and two fingers extended. Scott could have sworn that he'd seen Peter Falk do the identical thing, while holding a cigar in the same hand. 'Why would a

Russian schoolboy take a photo like this on an exchange visit to England, Mr Mitchell?' Vassiliyev ran his fingers over the picture. 'You see, it's a picture of two men standing on a river bank. Taken in the 70s, possibly. I had a jacket of the same style worn by the tall guy. In fact, I still wear it.' A wry smile appeared. 'I'm not paid as much as Columbo.'

'I've no idea Captain.' Any attempt to explain something that hadn't happened, a fiction, was a recipe for disaster. Shut down the avenue of enquiry at the earliest opportunity. It wasn't wise to have an answer for every question. 'No idea at all.' Scott clenched his fists under the table. His anxiety returned while Vassiliyev studied the picture of the hunters again and filled the room with smoke. He was waiting for the captain to ask him why two Russian men should be displaying an American dog tag.

Vassiliyev looked up.

'Any news on the other photo? At Mosfilmovskaya?'

Scott relaxed his fists. 'No, sorry. I can't help you with that either. You're no doubt aware that my client and her daughter are missing.'

The captain gazed at the ceiling and blew a smoke ring. 'You don't seem too concerned...about their disappearance.'

Scott was more concerned than anybody could imagine. But there was little he could do, especially as Gravchenko had told him to butt out. 'It's in the hands of the police and her husband. I've made my files available. I can't do any more than that.'

Vassiliyev licked his lips.

'Is that all, Captain?'

Vassiliyev squinted. 'Okay, Mr Mitchell, you can go.' The detective got up and opened the door. 'But don't leave the country without telling me.'

Scott couldn't get out of the room quick enough.

'A word of advice.'

'Yes, Captain?'

'Next time you acquire a nephew, remember to acquire a brother or sister first.'

When Scott entered the *Russkiy Izbar*, Rashid was stirring an extra-large cappuccino with a soup spoon in one hand and cramming a chocolate bagel into his mouth with the other. Scott sat opposite him.

'You should try this, chief,' Rashid said, showering Scott with bagel crumbs. 'Gives you energy.'

'I'm not in the mood, Rashid.' He couldn't believe Tom was dead. Perhaps if he hadn't asked Tom to...

'You're right,' Rashid said. He dropped the remains of the bagel onto the plate and wiped his mouth with a screwed up napkin. 'So what's the job?'

'Any more news about Petrov and the hospital?' Scott had neither the experience nor resources, much less any authority, to conduct an investigation into Tom's murder; it was a matter for the Moscow police. And he couldn't check on Ekaterina and Tanya until Ferlito called.

'I could get in the place,' Rashid said.' No problem.' He shook his head. 'But not you.'

'Why not?'

'Because, chief, your face is known from west to east, from Smolensk to Vladivostok. You wouldn't get in if you were disguised as a corpse.'

Rashid was right. The GRU guards must have Scott's mug shot imprinted on the insides of their eyelids. 'So, how would you get in?'

'The shit truck.'

Scott recoiled. 'What's that?'

'Once a week a truck takes away body parts, to the city incinerator on the outer ring road.' Rashid picked up the bagel again and began munching. 'It's diseased shit. Nobody wants to do it. I could easily take the truck in. It goes to the yard at the back of the hospital. The guards won't go near it.' He spoke with his mouth full. 'And while they're shoveling the shit on the truck I can take a smoke...' He winked at Scott. '...and a wander.'

Scott had to be the one to interview Petrov.

'What about face masks? The truck driver must be breathing in all this toxic stuff. Health and Safety.'

'Health and Safety?' Rashid choked on his bagel. 'Russia's only just got corrupt democratic elections.'

'So the driver's got no protection?' Scott asked. 'Hazchem mask or something?'

'Sure he has. An oily rag, tied over his mouth and nose. 'You know.' Rashid beamed. 'Like the Mexican *bandidos*.'

Scott could cover his face until he got to the pick-up point at the back of the building. How he would get into the wards without being recognized was another question. 'Okay, *bandidos* it is,' Scott said.

'Chief?'

'We're going in, *muchacho*.'

Rashid's bemused smile turned into a wide grin.

'Where's Petrov located?' Scott asked.

'Main building, north block, second floor, end of the corridor, last room on the right. But he's got a GRU guard with him, 24/7.'

'Is he awake? Well enough to talk?

'Sometimes awake. Sometimes not.'

Scott stood up. 'When's the next pick-up?'

'I'm not sure. In a couple of days. I'll check it out.'

'Can you get us on the truck?'

'I can do anything, with enough rubles, chief.'

'Rashid, you've just passed your medical exams... *summa cum laude*.'

'Chief?'

'Get two oily rags, two white coats and some of that stuff they smear under their noses at autopsies,' Scott said. 'We have an operation to perform.'

Chapter 30

Day Nine: 1.30pm

Pravda thumped three times in quick succession on the rear door of the surveillance truck and stamped his feet. The truck was parked in the grounds of the Exhibition of National Economic Achievements, near Prospect Mira, from where they were tracking Mitchell. Alexei opened the door and Pravda brushed him aside as he went in.

Vladimir, the tech ops, was sitting in front of a blank computer screen and banging the mouse on the desk top. 'Work, you bastard. Work.'

'Take a break Vladimir,' Pravda said.

'It's okay, Leon, I've just had one, thanks.'

'Now!'

Vladimir jumped up. 'Yes, sir.' He grabbed his coat and hurried out.

Pravda bolted the door behind him.

'What's up?' Alexei asked.

Pravda pulled a faxed copy of a photo of two men on a riverbank from his coat pocket and threw it onto the worktop in front of Alexei. 'Take a look at that.'

'What is it?' Alexei picked it up and studied it.

'Captain Vassiliyev at the homicide department has just sent it to my apartment. He called me. Tom Huxley was murdered yesterday evening, same MO as Sokolov, Karat and Grushchenko...minus the bomb.' Pravda felt a twinge as he mentioned the bomb.

Alexei looked at Pravda and his eyes widened. 'Fu—'

'Vassiliyev wanted to get some background information from Mitchell. Tom met with Mitchell earlier

270

yesterday afternoon, at the IKEA store on Khimki, and—'

'So that's why he was there,' Alexei said. 'We lost his signal in the morning and picked it up in the store's car park at 12.36.'

'And they discussed this photo,' Pravda continued. 'Tom had sent it to Washington—'

'What for?'

'Mitchell spun Vassiliyev some cock and bull story about his nephew collecting dog tags.' Pravda pointed at the metal-like object on the tall man's shirt. 'Which is exactly what this thing here looks like.'

'One of ours, you mean – Soviet? Russian?'

Pravda sucked in air. 'Unfortunately not.'

'So who are these two men?' Alexei asked.

'Get somebody from the identikit team to age their faces,' Pravda said. 'And get the metal object on the shirt enhanced. I want to be as sure as I can, before I commit myself.'

'What about Vassiliyev?' Alexei asked. 'How much does he know?'

'He's an old family friend. He knows when not to ask me any questions.'

Alexei nodded. 'Sorry about Tom. I know that—'

Pravda held up his hand. 'Thanks. My time for grieving will come. Meanwhile, where's Mitchell? With Romanova off the radar, I don't want to lose him as well.'

'He's parked in a side street off Strastnoy Boulevard and is making his way on foot to Pushkin Square. We have an eyeball on him.'

'Get the team there,' Pravda said.

'And?'

'Watch and wait.'

Scott sat alone in a booth by the window of the *Tutti Frutti* lounge in Pushkin Square. It was the quietest place in the restaurant, away from the Japanese DJ's obsession with Freddy Cannon's *Palisades Park*. It was Tom's favorite eatery in Moscow; he'd told Scott that he'd been brought up on 50s rock, thanks to a fanatical uncle. Scott began writing in his pocket notepad drafting a letter of condolence to Tom's two daughters.

A waiter brought his order to the table: a café latte, a blueberry muffin and a glass of water.

A man slid into the booth on the bench opposite him. 'Mind if I sit here?' the man asked. 'I like to watch the world go by.'

Scott looked up and stopped writing. He felt queasy. The man, in his thirties, had ginger hair in tight curls and a face full of freckles; an unusual, though not unique, complexion for a Russian. Two of the adjacent booths also had vacant window seats. 'Can't you sit—'

'Look at your chest,' Ginger said.

Scott obliged, and swallowed hard. A red dot roved around the left side of his upper torso. He'd seen the dot before, in the movies. He clenched his fists and froze.

'He's on the roof across the street.' Ginger looked out of the window.

Scott scanned the buildings; he couldn't see the marksman.

'And if you're thinking of making a run for it when a pedestrian blocks the line of sight, forget it.' Ginger squinted. 'Down below.'

Scott leant back and peered under the table. His eyes met a pistol barrel with an extended silencer inches from his crotch. He sat up. If they, whoever they were, wanted to kill him, the sniper could easily have picked him off on the sidewalk earlier. They wanted something from him. It wasn't the time to show his fear. He leant into Ginger's face. 'Okay, so you can kill me in the blink of an eye. Who are you and what do you want?'

'The list of names.'

Scott gulped.

Ginger's gun hand remained out of sight.

Scott broke the muffin into pieces on his plate. Had Ginger and his sniper friend killed the poor lad from Kiev? 'What list of names?' He ate some of the muffin; determined not to show anxiety.

'We don't have time to play cat and mouse,' Ginger said.

Scott looked at his chest again. The red dot had settled on his heart. Would they kill him without collecting the list? No. The list was more important to them than his life. 'I haven't got it with me.'

'We have transport. Get up. And walk towards the door.'

Ginger turned his head. He was wearing an earpiece.

Scott pocketed his notepad, stood up, threw some ruble notes on the table, and walked to the door, where he took his coat from a peg. He peered again at his chest. The red dot had disappeared. He could feel Ginger's hot breath on his neck. He assumed the gun was hidden in Ginger's pocket, and pointing at one of his kidneys. He hesitated. What would happen if he were to drop to the floor, clutching his chest and screaming? He felt a prod in his back with a hard object. He walked outside, and stopped.

'Keep moving,' Ginger said.

He felt another jab in his back. 'Which way?'

'See that white truck to your right, parked by the street sign?' Ginger asked.

'Yes.'

'Walk over to the rear doors. Take it easy, and don't look back.'

Scott glanced at his chest for the fourth time. The red dot was back in place. The street was crowded with lunchtime office workers and shoppers; he could lose his tail and the red dot with relative ease. But how many innocent bystanders would get shot in the ensuing drama?

'You haven't told me who you are. I'll need your name and address for the receipt.'

'Shut up.'

He felt two sharp prods in the back. He stopped at the rear doors of the truck. 'Now what?'

Ginger stepped up to Scott's side and raised his hand as if to rap on the door, but he hesitated.

Scott watched as Ginger turned and looked skyward, across the street.

Three whip-like cracks resounded across the square.

Scott and Ginger turned to see the pedestrians staring at the rooftops. Scott followed their eye line.

Silence.

Everything turned to slow motion.

A body had fallen from the roof and was floating like a feather towards the ground, arms and legs gently flailing in limbo.

The onlookers appeared to be wading through treacle as they parted.

The blood-soaked body kissed the sidewalk without a sound.

Scott blinked and people's screams pierced the air.

The truck's rear doors crashed open and knocked Scott to his knees.

Groggy, he looked up.

Two people wearing balaclavas hauled Ginger inside the truck and pulled the doors to.

The truck sped away.

Scott rose to his feet.

Two hundred meters down the road, the truck screeched to a halt.

The doors flew open again.

Ginger rolled out onto the road.

The truck sped away.

Ginger didn't move.

Scott stood rooted to the curbside.

His stomach turned somersaults.

His cellphone rang.

The screen was blank.

His hand was shaking.

'Hello, Scott Mitchell speaking,' he said in English. His native tongue gave him a momentary sense of sanity on Moscow's streets.

'Scott, this is Lieutenant-General Pravda.' He also spoke in English. 'It is time for you to come in from the cold.'

Pravda again parked in his favorite spot: the quiet cul-de-sac behind the Hotel Ukraina where he'd met Aunt Olga six days previously. He was fifteen minutes early for his meeting with Mitchell. He'd decided that a meeting in the open, away from GRU headquarters and his *dacha*, would be more likely to put the lawyer at his ease; threats and intimidation wouldn't work.

The Cherokee appeared in Pravda's rear-view mirror and flashed its lights twice. Mitchell parked a few car lengths behind the Moskvitch. Pravda kept his eye on the nearside wing mirror. Mitchell approached and got into Pravda's vehicle.

'Thank you for coming, Scott,' Pravda said. The lawyer was pale, and blinking excessively. 'Are you okay? Would you like some water?' He rummaged under his seat and produced a half-liter bottle. 'I've got—'

'No, I'm fine.'

Pravda swiveled the top half of his body to face Mitchell, full on. 'Now do you understand what danger you and Ekaterina Romanova are in?'

'Who were they?'

'FSB.'

'Why did they have a sniper on me?' Mitchell turned to Pravda. 'They know I don't carry a weapon. And I'm hardly likely to resist arrest.'

'They were independent contractors. The ginger guy

was known to us. A nasty piece of work. Even by FSB standards.'

'What are you saying? You saved my life?'

'Torture, then death,' Pravda said. 'That was his MO'

Mitchell rubbed his eyes. 'I guess I should thank you.' There was no warmth in Mitchell's voice; it was a half-hearted gesture, at best.

'It's not your thanks I want. It's your trust and your cooperation.'

'May I have that water now please?'

Pravda handed the bottle to him.

Mitchell drank the lot in three or four gulps.

'What did they want from you?' Pravda asked.

'The same as you guys.' Mitchell shrugged. 'What were Ekaterina and I doing at Mosfilmovskaya?'

'That's all?'

'Sure.' Mitchell licked his lips and twisted his watchstrap.

He was lying. 'What did you tell them?' Pravda asked.

'I pleaded attorney-client privilege.'

Pravda took a brown envelope from his pocket. It contained the photo of the two men on the riverbank. He was going to show it to Mitchell, to see his reaction.

'Do you know Tom Huxley of *The Washington Post?*' Mitchell asked, suddenly.

It was an unexpected question. 'I know he was murdered yesterday evening.' Pravda smoothed the envelope on his lap. 'He was a friend of mine, a good friend.' He looked at Mitchell. 'Which brings me to—'

'You're guarding a patient in one of your hospitals... His name is Petrov. He's been mumbling in English about being shot down.' Mitchell's speech was rapid and jumpy; it wasn't like him. 'Who is he?'

Pravda tensed his legs. He was losing control of the situation. 'I've not called this meeting to discuss street rumors.'

'Perhaps not,' Scott said. 'But that's why I accepted your invitation.'

Something had happened. The lawyer was hardening. Pravda opened the envelope and handed the photo to Mitchell. 'Where did you get this?' No more prevarication. 'And before you deny any knowledge of it, Captain Vassiliyev of the homicide department has told me about his interview with you.'

Mitchell glanced at it without expression, turned and looked at Pravda. 'I'm not going to tell you unless you let me interview Petrov.'

Pravda snatched the photo back and put it in the envelope. 'You're full of confidence at the moment, Scott.' The man was delusional. 'But as I've told you before, you're no longer in a court of law. There will be another ginger man. And when he comes, I may not be able to save you again.' Pravda's phone rang. He checked the screen. It was Alexei. He gazed out of the front window as he answered the call. 'Yes?'

'We've heard from Morpheus.'

'Good, I'll get back to you as soon as possible.'

'No Lev, you don't understand. You must come now. Before you discuss anything else with Mitchell.' There was an urgency in Alexei's voice that Pravda had rarely heard before.

'Okay. I'm on my way.' He disconnected and turned to Mitchell.

'Well?' Mitchell asked. 'Do I get my interview?'

'No.' Pravda leant over and opened Mitchell's door. 'You do not.'

Scott got out of the vehicle and watched Pravda drive off. Well, well. So Russian military intelligence was interested in the "A-16" photo. But also, a warning; Vassiliyev and Pravda were in league, somehow. Scott would have to be careful if he were to be interviewed by the homicide captain again. Why hadn't Ferlito called? It was approaching forty-eight hours. He punched Ferlito's number into his cellphone. It kept ringing and didn't default to voicemail. He tried another number.

'American Embassy, Commercial Section,' a woman said. 'How may I help you?'

'I'd like to speak to Frank Ferlito please.'

'Who shall I say is calling him, sir?'

'My name is Scott Mitchell. He knows who I am.'

'Thank you, Mr Mitchell. Please hold.'

'Mr Mitchell?'

It was a man's voice, but not Ferlito's.

'How can I help you, sir?'

'I would like to speak to Frank Ferlito, please.'

'He's on vacation, sir.'

Sure he is, and he's taken Ekaterina and Tanya with him. What did Ferlito say in the *House of Mirrors*, "nobody at the embassy knows what I'm doing here"?

'When will he be back?' Scott asked.

'In five days.'

'Okay. Thanks. I'll catch him later.'

Chapter 31

The moment he turned the key in the front door of his apartment and pushed it open Scott felt somebody's presence. It was dark; the timing device for the hall light must have broken. He halted, leaving the door open behind him. 'Hullo, anybody there?' he shouted in Russian.

'In here, Mitchell.'

'What the...' Scott recognized Gravchenko's deep voice coming from the living room.

The door slammed behind him and the light went on. He spun round. A medium-sized man, less physically intimidating than the finger-slicing thug Gleb, stood in front of the door with a gloved hand on the light switch. He was dressed in black and his short leather jacket was open, to reveal a muscular upper torso. His cropped hair was white; he could have been Al Pacino's personal bodyguard in *Godfather III*.

'I'm waiting, Mitchell,' Gravchenko called out.

Scott hurried into the living room. 'What the fuck's—'

A hand grabbed his neck and threw him into an armchair.

Gravchenko was sitting on the sofa opposite. There was a folded sheet of paper and a white envelope on the cushion beside him.

Scott turned round. The hand belonged to Gleb.

He turned back to his visitor. '*Now* what do you want, Mr Gravchenko?' Scott massaged his neck with his left hand and counted the fingers on his right hand, wondering whether they would still all be there by the end of the evening.

Gravchenko shook a cigarette from a packet that lay on the arm of the sofa. 'There's something I don't understand about you, Mitchell.'

Scott stretched to the table behind him and tipped out the paper clips from a molded clay pot. He handed the empty container to Gravchenko. 'Your cigarette.' Scott couldn't guess what the man was about to say.

Gravchenko balanced the pot on the sofa arm. 'You're not a wheeler-dealer commercial lawyer,' Gravchenko said. 'You don't swim with the sharks in the business world.' He lit his cigarette. 'You're a human rights lawyer. Your job is to care about people. Money isn't your motivation; compassion is.'

Get to the point.

Gravchenko tapped his cigarette on the side of the pot and watched the ash drop into the bowl. 'Yet when your client and her child go missing, you find the time to visit an amusement park.'

Fuck. More surveillance. Ekaterina had been so reticent about her relationship with Gravchenko, that the man could be one of Ferlito's bad guys or a jealous estranged husband – or both. Scott could feel his quandary manifest itself in his facial expression; he was losing color.

'You didn't imagine I was going to let my headstrong wife team up with a Chechen-loving human rights lawyer – a pariah in my country – without watching her back, did you?'

Okay, so not necessarily a bad guy. But Scott still needed to come up with a convincing response.

Gravchenko leant forward and narrowed his eyes. 'So tell me, what were you doing in the *House of Mirrors* – a kid's fun palace, closed for repairs – while half the nation was looking for my wife – *your* client – and my baby daughter?' Gravchenko relaxed back into the sofa and took a long hard drag on his cigarette. 'You have the floor, counselor.'

Shit. Scott had had no time to prepare his defense. He turned and looked at Gleb. The giant was cracking his knuckles. Scott had had to think on his feet before, but that had been in the tranquility of a court room, where the rule of law reigned supreme and he'd never been under any fear of physical harm. He wanted to remind Gravchenko that just two days previously he'd ordered Scott to stay away from his family, but he sensed the oligarch was in no mood for a "smart" riposte.

Gravchenko threw the white envelope at him. 'Maybe this will loosen your tongue. Open it.'

Scott caught it and fumbled with the seal. He took out a photo, and froze. It was a snapshot of his elderly parents in their local supermarket car park in England – time-stamped two days previously. 'Where did you—'

'The *House of Mirrors*, Mitchell.'

Scott looked at the photo again. His body shook. The sound of Gleb's knuckle-cracking increased. 'Okay, I'll tell you.' Sorry Ferlito, sorry GIs, but it's no contest. Scott told him about the meeting with Ferlito, though he left out Ferlito's view that Gravchenko himself might be a threat to Ekaterina's well-being.

'Is this the list?' Gravchenko asked, and handed Scott the piece of paper, unfolded.

Scott scanned it. 'Yes.' He assumed it came from Ekaterina. Scott and Ekaterina had been given it at noon. According to Tolik, she disappeared after 9pm. There was plenty of time to get a copy to her husband.

Gravchenko frowned. 'They're Russian names on the list, not American.'

'It doesn't make sense to me, either,' Scott said. He caressed the photo of his parents. 'Mr Gravchenko, as I said, Ferlito is worried about Ekaterina and Tanya's safety. He knows that we're looking for Ekaterina's father. She doesn't trust the Russian authorities. The car bomb. He's a diplomat. He knows people. He says he can help her.' Scott was talking too quickly. He slowed down. 'It might have something to do with the list. I don't know. Ferlito hasn't told me everything yet. But the main thing is, Ekaterina and Tanya won't come to any harm while they're with Ferlito.'

Gravchenko stubbed out his cigarette in the clay mold and fixed a cold hard stare on Scott. It reminded him of Ginger's roving red dot.

'Look, Mr Gravchenko.' Scott's heart raced as he searched for comforting words. 'Ekaterina asked me to check out Ferlito's story. She was calm. Not in the least bit fearful…' He took a deep breath. 'I'm expecting a call from Ferlito any time now. We're going to meet. And I'm going to collect Ekaterina and Tanya. I—'

'That woman is an idiot!' Gravchenko swept the ashtray onto the floor, spilling the ash on the rug.

Scott flinched.

Gravchenko leant forward. 'Now you listen to me, Mitchell. I know Ferlito. I've worked with him. Ferlito is a psycho, and he's got my daughter!' Gravchenko kicked the ashtray. 'Do you have any idea what you and that woman have done?' His eyes were on fire. 'Do you?!'

Stomach juices tickled the back of Scott's throat. He wasn't naïve, he knew that Gravchenko couldn't have amassed his fortune without silencing those who'd stood in his way. The paradoxical concept of state-sanctioned anarchy was a reality within the Russian business community. Why hadn't Scott heeded Sophie's wise counsel – and returned to the UK?

Gravchenko's cellphone rang. 'You haven't got a clue,' he snarled at Scott. 'Not a fucking clue.'

Scott clenched his fists and pressed his feet firmly onto the floor, to try to stop any visible shaking.

The ringing continued while Gravchenko toyed with a fresh cigarette.

Scott closed his eyes.

Gravchenko answered the phone.

Scott opened his eyes and turned round. Gleb was contorting his face; the smile of a sadist. He heard Gravchenko finish the call, turned and watched him light the cigarette. Gravchenko bent down and picked up the ashtray, leaving the contents scattered on the rug. His violent outburst disappeared as quickly as it had appeared.

'Mr Grav—'

'Shut up,' Gravchenko said. He produced a cellphone from his pocket and gave it to Scott. 'Take this.'

'What's it for?' It looked like any other cellphone.

'You'll call me when Ferlito calls you. Day or night. Immediately. Understand?'

'Yes, but I've got a cellphone.'

'Use this one. Nothing else.'

'Why? What's so special about it?'

'Do you know what the Echelon spy satellite is?'

'I've heard the name, that's all.'

'It's a global surveillance system developed by the National Security Agency in the States.' Gravchenko stubbed out the half-smoked cigarette in the ashtray. 'They eavesdrop on all telecommunications.'

'World-wide?' Scott couldn't see how that was possible. 'The traffic must be enormous; cellphones, e-mails, texts. How do they store it? And who has time to monitor it?' Edward Snowden's recent "Prism" revelations came to mind.

'Super computers, called Echelon Dictionaries. They sort out the wheat from the chaff by looking for key words.'

'Why do they do it? Do they think we're all terrorists?'

Gravchenko smiled for the first time that evening. 'Information is knowledge and knowledge is power. That's all governments need to control us.' He stubbed out his cigarette. 'The beauty of it is, even if the system doesn't work, the people think it does. That's enough for the power elite to manipulate us. We can have as much freedom as we want – as long as the motherfuckers can check how we're using it.'

'So what's all this got to do with Ferlito?' Scott fiddled with his new toy. Super computers? Echelon Dictionaries? Gravchenko may be an oligarch, but that didn't mean he couldn't also be paranoid.

'He'll have your telephones bugged.'

'And not this one?'

'It's encrypted. And registered to a US Supreme Court judge.' Another smile; it lingered longer. 'By the time Ferlito's cock-sucking geeks at the NSA decode it and work out what's going on, it'll be too late.'

An hour after Gravchenko and his goons had left the apartment, Scott was still sitting in the armchair, cradling a bottle of vodka and staring at the picture of his parents. His cellphone rang He fumbled for it in the pocket of his coat, which he'd been wearing since he'd first arrived home and met his uninvited guests. 'Yeh?'

'Scott.' It was Ferlito. 'A piece of friendly advice. Stay away from Gravchenko. Remember, the man's got different priorities to us. He doesn't give a shit about our boys. He has his own agenda.'

Scott sat up with a start. 'Ferlito.' He'd had enough. His parents' well-being was foremost in his mind. 'Please stop these games. When and where are we going to meet?' Doubts were beginning to creep in – but Ekaterina had been so calm and determined on the phone.

'Tomorrow night. 7pm. I've shaken off the enemy. We won't be disturbed,' Ferlito said. 'A few blocks behind the Olympic Stadium. The abandoned multi-story car park… top level. *Ciao*.' Ferlito ended the call.

A paranoid oligarch had told Scott that the eccentric spook he was about to meet was a psychopath.

He kissed his parents' photo.

Chapter 32

Pravda had spent late into the night and, again, early in the morning scrutinizing every dot and comma in the Morpheus file on Ferlito, supplementing the revelations with visits to corroborating websites recommended by Morpheus.

'Do you think Tom Clancy knew Ferlito?' Pravda asked Alexei.

'Lev?'

'If ever there was a "clear and present danger", Frank Ferlito is it,' Pravda said.

Alexei stopped his car 100 meters before the Novoarbatskiy Bridge. 'I could tell that from the summary I read.' He switched off the engine. 'The guy's a law unto himself.' He frowned. 'Why don't we bring him in?'

'I wish we could,' Pravda said. 'But we can't, without disclosing what's in the report, or some of it. And that's the last thing I want to do. Besides, he's got diplomatic immunity...and that's a political issue. Not for us.' Pravda opened the door.

'But—'

'Don't worry,' Pravda said. 'I have other plans.' He got out.

'Are you sure you don't want me to come with you, Lev?'

'I have to be alone,' Pravda said. 'That's the deal.' He slapped his hand on the car roof. 'I'll make my own way back to the surveillance truck.' The Moskvitch had a puncture; Alexei had driven him to the rendezvous. He closed the door and headed for the riverbank. Dark clouds had enveloped the capital, causing a premature switch on of the parliament building's lights. While the country's politicians were toying with the oxymoronic concept of Russian transparency Pravda was reverting to Soviet style subterfuge and opacity as he descended the steps to the slush-covered pathway underneath the bridge.

He was straying into the FSB's territory.

Two tramps were fighting over a cardboard box and a bottle of vodka; their twin shelters against the harsh Russian winters. Pravda didn't want witnesses, inebriated or not. He gave them each a thousand rubles and told them to skedaddle. They did so, after blessing their savior and praising his "Second Coming".

A man appeared from the half-light at one end of the underpass and approached Pravda; he was in no hurry, a silhouette in the shadows. 'Thank you for coming,' Pravda said. It was Major-General Dorogin of the FSB. Pravda had called him in the middle of the night. He hadn't been in contact with the major-general since Dorogin had instructed Colonel Kisletski to release Petrov into Pravda's care. But after reading Morpheus' report Pravda realized the scale of the threat he was facing. Enemies or not, the GRU needed the help of the FSB.

'Here's what you'll need,' Dorogin said. He handed Pravda a flash drive. 'He has the use of an embassy vehicle and personally owns a dark blue Range Rover Sport with opaque windows; the latest model.'

'Does he have a chauffeur?'

'We've never seen him with one,' Dorogin said. 'And he'll only be driving the Rover for the foreseeable future.'

'How do you know?' Pravda asked.

Dorogin checked his watch. 'Because the embassy Mercedes is being stolen from the garage under his apartment block as we speak. It'll be out of the country within three hours.'

Pravda cleared his throat and patted his chest. He waved the flash drive at Dorogin.

'It contains the Rover's registration number,' Dorogin said. 'Plus details of Ferlito's recent movements, and the software needed to pick up the vehicle's transmitter.'

'Thanks. I owe you.'

'You can repay the debt by not letting any harm come to him. We want him alive.'

'I understand,' Pravda said. He didn't like it. It had been too easy; Dorogin's readiness to meet with Pravda and to supply the information with little or no enquiry.

'By the way,' Dorogin said. 'Ferlito has met with Kisletski in Moscow on two occasions in the last six months.'

Pravda held his breath and counted to ten. 'What were the meetings about?' he said, careful not to betray his fears.

Dorogin shrugged. 'We only had them on visual.' The FSB officer turned and walked back along the pathway into the fading light.

Pravda looked at the flash drive in his hand. Ferlito equals Kisletski equals Arzamas equals Petrov and Danilov.

His left leg seized with cramp from his thigh to the tips of his toes.

'Who's the backup?' Scott looked around the *Bierstübe* in the Renaissance Penta Hotel, cupping a glass of lager in both hands. 'I hope he can shoot straight.' Scott had spent his career fighting the idea of summary executions, extra-judicial killings, but after the encounter with Ginger he felt the need to take his own extra-judicial measures. Besides, he also had Ekaterina and Tanya to protect. The FSB could pounce again at any time. Ferlito may well think he had shaken off the enemy, but the FSB had enormous resources.

'A sniper from Grozny, chief.' Rashid sucked in a seemingly endless strand of spaghetti. 'He's taken out more Ferlitos than you've had *blinnies*.'

Scott took a swig of beer and plunked the glass on the table. 'No, Rashid, as I've said before, Ferlito's not the problem. He's the good guy. No, it's the FSB. Jesus, they've already threatened to blow my balls off if I don't give them the list. I don't want them picking us off, like targets at a fairground shooting gallery.'

'Sure,' Rashid said, stuffing his mouth with a slice of garlic bread. 'The FSB. That's what I meant.'

Scott had reconnoitered the abandoned multi-story car park earlier in the day. The top level was exposed to the world; the only structure for an assassin to hide behind was a small brick building in the center which accessed the stairs to the lower levels. A sniper, with the benefit of night vision equipment and positioned on the roof of the high rise apartment on the north face, could monitor what was going on in the dark without difficulty. However, the lower levels were enclosed, with alcoves, buttresses and supporting pillars.

'Right,' Scott said. 'Finish your meal and get over to the car park. Search it thoroughly and tell your man that he's only there as an observer, unless our lives appear to be in danger...and that includes Ferlito's.'

'Sure, chief.' Rashid used a bread slice to wipe the plate clean of spaghetti sauce, ate it and stood up. 'No problem.'

'I mean it, Rashid. There's going to be a four-year-old child around. I don't want her to see any more bad stuff than is absolutely necessary.' He poked a finger at the gofer. 'No Rambo heroics. Understood?'

'Absolutely.' Rashid headed for the exit. 'Absolutely.'

'Rashid!'

Rashid turned round. 'What?'

'Aren't you forgetting something?'

Rashid spread his arms, palms upwards. 'Chief?'

'I'll need the list.' It was the copy that Scott had given to Rashid at the Hotel National, so Scott wouldn't be caught with it by Tax Inspector Chichikov.

'Ah.' Rashid gave it to Scott and headed for the exit again, muttering, 'No Rambo heroics, absolutely definitely no Rambo heroics.'

Scott tapped his fingers on the table.

'Let me guess. It's either Beethoven's *Fifth* or Meat Loaf's *Bat out of Hell*.'

Scott looked round.

'Sophie! What are you doing here?'

'Watching my client playing air piano.'

They lightly touched lips.

She pulled up a chair. 'So this is how you spend your afternoons, giving piano recitals for the deaf.'

'It's a bit more complicated than that,' Scott said.

'Explain yourself, counselor.'

Scott stopped tapping. He owed it to Sophie to tell her what was going on. She'd been with him all the way. He summarized the latest events. 'And I'm meeting Ferlito in a couple of hours to give him the list. He'll be bringing Ekaterina and Tanya. We're going to discuss how best to continue to keep them safe from—'

She raised her eyebrows. 'Let's get this straight. You give the list to Ferlito and Ekaterina returns to her homicidal husband. Ha, ha. Are you fucking cuckoo?' She began punching numbers into her cellphone. 'You need cavalry support.'

Scott snatched the phone from her. 'We've been through this before, Sophie. Gravchenko is not the danger.' He felt for the wallet in his jacket pocket. It contained the photo of his parents in the supermarket car park. 'Besides, now that Gravchenko has the list, he's got no reason to exert pressure on her.'

Sophie nodded. 'Okay.' She cocked her head sideways

and widened her eyes. 'But do you realize what's going to happen now?'

'What do you mean?'

'Scott, my oh so naïve counselor, no matter how you express it, in Gravchenko's eyes, Ferlito's care package for the man's wife and child amounts to kidnapping. And what do you think oligarchs do when their nearest and dearest have been kidnapped? Send the perp a begging letter?' She raised her eyebrows, as if expecting a reply.

Scott touched his pocket again. Gravchenko was capable of anything.

'So you'd better hope that the oligarch gets to Ferlito soon, because when Ferlito gets that list, he'll want to cover his tracks,' Sophie said. 'He's going to put a bullet through your head, and probably your client's – he might just let the kid live.'

This was nonsense. Ferlito hadn't kidnapped Ekaterina. She will confirm that to her husband. 'Sophie, I love you and respect your gut feelings...sometimes, but you can't go through life mistrusting everybody in power...not to the extent you do, anyway.' She'd gone too far this time. If she only knew. It wasn't Ferlito he feared, but another Ginger. However, if he told her about the *Tutti Frutti* incident, she would freak out even more.

Sophie sighed and stared at him with a disbelieving look.

'You've got it all wrong,' Scott said. 'You really have. Nothing bad is going to happen. Look, I'm well aware of the risks. Okay? I've read enough thrillers and seen enough movies to know how meetings in empty car parks work out.' He tapped her arm. 'I know you want to help. But there's no need for your cavalry support. Not this time.' He pulled back. 'I've done my research. Ferlito's story stacks up. And I want to help those GIs. No, it's not Ferlito who's the danger. It's Pravda...and God knows who else in Russia.'

'Scott, Listen to me, you arrogant dumb fuck. I've told you. You're playing with the big boys, and not in a courtroom. You're way out of their league. If Ferlito doesn't hit you, then somebody else will.'

'I've said no, Sophie. And no means no.'

'But—'

'No.'

Sophie rolled her eyes. 'Okay, you won't listen to reason, so ask yourself the following questions. Ferlito says that your list of names is a list of American GIs. How does he know that? And, anyway, how *can* they be? They're Russian names.'

'It doesn't matter what he knows or thinks,' Scott said. He was still trying to work out why the names were Russian and what Ferlito would say when he found out. 'All that matters is that we get the document to the right people in the US and to relieve any possible future pressure by the Russian authorities, on Ekaterina.'

Sophie cupped her hands around Scott's cheeks. 'Scott baby, you can walk away from all this shit. You know that, don't you? What's the use of a dead hero? Who's gonna look after your other clients and their human rights problems? Eh? With you gone, Putin's won. Don't you see that?'

'Huh, a few days ago you were telling me to return to London to advise on city zoning laws. Now you want me to stay in Moscow and look after my other clients. I don't understand you.' He watched as her eyes began to moisten. 'Sophie, do you know something about Ferlito that you haven't told me?'

She shook her head and stroked his lips with her thumbs. 'No baby, nothing. I promise. I just know those government shits; that's all. And I don't want to have to say "I told you so" at your funeral.'

Pravda and Alexei stood in the surveillance truck,

studying three separate computer screens. The first and second displayed a street map of the entire city within the outer ring road. The third showed the forensically-aged face of the smaller man in the photo that Tom Huxley had sent to Washington for Mitchell. Pravda also held a print-out of the forensic report on the metal object in his hand. It confirmed his suspicions.

A red dot blipped on the first screen, showing that Mitchell's Cherokee was still in the hotel car park. Pravda looked at the pulsating green and white dots on the second screen: green for Ferlito, white for Yelena. She was on her motorbike; dressed as a non-descript city courier, but armed to the hilt. She'd been dispatched to track Ferlito as soon as Alexei had installed the FSB flash drive. Pravda had insisted on using a pristine processing unit; he couldn't risk the FSB having included a virus with their software which would run amok in the GRU databases.

'Where's Yakob?' Alexei asked.

'He should be with the Cherokee.'

'Where's Ferlito going?' Alexei asked. 'Olympic Stadium? Penta?'

'Lev, all hell's broke loose.' It was Yelena on radio contact.

Pravda and Alexei could hear shouting and shooting in the background.

'Shrek's vehicle's being attacked.' This was the code for Ferlito.

The noise of the shots intensified.

'A truck and what looks like an army personnel carrier,' Yelena continued.

The sound of shattering glass carried across the airwaves.

'Seven, eight guys. They're smashing Shrek's windows. They—'

There was a loud explosion followed by more shouting.

'Shall I go in?' Yelena asked. 'Or call back up?'

Pravda's instinct was for her to remain undercover, for the moment. It was a simple case of logistics. There was no way he could get enough of his team to the scene in under five minutes. Yelena may have been able to neutralize three, four at the most, but not all of them. He didn't want to chance her getting shot. It wasn't a battlefield, where his soldiers were willing to accept the risks. If it was a choice between a member of his team or Ferlito being killed on the streets of Moscow, there was no contest. 'Not ye—'

'Wait! Wait!' Yelena said. 'They've got the rear doors open. Somebody's handing out a...a child. The men have taken the kid. Somebody...a woman. Yes it's a woman. She's getting out. I can't see who it...I can't... Another vehicle's arrived...a limousine. It's...Christ! I think it's Grav...Yes it's definitely Gravchenko's Lincoln. His goon, Gleb. He's got out and is helping the wom... it's Romanova...Romanova and Tanya...Gleb's guiding them into the limousine. Shrek is running away.'

'What the hell is Ferlito doing with Romanova and her child?' Pravda said to Alexei. The FSB tracking software wasn't so sophisticated that it could have detected how many people had got into Ferlito's vehicle when it had started its journey that afternoon.

Alexei raised his eyebrows and shrugged.

'And what is Gravchenko doing...? Unless.'

'What?' Alexei asked.

'According to Morpheus,' Pravda said. 'Some lawyers in the US Justice Department are convinced that Ferlito pulled strings...' Pravda hesitated. 'Or maybe destroyed evidence. To get Gravchenko off the indictments on that US time share scam five years ago.'

'And?' Alexei said.

'Rumor has it that our plutocratic comrade only paid half the promised fee.'

293

'So Ferlito kidnaps the wife and daughter for the other half?' Alexei said.

'It's a possibility.'

'But how did Gravchenko know that Ferlito had his wife and child?' Alexei asked. 'We didn't.'

Pravda tapped the computer which housed Major-General Dorogin's flash drive. 'Oligarchs pay well for their information.'

'Which means the FSB knows more about Ferlito than we thought,' Alexei said.

'It seems so.' Pravda spoke into the radio mike. 'Yelena, where is Shrek now?'

'He's disappeared into an apartment complex.'

Pravda was relieved. A dead diplomat was no good to him. 'Right, go to the house.' The code for the Renaissance Penta Hotel. 'Join Yakob and wait for further instructions.' He ended the call.

Pravda was concerned that Ferlito had been attacked a few minutes away from the Penta Hotel – and Mitchell. This was no coincidence. He looked again at the second screen. Ferlito's green blip remained stationary; the Range Rover had probably been reduced to a pile of scrap metal by Gravchenko's demolition squad. Yelena was heading for the Penta. He tapped the age-enhanced image on the third screen with the knuckle of his index finger. He could be wrong about the time share scam dispute. Pravda couldn't yet discount the possibility, no matter how implausible, that Romanova was acting as Gravchenko's proxy at the apartment on Mosfilmovskaya, Ferlito had found out and was angry for some reason.

'Do you reckon Mitchell knows anything about all this?' Alexei asked.

'I wish I could be certain what Mitchell does or does not know.' Pravda sucked in air. 'And particularly, why he wants to talk to Petrov.' He reread the forensic report on the metal object; it was an American dog tag. He looked again at the image of the smaller man on the third screen. It could well be the person he thought it was, but where had the photo been taken?

Scott drove the Cherokee up the ramp to the top level of the car park at 6.50pm. It had stopped snowing and much of the concrete floor space was dry, with the occasional sheets of ice. He was surprised to see a battered car parked in front of the stairwell access which led down to the lower floors. The vehicle hadn't been there earlier that day when he'd inspected the area. He parked his vehicle in the center, switched off the engine and gazed out over the capital. It was dark but the cloudless night sky and city lights helped provide visibility. He had brought Gravchenko's encrypted cellphone – just in case. His own cell rang. He checked the screen. It was Tolik. What a time to call him. 'Tolik, I—'

'Scott, where are you?' It was Ekaterina. Her tone was rushed; her voice panicky.

'Ekaterina? I'm here…I'm at the car park, waiting for you and Ferlito. I've—'

'Get out of there fast!' she said. 'Don't meet with Ferlito. He's going to kill you after you give him the list.'

Scott looked at his phone. 'Kill me? But—'

'Don't question me.' Her voice was commanding. 'Get out! Now! I know about Petrov's hospital. I'm going there.'

'Ekater—' Too late, she'd disconnected. Ekaterina had seen Petrov's name on the list. Tolik must have had told her about the hospital rumors. But what happened with Ferlito?

He switched on the ignition and began to accelerate when something caught his eye. The door of the battered vehicle flew open and a man got out, dragging a smaller man behind him. The smaller man's hands were bound behind his back and he was gagged. 'What the...' The taller man pushed the smaller man to his knees, grabbed a can from inside the vehicle and began emptying the can's liquid contents over the smaller man, and on the floor in a circle around him. 'Fucking hell!' Scott said. The man with the can was Ferlito, his captive was Rashid.

Scott jumped out of the Cherokee. 'Ferlito! Ferlito!' He scanned the high rise apartment, looking for Rashid's sniper.

The attaché lit a cigarette and held it over the trail of liquid.

Gasoline!

'Your backup's had an unfortunate encounter with an oxygen deficiency, Scott,' Ferlito said. 'Still, no harm done. I've replaced him with one of mine.' Ferlito waved the cigarette around. 'It was in my business plan. You gotta watch more than a few Bond movies if you wanna invest with the big boys.'

Scott scanned the high rise again, in the vain hope that he wasn't having hallucinations. It didn't make sense. Ferlito was still wise-cracking but his face was different, colder. This was a side of Ferlito that Scott hadn't seen before.

'You got ten seconds,' Ferlito said. 'Give me the list... one...two...three.'

Christ, the man really was going to kill Rashid. 'Stop! Stop!' Scott screamed. 'Throw the cigarette away! Here...' He took an envelope from his pocket. 'Look! Here! Here it is. Look!'

A shot sounded.

'Aaaaaagh!' Ferlito dropped the cigarette and fell to the floor, clutching his kneecap.

The circle of gasoline flared up.

Scott threw himself through the ring of flames and hauled Rashid up into his arms. He jumped back through the flames and rolled over and over on the floor with the gofer, trying to extinguish the fire that engulfed them.

It went dark. Somebody had thrown a coat or blanket

over them and was beating it. Scott choked on the smoke. The heat penetrated his pores.

The flames were extinguished and Scott pulled the cover off. A woman carrying a rifle was standing over him and Rashid. Scott blinked twice and stared at her chest. A red dot roved around her upper torso. 'Hit the ground! Quick!'

Two further shots sounded.

The woman tumbled backwards and fell to the floor.

Scott lay on top of Rashid, who was mumbling beneath his gag.

A deathly hush.

Scott lifted his head.

Ferlito was gone.

Rashid was writhing and groaning.

Scott eased himself up, untied Rashid and released his gag.

'Aaagh!' the gofer shrieked. 'I'm burning to death!'

Scott examined him. 'No you're not, a few blisters on your face and some redness around your neck. That's all. Stop exaggerating.'

'You're a lawyer!' Rashid screamed. 'Not a fucking doctor! I know when I'm dying!'

Scott ignored the tantrum. 'Get cover by the Cherokee and brush yourself down.' The shooting had stopped, but for how long? 'I'll get you to hospital.'

Scott knelt over the woman. There were two bullet holes in her clothing, but no signs of blood, and she had a pulse. He opened her leather jacket. She was wearing a Kevlar vest.

The sound of approaching sirens broke the silence.

Four speeding vehicles emerged from the ramp and screeched to a halt around Scott and the woman. All the doors seemed to open at once, as eight, nine or ten men poured out. They were in GRU uniforms. Three of them rushed to the woman and helped her to her feet. The other men spread out and searched the area.

Shots again rang out from the high rise, the bullets ricocheting off the battered car.

Scott hit the ground while the GRU men returned the fire. He kept thumping the ice cold stone floor with a clenched fist. How could he have been so wrong about Ferlito?

A fifth vehicle, a black limousine, appeared at the entrance to the ramp. The rear passenger window slid down. 'Scott.'

It was Pravda.

Rashid appeared from behind the Cherokee as one of the GRU men approached. 'We'll take this little one to hospital and check out those burns,' the soldier said. He grabbed Rashid's arm. The man was a giant. Rashid pulled back. 'Chief?' His face contorted.

Scott understood how Rashid must have felt; the Chechen's sworn enemy, towering over him, and ready to drag him away. 'It's okay. How are you going to eat with those blisters on your lips?' Scott put his hand on Rashid's shoulder. 'You need treatment.'

Rashid gently ran his fingers around his mouth. 'Ouch.'

'Go on,' Scott said. 'They'll patch you up. I'll be along later.'

Rashid hobbled away with his chaperone, muttering incoherently.

Scott walked towards the limousine. A rear door opened. Scott accepted General Pravda's invitation and crashed onto the seat. His head was spinning as he tried to rationalize what had happened.

'Drink?' Pravda held an open bottle of vodka and a glass in front of him.

Scott ignored the glass and grabbed the bottle. He took a large swig, hesitated, and took another, larger, mouthful. He wanted to flush the gasoline fumes, the flames and, most of all, his complete misjudgment of Ferlito, out of his system. He could no longer tell fact from fiction.

'What are you doing here with Ferlito?' Pravda asked.

Scott's senses returned. Ferlito had a secret agenda – he was a bad guy, but that didn't make Pravda a good guy. 'Who was that woman?' Scott would answer the question, but not yet.

'Yelena – Major Yelena Mikhailovna Grigoryeva.'

'I didn't get to thank her.' Scott was playing for time.

'Later,' Pravda said. 'Would you answer my question now, please?'

Scott returned the bottle to the general. Twice the GRU had saved his life. He must owe Pravda something. He put his hand in his pocket. 'He wanted this...' Scott stopped. The envelope wasn't there. He flashed back.

He's running towards the ring of fire to rescue Rashid, with the envelope in his hand. He drops the envelope the moment before he jumps into the circle. He searched his mind. He's dragging Rashid to safety through the flames. The envelope has disappeared.

'What?' Pravda said.

'I thought I still had it,' Scott said. 'The envelope. I must have dropped it by the fire.'

'Sergei,' Pravda said to his driver. 'Go over to the scene and look for an envelope lying on the ground.' Sergei got out and hurried to the spot.

'What's in the envelope?' Pravda asked.

'A list of names, Russians.'

Scott watched as Pravda squinted at Sergei and his men, scouring the ground for the envelope; Pravda remained phlegmatic and there was no sign that the list of Russian names meant anything special to him. 'Do you know who those people on the list are?' He'd heard Ferlito's version; it was time to hear Pravda's case.

'How can I answer that? I've no idea what names are on it.'

It was a dumb question for a lawyer. 'It contains ten Russian names: family name, first name and patronymic. They're each followed by a single number in brackets and a sequence of numbers followed by the English letter "N".' Let Pravda confirm they're latitudes. 'The names Sokolov and Petrov are on the list.' He thought he saw the beginnings of a frown from Pravda at the mention of the two names, but if he had, it quickly disappeared. 'You have shown to me that you have a connection to both of these people.' That was an exaggeration; he couldn't be sure it was the same Petrov.

Sergei returned empty handed.

'Drive,' Pravda said to him. 'To the hospital.'

'No need, thanks,' Scott said. 'I've no physical injuries.'

'It's not you I'm worried about,' Pravda said.

Pravda's left thigh was burning with pins and needles. 'Did Ferlito tell you why he wanted the list?' He must have done. Mitchell wasn't the type to surrender it without questions. It was a risk to let the human rights lawyer anywhere near Petrov, but Pravda had no time to do anything else and he preferred to have Mitchell at his side, than out of sight.

'I'm still waiting to hear your version,' Mitchell said. The lawyer's facial expression was uncompromising.

'How much do you know about Ferlito's background?' Pravda asked.

'He's a commercial attaché, so he says. And he's interested in the list. Apart from that…nothing.'

I'm not so sure, Mr Human Rights lawyer. I think you know more about him than you're saying, and about the list. Pravda had to find out how it got into the lawyer's possession. 'Are you ready to tell me what Ekaterina Romanova was doing at the apartment?'

'No, not without my client's permission...'

Pravda couldn't wait until Mitchell had discussed the matter with his client.

'...And I don't know when I'm going to see her again,' Mitchell said.

To paraphrase Uncle Nikolai, it was time to expose more of the genie above the parapet. 'Sit back, Scott. I'm going to tell you a story.'

'I'm all ears.'

'Frank Ferlito ran the *Phoenix Program* during the Vietnam War.'

'What was that?'

'His task was to neutralize the enemy and to track down captured American GIs who had special knowledge of American military equipment and to try to free them before they could be interrogated by the Vietcong.' He scanned Mitchell's face for reactions. None. 'However, Ferlito and a few of his cohorts were more patriotic.'

'In what way?'

'If he couldn't free them, he killed them.'

Mitchell jolted. 'He murdered his own men?'

'Yes.' Morpheus was never wrong.

Mitchell frowned. 'Let's get this straight, General Pravda; you're saying the American government deliberately sanctioned the murder of its own men, prisoners of war, by its own men, to stop them from revealing military secrets to the enemy?'

'I'm saying that Frank Ferlito deliberately murdered his own soldiers for that purpose. I have no evidence that the American government knew anything about it.' Pravda had no opinion on whether they did or did not; that was for the politicians to argue over. 'But, I expect you to believe that Ferlito recently murdered Yuri Vladimirovich Sokolov and...' He hesitated. He didn't have to mention Karat and Grushchenko.

'And, what?'

'…And his name, so you say, is on your list.'

'Captain Vassiliyev of the homicide department told me that Tom Huxley was killed with a single, very powerful, bullet through the forehead.' Mitchell said. 'It blew his brains out. I'm no forensics expert but wasn't that how Sokolov was killed?'

'Yes,' Pravda said.

'So it's conceivable that Ferlito also killed Tom?'

'Conceivable, yes. But we need a motive.' Huxley's remit from Mitchell was to check out the photo, but Pravda couldn't connect Ferlito to the photo.

Mitchell turned and gazed out of the window.

'Perhaps Tom Huxley was onto something,' Pravda continued. He wanted Mitchell to confirm Captain Vassiliyev's story about the metal object possibly being a US dog tag. 'What's more, if Ferlito is still alive, I am certain he will try to murder Petrov.' The mention of the threat to Petrov, too, might stir Mitchell into being more forthcoming.

Mitchell turned back. 'But what's all this *Phoenix Program* stuff and the murders of Sokolov and Tom got to do with a list of Russian names?'

The answer to Mitchell's question wasn't in the Morpheus Report. So far as Pravda was aware, only Uncle Nikolai, Alexei and himself knew why Sokolov's name was on the list, and its connection to the missing GIs. He had to tell Mitchell; eventually the lawyer would find out. 'If it's the list I believe it is, they are, were, American GIs with sensitive technological information who were passed on to us by the North Vietnamese, during and after the war.' Again, he looked for any sign in Mitchell's body language that Ferlito might have told him the story. There was none. 'They are the names my country gave to them when we resettled them here.'

Mitchell's eyes widened. 'Resettled? That's an interesting description of enforced captivity.' Mitchell scoffed. 'Like the Nazi resettlement of the Jews in Auschwitz and Dachau?'

'No! Not like Auschwitz and Dachau!' Pravda leapt into the lawyer's face and jabbed his index finger into the man's chest. 'Do not ever compare the Russians to the Nazis. We lost twenty million of our people in the Great Patriotic War, fighting to rid the planet of the scourge of fascism, for the benefit of the world.' He retracted his finger but let it hover a centimeter from Mitchell's chest. 'Do not ever say that again.'

Mitchell recoiled. 'I'm sorry, General. Really sorry. I didn't mean to...It was a stupid thing to say.'

Pravda removed his hand and relaxed his body. 'Okay.' He wasn't proud of his outburst. 'Okay.'

'What do the latitudes mean?' Mitchell asked. 'They are latitudes aren't they?'

'Yes. When matched with the longitudes they are the coordinates in Asia where the men were shot down.'

Mitchell's eyes were flickering. The mention of the word "longitudes" must have triggered something. 'And where is this list of longitudes?'

Pravda shook his head. Enough was enough.

'Well, at least tell me what the single digit number in brackets on my list means,' Mitchell said. 'It's between the names and the latitudes.'

Pravda saw no point in withholding that piece of information. Mitchell knew what the list meant and that there was a list of longitudes. 'It's a cross-reference with the names on the list of longitudes. For example, the given Russian name at number six on the latitude list matches the real American name with the same number on the longitude list.'

'Why is the latitude and longitude information so important to you?'

'One day we may have to convince the United States that these men were captured and brought to the

Soviet Union. I believe that some people in the United States…' According to Morpheus. '…The military, Vets' associations, investigators etc, call them the "Moscow Bounds". The Pentagon has records of where they were shot down – the latitudes and longitudes. It's our insurance policy. It's all part of the game. International politics.'

'Insurance! Game! Using the people as chess pieces, pawns to be precise.' Mitchell thumped his thigh with his fist. 'What's the fucking matter with you lot?'

Pravda wasn't offended at the outburst. It was to be expected from a human rights lawyer.

'But I don't get it.' Mitchell shook his head. 'Why continue with the murders today? The war was decades ago. Any sensitive information they had must be useless today. So what's Ferlito's motive?'

'I can think of only two reasons,' Pravda said. 'Either Ferlito is on a perverted mission of his own or the American government wants to close the history books, before the general public discovers the truth, beyond reasonable doubt, as you lawyers say.'

'Are you saying that the US government could today be sanctioning Ferlito's murderous activities?'

'I'm an intelligence officer. It's a possibility, no more than that. But I can't afford to discard the idea at the moment.' It wouldn't surprise Pravda if the US government were sanctioning, or turning a blind eye to, Ferlito's killings. Liberal democratic governments were not exempt from such acts, despite their protests to the contrary. But he wouldn't sit in judgment, he wasn't a court of law, or morals. He only wanted to persuade Mitchell that there were always two sides to a story, and sometimes more. Something lawyers were supposed to have learnt in their training.

'A possibility, perhaps,' Mitchell said. 'But it seems that the Russians also want to keep their part in this whole sordid affair under wraps...well, you do anyway.'

Time was pressing. 'Where is Ekaterina Romanova?' Pravda rubbed his leg.

'Who of these names on the list are still alive today, apart from Petrov?' Mitchell asked.

No more questions. 'Where is Ms Romanova?' Pravda asked. 'I need to speak with her.' He genuinely feared for her safety, with Ferlito loose in the city. At the same time, she was an unknown factor in the whole affair. 'Did Ferlito say where she was?'

'She and Tanya are okay.'

Pravda, of course, knew this much. 'How do you know?'

'She called me, just before the fireworks.' Mitchell picked at his watch strap.

The lawyer was hiding something.

Pravda made a call.

Scott was only half-listening to Pravda's phone conversation.

'Come on, come on, answer the phone...Gregor, how is he...? Good...I'm not sure, twenty minutes; depends on the traffic...Keep the door locked. Let no one in, except Dr Glasunov...No, especially not the nurse, there have been too many leaks...Okay.' Pravda disconnected.

Scott tried to reconcile Ekaterina's search for her father with Pravda's latest revelations; in particular, his confirmation that Petrov was a captured American GI from the Vietnam War. If Ferlito was on a crazy mission to kill any surviving GIs, Scott could understand Pravda's wariness about anybody who was trying to gain access to Petrov. But how did Ekaterina's father fit into the story? 'Was that Petrov's hospital?' Scott asked.

Pravda leant forward to Sergei. 'Put the sirens on.'

Sergei obliged and sped into the outer lane.

Pravda made another call. 'Anything...? Okay...Keep

a look out for a woman. Russian. Early thirties, looks younger. Expensively-dressed. Confident air...Detain her only. I don't want her injured in any way.' The call ended.

'You're talking about Ekaterina?' Scott asked. 'What if some trigger-happy GRU soldier mistook her actions?'

'So your client *is* on her way to the hospital?' Pravda asked.

'I didn't say that.'

'You didn't have to,' Pravda said. 'Where did you get the list from?'

Scott looked out at the traffic, while considering the pros and cons of giving Pravda the information.

'I'm not the threat,' Pravda said. 'Ferlito's still out there somewhere. The list has got Petrov's name on it.' He shook his leg. 'Ferlito must be aware of the Petrov rumors. Everybody else in the city seems to be.'

Indeed. And doubtless Gravchenko was now gunning for Ferlito. Scott could see how Ekaterina could be caught up in any crossfire between Petrov's protectors, the spook and the oligarch. 'But Ferlito took a bullet from your Major Yelena,' Scott said. 'In the kneecap, I think. He must have difficulty walking.'

'Only death will stop Frank Ferlito from completing his mission.' Pravda made a third call. 'Watch out for Ferlito...You have his description. He's wounded, probably limping, but armed. Only kill in self-defense. I want him alive. Tell Gregor and the rest.' Pravda rang off.

'What about granting me access to Petrov...under guard if you wish?' Ekaterina might succeed in getting into his ward, but Scott doubted she would be able to achieve much else before being detained and thrown out.

'Look,' Pravda said. 'I need more information on the list of names. Where did you get it?'

'Okay.' Scott sighed. Without Pravda's help, he was never going to get to interview the man. 'We got the list from a neighbor at the apartment on Mosfilmovskaya.'

'What neighbor?'

'A young man. He's dead; murdered by...I don't know who.' Scott assumed Pravda knew the story of Dmitry Yatsenko's killing. 'He was looking after his sick mother. She was given the list for safe keeping years ago.'

'Who gave her the list?'

'The young man said it was the owner of the apartment. Where your Mr Sokolov was murdered. He was the owner, wasn't he?'

'And so we come to the key questions,' Pravda said. 'What has your client retained you to do for her? And what were you doing in the apartment?'

The apartment was a direct link to the American GIs, with Sokolov's name also on the list. Pravda wasn't set on killing Ekaterina. And there was no reason, yet, to believe that Pravda would take any steps to prevent her from finding her father; assuming he could find out where her father was. It was the list that was occupying the General's mind, not Ekaterina's father. It was time to explain. Ekaterina's life could be in danger and it would be better to have the GRU on her side, than against her. 'Before I tell you', Scott said. 'Knowing for sure who owned the apartment may be helpful to my client.'

'It belonged to Sokolov,' Pravda said without hesitation.

'She's asked me to help her find her father.'

Pravda raised his eyebrows. His mask was slipping. He seemed confused. 'But why were you at Sokolov's apartment?'

'Ekaterina's mother died a few weeks ago,' Scott said. 'She left a letter telling Ekaterina that her father, who Ekaterina believed had died before she was born, had been taken by the KGB decades ago and she'd never heard from him again. Her mother also left Ekaterina an anonymous note she'd received a few weeks before her death, saying that her father was being kept in captivity without a trial and if she wanted to know more she should go to the apartment on Mosfilmovskaya.'

'And you believe her?'

What sort of question was that? 'I have copies of both the letter and the note,' Scott said.

'And where are the originals?'

'In a safe place.'

Pravda shook his head and sighed. It was obvious that he didn't believe Ekaterina's story. 'Does the note mention Sokolov by name?'

'No.'

Pravda received a call.

'Yes? What!?' He banged the back of Sergei's seat. 'Put your foot down! The hospital's on fire!'

Chapter 33

Day Ten: 8.35pm

As Sergei swung the limousine into the approach road Pravda could hear the piercing fire alarm coming from the hospital complex. They roared past the raised sentry barrier and screeched to a halt at the entrance to the north block, where the medical staff and their patients were assembling. All three men jumped out of the limousine, led by Pravda. 'Where's the fire?' Pravda said to a white-coated medic on the front steps. There was no sign of smoke, much less a fire or the emergency services.

'False alarm, sir. I've come to get them all back in.'

'Ferlito!' It was his doing. Pravda drew his gun and turned to Sergei. 'Get the others and seal all exits.'

'I'm on it.' Sergei began making calls on his cellphone.

Pravda dashed into the building and headed for the stairs; he wasn't going to hang around for the elevator. An unarmed Mitchell was close behind him and Ferlito was dangerous, but Pravda didn't have time to debate health and safety issues with the headstrong lawyer. 'Stick close to me...and do as I say, without question.'

'Would I do otherwise?'

The pair ran up the stairs to the second floor.

Fyodor Glasunov and Gregor were outside Petrov's room. Gregor was pushing at the door, it wouldn't open.

'What's going on? Pravda demanded. 'Where's Ferlito?'

'Romanova's in there with Petrov,' Gregor said. 'She's jammed the door.'

'What the...' Pravda said.

Gregor gave the door a powerful kick. 'Done it!'

The door shattered and Pravda burst in, followed by Gregor, Mitchell and Fyodor. They stumbled over a splintered chair. Petrov was sitting up in bed, with a puzzled look. Romanova, in a nurse's uniform, was at his side rifling in her handbag.

Looking for a weapon?

Pravda drew his pistol and pointed it at Romanova. 'Move away from the bed Ms Romanova. I will shoot if I have to. Move away.' If she produced a gun he would shoot to maim, not to kill.

Romanova didn't step back, but half raised her hands as if to surrender. She held on to her bag.

Pravda could see out of the corner of his eye that Gregor was also raising his gun. 'No, Gregor! No!' Pravda had Romanova covered, he could handle it. He didn't want any unnecessary shooting. Petrov already had one too many bullets sitting in his brain.

Mitchell yanked Gregor's arm upwards.

A loud bang, and a bullet hit the ceiling.

Gregor smashed his elbow into Mitchell's face.

Romanova's eyes widened, presumably with surprise, and she dropped her handbag to the floor.

Gregor kicked it under the bed.

Petrov appeared calm. What had Romanova been saying to him?

Fyodor checked Petrov's pulse.

Mitchell's nose gushed with blood. The lawyer was wiping his wound with a handkerchief. 'Are you alright, Scott?' Romanova asked. Mitchell managed a smile and nodded.

'Here, let me look at that,' Fyodor said. Mitchell tilted his head backwards. 'Can you move your nose?' Fyodor asked. 'It's lacerated and swelling.'

Mitchell twitched his nose. 'Yes, but it hurts.'

'Open your mouth.' Mitchell did so. Fyodor looked

inside. 'Teeth seem okay. Bloody gums, but no lasting damage,' he said, 'Still, I'd better staunch the blood flow. Come with me.'

'Later,' Mitchell said. 'Just give me some tissues.'

Fyodor obliged and Mitchell dabbed his nose and lips.

'Would somebody please tell me what you are all doing here?' Petrov asked in Russian.

Pravda stood at the end of the bed. 'Igor Alekseyevich, I—'

'If General Pravda would let me have my handbag, I will explain, Mr Petrov,' Romanova said.

'Well, General Pravda,' Petrov said to him. 'Are you going to let the lady have her handbag?'

Pravda couldn't connect the search for Romanova's father with Petrov; he needed the answer. 'Gregor.' Pravda kept his gun trained on Romanova. 'Get me the bag.'

Gregor retrieved it from under the bed.

Romanova made a grab for it, but Gregor was too quick and handed it to Pravda. He holstered his weapon and tipped the contents of the handbag onto the bed. He raised his eyebrows at the first two items to appear: two diamond-studded Apple cellphones, followed by her Russian passport in a Hermes crocodile skin cover, a leather cosmetics bag, some loose make-up and a manicure set, a diary and gold pen, a bunch of house or apartment keys, two car key fobs, a packet of tissues, a selection of mint candy, three child's crayons and a bottle of water.

There was no gun.

'My diary,' Romanova said.

'What about it?' Pravda asked.

'There are two photographs in it. Please give them to me. I want to show them to Mr Petrov.'

Pravda was intrigued. The only thing he was reasonably certain of was that Romanova wasn't the danger to Petrov that he'd thought she might have

311

been. It wasn't easy to kill or wound a person with a photograph. He nodded at Gregor who moved as close as he could to Romanova without touching her. Pravda flicked through the diary. The photographs fell out. The first – the picture of the two men on the river bank. What was Romanova doing with it? The picture was clear and the texture too smooth for the photograph to have been the original; nonetheless, he flipped it over out of habit, and had a sharp intake of air when he saw the legend "A-16 – Summer 1979". He looked at Romanova. Gravchenko had to be involved somehow. That was the only rational explanation. Romanova was far too young to have had any connection to Petrov and Arzamas. She hadn't been truthful with her lawyer; the search for her father was a smokescreen. Either, contrary to what Uncle Nikolai thought, Gravchenko knew about Pravda's covert activities and had found a way to make money out of the operation or the oligarch was working under Putin's patronage or, worse, his direction.

Pravda felt as if his blood had stopped circulating.

'Well?' Romanova asked.

Pravda opened his mouth; no words came out. He looked at the second photo, of a schoolgirl aged ten or eleven. She was wearing a 1980s dark blue three-piece suit, with a red necktie to show her membership of the Communist Party's Young Pioneers. The photograph looked to be an original. The date on the back was October 1986. 'Where did you get these?' Pravda asked Romanova. 'Where are the originals?' He wasn't concerned about the school photo, except to find out how it was connected to Petrov. The "A-16" photo, however, was a different matter. Gravchenko, Putin, FSB? It was a nightmare scenario.

Romanova straightened and held out her hand. 'If you let me show them to Mr Petrov, you will find out.'

Pravda half-smiled. Romanova wasn't in a strong

bargaining position – meddling as she and Mitchell were in matters of national security – yet she was trying to control the situation; an oligarch's wife to be sure.

'What are they?' Petrov asked. 'Let me see the photos.'

Pravda looked at Petrov. He was also holding out his hand.

'Well, General Pravda?' Romanova said.

'Give them to me, please.' Petrov eased forward and extended his hand further.

Pravda couldn't not give them to Petrov. The hemorrhaging of information had gone too far. It would be a meaningless gesture to refuse him. He offered them to his patient.

Romanova moved forward and snatched the photos from Pravda before he could stop her. '*I* will show them to Mr Petrov.'

Gregor took Romanova in a bear hug and dragged her back, away from the bed.

Pravda wasn't offended, more bemused, by her behavior. 'Okay, Gregor, let her be.' Matters were taking a comic turn – except of course, they weren't.

Gregor released her.

Romanova rubbed her arms and returned to the bedside. 'Here,' she said. She handed Petrov the "A-16" photo first. 'Do you recognize these men?'

Petrov stared at the picture for a long time without saying a word. His eyes moistened. 'Where did you get this?'

'Who are those men, Mr Petrov?' Romanova asked. 'Please tell me. I need to know.' She pushed her body against the side of the bed.

Gregor raised his arms. Pravda shook his head. He could see in Gregor's eyes that the young buck was itching for action. Pravda didn't want another shooting or any conduct that might cause distress to Petrov or, worse still, dislodge the bullet in his head. 'Take guard outside,

Gregor. Ferlito is in the area. I can smell him.' Gregor would also be out of earshot of whatever it was that was going to be revealed. Pravda himself was uncertain, but apart from him only Alexei under Uncle Nikolai knew the whole story of their operation. And that was how he wanted to keep it, though Fyodor and Mitchell would be allowed to stay, albeit for different reasons.

'Leon.' Gregor nodded and left the room.

'Where did you get this?' Petrov repeated.

'I found it. In an apartment, on Mosfilmovskaya, here in Moscow.'

Sokolov could have been given it by Danilov or Petrov when he'd visited them in Arzamas two weeks before his murder.

Tears came to Petrov's eyes. 'The smaller man is me,' Petrov said in a faltering voice as tears rolled down his cheeks.

Pravda's hunch in the surveillance truck had been right.

'And the other man?' Romanova asked, in a softer tone. 'Who is the other man, Mr Petrov?' She pulled up a chair and sat close to Petrov.

Pravda also wanted to know the answer to the question. He didn't recognize him in the photo. It made sense that it was Sokolov. The photo had been found in his apartment. If so, Sokolov hadn't only made a recent visit to Arzamas, as Danilov had said, but he'd also been there in 1979. Pravda edged closer to the bed, trying not to betray his increasing anxiety. Now he knew where Romanova had got the photo from, his concern shifted to how little he knew about the antics of the GIs. Did Uncle Nikolai know about the 1979 visit?

'A dear friend of mine,' Petrov said. He closed his eyes.

'What is his name Mr Petrov?' Romanova asked.

'His name?' Petrov glared at Pravda.

Pravda closed his eyes briefly and took a deep breath. He heard Petrov clear his throat. Pravda opened his eyes.

Petrov turned to Romanova. 'He's dead.'

It could still be Sokolov. Pravda hadn't had the opportunity to tell the sedated Petrov about Sokolov's murder while in Arzamas, but Danilov had been at his bedside while Pravda waited in Kisletski's office for the fax authorizing Petrov's release. Danilov could have told him during the man's lucid intervals.

Petrov looked at Pravda. 'You knew him as Lapin, General Pravda, Andrei Nikolayevich Lapin.' He turned to Romanova. 'But his real name was Damon, First Lieutenant George Petersfield Damon of the US Air Force.'

Lapin had visited Arzamas! And, like Sokolov, Pravda hadn't known about it. His leg tensed. His life's work was unfolding in public before his eyes. If Lapin was on Mitchell's list of Russian names, and Mitchell was ever to get hold of the list of longitudes, the lawyer would be able to cross-reference the name.

One down, nine to go.

'And what is *your* real name, Mr Petrov?' Mitchell asked.

Pravda stepped forward to assert control. He had to stop the questions; too much information was coming out. But short of marching Romanova and Mitchell out of the room at gunpoint, there was little he could do. And, apart from disconcerting Petrov, such a drastic course action would only delay the inevitable for a few days. Mitchell would find ways of getting the whole story. And Pravda had not yet established the nature and extent of Gravchenko's involvement.

'My name?' Petrov straightened up and looked at Mitchell. 'I am Colonel David James Pickering.' He spoke in English. 'Also of the US Air Force.'

Two down, eight to go.

'Ekaterina,' Mitchell said in Russian. 'Did you understand that?'

Romanova nodded and thrust the school photograph at Petrov. Her hand was quivering. 'Do you recognize this, Colonel Pickering?' she asked in Russian.

Petrov's eyes widened. 'Where did you get this?' His hands were shaking as he toyed with it.

Pravda didn't understand Petrov's reaction. He couldn't begin to imagine what Romanova was about to say.

'From my family album,' she said.

'Your family?' Petrov frowned. 'But that's not possible. The last time I saw this photograph, it was in Arzamas. You're not from Arzamas, are you? I would know if you were. You have family in Arzamas?'

Pravda was perplexed. Aunt Olga had told him that the FSB's file on Romanova was missing. Was it because of her apparent Arzamas connections? Or was it something to do with Gravchenko?

'No, no,' Romanova said. 'What you saw was a duplicate. My mother...' She began to sob. 'Where... where did you see it? Who had it? Tell...me. Please... you...must tell me. Who had this photo in Arzamas?'

'Who is this child?' Petrov asked, tapping the photo.

'Me,' Romanova said, wiping tears from her cheeks. 'Me.'

Petrov's eyes widened again. 'You're the girl in the picture?' He began nodding.

'Be careful, Igor Alekseyevich,' Fyodor said. 'Keep your head still.'

'Yes. Mr Petrov.' Romanova reached over and laid her hand on Petrov's arm. 'It's me.'

The plot thickens. Why would Petrov have seen Romanova's schoolgirl photo?

Petrov took hold of Romanova's hand. 'My child,' he said. 'It was a friend of mine who showed me this photograph. He said the girl...' He fixed his tearful eyes on Romanova. 'He said the girl...you...He said that she was his daughter. The daughter he'd never seen.'

Pravda felt a tingling sensation in his leg.

'Who?' Romanova asked. 'Is he still alive? What is his name? Please tell me Mr Petrov. You must tell me, please.' Her whole body appeared to be trembling.

Petrov squeezed her hand and smiled. 'Yes, my child, your father is still alive. Very much so. His name is Colonel David Scott Berkowitz of the US Air Force.' Petrov turned to General Pravda. 'You, General, you of course know him as Mikhail Konstantinovich Danilov, aero-physicist and reluctant Hero of the Soviet Union.'

Romanova collapsed onto Petrov and embraced him.

Fyodor rushed forward and put his arms on Ekaterina's shoulders. 'Please, Ms Romanova. Mr Petrov's head.'

Petrov gently waived him away.

Pravda couldn't move his leg. His stomach churned over, and over. Danilov had never said anything about having a Russian daughter. And how had it been possible?

Three down, seven to go.

Then it dawned on him, she'd been telling the truth; Gravchenko and Putin weren't involved. That was some compensation, but not enough. An eerie silence engulfed the room. Pravda sat down on a chair in the corner. He had visions of Uncle Nikolai's express train emerging from the tunnel and colliding with the freight cars. The faces of Karat, Sokolov and Grushchenko were imprinted on the dead and injured lying on the embankment. The world's media were on the scene with their intrusive arc lights and sky-scraping satellite masts. He thought of Anna and Stepan; their dreams of going to America. Would those dreams ever be realized?

Scott wiped a tear from his eye as he watched Ekaterina ease herself away from Petrov and exchange fond smiles while holding his hand. Petrov's face, too, had come alive; there were fewer wrinkles and more color in his cheeks. If only all Scott's clients' problems could have such a happy ending. However, there were still other human rights issues, involving Pravda's "resettlement" of the "Moscow Bounds", which should be investigated. He approached the bed. 'Colonel Pickering, my name is Scott Mitchell,' he said in Russian, for Ekaterina's benefit. 'I am Ekaterina's lawyer. I specialize in human rights cases. May I ask you a few questions?'

Pravda rose from his chair. 'I don't—'

'Dr Glasunov,' Petrov said. 'Would you please help me sit up?' The doctor and Ekaterina plumped up the pillows. 'Thank you.' Petrov looked at Scott. 'Go ahead young man.'

'Did you ever try to make contact with the West while you were held in Russia, either before or after 1991?'

Petrov looked at Pravda, who opened his mouth, presumably about to speak. 'No...I didn't,' Petrov said.

Scott was surprised. Petrov's conditions couldn't have been as wretched as he'd thought. He looked at Pravda, searching for a sign of satisfaction with Petrov's response, if not smugness. But the GRU general remained inscrutable.

'Why not, Colonel?' Scott asked. It had been regarded as a duty for British captives to try to escape in the Second World War. He presumed it was no different for Americans in Vietnam.

Petrov turned to Ekaterina and patted her hand. 'Do you understand English, Ekaterina?' He asked the question in Russian.

'Very little, Mr Petrov, I mean, Colonel Pickering.'

Petrov smiled at Ekaterina and squeezed her hand. 'You may call me Igor, my child. And I shall stay in Russian.'

'Thank you.' She returned the smile.

He turned to Scott. 'Young man. Do you have family, parents, siblings, wife, children?'

'Just my parents, sir. I'm an only child. Never married and...no children.'

Petrov toyed with the photo of Ekaterina, the schoolchild. 'I'm an orphan. I've no idea who my parents are, or were, or if I have any other relatives.' He looked at the faces in the room. His eyes glazed over. 'I spent my childhood being shunted around orphanages in California. I joined the US Air Force when I was seventeen.' He coughed. 'Excuse me...The Air Force became my parents. It fed me, clothed me and educated me...It was the only real family I ever knew.' He stopped and wiped his eyes.

Nobody said a word.

'Then came Vietnam. As a trained pilot, I volunteered. I wanted to repay my family. But my family deserted me.' He choked. 'First my birth parents, then my adopted parents. They both deserted me.'

'In what way did your adopted parents, the US Air Force, desert you?' Scott's thoughts turned to Sophie's bitterness about the way the US authorities had treated her father and, allegedly, treated the returning GIs generally. Was Petrov going to be another example of such treatment, but this time as a MIA?

'Would somebody please get me some water?' Petrov asked.

Ekaterina poured a glass and handed it to him.

'Thank you.' He drank half and returned the glass to Ekaterina. 'I was shot down and captured by the VC. I spent two years in the camps. I was caged, tortured and fed a starvation diet. Then in 1973 the news came through of Nixon's "Peace with Honor" speech. He'd agreed with the North Vietnamese that all American prisoners of war would be released.' He sighed. 'But the North Vietnamese used the broadcasts as further torture, mocking and goading us that we'd been abandoned by the US government, and left to rot in hell.'

'But,' Scott said. There was another side to the story.

'Wasn't that so much Vietnamese propaganda? I've discovered that over the years the American government has made, or at least contributed in some way to, many attempts to find you guys, the MIAs.' If that was true, there wouldn't have been much more the American government could have done – short of restarting the war against the North Vietnamese.

'Perhaps,' Petrov said to Scott. 'But they never found me, or the others.'

'Then what happened?' Scott asked.

'I was sold to the Soviets in 1974.' He looked at Pravda. 'Well, that's what the VC told us.'

Pravda was rubbing his leg and appeared to be uncomfortable. 'A deal was done,' the general said.

Scott glared at Pravda. These men were human beings, not commodities to be exchanged for arms shipments.

'I was flying the latest Phantoms,' Petrov said to Scott. 'Their MIGs couldn't compete.'

'Hmm,' Scott said. 'From one cage to another.'

'Lawyer's license, Mr Mitchell?' Petrov grinned. 'In fact, I wasn't badly treated, when I come to think about it.'

A faint smile appeared on Pravda's face.

Naturally, Scott was pleased that Petrov considered he hadn't been badly treated. He knew from his own experience that most Russian individuals were decent people, as in other countries, and the problems were with the agencies and institutions – the "collective individuals". Nonetheless, such testimony wouldn't help his proposed case that the man's human rights had been breached. 'Even so—'

'I was clothed, fed and watered,' Petrov continued. 'They gave me a modest, clean, apartment with all basic necessities. They further educated me to Masters' Degree level, in aero-physics.' He folded his arms. 'You could say they became my new family.'

Pravda stopped rubbing his leg.

'That's fine, as it goes, Colonel,' Scott said. 'On the other hand, you could say they deprived you of your basic human right. The right to return to your homeland, or at least to contact the outside world.' No amount of clothing, feeding and watering could compensate for that.

Pravda winced.

Petrov took time to respond. 'Yes, you could say that. But the real question is: did I want to go back to the States? Or even to contact them?'

'Did you want to, Igor?' Ekaterina asked.

Pravda edged further forward.

As did Scott. The reply would be crucial to the Strasburg petition he was preparing in his mind.

Petrov again hesitated before he spoke. He focused on Ekaterina. 'To be honest, I didn't think I had anything to go back to.' He looked at Pravda. 'Don't get me wrong. I never became a communist. I've never had time for political ideology...of any persuasion.' He looked at Scott. 'I saw the media reports of how the American government was treating the returning GIs...as pariahs.'

'But, Co—'

'Yes, I know, Mr Mitchell. Much of it could have been propaganda, the Soviets taking it out of context. But much of it did happen. We knew that for a fact. We were, after all, fairly well-educated in technology, including communications.' He glanced at Pravda. 'We had some, limited, success in circumventing the restrictions on access to information that were placed on us. We managed to get some information from the West and share it among ourselves.' He clasped his hands and grinned. 'In fact, I think we did quite well, bearing in mind the internet and e-mails hadn't yet been invented...for public usage, anyhow.'

Petrov was looking tired. His eyes were drooping.

'Only two final questions, if I may,' Scott said. 'Please Colonel.' Scott didn't know how soon he would get another opportunity to question Petrov, if it all.

'No,' Dr Glasunov said. 'My patient is—'

'Go ahead, Mr Mitchell,' Petrov said. 'It's alright, Doctor.'

'Were you working with nuclear arms at Arzamas, or Sarov, as it's called again?'

'Stop,' Pravda said. He straightened. 'That's not a matter for public discussion. I won't allow you to ans—'

'General Pravda,' Petrov said. 'The whole world knows that US and Canadian scientists have been on exchange visits to Arzamas for nuclear arms and production talks since the 1990s. Go on the internet.' He turned to Scott before Pravda could respond. 'But as a matter of fact, no, I've no nuclear training. Besides, whenever these exchange visits took place Danilov and I were taken out of the city.'

'In case you tried to make contact with the Westerners?' Ekaterina suggested.

Petrov smiled and looked at Pravda. 'Perhaps you should answer that, General.'

All eyes turned to Pravda.

'We've all done things that we might find difficult to justify at a later date,' Pravda said. His shoulders slumped.

But not with such monumental consequences as your actions, Lieutenant-General Leonid Igorovich Pravda of Russian Military Intelligence. Scott turned back to Petrov. 'Last question, Colonel.' This was the key. 'Do you want the world to know what happened to you?'

Pravda stared at Petrov. The GRU general looked as though his life depended on the answer.

'I haven't made up my mind,' Petrov said.

Pravda's heart missed a beat. He wondered if he could persuade Petrov not to go public. His phone rang.

'Pravda.'

'This is reception, General. Mr Konstantin Gravchenko is here. He would like you to come down. He asked me to mention the name Ferlito.'

Pravda was ambivalent. Of course he wanted to know immediately what the oligarch might have to say about Ferlito, but he also wanted to hear what else Petrov had to reveal. He looked at Romanova. He wouldn't mention her husband's arrival until he had spoken with the man. He addressed Petrov. 'Igor Alek...Colonel. I'm needed in reception for a moment. But I would like to hear what—'

Petrov looked at Fyodor. 'Doctor, I want to sleep now.'

Fyodor turned to the others and put his hand on Mitchell's back 'Ms Romanova, gentlemen. Would you please leave and allow my patient to rest.'

Romanova kissed Petrov on the forehead and made her way out.

'Thank you, Mr Petrov...Colonel Pickering,' Mitchell said and left the room.

Pravda followed them into the corridor and closed the door behind him. 'Would you both please go with Gregor,' he said to Romanova and Mitchell. 'He'll take you to the visitors' waiting room at the end of this corridor. I should be back in ten to fifteen minutes. I would like to have a word with you both.'

'But, General—'

'And before you ask, Scott,' Pravda held up his hand. 'You're not under arrest. You are free to leave whenever you wish, but I would ask you to indulge me, please, this one last time.'

Pravda turned and hurried downstairs.

A crowd of medics stood huddled together in the middle of the reception area.

They parted when Pravda approached.

Gravchenko was standing over a blood-soaked body on the floor. 'Good evening General Pravda.' He kicked at the body. 'My men found him a few streets away.'

Pravda moved in for a closer inspection. He recognized

the face from his files; it was Frank Ferlito. His hands had been severed at the wrists; his feet were torn from his ankles and his penis was protruding from his mouth.

'Looks like a hit and run,' Gravchenko said. 'Here.' He handed Pravda an envelope. 'We found this on his body.'

Pravda didn't need a doctor to tell him that Ferlito was dead. He opened the envelope and took out a piece of paper; it was Mitchell's list of Russian names. A wave of relief surged throughout his body. He looked at Ferlito. No Russian agency would find the energy to spend much time investigating the "road traffic accident". Moreover, unless witnesses came forward, it was going to be difficult for the American Embassy to make any progress in tracking down the perpetrator, assuming they would want to. Pravda had literally come to a dead end. He was in two minds. Any investigation of Ferlito would have exposed Pravda's operation, but the absence of any such enquiry meant that he would never discover the real reasons behind Ferlito's actions and how far, if at all, the US government was involved.

He turned to the assembled medics. 'Okay.'

They moved in and carried Ferlito away.

'What brought you here Mr Gravchenko?'

'Tolik Bron, Katya's cousin, told me they were coming here, to check out the rumors.'

'Would you like to see your wife?'

'No, that won't be necessary. She's got to do what she's got to do. Tolik's gone home. I'll leave a car and driver here to take her back to her apartment when she's ready. I'll catch her later.' He nodded. 'Goodnight, General Pravda.'

'Goodnight, Mr Gravchenko.' He watched the oligarch leave the premises. 'Until we meet again.'

Epilogue

Three weeks later

After Colonel Kisletski's not unexpected death from liver failure, Pravda was free to enter Arzamas without fear of being shot on sight. Uncle Nikolai arranged through a – suspiciously to Pravda – cooperative FSB, for Romanova to visit her father. It rattled Pravda that he still couldn't be sure how much the FSB knew of Danilov and Petrov's American history, or that of any other members of the group. Whichever way the case ended, Pravda was determined to have "full and frank" discussions with Uncle Nikolai. His more immediate concern, though, was that Romanova had insisted on Mitchell accompanying her to Arzamas. The lawyer had enough material to generate public interest if Petrov, and Danilov, would let him use it. And Mitchell would doubtless be far more probing if the opportunity arose. Pravda's head told him it was his duty to try to limit the damage caused by any public disclosure, but his heart was questioning the morality of such an approach.

As the helicopter flew east across Moscow's night skies Pravda sat silently watching Romanova blowing her nose while turning the pages of the family photo album she had prepared for her father.

What had the system, his system, done to her and her father?

Mitchell, meanwhile, was flicking through the pages of his pocket notebook and underscoring texts. 'General,' Mitchell said. 'During these past few weeks I've been trying to research the other Russian names on the list. Not an

easy task, in the absence of their real American names...
although...' He smiled. 'I have three of them now.'

'You know I can't disclose this information.'

'So you say.' Mitchell read from his notes. 'We have the following: 1. Alekseyev, Sergei Yurevich; 2. Grushchenko, Mikhail Semeonovich; 3. Kulachenko, Vladimir Grigoryevich; 4. Karat, Fyodor Sergeyevich; 5. Redchenko, Anatoli Igorovich; 6. Petrov, Igor Alekseyevich...aka Colonel Pickering; 7. Lapin, Andrei Nikolayevich...aka First Lieutenant Damon; 8. Poltoranin, Gleb Mikhailovich; 9. Danilov, Mikhail Konstantinovich...aka Colonel Berkowitz, and 10. Sokolov, Yuri Vladimirovich.' He looked at Pravda. 'Do you agree?'

Petrov's frankness, and his current indecision about whether to go public, was making Pravda's reticence less and less effective.

'We know,' Mitchell continued. 'About Mr Petrov, Colonel Pickering, and his reasons for not trying to escape or contact the West.' He turned to Romanova. 'And I assume, Ekaterina, that your father will tell you why he, apparently, chose to keep quiet.' He smiled at her. 'And whether he would like to go public.'

Pravda studied Romanova. Her blue eyes sparkled one moment and hazed over the next. He thought about Anna and Stepan and how comforting it was to be a part of a complete family unit.

'I will ask him your questions,' she said, softly, and returned to her photo album.

'Thank you,' Mitchell turned back to Pravda. 'What about the other eight? Did they remain...compliant?'

Life was so simple for the human rights lawyer. Pravda sat up. 'I trust you will accept the truth of what I am going to tell you.'

'As long as you don't expect me to suspend my disbelief,' Mitchell said.

'Alekseyev, Kulachenko, Redchenko, Lapin and

Poltoranin all died before I took over in December 1991 and...' Pravda hesitated. He knew what Mitchell's reaction would be. 'I have never seen their files.' The beginnings of a supercilious smile appeared on Mitchell's face. 'I was told that they were lost.' Mitchell raised his eyebrows. 'I know nothing about these men, other than their Russian and American names.' Pravda didn't how Lapin had managed to persuade the KGB, as it then was, to let him into Arzamas in 1979. Neither did he know whether Lapin had ever tried to escape. He hoped Petrov or Danilov would tell him the answers to both questions. It was obvious that Mitchell didn't believe a word he was saying. 'It's true.' Uncle Nikolai, the first and only other guardian of the Americans, had told him in 1991 that the other five men were dead and their files had disappeared from the archives.

'And convenient,' Mitchell said.

'That doesn't make it any the less truthful,' Pravda replied.

'Maybe. But what about the other three: Karat, Sokolov and Grushchenko?' Mitchell frowned. 'Is Grushchenko available for interview, by the way?'

'No, he isn't,' Pravda said. 'He's dead. Killed recently, we believe by Ferlito.' There was no other credible suspect.

'Same MO?' Mitchell asked.

'Yes.' Pravda saw no point in adding the bomb. Though he was surprised at how freely he was answering Mitchell's questions. His default position of not revealing anything was ebbing away.

'Did he ever want to leave Russia?'

Pravda checked the screen on his cellphone, to give himself thinking time. 'Initially, he was considered an escape risk so we held him under close supervision.' It was Sakhalin Island on the eastern seaboard near Japan, though again, Mitchell didn't need this information. 'But he was a very bright young man, with an American post graduate degree in physics as well as being a Phantom pilot. We needed him elsewhere.'

'Where?' Mitchell asked.

He wasn't going to tell Mitchell that. 'He got into Marxism…and became more compliant.'

'Could he have been faking the politics?'

'Yes, then, perhaps not. We'll never know. They say that political and religious converts are often the most fervent. But they can also be the most unstable. Anyway, we kept a close eye on him until he married a Soviet woman and appeared to settle down.'

'But you moved him. Brought him in from the Siberian cold, so to speak. Nearer to Moscow?'

You never give up Scott Mitchell. But Pravda was beginning to feel that a great weight was being lifted from his shoulders. 'Karat, on the other hand, never presented an escape threat. Like Petrov, he always said he had nothing to go home to. His mother left him to his own devices after his alcoholic father committed suicide when he was eight. His childless teenage marriage ended after two years. He was happy to stay with us.'

'And Sokolov?'

Yes, Sokolov. 'He was a strange mixture,' Pravda said. 'He said he was a pacifist and wanted to be a draft dodger. But when his number came up he got cold feet. He was fascinated by gadgets and problem-solving. He could turn his hand to anything and he was the quickest learner I'd ever encountered; Russian or American. He became a Phantom pilot because of its technological wizardry. He claimed to know more about the aircraft than the manufacturers.'

'I can see how useful he would have been to you,' Mitchell said. 'Didn't he feel any loyalty to America?'

'We educated him in nuclear physics, which he took to like a duck to water. He wanted to contribute to the body of learning that would show how nuclear fusion could be used for peaceful means, by all countries.'

'What? As an American held captive in the USSR, in the middle of the Cold War?' Mitchell sighed. 'You expect me to believe he was *that* naïve?'

'You will doubtless want to check it out with Petrov,' Pravda said. He could no longer prevent Petrov from talking. He wasn't so sure that he wanted to. The question and answer exercise felt cathartic. 'Scientific, technological, problem-solving was all Sokolov was interested in. Apart from his professed pacifism, I don't think he had a political, or ideological, thought in his head...like Petrov.'

'Why was he living in Moscow? It's not a secret city.'

'He'd served us well and—'

'Making bombs?' Mitchell asked.

'No.' He glared at Mitchell. Don't put words into my mouth Mitchell. 'He was working on other uses, as I've tried to explain to you. Anyway, when he retired in 1999 he asked if he could live out his days in Moscow. His knowledge soon became outdated, so there was no tangible risk to our national security. He remained under moderate surveillance by the GRU. He could have made contact with Western press agencies and told his story. But he appeared never to have done so.'

Mitchell closed his notepad. 'Did you ever consider, General, that with all the information you were feeding these men about the Soviet and Russia's arms and technological situation, they might secretly turn and become spies for the US?'

'Of course we did. It was never out of our minds.'

'So how did you contain the risk?'

'We had our methods.' Come, come Mr Mitchell, you know better than to ask that.

'Constant surveillance, 24/7? Old tricks die hard, eh?' Mitchell said.

'Like the West, after 9/11.'

'What do you mean?' Mitchell's tone was indignant.

'I read somewhere that there are over 422,000 CCTV cameras in London working round the clock; that's one for every fourteen people. I would say that's not only constant, but all-pervasive, state surveillance.'

'And I read in a Moscow Interfax news agency report,' Mitchell said. 'That during the war the North Vietnamese transferred fifty-one American GIs to the USSR, of which seven have now been named. Any of them on your list of longitudes, General?'

Pravda had seen the report, but he didn't know the identities of any of the fifty-one. Uncle Nikolai had instilled in him the need for absolute secrecy about their operation, so Pravda had never enquired about any other group of GIs, for fear of having to reveal details of his group. He'd assumed that the structure was deliberately set up like a spy cell network, where each cell was discrete and nobody knew anything about the other cells, much less the identities of their members. 'I don't know the names of any of the fifty-one,' he said.

The first draft of Scott's second petition to the European Court of Human Rights was nearing completion – in his head; but he would have to respect Petrov's wishes if the man decided he would prefer to retain his privacy. And Scott would be bound by client confidentiality if Ekaterina and her father also wished to keep quiet.

However, he owed no such obligation to the eight US airmen who weren't his clients and who were dead. In their case Scott's duty, as a humanitarian and not necessarily as a lawyer, was surely owed to their American families and descendants. They were entitled to know what had happened to their loved ones. But, Grushchenko had married a Soviet woman. What Soviet/Russian families did the others have? Scott didn't know. Moreover, if they did have such families what did they know of their loved one's American background? If he could find them and were to tell them the story, how would it affect them and their feelings for their deceased husband or father?

Maybe they had a human right *not* to be told?

On a practical front, he couldn't prove anything specific. Pravda had refused to open his files to him. Scott would have to get his hands on the list of longitudes if were to make any more progress.

Until then, his story would be difficult to believe.

It was neither the fading white scar on his right arm, nor the two bottles of Jack Daniels on the kitchen shelf that convinced Ekaterina that Mikhail Konstantinovich Danilov was her father. She recognized him as soon as she entered the room and came face-to-face with his cobalt-blue eyes. The eyes she saw every time she looked in the mirror.

DNA testing was unnecessary.

She sat on the sofa and watched him at the table, leafing through the photo album. It was a brief pictorial history of her life so far, with many snapshots of her mama and baby Tanya. She studied her father as he edged his glasses to his forehead and leant forward for a closer look at a picture, sometimes reaching out to the figures and gently stroking their faces with his fingers.

She watched her father wiping the tears from his eyes.

She was numb. It was as though her conflicting feelings of joy and anger were of equal strength; they had locked horns and forced her into a state of immobility. Part of her wanted to shower her papa with hugs and kisses, to make up for the lost opportunities of the past, yet another part of her wanted to scream at the man and pummel his chest ferociously.

Why had he taken three decades to come into her life?

She was certain she understood it wasn't his fault, he couldn't have done anything, he was a prisoner of the cruel Soviet system, and he had no control over what had happened to him. Any freedom in a closed city would be monitored and severely limited; although hadn't Petrov said that they managed to communicate with other GIs scattered around the country? And when she saw him, when she saw a healthy living individual with no apparent physical disabilities, a man in full possession of his mental faculties, living in an apartment without bars or guards at the door, she asked herself, why couldn't he have done something? If not during the Soviet regime, then in the years after 1991. Yeltsin opened up all sorts of "freedom avenues" during the 1990s.

She hesitated.

'Papa.' She felt the hairs stand up on the back of her neck and her spine tingled. She had only just met the man, yet she was already calling him "papa".

He looked up from the album. 'Yes, Katyushka?'

'How did you meet Mama?'

He laid his glasses on the table. 'I was brought to Russia in 1972, and to Arzamas in 1974. I tried to escape in the spring of 1975. I made my way to Alma Ata, in Kazakhstan. It was a Soviet republic then. I heard that there was an escape corridor that could get me home to the USA.'

'So why didn't you escape?'

'I couldn't find the corridor.' He smiled. 'Then I met your mama.'

'You told her you were teaching at a local junior school.'

'That wasn't true. I was sleeping rough. I had no papers. I wasn't able to work.' He shook his head. 'Anyway, at that time, I didn't want to work. I wanted to get out of the USSR and back to the free world.'

'But the KGB caught you?'

'Yes.' He wiped his eyes.

'Did you try to escape again?' That was her lawyer's

question. 'Do you want to go back to America?' This was her question.

'No, my darling, that was my only attempt. Your second question? Both my parents died in a car crash when I was ten. I was brought up by an aunt and uncle. They didn't have any children; they must be dead by now. I'm happily married. My wife, Ludmilla, knows nothing of my American origins. Neither do our two adult sons, both doing well in academia.' Tears welled up. 'And now, Katya my darling, I also have a daughter...' He took out his handkerchief. 'And...a granddaughter. A beautiful little granddaughter.' He sobbed. 'Katya, my darling, my dearest darling Katyushka. I'm sorry. I'm so, so sorry.'

Ekaterina went to her papa and cradled his head in her arms. 'Papa, please tell me you tried to contact us, please tell me, even it was only the once.' She began to cry and stroked his head. 'Please tell me, Papa.'

He put his arms around her waist and hugged her tightly, burying his head in her body. 'I was confused Katyushka. I had a settled life. I was confused.'

Ekaterina cupped his face and gazed down at him, both their faces were sodden. 'Did you at least think of us, Papa?'

A torrent of tears poured down his cheeks. 'All the time baby, all the time. I thought of you and your mama all the time. I never stopped thinking about you. Every single minute of every single day I thought about you and your mama. You must believe me, Katyushka.' His grip tightened. 'Forgive me. Please forgive me.'

Ekaterina's body shook.

She kissed the top of his head and pulled him tightly into her body.

'There's nothing to forgive, Papa. Nothing.'

Postscript

A month after his visit to Arzamas, Scott returned to the UK for a vacation at his parents' home, where he received a courier package. The return address was a USPS post box in Miami. Inside the package was a sheet of paper on which ten American names were typed, each followed by a single number in brackets and a series of numbers ending with the letter "E".

Attached to the sheet was a handwritten note, bearing three Russian words – "Your insurance policy".

The End

Acknowledgments

My sincerest thanks must go to Beth Jusino of The Editorial Department of Tucson Arizona, who teased out of me structure, scenes and dialogue that I never dreamt I could have created. This book would not have been written without Beth's painstaking guidance and expert attention to detail. Many thanks also to the other members of The Editorial Department team: Karinya, Jane and Ross for their efforts and continued encouragement. Last, but not least, I would also like to thank Emily and the design team at Silverwood who have brought this project to life.

Lightning Source UK Ltd.
Milton Keynes UK
UKOW05f0257220714

235540UK00002B/33/P